Street Smart x 7

Street Smart x 7

A Street Smart Series Omnibus

from

Frayed Edge Press

Edited by

Alison M. Lewis

Frayed Edge Press
Philadelphia, PA

Library of Congress Control Number: 2022947902

Cover illustration by Daniel Hales

Illustrations opposite pages 1, 127, 157, and 209 by Bruce Orr
Illustrations opposite pages vii and 57 by seeratf0003
Illustration opposite page 181 by graphica013

Publisher's Cataloging-in-Publication Data

Names: Lewis, Alison M., editor.
Title: Street smart x 7 : a street smart series omnibus / edited by Alison M. Lewis.
Other titles: Street smart times seven.
Description: Philadelphia, PA : Frayed Edge Press, 2022. | Illustrated. | Summary: An omnibus collection of the first seven stories in the Street Smart Series from Frayed Edge Press.
Identifiers: LCCN 2022947902 | ISBN 9781642510430 (pbk.) | ISBN 9781642510447 (ebook)
Subjects: LCSH: American fiction -- 21st century. | French fiction -- 20th century. | Short stories, American. | Short stories, French. | BISAC: FICTION / Anthologies (multiple authors). | FICTION / Literary. | FICTION / World Literature / American / 21st Century.
Classification: LCC PS536.3 L39 2022 | DDC 813 L39--dc23
LC record available at https://lccn.loc.gov/2022947902

Contents

"Visiting the cats at the wall became the high point of my day, and made my bleak existence a little less bleak."

(from Street Smart #2, *Down and Out in Paris, with Cat* by R.A. Bolo.)

Editor's Introduction

It seemed like a good idea at the time—small, pocket-sized books that could slip easily into a bag or purse; stand-alone stories of "novelette" length (between about 10,000 and 20,000 words); uniform covers but nicely illustrated inside with original black-and-white line drawings. The title and theme of the series would be "street smart"—works with urban settings, well-drawn characters, and engaging plots. We imagined stories influenced by detective noir, urban fantasy, urban fiction—mixed-genre works that would highlight the cities in which they were set. Who wouldn't love them? Who wouldn't want to "collect 'em all"?

The original impetus for the idea was our admiration for the series of small, pocket-sized fiction sold in French train stations and consumed there by commuters and travelers. Who doesn't love having something fun to read, just the right length for a short journey or long commute? These stories were easily recognizable by their uniform covers and some people did collect them and seek out stories by particular authors.

One "star" in the universe of French train station fiction is Jean-Bernard Pouy, a popular and prolific author probably best known for his *Le Poulpe* series of detective novels. Pouy is notoriously difficult to translate, not only because of his use of French vernacular and slang, but because he is a practitioner of *Oulipo*—an act of writing within pre-determined literary constraints (such as never using a particular vowel)—making that aspect of his work particularly impossible to translate.

However, Pouy's work has indeed been translated—just not into English. That is, until a crack team of three Franco-American translators finally rendered his *Plein Tarif* train-station story into English. The manuscript of that translation, along with a brilliant set of illustrations created by comix artist Bruce Orr, sat in a box in the closet of my office for years.

They finally got pulled out after we'd gotten our ducks in line to start the press. But what to do about obtaining rights to publish the translation? Despite one of the translators' assurances that "J.B. is an anarchist—he doesn't care if you publish his story," I suspected that his publishers were not anarchists and might care. I then started to research the original French publication and found out that its small press publisher had been bought out by another press—and that that press had been bought out by another, and then another, until the catalog was in the hands of one of the nastier "Big 5" behemoths currently strangling the publishing industry. Ugh. The last people in the world I wanted to deal with!

I obtained contact information for Pouy from one of the translators and reached out to him directly for advice. He was surprised to hear the history of press buy-outs and was unaware that these stories were now in the hands of "they-who-shall-not-be-named." He offered to contact them himself and request that they revert the rights of those old stories back to him. This was mercifully accomplished quickly and without fuss. Frayed Edge Press then paid a small fee to Pouy for the English-language publication rights for *Plein Terif*, and the *Street Smart Series of Short Fiction for People on the Go* (as it was originally characterized) was born.

Thus, *Full Fare* (perhaps we should have gone with the translators' alternate title suggestion of *No One Rides for Free*?) officially became #1 in the *Street Smart Series*. Fittingly, the main action takes place aboard a train. Paris officials have decided to round up the homeless and place them in unused train cars to prevent the fallout from having them freeze to death on the streets. Although the plan initially works, the homeless soon come into conflict with the authorities, prompting young anarchists and other radicals to come out in support of the train-dwellers. The story's narrator is one of those young radicals and his alcoholic "bum" Uncle Guy (who has his own story of activism back in the civil unrest of May '68) is one of the homeless. Things start to move when an engine is connected to the homeless train cars and the story rolls toward its inevitable unhappy ending.

Although it was not consciously planned this way, the next two numbers in the Street Smart Series also involved anarchists. #2 was R.A. Bolo's *Down and Out in Paris, With Cat*, the title alluding to Orwell's *Down and Out in Paris and London*, among other things. In this story, an American expatriate anarchist living in Paris falls down on his luck after relapsing into alcoholism. It is through the eyes of this unreliable narrator that we see the people he interacts with and the situations he faces. But his love and care for a poisoned stray cat places the reader firmly on his side and rooting for both to survive.

The Accidental Anarchist by A.R. Melnik, #3 in the series, spins out a "What if…?" tale—what if, instead of heading to work as usual, you just kept going? That's the snap decision the middle-aged protagonist makes as she circumvents her college-teaching responsibilities in Philadelphia for the day and heads to New York City. This low-key act of rebellion turns into more than she expected when she crosses the path of activists battling human-traffickers and winds up getting involved in a genuine "anarchist bomb plot." The story features not just one, but three strong female characters and includes the "tale within a tale" of Nusara being trafficked.

With the publication of these first three numbers in the series, another "good idea" evolved at the press. Since sales were slow, we had no way of selling the stories in train or bus stations, and the small format was unappealing for libraries and bookstores, what if we sold the stories in sets? We could offer a price break on two or more stories packaged by a common theme! Thus, numbers one through three were briefly marketed as "The Anarchist Set" and the following two numbers were packaged together as "The Crime Set." Well, anything was worth a try!

The first "crime" story and #4 in the series, *Stealing MacGuffin* by Matthew Kastel, is contemporary detective fiction set in Baltimore. Heavily influenced by classic noir, it ticks all of the boxes: down-at-his-heels private eye, faithful sidekick, dastardly villain, a dame with a secret, and a plot for stealing an unusual Hollywood artifact that turns into murder. It even has a twist ending as the cherry on top.

#5 in the series is Albert Tucher's *Pele's Domain*, a police procedural featuring a rookie female police officer trying to solve the *almost* perfect crime on the big island of Hawaii. Someone is murdering young mixed-race women resembling Officer Jenny Freitas and leaving their bodies in houses about to be engulfed in lava. Jenny goes undercover to bait the murderer and finds herself up against not only time, the criminal, and the wrath of volcanic Pele, but also the dark forces within her own ranks.

Stephen St. Francis Decky's *"Make the Bear Be Nice"*, the sixth number in the series, somewhat breaks the urban setting mold by taking place in South Jersey/suburban Philadelphia. The unusual title refers to the cutesy and annoying summer kids' movie that seems to be everywhere. It complicates the life of the homeless teen protagonist who works nights cleaning a multiplex cinema, and becomes the scene for a chaotic uprising instigated by the protagonist's unhinged friend. This story made me laugh out loud the first time I read it and it also contains some of the most memorable descriptions of filth that I've ever read.

The Day is Gone by Shelonda Montgomery, #7 in the series, fits in the genre of urban fiction. A Chicago family is impacted by inner-city violence, and also faces the challenges of unemployment, alcoholism, and the breakdown of a marriage. Despite these dark and unsettling themes, there is a lot of love and hope in this story, as well as humor. The author expertly captures the way children talk and interact with each other, and with adults. If we were to have made another set consisting of the last two numbers in the Street Smart Series, it probably would have been called something like "The Dark But Hopeful Set."

So, all seven of these stories are now gathered together here under one cover. We've also included a representative illustration from each story, including three more numbers that were illustrated by Bruce Orr after #1. This collection may represent the swan song of Frayed Edge Press' *Street Smart Series*, although we still love the concept of "commuter" length fiction and may look for other ways to present it to readers in the future. We also still admire the stories in this collection, and their authors, and hope you enjoy reading these works as much as we have enjoyed bringing them to you.

Alison M. Lewis
Philadelphia, 2022

"Finally, on the evening of March twenty-second, the henchmen took a serious beating during an encounter with some eager young anarchists who had rushed over to provide security for the train-dwellers."

(from Street Smart #1, *Full Fare* by Jean-Bernard Pouy)

#1 Full Fare

Jean-Bernard Pouy

translated by Carolyn Gates, Jean-Philippe Gury, and Robert Helms

First, there's the smell. It's a wall of stench, somehow concentrated: a mixture of the foul reek of cold cigarettes, the smell of feet, whiffs of burnt fat, the mildewy funk of cheap wine, and farts blowing at force twelve on the Limburger scale. One hit of it made you want to immediately turn around and go back, made you want to scour out your mucous membranes with Ajax.

But all this could have been just some sort of rite of passage. If you could reach the point where you could mentally plug your nostrils, if you managed to block the work of the olfactory nerve between the nose and the brain, you could go on.

I had just climbed into the train car, as relaxed as an American entering an abandoned cheese cellar. But thanks to a chronic sinus infection, my nasal passages were not exactly sterile and I could stand it.

I had come to visit Uncle Guy. I found him in the second compartment, in the company of a fat woman in a duffle-coat, who snored on the seat with her head leaning against a mutt as filthy as his mistress. It started barking like a hyena as soon as I stopped in the doorway.

"Fuck! Here's my family!" bellowed my uncle. "And they sent the little louse in the vanguard!"

"Hello, Uncle. I thought you hated to travel."

"Shit, it's taken me seventy years to find a train that doesn't budge! It reminds me of the old transit strikes."

"How are you?"

"What do you care?"

"Have you got your ticket?" I joked. That gave him a good laugh.

"That's good. You may be a bastard like the rest of them, but at least you're not as stupid."

I was used to this abuse. The insults weren't really about me. Even though Guy bitterly told me to leave him alone on a regular basis, I knew he really loved me. These epithets were really directed at people in his previous life. It was precisely against them that he had built this barrier, as smelly as it was effective.

My uncle is a hobo. That's just how it is. After my aunt's death, from as cutting-edge a cancer as you could ask for, including final moments so painful and horrible that it actually became irrefutable proof of the non-existence of God, he'd been in a depression as deep as 1929. And then, upon returning from a treatment of prescribed rest, he'd dropped everything, sold everything, spent everything, and become a tramp. But not exactly the "saintly" kind. He was a typically Parisian, Place de Vosges section-type tramp. As long as you're bumming around on the street, you might as well choose an historic district; as long as you're crashing under an arch, it might as well be from the 17th—the Century, not the *arrondissement.*

When winter came, the whole family tried to take Uncle back under its wing, trying to assuage the guilty conscience they felt for not having taken such good care of Auntie during her illness. They'd tried to settle him in a warm place, with the secret hope of seeing him abandon this lifestyle, which had cast a purulent shadow over the dignity of the whole clan. He refused, telling all of us to take a hike, and remained out under the stars, even though they were invisible in the city sky.

He had enough dough to survive, Camembert, cheap wine, and whiskey for the holidays; all his junk was stuffed into a disgusting leather bag. His distinguishing mark was his shoes. There was no way he would ever go barefoot in the cold, and his last remaining vanity was that he would never wear slippers split open by the roughness of the asphalt. He was the only beggar walking around in Clarks. He always had great shoes, even if he never washed his feet.

"People put stinky cheese on silver plates, so, fuck it!" he would howl at me.

Whenever I was passing through the Marais district, I would always end up finding him in one of the usual corners of his territory. We would chat for a moment and he'd invariably end up calling me a slave and telling me to go back to my precious studies; his advice was that I should instead use my energies to wreak havoc in the family, the factory, or in society.

I liked him a lot, Uncle Guy. There were people who had generals in their families, or government ministers, but us, we had a tramp.

"You must have thought I'd croaked, huh? Did they pop open a bottle of champagne, those pricks?"

"Not really. Me, I was a bit worried. Them, I don't know."

"Them, they can drop dead."

"They're dead already, you keep saying."

"They can drop dead again."

I had found him in the second compartment of the third coach of the last train. I was relieved because Uncle had disappeared for at least two full weeks and we'd even called the morgue. They indeed had two vagabonds in their drawers, frozen, of course, but they were two younger ones.

I had looked in all the usual homeless shelters until I realized that it could only be here that I would track him down: the homeless train.

"You're cozy here," I said. "It's almost like a Pullman. Or the Orient Express. At least it's warm."

"Forget about it. You wouldn't understand. But I'm happy to see you and I'll introduce you to my pals. It'll be good for your education; a nice change from those turkeys you hang out with—because you're a chickenshit."

Then, very carefully, I sat down on a green vinyl seat and quietly contemplated the fat lady who was still snoring. The dog, on the other hand, had at least shut up. He was looking at me from the corner of his eye. He could tell I wasn't a friend, but I wasn't an enemy, either. Uncle slipped me a piece of Camembert cheese. He seemed to me like a Yaqui sorcerer, handing me my first hallucinogenic mushroom.

"You know, it's terrible," he continued, "of course it's warm here. But all of a sudden, all this chaos. People should come and visit us. The homeless, they're not just penniless guys. They're drunks, too. Only the rot-gut warms you up out there. When the blood boils, the meat doesn't freeze. They're living garbage dumps. The grime keeps them warm the same way. They are sick people. It's incredible how many diseases there are, lying around on the sidewalks. Poor folks, it's sad. It's mean. Every man for himself, since there's nothing to expect from others."

I had to agree, and I had my reasons.

"Yesterday in the Metro," I told him, "I saw a homeless woman, begging. Not too dirty, not too drunk, as you'd say. She was passing between the riders, her little hand cupped in front of her. She seemed to be thinking aloud. She was telling people that, the day before, someone had actually spit in her hand. Well, there was a guy sitting on a jump seat, and he gave her a 200 franc note. She was stunned. She tried to give the money back, saying that it wasn't possible, that he shouldn't. The guy told her that he too was from the North, and that he'd recognized her accent. The woman started crying, holding onto the bar by the door. At the next station, in tears, she said to the guy,

"I'm sorry, I have to get off." She sat down on a bench right in front the door and kept crying, all hunched up.

"You see? You see?" Uncle bawled, sure of himself.

I didn't see anything, but I kept my mouth shut. The Camembert was sticking to my teeth. Guy passed me his bottle of red. I didn't even wipe off the mouth.

It had been a month since I tracked down Uncle in this fucking "homeless train," and now I was camping out there almost permanently.

The Empty Pocket Express. The Super Sleaze Special.

It had seemed like a good idea in the beginning.

It came into existence after the first time it dropped below freezing one December night. The entire northern half of France was iced over, and public officials started to have the same original ideas, all over again, as they'd come up with the previous year: opening up the dilapidated Metro stations and First Aid centers; school cafeterias expanded for use by the homeless; gymnasia transformed into overnight shelters—and into a Charlie Chaplin movie. The whole kit and kaboodle, the intense Mother Theresaization of the first days of winter.

But the state-owned French National Railway Company had for once distinguished itself: "*Everything is Possible*," ran their slogan. This time it wasn't a lie, and a few good ideas had led to one that was nearly ingenious. In the sorting yards between the Masséna station and Ivry, not very far from Paris-Austerlitz, there was a station that had been almost abandoned by travelers since the real trains—the ones that look like Boeings without wings—now leave from Montparnasse. The railway headquarters had had to pull one hundred mismatched cars for not being up-to-date or just too old. Some round-the-clock crews had attached them in a line, ten trains in all, on ten tracks. Other crews, paid for by both the Railway and the Ministry of Public Works, had made haste, so to speak, to connect the cars with electricity (provided *gratis* by the electric company) and water. Some plumbers had linked all of the cars with PVC pipes, with the whole thing running into a septic tank which had been hastily dug at the end of one of the tracks.

So, here were a hundred train cars, packed seat by seat with two thousand homeless people, perfectly housed in a cozy myth. The shitters were at one end of each car, kitchenettes at the other; they had doors that close, heat, easy-to-clean vinyl, curtains for those who prefer darkness, and the incredible illusion of stationary travel. Teams of social workers acted as dispatchers, sending an entire mob into this unique form of government-provided housing. A few people raised their voices in protest against the rounding up and "penning" of this crowd of destitutes, noting that there were certainly some ghastly historical precedents. In the Nazi "death trains," people had traveled for free. Some others were offended by such an ugly thought, and an intense media barrage had the effect of calming the public's guilty conscience a little bit. They praised this new-found comfort, the bodies rescued from the impending ice age, and the generosity of the French National Railway. From all this emerged a politically correct ad slogan: "Save Our Frozen Tramps!"

Inside the trains, it was a demented microcosm.

The coaches were full, but not overcrowded; there were various groups forming by affinity, there was the stench, the party-shouts, drunken screams, barking animals, and brawls for the conquest of rediscovered love or over the protection of some paltry territory. There was some semblance of order, a little of the civic spirit that had been disappearing from modern life: forming a line at the toilets, for example, the first thing that separates humans from other primates. People took their empty bottles to the trash can; they helped the cripples get up and down from the cars, because without platforms the steps were pretty high. Inside, most of the population was ill, staggering along, desperate. There were wounds, mostly unseen, and a pessimism that sometimes carried infection.

Outside, there were some social activists, people distributing food, and charitable organizations. There were journalists, all believing they could win the Pulitzer Prize, and some film makers, re-making *Viridiana*. And of course there were cops, watching out for trouble and making sure this survival zone didn't become a den of thieves.

It sustained the life of the body, but it was the death of the soul.

"Better be careful with your dogs," a police official said, "you should put them on leashes!"

"Hey, who's the dog here?" a tramp responded. "Where's your leash, pal? If your boss tells you to sit, you sit, right? Well, my mutt's the same way."

"Watch your mouth! I'm not your pal!"

"Run along back to your dog house!"

"You and your dog house. We'll send you back there sooner than you think. You'll see. If you think we're paying taxes just to pamper your gang of freeloaders..."

There were other such terms of endearment. The paupers were cozy, but that was no reason to start liking the dicks.

All of the surroundings were freezing under an ice-blue sky. Viewed from the outside, the camp had a Siberian quality; it was an inner city, but with a Mongolian tendency. One could almost see the horses and yaks grazing outside on the sparse, icy grass growing between the tracks. But friendly steam was escaping from the ten trains, and into the dominant shades of dark green, some new curtains were timidly reappearing, some laundry was trying to dry without crystallizing.

Some taggers and graffiti artists in the area had even repainted the sides of some of the cars, but they were getting bawled out by homeless people with a different aesthetic.

"You little bastards! Go tag the police cars instead of messing up this place!"

"Yeah, go on, call the pigs," came the reply. "What are you protecting? Your suburban house? Your garden- gnomes?"

"Buzz off, zombies, or we'll set the dogs on you!"

"You're the dogs!"

A few local bands wouldn't have minded playing some basic rock 'n' roll there, but the security force let them know that this was not a captive audience, not a zoo filled with endangered and exotic species. And even less was it some discounted version of the Hollywood Bowl.

In short, the poor should be left in peace, especially since the state, via the ever-so-nice French National Railway, had informed the population that all of this would be only a short-term situation. Come spring, as soon as the temperature was no longer synonymous with bronchitis and fatal pneumonia for Joe Homeless, the company would retrieve its equipment, completely bleach and disinfect it, and stow it away for the following year and the next round of cold weather. It was not something permanent. The whole thing was an experiment, and like all experiments, they had to draw some conclusions, put their bigwig sociologists and ethnologists on the job to decide how to do it again, and how to do it better.

In view of the operation's success, some voices, this time many of them sharing the same opinion, had spoken up for maintaining what were then called "the trains of life." These people knew very well that the authorities could not easily discontinue the project for at least one reason: the homeless people and other riff-raff, penned in so far from the downtown area, would no longer make the streets of the capital and the Metro tunnels all messy just when the tourists would arrive *en masse* to see the most beautiful city in the world. Maintaining the trains would mean the end of open-air bathing in the public water fountains; the end of public park benches being used as hotel rooms.

Additionally, since the authorities had them—these rejects, these outcasts—right in front of them, they could finally count them (in order to provide services, they'd say), and watch them (to help keep them safe, they'd say), and manipulate them (to prepare them for re-integration, they'd say).

The theoretical battle was rough. There were a few public demonstrations, but they brought together only a handful of activists. The "fourth world" of urban homelessness always discouraged the ideologues. But in article after article, declaration after declaration, the partisans of train-suppression won the day with their iron-clad motto, which had already been frequently used: *"We must not manage want with indignity."* The problem was not with the ghettoization, but with the integration. These were big words.

"I don't want to be integrated!" Uncle screamed.

What followed were three months of peace. These were strange weeks during which I was very often making the trip between my little room on Rue de Charonne and the train tracks near Masséna Station.

All around this immobile pandemonium, redevelopment activities were going on full bore: the big new national library opened her four gigantic book-like wings of glass and steel, like the thighs of an intellectual courtesan. Masséna and its surroundings were passing from an old-fashioned life into a modern death. The thunderous snores escaping from the train cars hardly covered the roars and crashes of the cement mixers.

I really don't know what was pushing me toward the homeless trains. Without having any ready answers in my mind, I was telling myself that, by helping Uncle, by bringing him smokes and, often, alcohol, I was doing my social duty. It was a bit like some do-gooder who visits prisoners. I went to the slammer once, the visiting room of the local jail, to see a friend. It had been scary. Uncle was right; you have to see it to believe it. You have to really know the situation if you want to judge it. Now I was speaking with the train people, trying to understand what was coming out of their generally wine-soaked minds. I didn't argue, just agreed. Sometimes—rarely—some of them would develop an actual philosophy which was organized, coherent, and vengeful. They saw their fate as a punishment. They flogged themselves frequently for their cowardice and lack of culture. They considered themselves an underclass, and very few of them had the hope, and even less so, the strength to fight with. Rather, they were participating in a long, slow suicide. Among these homeless, many called themselves "terminally unemployed." These were terrible, lucid words.

It was probably the "traditional" tramps who were the most wound up. Among them, there were some who were advocates for the total rejection of any social order. They had lived very different lives, but almost always, there was an underlying resolve, healthy and definitive: "Down with work" and "Death to the pigs." This was what brought them closer to the anarchist activists who had rushed up there and were camping near the site. The color black united them: that of the flag on the one hand, and that of grime on the other.

Since setting foot in this little world, I had felt useful. I could handle a fight. However, most of my time was spent making sure that supplies were arriving. Cheap wine was flowing in rivers, but I also had to convince a few doctors to come and work overtime to provide health care on board. Mostly it was skin problems, and a few ill-treated wounds. There were follow-up treatments for bedsores and psoriasis. I was delighted to be elbow-to-elbow with these bums, these romantic libertarians who my family had made me swear never to hang out with nor ever approach. They had convinced me by daily proselytizing and soft-core brainwashing that entropy and chaos were barbarism, that the future lay in Social Democracy, and that everything else is just hard drugs.

Uncle had little by little introduced me to his buddies and pointed out his enemies. His paranoia had chosen some who were very obvious, such as the ones who wanted to take his shoes. He showed me around the place. The homeless, now that they had homes, were starting to decorate their compartments, trying to lighten the place up with some recycled junk, as though they wanted to perfume over the atmosphere of filth and abandonment. We were far from a basic IKEA store, but one couldn't help being surprised by the number of knick-knacks they'd already accumulated. It hadn't occurred to them to tidy the place up, and they had not yet decided to form a neighborhood association, but it didn't matter. They weren't just passive, which was grist for the mill for those who advocated for a second chance for the destitute. Suddenly it became a vast wasteland of metal, a shanty-town on wheels, described by the authorities as a regular petri dish, a shameful canker on a district that served as home for the world's most beautiful library; it had become a danger zone. Some people spoke of cholera. Others spoke of it as an illegal psychiatric hospital; still others, as a hospice for dying alcoholics. Among the more radical, it was called a concentration camp.

It was filthy, this is true. But it was also a lot of fun! The idea that it would all come to an end was just intolerable.

The nice weather returned in the shape of a wandering high-pressure system, ahead of its summer schedule. The social workers tried, at first gently, to evict the stationary travelers by using persuasion and dangling various carrots in front of them. With the exception of a few long-time tramps who returned without balking to their old haunts on the streets (the haughty solitude in which these flowers will bloom at all costs), most of "the relocated," against all expectations, formed an unmovable block. It was out of the question that this railroad squat, given to them with one hand, could be taken away by the other. Below the surface some fights simmered, there was some squabbling of striking rudeness, and there were even some actual distress calls. One guy died of natural causes, his liver scratching to get out; two others had to be hospitalized as emergency cases. But that was the worst of it.

The numerous dogs accompanying these shaggy paupers had bitten a few shins and were barking as loudly as those Dobermans guarding the small homes of their owners, behind the apartment towers a bit farther away. The press got involved, and viewed from, say Limoges, the scene looked almost Somalian. The henchmen for the Railway (who had been given a rude nickname by the anarchist paper *Liberatión*, meaning "five out of nine are fascists") manhandled a few people and indulged in a few brutalities. Because of this predictable malfeasance, they got called vigilantes, Vichy cops, and collaborators. Finally, on the evening of March twenty-second, the henchmen took a serious beating during an encounter with some eager young anarchists who had rushed over to provide security for the train-dwellers.

Nobody had really planned that. The red squads were not what they used to be, being too busy infiltrating the Trotskyists, who in turn were infiltrating everybody, so they had not seen the sudden mobilization of the young anarchists, who had just been waiting for this sort of chance to play cops and robbers: the Austerlitz sorting-yard as Parisian battlefield.

The whole affair became bluntly ideological, and suddenly small groups of every kind turned up, all at once, finding their second wind. But the anarchist group, snickering, was more than happy to show the suddenly re-appearing Leninists that they were armed to the teeth with axe handles, slingshots, and Molotov cocktails. They were a Black Revolutionary Guard for the hungry, consciously committed to defend the trains and to not re-live Kronstadt or Barcelona. The closet-commies were accused of train-hopping (hahaha), but they contented themselves with circulating leaflets and petitions, and timidly attempting to lure new recruits. The political big shots didn't even bother to show up. The Right eats at Maxim's, not the soup kitchen; the Left eats caviar, not Campbell's Pork & Beans. The "fourth world" is just too "fifth of Night Train" for them.

Everyone in this weird little world coexisted. Inside, in the cars, a complex humanity had found its niche. Outside, the political and social activists were bent on protecting what they considered to be a victory in the class war.

During that time, members of Parliament from every party made strong, dramatic speeches when the Railway had asked, with a heavy heart, that the Minister of the Interior help them clear the flea-bags out. And they had to act quickly: in the field, their opponents were rapidly reinforcing and getting organized. They had to avoid the recurrence of scandalous episodes like when they forcibly evacuated Berber immigrants from the Sonacotra hostels: the burnoose against the bulldozer. It wasn't good for the image of France, the land of welcome, a nation trying to fight against discrimination, a society reputedly rich and responsible. The high-ranking Railway administrator who first had the idea for the "trains of life" (once seen as generous but now seen as cumbersome and almost unmanageable) had been transferred to Marseille. He had his work cut out for him down there.

I had never seen Uncle like this before. He was almost enjoying a social life again. He was becoming less isolated, having met people like himself, something he didn't think was possible anymore. However, inside this paradoxical village, some forms of discrimination had started to appear. The unemployed and homeless had slowly created an internal selection process, first by screaming matches, then by smacks upside the head. They thought of themselves as being on a sinking ship, but not voluntarily. They managed to slowly eliminate from the cars anyone who didn't look like them.

At the end of March, there was a territorial partition, not very different, I have to admit, from what is seen anywhere else. Uncle, and people like him, the old-fashioned tramps, the stinkiest and loudest ones, the sickest also, the ones who knew almost genetically how to avoid rides in the squad cars, had regrouped in the last train, the one at the back, the one least exposed to view, as if the ones who had put them there wanted to give the world a good impression of their village. Even if geraniums were conspicuously absent from the windows, there was no way you could leave the dirtiest people on full display. It was a question of appearances.

There were two train cars where the people of color had wound up, by no accident, even if the others were saying that it was they who had seceded. The leftists had tried to make the train inhabitants respect the diversity, the integration, the mingling of races, but they broke their own morale in the attempt. It was a ghetto inside a ghetto, a tale within a tale.

Some young runaways had tried to find lodging and meals in the more respectable cars, but they were thrown out. They were told, "Go swipe what's available from your bourgeois parents and redistribute all of it here." A crypto-commie had remarked that this was a class reaction of good omen.

Then the neo-fascists conducted a raid one night. These cretins had succeeded in making a "holy alliance" between themselves, but they only succeeded in bringing everyone on the trains back together as one. The brawl had been quick and brutal; the men on the train had not held their ground, but the dogs quickly made the difference. The distinctive green hunting jackets of the fascists were left in red shreds.

The government couldn't take it anymore. France couldn't brag about having a little Bogotá. It was jarring; it had become dangerous, out of control. The lack of security was on everyone's lips. Only drugs were missing from this confluence of evil deeds, probably because they were too expensive. The homeless train was becoming a more and more unbearable provocation. But still everything remained more or less on the level of "big words and little sorrows."

On April 2nd, there was a death. It had been a quarrel, a squabble over a seat or a stolen bottle, we will never know for sure; in the end, it was simply a story of drunkenness and misfortune. Knives had been drawn and a guy was stabbed to death. Before the paramedics could arrive, the green vinyl seat cover had changed color. The ambulance and the cops arrived later, but everything had been settled. The murderer didn't even hide himself, but was sleeping it off, stretched out in the aisle, his head resting against some empty beer cans. The TV channels, like buzzing shit-flies, followed the cops to the stench, looking for the best turd to film.

Among the anarchist comrades, we knew this was the signal of the end. The media finally had enough bad news to make the viewers sick, to assuage any remaining guilty feelings, and to prepare the ground for what would come next. Since everything had gotten out of control here, in this little Rwandan slum ruled by senseless death, some of course unpleasant but now necessary measures were in order. From now on it was a question of prevention. The time of arrival was announced. The train had never started, but the end of the line was now appearing on the horizon.

We were as jumpy as fleas. At last, we'd be able to fight, to show them what we're made of, to test ourselves in the field of political strategy. We'd whack the good old axe handle on the right helmet. It would not be the "great night" of our ancestors, but it would be a little evening very much appreciated.

The riot squad appeared two days later at 6 a.m., when our dear Babylon was still asleep. The dogs howled with one voice, but they could not cover up the snoring coming from the cars. The poor panicked animals quickly took flight from the tear gas, which clouded the rising dawn. There were not many Trotskyists on duty that day and, even if they showed undeniable courage in trying to block all the doors, they didn't understand the tactics of the forces of order, which were more clever than usual. They didn't launch a frontal attack on the entrenched but dazed camp. Instead, they savaged only the first car of the first train without going further, without going into the whole train to drag out its occupants with iron fists.

We quickly understood why—an engine was coming.

It was an old one, my Uncle told me, but it was one of those which had a long time ago broken the speed record of over 200 miles per hour. I was rediscovering, little by little, my uncle's old passions, each one more surprising than the other. I had realized, for example, that he was passionately interested in history, especially with facts, and that his favorite period was the beginning of the 17th century; that explained why he always used to hang out around the Place des Vosges historic district.

The huge engine brutally slammed into the train, destroying all the sewer pipes and bursting the water lines. There were some sparks, the lights went off, and some of the pipes dumped out their contents. Inside the train, there was a lot of fierce yelling: the Holler Express. Then, protected by triple ranks of black-helmeted police with shields, some railway workers came and attached the engine to the train. It started squealing, pulling away the ten cars behind it at low speed. A few people jumped from the moving train, falling into the stinking mud and the geysers of running water, but most of the occupants, screaming obscenities and insults out the windows, were dragged along with the train out of the sorting yard.

In the near-silence due to astonishment and surprise, the newly-besieged watched the departure of this ghostly train, creaking along in the early morning light, this Breugel painting on wheels, until it disappeared at the end of the tracks.

And then the fighting started up again at pace. The riot squad retreated in good order, under a rain of various projectiles, and after a ten-minute break they attacked the first car of the next train, because another older model engine was approaching at low speed.

"They could have at least sent us a classier engine, so we could travel in style!" Uncle laughed.

Some people tried to lay down on the tracks but were cleared off by the law, feet first.

Three frenzied guys reached us from the outside, having snuck into the yard by going around by the huge waste incinerator. They told us that the whole neighborhood had been sealed off, from Austerlitz to Ivry, and that we could only count on our own meager forces. Reinforcements would not be coming; waiting for the cavalry was not an option. Our eyes were already red, but bright. Bandanas concealed faces, cases of Molotov cocktails appeared as though by magic, and different tactics were discussed and adopted. The anarchists regrouped in and around the last two trains, thinking that the cops would probably attack them from all sides. The rest of the troops dispersed with the objective of delaying the mopping-up of the trains as much as possible, until the friends, concerned parties, comrades, and maybe even the Parisian populace intervened, raising an enormous demonstration, joining hands and defending the wretched of the rails.

Uncle was ecstatic. It reminded him of the revolutionary activities of '68, he said.

"Oh, right. Like you were there in 1968? At forty years old?" I shot back at him, sure that I could learn some things by pushing him onto this slippery ground. Back then he had been the manager of an insurance company, so I could hardly imagine him manning the barricades.

"You weren't even born, you little squirt, so what would *you* know?"

"My father never told me about this."

"*That* moron? All *he* did in '68 was debate at the Odeon. For him to have been there and to have put out his bullshit gives him the right to say he took part in the revolution. Myself, I didn't participate in the revolution. I didn't know a thing about the revolution. All I know is that on the 24th, I was on the street in my business suit."

"No kidding..."

"Yep! Just wear a tie for thirty years, and you'll find out that you don't want to wash your feet again either. I didn't know what to do. All these young people were giving me funny looks. Maybe they thought I was an undercover cop. In any case, I told myself, 'I have to leave my mark; I have to leave my signature.' At the corner of Boulevard du Maine and the Rue Froidevaux there was some construction work: a heap of rubble with fences and a backhoe. So, I climbed into the backhoe and started it up. They're no harder to drive than a car, those things. It took me fifteen minutes to flatten one of those disgusting public urinals built up against a wall. After that, I left. Everybody was laughing. I came back a month later. The smashed urinal was still there, like some sort of iron sandwich. But, hey, at least my signature had been there for a month!"

Uncle was right: I didn't know what to say.

Then the trench warfare began, train after train, with incessant victories for the reactionary forces of order. The always-well-to-do were defeating the newly-poor, skirmish after skirmish, ambush after ambush, charge after charge. The riot squad was taking a beating, losing shitloads of helmets, but it still advanced, inevitably. Gasoline bottles exploded in their faces, and they answered this with tear-gas grenades, fired point-blank. The paupers dropped to their bellies in the train compartments and aisles, few among them taking part in the fight, leaving the struggle mostly to the outside combatants. In the corridors, a few of them did take part in the fight. Some, sensing deep inside that they had nothing to lose, charged straight ahead and hurled themselves, screaming, into the big, hairy arms of the forces of order. The most energetic of the combatants were dragged away, clubbed, and thrown into trucks, to be taken away for another beating elsewhere. We learned over the radio, thanks to the two or three squawk-boxes that were still crackling away, that all around the battlefield, everything was calm. No demonstrations were on the horizon. No journalists had been invited to the party, so they were making do from the windows of surrounding apartments, to follow the carnage at a distance. One journalist saw the battle from so far away that everything he said was bullshit, talking about "hundreds of injured," "the war in Paris," and "Sarajevo at our gates." Another more serious guy managed to get closer to the theater of operations, but he was severely trounced.

"The Press is in danger!" he screamed. "Free speech is being murdered!" But we were alone, as on a stage, with very few spectators. It was a clean-handed operation.

On the other hand, our freedom of speech had not yet been murdered. Insults, filthy names, and other rhetorical devices poured down like rain. I learned a lot of new words. The tramps had one hell of a vocabulary, and they tried it all out in a coughing, spitting barrage. I didn't know that a cop could be fucked up in so many different ways.

We also learned that the trains conquered by the Law and the State were being taken a bit farther away, between Vitry and Choisy, and that the passengers were being handed over to the regular cops there, who in turn brought them to Nanterre, where there was an infamous homeless "shelter." Those who were willing to clear out on their own were set free without too much violence. This was the carrot and the stick, the on-going story of life.

As a result, many of our homeless "protégés" began to exhibit some reluctance. They wanted to surrender. They were scared. Since they knew they'd be set free only a little farther down the line, they preferred to leave right now, rather than going through another hell. Some of them even started to insult us, saying that it was all our fault, that they didn't want anything other than to be left alone, and that little fools like us with our big words weren't going to tell them what to do. Many avoided the persuasive guardianship of the anarchists and left, coughing away. For them, cheap wine in some other place would still be cheap wine.

Uncle himself was holding on just fine. He was having fun, feeling like a kid again, rediscovering his youth: Ah, '36': the demonstrations in espadrilles, the shoulder-bags full of nuts and bolts, the flatfoots who high-tailed it out of there. Ah, '68: the trees felled along the boulevards, and the enormous, flooded hole at the intersection of Boulevards Sainte-Germain and Saint-Michel. In our train—that of the smelly bums—there was a wonderful ambiance, a death-to-the-pigs mood after the hasty withdrawal of the least faithful and the most sickly. Wine is wine, and it makes you warm when you piss it. Some of them had started the battle by hitting the bottle, and the events must have looked to them like the unreal decor of a nightmare, or a party that ends in a fight. Others were angry at the whole world: No mercy. Liberty or death. Fuck those assholes. No gods, no masters. Anarchy rules. Jail the rich and send the teachers to the beach.

It was a glorious day for everyone, a redemption. Silent Night, Drunken Night. We'll probably be the last ones to fall, but we'll keep on fighting till the end; until death; until we quench our thirst.

Time was marked by the waves of attack. It was all happening pretty quickly, not taking them more than fifteen minutes per train. Needless to say, the homeless were not crack troops. Drunk, sick, blinded by the tear gas, drained of strength, they were getting picked off, one by one, just like in 1914. The young leftists learned quickly how to respond, but they were too few in number and they were hampered in their movements by the haphazard and disorderly comings-and-goings of the panicked homeless. The riot squad was throwing them into paddy wagons left and right. Some of the cops had even discarded their shields—too cumbersome—and were clearing out the areas around the cars with billy clubs. They even ventured to do some sorting: the younger ones were herded to one side and thrown into trucks, bound for jail; the older ones were pushed back into the trains by force.

The trains started up with squealing noises, but they gradually became less wild and vocal. The last one we saw leaving had a downright shameful silence to it.

"Destination, Auschwitz," Uncle mumbled through his rotted teeth. "These Nazis won't get me."

By morning's end, eight of the trains had been cleared out, and the terrain had become a total wasteland: a mixture of rails, mud, shit, and garbage. It was not a very cheerful sight, especially under the thick clouds of teargas. Within a few hours, we had gone from Bruegel to Hieronymous Bosch. Hundreds of flashing lights on the cop cars and ambulances were piercing the fog, tracing the almost monolithic silhouette of the riot squad and gendarmes' army, withdrawn for a while before the attack on the ninth train.

I myself was excited, eyes red, exhausted by incessant trips back and forth, trying to persuade the wine-sodden wrecks of humanity to organize themselves for the final clash. Our car was finally ready—it was a real mobilization. Some were laying down under the seats. The doors were blocked by miniature barricades made of stacked objects. Each window was manned by the same number of warriors. The supply of projectiles had been distributed.

But a quarrel had divided the defenders of our castle. Some had suggested that we detach all the cars. That way the invaders would have to do battle at least ten times, and the engine would be able to take away only one car at a time. Others thought the fight would continue in another place, with lower odds, and that we should all stick together. Negotiations took place, and we ended up dividing the train in two. There would have to be two battles instead of one for the attackers, and each train of five cars would still be an army on the march.

The battle for the ninth train was really Dantesque. I was able to see up close that, aided by fatigue and high stress, the violence was becoming very real. The combatants were carried away, often covered in blood, by riot police who had become pit-bulls without leashes. The last organized leftists lost their bet in a gallant manner. They knocked out some members of the enemy forces with the sheer energy of their desperation. All this happened right in front of our eyes. The tramps on my train were terrorized: they almost weren't shouting anymore. They stood there with arms dangling and wild hair, and started to drink again, in order to forget. It was like they were waiting for death.

I was, too. I was living with a bizarre sensation of inevitability. We were definitely going to have our faces smashed in. And this certain fact, instead of scaring me, actually gave me extraordinary strength and energy. I'd never felt like that before. There were no more questions to ask ourselves; we knew we had already lost. But this somehow prevented the anguish, suppressed the fear of physical pain. I thought about all those stories of hopeless battles, such as Camarone or the Alamo, about all those cornered guys who no longer seemed to fear anything. It was as though certain defeat was giving birth to invincibility and a kind of courage. In my street fights I had learned that only the first blow is painful, and after that you don't feel anything. You defend yourself, that's all.

When the ninth train started moving, we saw that many members of the forces of order were on board, blocking the doors. The ride was going to be rough. Some guys escaped from our car through the windows and lurched off, absolutely refusing to face this kind of conclusion. As for myself, I was starting to tremble, unable to stop. Our turn had arrived. It was like being at the dentist's office. As long as there were three people ahead of you, it's OK, but after that it's scary, and you find yourself continually watching the door. I finally realized that I'd felt like running off myself for a long time, that there was nothing to do here but get one's face smashed in or to get shipped off, as if this were a fucking death-train, and wait for the big wash-down a half a mile away. But acting on this idea was becoming impossible. A fight without any hope of victory is no longer a fight: it's suicide. The tramps were moaning, and I saw one crying. Only a few loud ones were rediscovering their youth, with Uncle in the lead. They joined the dozen or so anarchists there defending the train, wild and excited like birds of prey. But there were not enough of us anymore. The police fury was about to sweep us away.

The anarchist next to me seemed to read my mind. He was a tall fellow with a romantic, disabused attitude, but not hiding the tough, complicated tattoos covering his forearms. He was tearing his clothes apart on purpose, rubbing them on the ground to make them filthy, and smearing his face with dirt.

"Don't fall apart," he told me, "If you split now, if you surrender, they'll have time to see who you are, where you come from. They'll have all the time they need to get you. In the heat of the battle, you can blend in. But it's really up to you to decide. Personally, I just *can't* get nabbed. I've been a draft dodger for four years now, and I walked myself right into this stupid trap. I'm going to fight, but at the last moment I'm going to try to get rounded up with the tramps. It may work. I have to believe it will work. Otherwise, I know I'll soon enough find myself serving in a disciplinary unit in Bosnia.

"But—there's only volunteers over there..." I objected.

"You—you believe everything they tell you?" He looked at me as if I was a young novice from a convent. "As soon as things start getting hot, play dead, as if you're unconscious. That way they'll beat you a little less violently. With a little luck you'll get an ambulance ride. It's always better than the paddy wagon."

This draft-dodger was bugging me with his veteran's advice, but at the same time I had to admit that I admired his courage. I suddenly realized that there were plenty of people, roughly my age, who were living very different lives from mine—more thrilling, dangerous, unpredictable—and all this was happening right here in our beautiful society, apparently so tranquil and comfortable.

We watched in stiff silence as the riot squad withdrew to recuperate, to regain some strength, to reorganize themselves, and to reload their guns and weapons. I thought about all those movies that had the same cliché scenes: entrenched before the assault, behind the wagons, before the Apaches arrive, in the belly of a plane before the big jump, with all those idiotic dialogues that everyone knows by heart:

"*If you manage to survive, go find my wife, and tell her that I died bravely...*"

"*If I get out of here somehow, I'll spend a week at a classy hotel, down on the Riviera...*"

All of those stupid lines! And the photo of the child that the hero looks at tearfully, the love letter that he dreamily smells. Whatever. In short: There was an incredible tension in the air—like before an injection of sodium pentothal, before utter agony, yeah.

It had been a while since my uncle was by my side. He'd been hanging out with the little group of four or five anarchists who acted, more or less, as the train conductors. They were debating in low tones; one could have called it a council of Sioux elders before the buffalo hunt. I was wondering what they could be saying, or what they might be cooking up. My uncle was in high spirits, not at all worried, and he nodded his head often and started laughing, a bit hysterically. I was thinking what a catastrophe it was that I couldn't tell all this to the family. They would never believe me. Maybe my uncle had been in Diên Biên Phu. You never could tell with him. He was no doubt sharing his own experience as a veteran. Yeah, right; he was probably telling them the public urinal story.

Then, almost transfigured by the importance of having a secret mission, he rigged up a sort of white flag using a scrap of an undershirt, stuck it on a stick, and rushed outside. My uncle was going to sacrifice himself!

I tried to stop him, shouting like a madman: "Come back, Uncle! They're gonna kill you!"

He dodged back through the mud, zig-zagging between the jets of water spilling from the broken pipes, came up to the window where I was, and advised me, with grandiloquence, to observe the lesson of courage I would later be able to report to our flabbergasted family, that family of cowards and living-dead bourgeois.

"And you'll tell them, 'That was a brave man!'"

Then he began to laugh. Even on the edge of tragedy, he had an air of being surprisingly sure of himself. I, however, was ill at ease. Nothing made sense anymore. The tramp of the family had been transformed into a herald. Or into a hero—who knew?

He advanced through the devastated field, stepping over the rails and debris with difficulty. He was going, all alone, towards that pack of black dogs, the uniformed police, who were waiting for him further on, standing around their trucks. I headed to the end of our train car, to the group of anarchists he'd been speaking with. I wanted to find out what their secret meetings had been about, to understand this family sacrifice.

It was quickly made known to me, and I was floored by the naïveté of the thing. My uncle, he was going to parley. He was going to say that we would give ourselves up, but that beforehand, he wanted an eminent member of the French National Railway, accompanied by a representative of the Police Headquarters, to come and see the state of the people that the police were planning to attack, as if they were all potential Mesrines, the infamous "Robin Hood of the Paris streets." They needed to simply see the sickness, the fear, and the fatigue, and realize what was going on. That's all. To see. To know. And afterwards, we would let ourselves be transported away to that other dispatch area, farther away, but with those two VIPs as guarantees. All of this was cooked up as a way to avoid unnecessary violence.

Of course, the whole idea was completely insane. It was obvious that he was going to get clobbered and thrown in the police van, and that would make one less on our side. The cops had not beat the hell out of nine trains full of people in order to make peace with the tenth. They wanted to win ten to nothing, and I didn't see any way that they would let us score at the last minute.

I even thought for a moment that my uncle had found the right plan for escape from the massacre, that he was playing a quiet little treason and that he was utilizing the same methods of escape that he had always used with his own family. Bum for a day, bum forever.

But everyone left me alone to my thoughts, and those who were not yet paralyzed by the cheap wine began to speculate. The cops had had too many casualties. This would be a convenient exit door for them as well. If they attacked again, their image would become too deplorable, now, in the eyes of instantly informed mass opinion. The battle had lasted three hours. They owed it to themselves to accept this opportunity, to show that they were not just acting like starving wild beasts maintaining public order, but that they were also clever negotiators. Humanitarians. Intellectuals, almost.

In any case, the anarchists seemed to believe it. The situation in the car was tense, but cheerful, with the Draft Dodger, the Chief Desperado, in command. But I sensed there was a problem somewhere. I worried that they had sacrificed my uncle in their romantic fury for their lost cause. No, they really had a confident air. One of them had even said that this guy, my uncle, was brilliant and that this would be a great day for the cause.

It was then that I saw the weapons. Two guys had guns, one of which was all shiny and nickel-plated. They hid them behind their backs, thrust into the belts of their jeans, under their jackets.

This—this changed the tune for me. The fear that was roiling my stomach was suddenly no longer shameful, there was a reason for it. These bastards were going to put the lives of numerous people in danger for a chance to play out their little war. Weapons. I just couldn't believe it. Reality hit me hard. I had learned that in big demonstrations, there was always one line that was never to be crossed: that of having firearms. It was this line that avoided, for quite some time, many casualties in France. Now, everything was changing, switching into high gear. I decided that if these jerks wanted to get shot at, it would be without me.

I rushed immediately to the middle of the train, fleeing the front line, but I couldn't go farther than the fifth train car. After that, it was the other half of the train, the other fortress. Maybe it was loaded with bazookas. Or rocket launchers. I huddled on a seat. Outside, everything was grey, almost white with smoke and tear gas, like the end in *Gordan Pym*.

Everything was relatively quiet. There were a few sirens in the distance; some barking, some shouting. The sound of water; some creaking. The clatter of the commuter trains, passing nearby. A radio in one of the compartments. There was still no demonstration coming to our rescue, but some slum kids had started torching cars near Bercy. A few store windows had also been smashed, but the forces of order were on top of it. It was nothing but isolated incidents. And there was monstrous commentary on our "village": one of filth and lice, alcoholism and vermin, vague testimonials about the homeless being happy to be free of it. The journalists didn't hold back on the jargon: "The dispatch of horror." "The trains of shame." And also, Abbé Pierre, the activist priest, was requesting an emergency audience with the President.

Twenty minutes later, along with everyone else whose eyes searched the fog, I saw my uncle come back to the train—staggering, but still brandishing his ridiculous flag, which he was using more like a prod. Indeed, in front of him, two more shadows were advancing towards us. My uncle had succeeded: two officials were coming to visit.

I thought again of the guns and began to tremble, sick to my stomach. They weren't going to shoot them, I told myself. It was impossible. I forced myself to head back up the train cars, stepping over all those silent and resigned bodies. Several tramps had sunk into comatose sleep. No doubt they wouldn't even remember their last battle.

I arrived too late to witness the reception. The first thing I saw was the two guys in raincoats and suits, tied up with ropes, their wrists attached to a window bar, looking bewildered and pale. And then the two anarchists with guns in their hands. My uncle was dancing around, in seventh heaven.

"We won! You lost! Nyaah-nyaa-na-nyaaah-nyaaaaah!

"Guy, fucking hell! Explain this to me!"

"Napoleon was an amateur compared to us, I tell you!"

"What's going on, Uncle?"

"What's happening is that we're going on vacation, to the sea!"

As soon as the railway official and the police chief had boarded the first train car, the welcoming committee had acted. Voilà, they were all tied up. Then the anarchists had chosen one of the tramps who was in the worst state, gave him a letter and sent him out towards the forces of order. In this letter were "our" conditions, as set forth by the occupants of the "Makhno" train, taking the name of the Ukranian anarchist leader who had raised an army and resisted the incursions of both the White and Red armies during the Russian Revolution. Henceforth, the Makhnos were holding hostage two servants of Power and Capital. They wanted a locomotive. They wanted open rails all the way to Marseille. There, by the time they reached the sea and the end of the line, all France would know about their just cause and then they would surrender.

If not, the two civil servants would be shot.

The two anarchists fired three gunshots into the air as soon as they were sure that their letter of demands had arrived at its destination.

The two tied-up big shots were terrified. There was the smell, the pandemonium, and also the fear.

We waited. Outside, there was silence. A few sirens wailed, farther away.

Inside the train, there was chronic coughing, throat-clearing, and drunken mumbling.

My uncle was sitting on the floor. He was back on the bottle.

"Let's celebrate! I've never had so much fun. They didn't want to come, these bastards. But the TV people were there, I saw the cameras. So, I started bawling. Man, that settled it! These two guys followed me straight away."

"What the hell is this stuff about Marseille?"

"You can send a postcard to my fucking brother!"

"I don't know if you realize, Uncle, but we're at Austerlitz Station! Getting to Marseille is going to be a bit complicated! That's the Bordeaux line. Or through Toulouse."

"We'll go by Béziers!"

"But I don't want to go to Marseille!"

"You fucking idiot, we're not going to Marseille! Marseille? What the hell would I do in Marseille? You're not getting it! If this trick works, in one hour we'll stop the train in the middle of the countryside, and we'll jump out, scatter, and disappear. No one sees or knows anything. Made in the shade!"

I was stunned. They thought they were in the Three Musketeers.

"But these tramps won't be able to go thirty feet in the countryside! There's no one here who could climb over the barbed wire fences."

"Stop whining, damn it. You're not being forced to come along. You're not my babysitter. Go back and join your tight-ass family. Tell them I've moved south. Hey, tell 'em I've become a Green, that's what you should tell 'em."

"Here comes the engine!" shouted one of the lookouts in the front of the train.

We rushed up front in order to be able to see, at crawl speed, an old, bright green engine piercing the haze little by little. Farther away, some shadowy riot squad troops approached, keeping a respectful distance. It seemed like the authorities had accepted the deal. They must have thought of some other way to arrest us. And besides, holding a police chief meant something. And a police chief with a pistol to his head, that was a first.

The engine bumped into the train gently, but everything cut out immediately. There was no more juice, the water pipes were torn out and the PVC toilet hook-ups creaked eerily. A powerful odor of human waste succeeded in imposing itself over the already strong general stench. A guy in blue work overalls came and attached the engine to the first car and ran off, following in the footsteps of the engine conductor who was running away, skirting the rails.

The Draft Dodger and one of his buddies untied the railway official and pushed him out, a gun barrel stuck against his jaw, in full view of everyone. They clambered into the engine. My uncle explained to me that all these train-bosses were able to drive a train. The police chief tried to tell us to cut our losses before things got any more serious, that all this was a big mistake, but my uncle threatened him, saying that if he didn't shut up he would stuff his bottle of cheap wine down his throat and then gag him with his own socks. The guy blanched, ready to faint.

We waited another long moment.

My uncle, on the foot-rail, hanging on to the iron handrails, was looking off into the distance. The signal was still red. Everyone was tense. No one quite believed it yet. It all seemed incredibly insane.

"It's green!" shouted my uncle. "They've opened the track! We've won!"

A blast of the whistle, coming from the locomotive, replied.

The train started its engine. Everyone started cheering.

At slow speed, the five train cars passed in front of the riot squad, who came nearer to see their prey escaping. There was a volley of insults, with unexpected variations, shot out from all the lowered windows. Stylish exercise routines based on giving the finger were spontaneously invented. There was intense mocking laughter, and the drunken feeling of certain victory.

I relaxed a little bit. I couldn't see any viable outcome to this ghostly trip, but we had escaped a police beating, so we could breathe a sigh of relief.

We passed Choisy-le-Roi at slow speed.

It was a beautiful, sunny day and a little fresh breeze came in through the open windows. Exhausted and worn out by the fighting and the tension, many guys were already asleep, often on the floor, in the middle of empty beer cans and the residue of the siege. In certain compartments there was loud snoring, despite the noise coming from outside, despite the flapping curtains. We passed alongside other deserted train cars, lined up head to tail on a garage track. Two police cars stood guard. We shouted, vengeful fists raised, we laughed, everyone was hysterical. We were crossing a sort of border. We were going farther than where society had wanted to push us. The victory was complete. It was a grand slam, a bloodbath.

"But they will block the track at some point," I said to my uncle. "At a switch. We won't be able to go on. It'll be someplace quiet, far from everything, where they can massacre us without any journalists present."

"Stop worrying, there's no risk of that," he replied. "Don't forget two things: we have two hostages, and, in the locomotive, there is a radio. And you can count on those two dudes up there to keep the pressure on and scare the shit out of everyone."

I looked at the police chief. He was as white as the middle of the French flag that he represented. Still tied up to his bar, he watched the landscape flash by him with an astonished disbelief. It was all a bad dream; this was completely beyond him. It wasn't possible for him to be on an adventure like this. He was handcuffed on a train with a bunch of stinking, dangerous crazies. I didn't really know what he could be thinking. In any case, he didn't seem to be listening to the grumbling of certain people who at last were beginning to balk. These were the kind who are never happy. It's only to be expected, it's a kind of lifestyle. They were saying things like: "The countryside is boring," "Only in Paris can you get a decent bite to eat," "Go begging around the cows, yeah right," "Gendarmes are stupid," "It's getting too sunny," "There's no metro down south." Some guys were regretting the trip; they felt almost homesick already. They started believing that, farther on, it was going to be hell, because they were likely to find people there even poorer and more helpless than themselves.

Outside, everything was becoming more and more green and gold. The suburbs had petered out. There were fields, small villages, steeples.

The platforms of the station at Dourdan were full of people who had come to see the phantom train go by. They were the curious. I saw some cameras. All of France knew about our train and wanted front row seats; we weren't going to pass by unnoticed. They shouted as we went by, some waved, but most gaped. So, this train really did exist. It wasn't just a joke.

Aboard, some people were getting sick. The bad wine had led to violent puking. The police chief himself had taken a good hit of purple splatter on his shoes and was on the edge of collapse.

Those who were not sick, those who were not plunged in comatose sleep, started complaining. They wanted water, they wondered what they were going to eat, and they looked for other reasons to be unhappy. My uncle shouted at them, calling them sheep-brained losers, and harshly advised them to figure out what they wanted, once and for all. They were going to see the ocean—shit, what did they have to complain about?

My uncle seemed to be growing younger. I no longer noticed his seventy years. He belched, pitching along the corridors, sometimes dropping down onto a seat, his face profoundly flushed but with an Olympic glow.

And then the train slowed and stopped in the middle of the countryside.

Some of the Makhnos got out immediately, in order to meet up with those in the locomotive. My uncle also jumped out onto the gravel. Through the window I heard them discussing things, just below me. Everything was fine. The Railway, for the moment, had opened the track, on the condition that we didn't go faster than forty-five miles per hour. They wanted us to stop at the station in Aubrais in order to renegotiate. The Draft Dodger, speaking for our group, had accepted this on the condition that our side could take advantage of situation to have supplies brought to us, something to drink and eat. Then we would see. Over the radio, numerous people had tried, with serious words and voices, to ask us to be more or less reasonable, that this couldn't go on forever, that there would be no repression or lawsuit started, but that we had to stop, that the distance already travelled was really far enough, that we had proved our case, that now we were front cover news, that we should be happy, that the homeless had had their trench-battle, but that this was now something unmanageable, that it was dangerous, all this. They contradicted themselves, not knowing how to put forward a package neatly tied up with threats, paternalism, and panic. Someone might fall off the train and we would be responsible—they had warned us.

My uncle was laughing at least as much as the Makhnos.

A first negotiation had already taken place and had concluded with no progress. It was out of the question for the Railway to let us travel on the southeast train line; there was too much traffic, it was too dangerous, too complicated, and not all of the secondary lines were electrified.

"There's no question of us backing down," the anarchists retorted. "We're going to see the great, blue ocean."

The other side had a counter proposal that would allow us to see the sea: to let us go on to Sète. This offer was accepted. To go to the hometown of Georges Brassens, the anarchist musician—that was fair, my uncle judged.

But that was when a bunch of guys jumped off the train, and some began to run like rabbits into the nearby fields. My uncle was shouting after them, trying to get them to stop, but it didn't do any good. They were running away from a nightmare that they had decided they couldn't handle. Our five train cars were now half empty.

Wounded to the core, the anarchist leaders nevertheless decided that no one would be forced to continue. This wasn't Kronstadt. Everyone was asked to choose, and we did the sorting. We got rid of everyone who didn't want to continue—many of them didn't even know why. Inside the thick fog of their drunkenness, they no longer knew where they were. A few were crying, begging for the shouting and arguing to stop. It was necessary to carry some to the bottom of the foot-rail. There was some sweettalking, some grandiose speech-making about cowardice, and some radical injunctions to go get screwed.

I was tempted for a brief moment to leave then, too, and do what I could on my own to get back home. It wasn't out of fear, but simply because everything was so green around us, and those quiet fields bordered by rustling trees suddenly seemed to me to be the most calm, restful, beautiful place.

But I was starting to care more and more about my uncle's respect. Despite his rags, despite his drunkard's face, I gradually understood the hostile and unfair ways in which our family had treated him. He was a real desperado, the kind of guy who did not live well except under galloping entropy. I was beginning to understand why he had given up on everything in order to slowly commit suicide beside the gutters in the Place de Vosges. He couldn't help himself. He knew that the family would never really understand his unhappiness. And now, through this grotesque and incredible adventure, he was gradually coming back to the world. He was doing it in opposition to the others, in opposition to the family, but not in opposition to me. It was *for* me, maybe. It was in order to leave me a small, positive image of him, something that I could keep for a long time in the wallet of my memory. I had to stay.

And then, once again, he distinguished himself. He remembered the mechanic in Buster Keaton's film *The General*, and persuaded us to detach the last train car, in order to avoid being pursued. We did it quickly.

Then we set off again. The engine groaned, as did the train cars. We watched as, at the end of a straight line of track, the lone train car we'd left behind disappeared, looking ridiculous and lost on the gleaming rails.

We made ourselves at home. We opened the doors and chucked out everything getting in the way. We cleaned house, leaving a real garbage dump alongside the tracks. From the back door we saw greasy papers and pieces of cardboard flying, we saw the glittering shards of numerous broken bottles.

"It's all biodegradable!" shouted my uncle. "Just like us!"

We divided ourselves up. From now on everyone had their own compartment assigned. Then, we divvied up the supplies. We collected everything that could serve as a projectile, we brought together the rest of the food, and all of the wine. We made plans. The trip became organized. Our surroundings became almost acceptable. We were going to leave this place in the state in which we had found it—well, almost. This train was, however, a sort of scenic railway for the broke, from the blocked johns to the half-gutted seats, with a strange group of clandestine passengers. There were about forty disheveled tramps, with weeping eyes and filth getting the upper hand, and a dozen madmen in leather who thought they were the Jesse James gang riding on the Pony Express.

Everyone sat down in their compartments, letting themselves be gently rocked by the regular rhythm of the rails. A few look-outs stayed at the windows to keep an eye on the roads, bridges, and stations, and to try to spot any pursuit or tail on us. At smaller stations, there was sometimes a crowd that waved to us. The engine often whistled. It now felt like a kind of traveling summer camp.

For a while, before we reached Orleans, my eyes followed the long, unfinished concrete track meant for the aerotrain. It ran alongside our track for fifteen miles or so, a completely useless thing. I couldn't help but think about all the dough that had been invested in that dead-end project, money that could have supported the occupants of our train for the rest of their lives.

The train slowly rumbled over the switches at the Aubrais station. Each time our train passed a switch, my heart was in my throat. At low speed, the Railway could have derailed us, immobilizing us forever. They had steered us onto one of the last tracks. We noticed a lively crowd around the station. There were also a lot of cops, and the riot squad must have been guarding all the entrances and exits.

When the train came to a stop, a heavy silence fell over us.

We were all at the windows, watching the movements of the crowd, three platforms away.

A small electric cart with three trailers hooked up to it drove along the platform to meet us. It stopped beside us and the driver immediately left on foot, going back towards the station.

"Those pigs," grumbled my uncle, "they've only given us water!"

Sure enough, there were several bundles of Evian bottles on the little carts. Nothing to burn our brains—safety precautions. The detox program was already starting, long distance. Two anarchists jumped out to load the stuff onto the train. There were also some of the usual French National Railway sandwiches, in their crackly plastic wrap.

"Check the expiration date," Guy muttered. "They might be trying to poison us!"

"It's paté," replied one of the guys on the platform.

"Be careful!" One of the anarchists from the engine started shouting, pointing to a small group of men in dark blue spilling out like magic from a stairwell in the middle of the platform. They were the SWAT team or some shit like that. One of the anarchists who had been loading the water jumped up on the foot-rail and fired two shots in their direction, aiming above their heads.

"Go back or we'll shoot the police chief," shouted my uncle.

The police athletes immediately disappeared down the stairway. We returned to an impasse. That must have been a fucking setback for them, and it was for us, too. At this rate, the police chief wouldn't last much longer.

At my window, I was breaking out in a cold sweat and had started trembling.

This was a fucking mess. Once considered the buddies of the respected Abbé Pierre, now we had become die-hard terrorists. Stealthily, we had been pushed down a slippery slope with no escape route. We would be hunted down like rabbits. Things were looking grim. The Special Forces were not far away, and probably helicopters, snipers, all that stuff; they were just waiting to put a bullet in your head while you slept.

I wasn't the only one thinking this way, because about ten loud-mouth tramps and three nervous younger guys chose that moment to jump off the train and run towards the station across the tracks.

"You bunch of idiots!" my uncle shouted, "They'll slaughter you! You'll pay for all of us! Fools!"

In front of us the signal was still red—we couldn't start off yet. It felt like something was getting ready to happen. At my feet, a guy was snoring heavily. When he woke up, it would take him a while to understand the shit he was in, far from Paris, an outlaw on the front line.

We stayed there for a long moment. Then a strange thought ran through my mind. I no longer felt afraid and I no longer wanted to leave, to get away. I only wanted one thing: that this would be over. It didn't matter how. I was practically sure that whatever happened would be in some sense a liberation, something which I would be able to claim for myself for a long time to come. It would be my own valorous deed, my own 1968. My battle. I had been there, not you.

Then another guy showed up, all alone. He was a station master or something like that, wearing a cap with four stars. He was a train general, at least.

We let him come all the way to us.

"This is getting to be some kind of joke, guys," he said, out of breath.

"Who's joking?" replied our spokesman, the Draft Dodger. "All that we want is to get to the sea. Then we'll surrender."

"But that's stupid!"

"It's not stupid, it's vital."

He took off his cap to wipe his large forehead.

"Just come with us," said the Draft Dodger, laughing. "We'll pretend to take you hostage and you'll see the big blue sea, too."

"Right. Like I've got the fucking time for that. I've got 200 riot police on my back in the station, plus the SWAT team, plus my boss, plus two slicks from the Ministry of the Interior, and a shit-load of journalists."

"It'll be good advertising for the company."

"Don't laugh."

"We're not laughing."

The station master breathed loudly. "OK, here's the deal: they want you to release the police chief—it seems he has a heart problem—and take a doctor and a ministry official in his place. They're both volunteers."

"Tell them that heart trouble or no, the chief is gonna die if this track isn't clear in five minutes."

"But I can't just tell them that. I have to take them something."

The Draft Dodger, out of patience, started shouting. "That's their fucking problem. They were the ones who shot first, damn it! You just tell them that we'll stop at Vierzon. By the time we get there, we'll have thought about their proposition. You've got five minutes! No more!"

And then he fired a shot in the air. The guy with the cap took off running.

"Now he's really screwed, that station master," a tramp said, quoting a popular Brassens song.

Nobody laughed.

Two minutes later, the signal changed to green.

It started all over again, just like in '14.

We had a nice trip. It was an hour and a half of peaceful travel. Everyone was sprawling on the seats, with the warm breeze coming in the windows.

The stench, little by little, was swept away by the wind and it became breathable in there. There weren't many people left in our train—barely thirty passengers, including three women. There were about twenty tramps, ten excited Makhnos, and the two hostages, who seemed not to be enjoying the trip, based on the completely panicked look of the police chief who was still attached to the window bar.

Spirits lifted a bit; we started believing in Sète. My uncle described the station, with its awning, just next to the port, where the boats lolled about. And these were not just any kind of boats—they were wine boats, those carrying the cheap Hérault wine to vinegar makers around the world. His audience was laughing. Some of them already had the desire to get on board one of those boats and dive into the wine tanks, leaving for faraway parts while swimming in red wine. It would be paradise!

A helicopter had been following us for a while, like a shit-fly. Since there might be cameras on board, the guys took turns making obscene gestures towards it, in order to keep up the pressure.

The problem at the moment was that there was only water on board. That was serious. Thank goodness for Vierzon.

The train stopped just underneath the big colored bridge, all the way at the end of the Vierzon station. The Makhnos had already negotiated by telephone with the authorities. There would be a trade: beer, lots of it, in exchange for one of the hostages. They had decided to unload the Railway official.

"You wanted to see Vierzon, well, you've seen Vierzon," laughed my uncle, quoting Jacques Brel.

He was of no use anymore, our train-boss, since the anarchists had figured out how this kind of machine operates. As a hostage, he wasn't much good, but his liberation for a palette of beer cans seemed like it would be another victory for us. The police chief could still serve amply as our shield.

From where we were, we couldn't see much of what was happening in the station. We could see some sort of a commotion and people in uniforms, but it didn't seem like anyone was going to try the same trick they'd attempted at Aubrais. They understood now that we were dangerous and determined. There was no hurry. As soon as the engineer set his foot on the asphalt of the platform, a tire cart filled with cases of six-packs started towards us, pulled by two guys in blue overalls.

What seemed strange to me was that there was no one on the bridge above us. It was such a pretty bridge, painted in psychedelic colors. They must have blocked access to avoid mobs of supporters. They didn't want a crowd coming to cheer us while eating grilled hot-dogs, since we must be the headline of every news story. Seeing something like this, live, was candy for the carrion-gobbling spectators. We'd already noticed it on the little radios we still had in the train. It was really ramping up: "The Tramps from Hell." "The Train Trip to Shame." "They have nothing to lose except their alcoholic delusions," etc. And, of course, saying that the police chief was a good father, with two young children.

While everyone was laughing and watching the cases of beer arrive, I couldn't take my eyes off the steel girders above us, which seemed like a mute menace, a foreboding image of brutality. Far away, on the station side, there was still the same silence.

"They're being very quiet, these pigs," belched my uncle. "It's almost as if they're full, like wild animals after feasting on the kill."

When the cart carrying the beer reached us, four guys got off the train to load everything on board the first car. They grabbed hold of the cases of six-packs and started throwing them into the corridor.

On the bridge, I saw some sort of Batman-like figure. I wanted to say something, but everything got stuck in my throat. And what would I have said? Look out? Death is above us? It was completely ridiculous.

My eyes were still glued up above when I heard the first beer can pop open.

Then the guy in a black body-suit jumped from the bridge.

All the rest happened very quickly. My hands never stopped clenching the window bar.

The batman landed on the roof of the third car, a wire in his hands. It was a cord of steel upon which were sliding, at high speed, a dozen more guys in ski masks, fucking flying spiders.

Not one sound came from my throat. My mouth was dry. My finger pointed at them.

The Draft Dodger spotted me, understood that something was wrong, and jumped off the train with his pistol in his hand. He too looking up in the air. I saw his chest jolt as if he was struck with an epileptic seizure and he fell backwards onto the middle of the tracks.

I never heard a single shot. The other armed anarchist, just like in the movies, fired two or three shots through the metal roof of the train car. But one of the assailants was already at the end of the car, with a strange, long weapon in his grasp. I saw the head of the Makhno disappear as if by magic. There was a pink cloud around him.

I threw myself on the ground. Everything went white as if there was ether in the air.

I guess that my uncle had jumped on one of the pistols that had fallen on the ground and was brandishing it and shouting. And then he disappeared, falling back under the impact of bullets, into the compartment from which he had emerged.

I just had time, before screaming, to see a huge black spider jump on me, flip me over like a pancake, and crush my nose into the floor, warning me not to move a muscle, not a single muscle.

I heard the crackle of a walkie-talkie.

Then a voice, calm, poised, and cold: "Mission terminated. All secure."

#2 Down and Out in Paris, with Cat

R.A. Bolo

Yeah, I know—for a lot of people, it would seem like I was living the dream life in the beautiful "city of lights" of Paris. I'm sure it looked that way from the outside: cushy, well-paying job as an English-language researcher; sexy young French girlfriend; cheap rent for a decent apartment owned by my girlfriend's aunt in the nearby suburb of Noisy-Le-Sec; easy commute of just two stops on the RER Magenta line from *Gare du Nord*; and access to all the sights and sounds and food and activities that Paris has to offer. And the food—did I mention the food? Not just the butter and cream-infused concoctions that the French are known for, but the variety of meats I could get on a regular basis from the local butcher: entrails, goat, horse. Shocking to friends and family back home in the States, but I have to admit that I really like horse. To me, there's no difference between eating a horse and eating a cow, and the French know it. I appreciate that streak of no-nonsense in them. If it were possible to make billions by factory-farming horses, or if it weren't only the rich who could keep and love a pet horse, nobody would give a second thought to *les boucheries chevaline.*

So, yeah, it was a regular "life of Riley" in Paris for me, except that it wasn't. I'd left Boston and moved to be with Marie-France in Paris after my Boston girlfriend Julie threw me out of the house. Julie's a smart, hard-working academic, but way too possessive and controlling, and way too intolerant of a minor indiscretion like Marie-France. Julie always had to be talking about and negotiating "the relationship" and it all just got too heavy. As for me, I'm an anarchist and more of a free love advocate, which I really think is better for everyone involved. Julie argued that it wasn't really "free love" or polyamory if everyone involved didn't agree to it, and I could never get her to see my point of view. Then she found out about Marie-France and kicked me out.

So, I found myself on the other side of the Atlantic, living with Marie-France, and to be honest, Julie was starting to look good to me again. I mean, Marie-France definitely had her points. She was young and energetic in bed, and she was an artist and musician with a lot of creative ideas. But she was perpetually encased in a cloud of smoke and it seemed like something on fire was always in her hand, whether it was a *Gitanes*, a clove cigarette, or a joint. It may have been the language difference, as neither of us was completely fluent in the other's native tongue, but I was also irritated by the shallowness of her intellect and her constant retreat into the creative process. I'd come home from work and the apartment would be a disaster area with dirty laundry piled up and the kitchen covered in paint, but nothing to eat and no food in the refrigerator.

"What have you been doing all day?" I'd bark at her, waving the smoke out of my eyes. "I've been working my ass off and I'm ready to eat!"

"I've been *painting*, darling," she'd reply languidly, as if there was all the time in the world and no need to worry about eating. At that point, I'd storm out of the apartment and go to the café down the block and order something to eat. Then I'd walk the streets of Noisy-Le-Sec enjoying the sounds of music slipping out the doors of some of the clubs. I'd look into the eyes of some of the African immigrants who I'd pass on the street, wondering if they could possibly feel more alienated and alone in France than I did. Then when it was late enough that I was sure that Marie-France had gone to bed, I'd finally go home, sleep, wake up the next day, and do it all over again.

After living in this state of non-conjugal non-bliss for several months, it turned out that Marie-France was the one with the lowest tolerance for our constant bickering. I arrived home to the apartment one evening to find her gone, along with a good portion of her clothes and art supplies. There was a note on the paint-spattered kitchen table that read, "Darling, I just can't take it any longer, off to stay with mes amis en Rouen, talk later, ciao, MF." A sent of clove cigarette lingered in the air. I left the apartment and headed to the café once again.

After Marie-France had fled, I was afraid I'd have to move out of the apartment; we'd been paying extremely cheap rent for it because it belonged to her aunt, Marie-Anne. But Marie-Anne completely understood what a flighty, pain-in-the-ass Marie-France could be and offered to lower the rent even more since it was only me living there. I kept her happy in return by making my handyman skills available on weekends for help around the apartment building: re-writing a light fixture, replacing a rotted window sill, clearing a blocked drain.

But things seemed to start a steep downward slide after this. Julie refused to take my late-night, long-distance calls and I heard from Boston friends that she was dating someone else. The few phone calls I had with Marie-France started out friendly enough, but ended with tears and angrily slammed phone receivers. Even though it was the proverbial "springtime in Paris," the "*Temps des cerises*" or "time of the cherry blossoms" that intoxicate with feelings of love and perhaps revolution, the weather seemed unnaturally cool and the Paris sky was perpetually overcast, which perfectly matched my mood.

Then one evening, I was eating at the usual café and there happened to be a new waiter on duty serving me. I was a "regular" there by now and all of the waiters knew me—and knew that I didn't drink. But this new guy didn't know that, and he was pushing me.

"Mais, pourquoi pas, monseiur?" he asked, aggressively pushing the wine list in my face. I was either going to punch the guy or order some damn wine. I ended up doing the latter, breaking over twelve years of sobriety. After that, the steep downward slide turned into a plunge off the cliff.

My job of course started to suffer. I was late almost every day, I called out sick a lot or just didn't bother to show up, and when I did come in, I was hungover and surly, and not in a mood to get much work done. My boss Marie-Claude went from being an occasional grouch to being a full-time bitch. She was laying on the passive-aggressive schtick big time, with every interaction being, "Could you *please* do this" or "Thank you *so very much* for that." I couldn't stand being there but it was a paycheck, even when they were docking my pay for missed hours. It was obvious Marie-Claude wanted to fire me, but she needed my native-English-speaker skills until the research project we were working on was over. I knew I had job security, at least for a while.

Then my health began to suffer as well. My paycheck was getting smaller and a good portion of it was going for booze. I couldn't afford to eat out, so I had to go shopping and try to cook for myself. I started to wait in line with the other poor immigrants for charity handouts of food once a week, just so I'd have some food on hand and more money for booze. I couldn't afford to pay to heat the apartment, so it was cold all of the time. I was getting sick on a regular basis and had a perpetual cough that I just couldn't shake.

At night, I'd often walk out in the streets, too angry and agitated to stay at home. Sometimes I'd try to chat with a prostitute or another drunk that I'd encounter on my walks, but usually the language barrier and my own impairment prevented any meaningful communication. My normal pattern was to stumble back to my apartment after midnight and try to get some sleep, but on more than one morning, I was awakened by an angry shopkeeper or resident who found me passed out in their alley or doorway. Once I was even picked up by the police, but was released with a stern warning after playing the part of a poor, ignorant foreigner.

My dream life in Paris was turning into a real nightmare. Every day on the train platforms on my commute to and from work, it seemed like at least one of the schedule-boards would post a thirty-minute delay on one of the train lines, due to an "*accident du personne*." This meant that someone had jumped in front of a train. I wasn't quite ready to buy that ticket, but I started to understand the feeling, to get a whiff of why it was such a common event in France.

Then one evening when I was walking home from the train station, a bright spot entered my life. I took a slightly different route home and, on the street that was behind the street that I lived on, I noticed a house with a *clos*, or enclosed garden, where someone had put food out for the street cats. There was a black-and-white mother cat there with three half-grown kittens, all having their supper on top of the stone wall. Seeing them made me so totally, inexplicably happy that I almost cried right there on the street.

I stopped on the sidewalk next to the wall and watched them as their little pink tongues lapped up the food left on an old, chipped plate. They reminded me of cats that my family had taken care of in our yard when I was growing up. I also had bittersweet thoughts of cats of my own that I'd had as an adult—some lost long ago to disease or old age, some left behind in Boston when I had moved. Watching these cats made me feel so good that I went home and cooked a delicious stew of chunks of horse meat and vegetables. I stayed inside all night, and only drank a little.

Passing by the house that fed the cats then became part of my regular routine and I'd often see the mother cat and her kittens there eating. There were some other street cats that would show up there as well: a crusty old grey tom who the mother cat would give a wide berth to, a grey tabby of indeterminate sex, and a couple of youngish calicos that looked like they could be sisters. The people feeding the cats appeared to be a young family consisting of father and mother and two or three young children. I'd sometimes here the kids yelling and playing in the yard, or the parents calling out to them from the house. It seemed like such an idyllic situation—a young, healthy, happy family caring for cats who needed their help.

Visiting the cats at the wall became the high point of my day, and made my bleak existence a little less bleak. I started sticking a can of sardines in my pocket when I left for work in the morning, and then opening it up to share with the cats on the wall on my way home. They were gradually getting used to me, and would react when they saw me coming. Some of the older ones were even open to letting me pet them. Eventually I started hoisting myself up to sit on top of the wall, petting and playing with the cats, and grabbing the kittens to hold them and try to socialize them so they'd be less feral. Everything else in my life was still pretty much sucking, but being with these cats gave me one glimmer of hope and purpose.

Then one day, that came crashing down as well. I stopped by the wall on my way home as usual, but when I got there I was shocked by a new development. A hand-drawn sign on a plain white piece of paper, that looked like it had probably been made by one of the children, was taped to the wall. It read: "Rester loin de notre mur!"—which means, "Stay off of our wall!" An unhappy or angry face was drawn at the bottom. The message was clear: my presence was not welcome, and the joy I received from interacting with the cats was now at an end. This simple sign felt like a punch in my gut, and I avoided walking down that street from then on.

The weeks rolled by, and I was adrift in a black sea of depression and hopelessness. My drinking increased, my attendance at work decreased, and my health (which had actually been improving) was now taking another nose-dive. I was coughing so much and so hard that it would sometimes keep me awake at night. I was never sure if I had a fever or not, but I always felt kind of low-grade terrible. I was surly and argumentative and would snap at anyone I interacted with. Life was not good.

One day when I'd actually managed to make it into work, Marie-Claude stopped by my cubicle with a young, well-dressed man. His dark hair was perfectly styled, he wore trendy fashionable glasses, and he exuded that kind of energy and exuberance found only in the young. I hated him on sight.

"This is Jean-Philippe," Marie-Claude told me, and I grudgingly shook the young man's hand. "He may be doing some work for us in the future and I'm showing him around the office. Would you *please* take a few minutes to speak with him and explain what it is that you do here? Thank you *so much*!" And off she went without even waiting for a reply from me.

Jean-Philippe pulled another chair into the cubicle and sat there beside me, asking some questions about the work I did and dotting the conversation with some information about himself. It turned out that he had studied in the United States for a few years and his English was actually pretty good. I answered his questions in the most basic ways possible, not going into much detail unless he specifically asked. Then it finally dawned on me why he was here: he was someone Marie-Claude was considering as my replacement.

Once that lightbulb turned on, I turned off. I got shorter in my responses and ruder in my demeanor until he finally took the hint, thanked me politely, and left to track down Marie-Claude. Later in the day, when I was sure that Marie-Claude was within earshot, I loudly said to Marie-Thérèse in the cubicle next to mine: "Hey, what's up with that guy Jean-Philippe? He seemed like a nice enough fellow, but his English is *absolutely terrible*!" We never saw Jean-Philippe after that. I had won this round, but I still had enough brain cells left to know that I'd only won a battle and not the war. My days on the job were numbered and Marie-Claude would eventually take me down.

A feeling of desperation started to set in. I was a hopeless drunk in a foreign country where I didn't speak the language, had difficulty in navigating my day-to-day activities, and had no hope of finding another job once this one ended. I'd never get a good recommendation from Marie-Claude and there wasn't a lot else I could do. Sometimes at night, I'd drunkenly walk along the canal, staring into the dark waters and wondering if it wouldn't be better if I just threw myself in and ended it all.

Just as my despair was becoming more palpable, and the thought of the dark canal waters embracing me was becoming more comforting, I was once again saved by an angel on four furry feet. The kitchen window in my apartment looked into the small backyard of our building. I happened to glance out of it one day, and I noticed a young, scrawny, black-and-white cat sitting on the wall at the back of the yard. I'm not really sure that he could even see into the window, but it seemed at the time that he was looking straight at me. I felt an immediate need to spring into action. I grabbed some leftover food from the refrigerator, and took it out on a small plate to the backyard.

The cat eyed me warily from his perch on the wall. He didn't come for the food when I set it down, but he didn't run away, either. He watched me closely and waited until I left. Then I could see from my window that he'd come for the grub, gobbling it down hungrily. That evening I bought a bunch of cans of cheap cat food and began a new routine of feeding the little guy every day.

I gradually went about trying to gain his trust. First, I stopped going all the way back into the building after I set the food down; I'd just go to the door and wait. He could still see me there, but his desire to eat made him brave enough to come down from the wall and enter the yard for the food. Then I started to just sit on a bench in the yard, after leaving the food about halfway between the bench and the wall. The cat was still hungry enough, and starting to see me as less of a threat, that this arrangement was acceptable to him as well. I'd talk to him in a soothing voice while he ate, trying to help him get used to me. He didn't seem to mind this, but he still wasn't drawn into contact with me; he'd leave the yard as soon as he was finished eating.

After about a week of this, I sat on the bench and put the dish of food next to me, then waited. If he wanted to eat, it would cost him a head scratch this time. Sure enough, the beast crept up to his dish and ate while I petted him and scratched his furry head. Our real friendship began at that time. He was now open to interacting with me, and would run to greet when I entered the yard in the evening with his food. Now he would hang out with me even after he finished eating, lounging on the bench next to me and waiting for head scratches and belly rubs. Seeing him close up, I noticed the distinctive teardrop-shaped white blaze on his chest, and knew that he was one of the kittens from the litter I'd played with at the house at the far end of the block. He was almost fully grown now, probably about ten months old.

As I continued to feed my new black-and-white buddy on a regular basis, he filled out and put on weight. He was no longer a scrawny, skinny little cat, but a strong, healthy-looking feline with some meat on his bones. Pretty soon he'd be ready to own the neighborhood, or at least our small section of it. But there's a funny thing about cats sometimes. We think we're helping them out, that we're rescuing them, but it actually turns out that at the same time, they're also rescuing us. I now had something to distract me from my sorrows; I had someone to come home to and something to look forward to every night.

Things were looking up all around. Ever since the Jean-Philippe incident at work, I'd made more of an effort to make it into the office every day and to get at least some work done while I was there. I had another mouth to feed and that was an incentive to put the hours in and get as full a paycheck as possible. Marie-Claude seemed to appreciate my new-found work ethic and eased up on the bitchiness somewhat. I knew that my position there was still in jeopardy, but I now felt more hopeful about the future. I was drinking less, spending more of my money on food and less on booze, and I no longer entertained dark thoughts at the side of the canal.

I was generally in a better mood all around, and Julie even started taking my calls again. She was still seeing the guy she'd started dating after I left, and I think that gave her enough confidence to re-open contact, keeping me clearly in the "friend zone." It was great to chat with her and she loved to hear stories about my new cat friend. Being a real "cat person" herself, she always had news of her own cats, as well as of some of our mutual friends back in Boston. Talking to her helped give my life another sense of normalcy, and provided a tie to the happier times back home. I never told her that I'd fallen off the wagon, but I was sometimes drunk when I was talking to her and I imagine that she had begun to suspect.

So, I'd managed to establish a new, more sustainable pattern in my life—but it wasn't long before that, too, got thrown off the rails. One evening in mid-November, I brought the cat food out to the yard as usual but there was no cat there. I was disappointed, but I didn't think too much about it at the time. I figured my cat buddy was "otherwise engaged" elsewhere, and would show up the next day, hungry as usual. But he didn't show up the next day, or the day after that. Three whole days went by without any trace of him. I tried not to think of it as a rejection but consoled myself somewhat with the thought that, "Well, either he's been adopted by somebody else or he's been squashed by a Peugeot." I continued to hold out hope of seeing him again ("maybe he was accidentally locked in someone's basement!") but in truth a bit of light had gone out of my life once again.

On the Friday afternoon following the cat's disappearance, I had come home early and was startled to hear a long, horrible moan through my rear window. I looked out and there was my *chat du rue*, stumbling across the yard, falling on his side after every two or three agonized steps. This was accompanied by the most pathetic, heart-rendering, drawn-out yowling that I had ever heard: "Mmmmmrrrraaaaaaoooowwwww!!!" I rushed down to the yard, snatched up the poor, suffering beast and brought him inside. He kept trying to stand but continued to topple over on the kitchen floor. There was no obvious evidence of injury or blood, and I could find no broken bones as I felt along his legs and body. I was in a real panic and not sure what I could do to help him. I threw an old sweater into a box and put him in it, hoping that he might settle down. Unfortunately, the cat's distress and his awful yowling continued.

I knew absolutely nothing about veterinary care in France, so I figured that I needed to find someone who did. I tried to call Marie-France, but she didn't answer. I was then desperate enough to do something I really didn't want to do, which was to call my work colleague Marie-Thérèse and ask for her advice as a favor. Marie-Thérèse spoke English well enough and she'd always been friendly to me, if a little distant. I managed to reach her, and between what she knew and the advice that her boyfriend chimed in with, I got some useful information for next steps to take.

It sounded like the vet school would be my best bet; I called and they said that they would be willing to see the cat free of charge if I got him there before 5 PM. Unfortunately, the school was on the opposite side of Paris from me, and I'd have to change trains at least a couple of times after getting to the city. It was not likely I'd make it there on time. Plan B was to take him to the local vet in Noisy-le-Sec, which luckily happened to be open that evening.

I carried the groaning cat in the cardboard box as a cold, steady rain started to fall on the lamplit streets. A young veterinarian, a man who I could see was not the boss, and a young woman who seemed to be in training, received us. I explained the situation in my clumsy French as they began to examine my little friend. The verdict was that he'd probably gotten into a poison trap for rats or mice that someone had left in a shed or basement. Ingesting this kind of poison was unfortunately commonly fatal for stray cats. They said that they could hydrate him with an intravenous line and if he survived the night and didn't show signs of too much organ damage, they'd castrate him the next day and give him back to me. If he was too badly damaged, they would just euthanize him.

The quote that they gave me for their services was more money than I even had. I think that they could tell that by the shocked look on my face. In return, I gave them my sob story about being a poor immigrant and asked how much they would charge for just the minimum life-saving treatment. They conferred together quietly and seemed to take pity on me, but said that ninety euros was the best they could do, dead or alive. That was about three quarters of everything I had in the bank, but I agreed.

The following afternoon I returned to the vet's office and, to my delight, there was my brave critter, all cleaned up and standing on his own four feet. I thanked the vets profusely, paid them, and brought my boy home. Unfortunately, "NO PETS" was one of Marie-Anne's iron-clad rules for the apartment. She had endless horror stories about how woodwork had been damaged or carpets "absolutely destroyed" by thoughtless pet owners and their filthy, vicious animals. When we moved into the apartment, Marie-France had to turn over custody of her beloved pet snake to a former boyfriend. Once, after we'd been there a few months, I'd asked Marie-Anne about having some small, caged animals like hamsters or guinea pigs in the apartment. She had looked at me in horror, imperiously declaring "NO RODENTS!"

So, I knew I was wantonly breaking one of the cardinal rules for having access to the cushy deal for this apartment. But it was almost like I didn't really have a choice; it was really a life-or-death situation that called for protecting an endangered friend. I named him Georgie that night, after the son of George Brown, a long-dead anarchist of Philadelphia who I'd researched and written about during the preceding year. George Junior was born in 1892 and had a fairly idyllic childhood, but he had returned from the Great War shell-shocked and alcoholic, leading a dreary life thereafter. It was a little surprising to think that the cat had remained nameless this long, but now he was here in the apartment with me and the name seemed to fit.

The cat's journey back to health continued through his first night indoors. Georgie paced the floors growling, avoiding me, and only nibbling at his favorite food that I put down for him. I went to bed, hoping that he would feel more settled by morning. In the middle of the night, I was awakened by a thump as he jumped up on the bed, and I was gratified to feel him curling up by my feet. It was cold in the apartment due to my non-payment of the heating bill, and even if he was scared and disoriented, he knew where to find warmth. We both drifted back off to sleep. Later in the wee hours of the morning, I was awakened by him again as he started scratching at the comforter on my bed. It wasn't the loving kind of kneading that cats do, but rather the kind of digging they do when they are ready to do their business. Realizing he was getting ready to have a crap, I jumped out of bed and grabbed him. As I carried him to the kitchen where I had left a makeshift litter box, he was dropping small, hard turds along the way. The vets had warned me that the poison he'd eaten may have made him constipated; this was his painful moment of "clearing the pipes."

In the morning, he did seem more settled and he undoubtedly felt better physically after having gotten rid of the bad crap that had plugged him up. Being the fastidious genius that most cats are, he immediately recognized the value of the litterbox and never had another "accident." I now officially had a pet in an apartment where pets were strictly prohibited; Georgie was now an indoor cat and my new best friend.

We fell into a new routine where I would arrive home from work, lie down on the couch, and softly call his name. He would immediately appear and jump up onto my chest, and I'd pet his purring body and stare into his round, dark eyes. Georgie had long, black fur with two white paws in the front, a narrow white mask on his face, and the distinctive white teardrop blaze on his chest; I was in awe of his beauty. After cuddling on the couch and relaxing from my day, we'd both have dinner together. I was still drinking too much at night, but at least I was no longer drinking alone. I had Georgie for company, and he was never judgmental.

Despite the joy that my new friend brought to my life, I was still struggling and in a constant state of anxiety. I was trying to make it into work every day, as much as I could, and trying to draw as much pay as possible. But I'd finally gotten an official letter of dismissal from the "big boss," Marie-Claude's superior, thanking me profusely for my contributions to the project, while at the same time stating in no uncertain terms that my services would no longer be required once the project ended. I estimated that I had another six to ten weeks on the job, and made the conscious decision to slow my pace at work to help ensure that number was as close to ten as possible. I also had to take steps to economize again, saving as much money each week as I could and only buying the cheapest food for both myself and Georgie. I was once again standing in line for the charity food handouts at a *Resto du Couer*—"Restaurant of the Heart," coming home with a sack of rice, some wilted vegetables, an odd assortment of canned goods, and some frozen meats. It wasn't the best grub in the world, but it definitely helped.

When I had courage enough to face facts, I knew that this couldn't go on forever. No matter how much I economized, no matter how much free food I stood in line for, no matter how often Marie-Anne "forgot" about the rent in thanks for my small repairs around the building, it just wouldn't, it just couldn't last. My job would eventually end and my money would eventually run out. I saw no hope of finding steady work elsewhere. I had few friends and fewer opportunities on the horizon. I felt completely, utterly stuck. If it hadn't been for Georgie, I'm sure that the idea of jumping onto the train tracks or throwing myself into the canal would have started to look good again.

Then one night, a door cracked open for me. I was talking to Julie on the phone and I know I'd probably been going on at length about all of my problems and how hopeless I felt. I felt stuck and didn't see any way out of my troubles. Julie finally interrupted me, saying, "I have an idea. Why don't you come home?"

"Haven't you been listening?" I'd retorted irritably. "I have sixty euros in the bank. That would probably buy me a second-class train ticket to London from here. If by 'home,' you mean 'Boston,' it's going to be a long swim."

"No one's expecting you to swim!" she snapped back. "I've been talking to Jacob and Alexandria and some of your other friends here. We're willing to spring for a one-way plane ticket back."

"You...you are?" The offer was entirely unexpected and threw me off guard.

"Yes, we are," Julie went on. "We've been talking about your situation and everyone agrees that it would be better if you were back in the States."

"Well, thank you. Let me think about it. It's a generous offer and it certainly has its appeal." We agreed to talk again in a few days, after I'd had more time to think it over.

In the intervening days, the offer of plane ticket back to Boston got even more appealing. My situation in Paris was seeming more and more like a dead end. Back in Boston, I'd have more resources: more friends and more work opportunities. It was looking like my salvation, my way out, had arrived. There was just one problem: what to do with Georgie.

When I next talked to Julie, I told her that I'd gratefully take up the offer of the plane ticket back to Boston. "But I'm wondering about Georgie," I said. "Can he come, too?"

"I've looked into it," Julie responded. "Honestly, it's just not doable. The cost to take him on the plane would be almost as much as a second ticket. You'd have to have a regulation-sized carrier to bring him into the cabin. And he'd also need to have a completed health form from a veterinarian, and even with that, he'd have to stay in quarantine for three months."

"Really?" I asked, trying to take it all in. The thought of another visit to the vet, and paying for it, seemed daunting on the face of it, not to mention having to buy a special carrier.

"Yes," said Julie. "And just think about it from his perspective: how happy would he be on a long international flight? And how happy would he be, sitting in a cage somewhere for three months? He's a French cat; he needs to stay in France. You need to see if you can find a home for him there, or a shelter that will take him."

Julie was always the practical, logical one and I usually heeded her advice on most things. But I really couldn't stand the idea of leaving Georgie behind. I made a mental note to find out how much it would cost to get the medical form from a vet, and to come up with a good plan for paying everyone back if they'd spring for the cost of Georgie's flight. I tried not to think about the quarantine for the time being.

I made some non-committal noises to her in regard to the fate of the cat, and we went on to discuss other aspects of my return to Boston. Julie was now living with her boyfriend, so I wouldn't be able to stay with her. She told me that our mutual friend Damien had a spare room at his place and was willing to put me up for at least a few weeks on my return to Boston. Things were slowly starting to come together for my return to the States.

The next day, I blew off going in to work. Since my time was officially nearing an end there and I had a new plan in place for my next steps, my motivation to do any work at my job had taken a steep nosedive. Instead, I ventured back to the local vet's office to see what I could find out about the needed medical form for Georgie's travel. As luck would have it, the young veterinarian who'd provided Georgie's life-saving treatment was there and available to speak with me. I thanked him again for his help with my poor cat and assured him that he was doing well. As best as I could explain in my poor French, I communicated to him that I planned to return to the U.S. and needed a health form for the cat to travel. In turn, he explained back in a mixture of French and English that he wasn't familiar with this, but that he would look into it and give me a call when he had more information.

After that, I went home and thought about what I'd need to do in order to leave. I'd been in France for over a year and I'd accumulated various possessions in addition to what I'd brought with me. Now I needed to think about how much I could pack into suitcases and what I needed to get rid of. Georgie sat on my bed, watching with intense interest as I went through my clothes.

"What do you think, Georgie?" I'd ask, holding up a sweater. "Pack it or sack it?"

Georgie wasn't particularly opinionated, but that didn't stop my banter with him. "What do you think about moving to the United States?" I asked. "You'll have to learn English, but there's some nice girl cats in Boston that I'm sure will be charmed by your French accent."

I was making progress on creating "keep" and "discard" piles of clothing when my phone rang. It was the vet calling with information about the required animal travel form, and the news wasn't good. It turned out that Georgie would need a complete physical work-up, including blood work and various tests for illness, and would need to get several vaccinations as well. The best price the vet could offer was a hundred euros, more money than I had to my name. I thanked him for the information and told him I'd get back to him.

This news was enough to send me into another dark funk. I spent the rest of the afternoon drinking and trying to figure out a way to make bringing Georgie home with me a reality. But every train of thought I started on ended in a black tunnel with no light at the end. I lay half dozing on the couch with Georgie resting on my chest when the phone rang again. This time it was Julie calling from Boston. She wanted me to give her a departure date as soon as possible so that she could purchase the plane ticket for me.

I normally didn't want to talk to Julie when I'd been drinking because I didn't want her to know that I'd fallen off the wagon. But I was feeling sorry for myself, and sorry for Georgie, and I needed someone to talk to. I told her what the vet had said and she was not particularly sympathetic.

"I already told you that bringing the cat back wasn't going to work!" she said. "I don't know why you're even pursuing this. You need to put your time and energy into getting ready to leave, and that includes finding a home for him."

"I know," I whined. "But poor Georgie! I saved his life! He saved my life! I just can't bear the thought of leaving him! Do you think you could lend me the money to pay for the vet visit for the form?"

That's when Julie lost it. "Listen to me!" she yelled. "I don't think you're fully grasping what's going on here. You can't even take care of yourself! How do you think you'll manage taking care of a cat? Your friends are paying to get you home. We're providing you with a place to stay, and help in getting back on your feet. You need to start cooperating with the people trying to help you, and stop feeling sorry for yourself and coming up with new problems we have to solve for you." At that moment, I knew that she understood the full extent of the trouble I was in.

"You're right," I conceded. "I'm sorry. I do appreciate what you and the others are doing for me. I'm going to work on finding a home for Georgie." I promised to give her a date for my return soon and we hung up. As much as I didn't want to face it, I knew I'd have to be leaving my beautiful boy behind. I buried my face in his luxurious fur and told him, "I'm sorry" over and over again. Then I opened another bottle.

The next day I woke up on the couch with a terrible hangover, but with a gorgeous black-and-white cat still snoozing on my chest. It was almost noon, so there was no room for any thought of going in to work that day. I fixed a pot of coffee, had some "hair of the dog that bit me," and warmed up some leftovers I found in the fridge. After feeding myself and Georgie, I knew I had to accomplish something productive that day.

It seemed to me that there had to be animal shelters somewhere in the vicinity, just like there were back in the States, although I'd never noticed one in any of my travels around the city. But I did some searching online and found what looked like a good bet—a place that was in a nearby suburb and that adopted out dogs and cats. I called the number on the website and in my lousy French, tried to explain my situation to the woman who answered the phone. Between my French and her English, I finally got my message across. But she told me that there was an eighty-euro fee to surrender an animal at their shelter. I could afford that about as much as I could afford the airline ticket for the cat.

It was discouraging to get more bad news, but I also figured there were other shelters in the greater Paris area. Maybe some of them were cheaper or would cut me a deal. I would do more research and make more calls later. Now I needed to get out of the apartment and get some fresh air. I pulled on my coat and walked around the neighborhood for about an hour and then decided to go home by way of Marie Anne's house, which was a couple of blocks away from my apartment. She was always happy to see me and I needed cheering up. I also had to let her know that I would be leaving the apartment, and it would be good to get one more task out of the way.

I wasn't disappointed when Marie-Anne answered the door. Her gray hair was pulled back in a neat bun, and she wore a nice dress and jewelry even though she was just sitting around at home—a typical elegant French woman. She broke into a smile when she saw me, saying "Come in! Come in! It's been so long since I've seen you! How come you never visit me?"

"I'm sorry, Marie-Anne," I said, taking off my coat as I entered her small, tidy house. "I've been really busy and I've been having some difficulties. I didn't want to burden you…"

"It's no burden! I'm always happy to see you, no matter how your life is going. Do you want coffee?"

"Yes, I'd love coffee," I responded, following her into the kitchen. I sat at the table while she busied herself getting water started for the coffee. "I'm afraid I have a couple of things I need to tell you, and I'm afraid you're not going to like either of them."

"Oh, no! What is it?" she asked, looking at me with concern. "It's not that wild child Marie-France, is it?"

"No, it's not Marie-France. I haven't spoken to her in months and I'm not even sure how she's doing. I don't think she wants to hear from me."

"That's alright," said Marie-Anne. "You can do better."

I laughed at that, but got more serious when I responded to her. "I have to tell you that I'm going to be leaving the apartment soon. My job is ending and I don't think I'll be able to find more work here. My friends in Boston have offered to buy me a plane ticket home, and I think I'm going to take them up on it."

"Oh, is that all? I thought something was very wrong. Going home is good. That is probably the best thing for you. I'll miss having you here; you've been such a help to me. But don't worry about the apartment—I never have any trouble finding a new tenant. When do you plan to be leaving?"

"I'm not sure; I think in a couple of weeks or so. I need to let my friend in Boston know so she can buy the ticket. But there's another problem as well, and I need to take care of it before I leave."

"What's that?" she asked. She'd brought a loaf of bread to the table and now was pulling a leftover baked ham and some cheese out of her refrigerator. I could always count on Marie-Anne to feed me when I came to her place. Now I wouldn't have to worry about dinner.

"I don't want this to upset you," I told her, "but I have a confession to make. I have a cat in the apartment and I know I'm not supposed to. I'd been feeding him in the yard and one day he got poisoned. It was really terrible; he almost died. I had to take him to the vet and they said he needed to stay inside to recover, and I just..."

"A cat! You know that animals are against the rules!"

"Yes, I know and I'm sorry. I didn't mean to have him inside; it just sort of happened. Now I need to find a home for him before I leave."

"Well, I'm sure you didn't come here thinking that I would take the creature in!"

"Oh, no, of course not. I was just hoping you might have some advice about what I should do. I tried calling a shelter earlier, but I don't have the money for the fee."

"Animal shelters are a scam," replied Marie-Anne. "You don't want to give them money for anything!"

"But what should I do, Marie-Anne?"

"You put up flyers. You say, 'free cat to good home.' Someone will take it."

"Do you think so? That would be great if I could find someone to take him. He's a very nice, very clean cat," I assured her.

We chatted for a while longer, and I ate my fill of bread and ham and cheese. As I was getting ready to leave, she cut a large hunk of ham off the bone and sliced off a chunk of cheese, wrapping them in paper for me to take with me.

"Pour le petit chat malade," she said, pressing the package into my hands. Then she gave me a stern look. "Get rid of it soon."

When I got home, I took some photos of Georgie and wrote up some text for a flyer. All of this was enough motivation to get me up the next morning, and drag myself into work. I wanted to run the flyer past my colleague Marie-Thérèse and also use the printer and photocopier at work to make copies.

Marie-Thérèse was sympathetic, as usual. She corrected my French on the flyer and gave me some tips to make it more appealing. She and her boyfriend had a couple of dogs and so they weren't interested in adopting a cat, but she promised to mention Georgie and his situation to friends. I printed out the finished copy of the flyer and then made forty photocopies. I put one on the staff bulletin board in the break room and stuffed the rest of them in a folder which I put in my backpack along with a stapler and a tape dispenser I'd taken from my desk. I could hear Marie-Claude's voice coming down the hall as I headed to the door and so I narrowly missed running into her on my way out.

I decided to concentrate posting the flyers in my own neighborhood, as that was where Georgie was from and it would be easiest to turn him over to someone in the area. I stapled my flyer to wooden poles and fences, and taped them on metal rails and the sides of bus kiosks. I asked some shopkeepers in the area to post them in their windows for me and several of them obliged. I even taped one to the wall where I'd climbed up to pet Georgie, along with his mother and siblings, at the very start of this adventure. I knew that the flyer wouldn't stay up very long but I felt I had to post one there on principle.

When I got back home, I tried calling two more animal shelters and got more or less the same answer that I'd gotten from the first place I talked to. It seemed that there was no solution for poor people to surrender their animals in the greater Paris region, other than to dump them on the street. It was discouraging, but I tried to remain hopeful that the right person would see one of the flyers.

Later I talked to Julie on the phone. She was pleased to hear of the developments on my end and my efforts to find Georgie a new home. We settled on a date for me to return to Boston, and when I checked my computer awhile later, there was already a copy of the travel itinerary from the airline in my email. Now the fact that I was leaving Paris seemed solid and real; I now had a hard deadline for dealing with all my loose ends in Paris, including finding a new home for my feline pal.

By now, I didn't see any point in going back into work for any reason, other than to pick up my final paycheck. So, I stopped in one day to collect that check, and to clean out my desk and say good-bye to Marie-Thérèse and a couple of other co-workers who'd been friendly to me during my time there. I also stopped by the photocopier and made another twenty copies of my flyer. I was hoping to not have to see Marie-Claude while I was there, but this time she proved impossible to avoid. She came into the copy room just as I'd finished stuffing the flyers into my backpack. She was surprisingly cordial to me and seemed to be genuine in thanking me for all the work I'd done on the project. That caught me a little off guard, and caused me to venture telling her about Georgie and my need to find a home for him before I left.

"A cat?" she said, wrinkling her nose in disgust. "No, I definitely wouldn't want one of those dirty animals and I can't think of anyone I know who would."

That was the final nail in the coffin for any stray good thoughts I might have entertained about Marie-Claude. I abruptly ended the conversation there, and walked out of that office with the intention to never darken the door again.

Since I was in town, I decided to go by the anarchist bookstore that I sometimes visited. Marie-France had connections there, and I'd had an article published in their monthly newspaper the year before. I'd also bought plenty of books and other materials from there during my time in Paris. I didn't recognize the person on staff when I walked in, but he was friendly enough and willing to engage in a conversation with me despite my poor French. I explained Georgie's situation to him and made a case for Georgie being an "anarchist cat" as best I could, just for some light humor. He took two of the flyers, promising to put one in the window and to make additional copies for the literature table with the other.

I thanked him and was starting to leave when he stopped me. "Hey, you know what?' he said. "Jean-Michele is in the back, in the radio studio, doing his show. I can ask if he'd interrupt and let you do an announcement about the cat."

"Oh, I don't know," I replied, feeling shy at the thought of being on the radio. "My French is terrible, and I wouldn't know what to say."

"Just hold on; let me ask him." Then he was on the phone, talking rapidly to someone who I assumed was Jean-Michele in the back. I couldn't catch most of what he was saying, but I did hear the phrase "*chat anarchiste*" at least twice.

"Yeah, yeah, it's OK, yes, go on back," he told me when he got off the phone, smiling and waving me toward a door at the back of the shop.

"But, my French..." I started.

"It's OK, you can speak in English. Jean-Michele will translate for you and people will understand; just go on back."

With some trepidation, I went to the door and entered the studio space for on *Radio Libertaire*, the anarchist station operated by the same collective that ran the bookstore. A young man with curly dark hair invited me in, and pointed to a seat next to him at the console. A record was spinning on a turntable, and I could hear the muted sounds of the thrash punk song that was playing.

"We go on at the end of this song, OK?" Jean-Michele said to me. "Just pause every once in awhile and let me translate."

"OK," I replied back, feeling somewhat panicked and backed into a corner.

When the song ended, he flipped a switch and spoke into the microphone in front of him on the table. I could pick up some of what he was saying and knew that I was the "Camarade américain" with the "chat anarchiste" that was under discussion.

Then he flipped a switch and a signal button on the microphone on my side of the table lit up. He gestured for me to speak into it.

"Um, hello," I said. "Bonne après-midi. My apologies for addressing you in English. I'm here to tell you about my cat: Georgie, the anarchist cat." I paused and Jean-Michele translated what I said. Then I continued, pausing periodically for Jean-Michele to render what I was saying into French.

"He's very beautiful—black-and-white, with lovely long fur and dark, golden eyes. He has a tear-drop shaped blaze on his chest because he's had cause for tears in his short, hard life. He was born on the street in Noisy-Le-Sec to a homeless single mother…He came into my yard as a starving street cat and I started feeding and caring for him. Then he almost lost his life to rat poison manufactured by the capitalist chemical industry… Thanks to some veterinarian comrades who heroically treated him, his life was saved. He's been living happily with me for the last four months, but I have to return to America and I can't afford to bring him with me…The animal shelters I've contacted are all full or require too big of a payment for me to leave him there. But I can't stand the thought of turning him back out on the street again…If anyone listening to this would like to adopt this brave, beautiful, anarchist cat, I can guarantee that your life will be the better for it." I ended by thanking the listeners and giving out my phone number.

Jean-Michele followed up the final translation by saying something quick about the upcoming music, then flipped switches on the control panel to turn the microphones off and play the next song on the turntable. I shook his hand and thanked him, and gave him one of the flyers. He promised to make additional announcements about the cat when he could.

I felt buoyed by this tremendous support from my anarchist comrades, and it gave me the confidence to enter some of the other shops in the area to ask to leave flyers with them. When I got home later in the day, Georgie was there to greet me as always. I stroked his silky fur and told him, "You might not know it, but people were talking about you on the radio today." He blinked his beautiful golden eyes, rubbed his head against my hand, and started to purr. It felt good just to be around him, but I fought back a sickening feeling in my gut. He loved me and trusted me, but here I was, working to get rid of him. My logical mind kept reminding me that it was really the only way to move forward, but my emotional reaction told me something very different.

My departure date was drawing near. I had sold or given away my surplus books and other belongings. I had whittled down everything I owned to what could fit into two carry-on bags and two oversized duffle bags that would cost me some extra baggage fees. I was cleaning the apartment and scrubbing down the kitchen one last time—I didn't want to leave a mess for Marie-Anne to have to clean up before another tenant could move in. I was saying my good-byes to friends and neighbors, and I was doing some of the things I had been meaning to do since I had arrived twenty months earlier as a new resident. I saw a wildly spectacular performance of Shakespeare's play *Julius Caesar* at the national theater on the Trocadero, and during the intermission I had a coffee by a fifty-foot-tall window that perfectly framed the Eiffel Tower, standing about a block away. I also had an enjoyable evening around the Tuilleries Palace with Marie-Thérèse, her boyfriend, and some other friends during an annual music festival when every musician in France, from the ragged busker in a small town to the national orchestra in the Louvre, turns out and plays for the public, free of charge. There were sentimental tears in my eyes for days on end. It was as though this great enchanted city had dressed to the nines and invited me out, just to say farewell. But how would Paris keep my sweet Georgie?

I continued to brainstorm about where I might leave Georgie. In the Bois de Boulogne, where the prostitutes might feed him? Along the Canal de l'Ourcq, where there were many empty factory buildings where he might take shelter? Maybe somewhere out in the country? Or how about in front of the old cat lady's home? There was a hardcore cat lady in Noisy-le-Sec who walked the streets at 3am with big bags of cat food, making her rounds. I used to listen to her roaring advice about Georgie under the streetlamps—advice I sometimes disagreed with. She was a regular fanatic about how a pet owner should care for their animal. She wouldn't budge on anything even if the humans were poor. Still, I enjoyed talking with her, and she seemed to know every single stray in the town. She wasn't my first choice for a caretaker for Georgie, but at least I could be sure she would feed him.

My shelves were near empty and most of the "to-do" items on my list were crossed off. I was thinking of who I needed to call before the telephone service would be shut off when the phone rang. A man on the line was speaking English with a heavy French accent.

"Is Georgie still available?" he asked.

I was astonished. "Yes, yes he is!" I replied. "How do you know about him?"

It turned out that he and his partner had been listening to *Radio Libertaire* and had heard my announcement. He was reminded again that day when Jean-Michele made another public service announcement on the air, and he decided to call. The next day was a Saturday, and the caller asked me to bring Georgie by his apartment so that he and his partner could meet him. I jotted down the address and agreed to bring the cat by at two in the afternoon.

The journey the next day, first by train and then by Metro, was one that took us from the working-class suburb of Noisy-le-Sec in the militantly left-radical outskirts of Seine-Saint-Denis to the 6th arrondissement, or sixth district, one of the oldest and most desirable neighborhoods of Paris proper. A short walk from the Metro stop will take you past the Sorbonne, through Place Saint-Michel, to the Île de la Cité where once upon an ancient time, the sheep and cattle were forded across the river and the original settlement was built along the Seine. This is one of the most expensive neighborhoods in the world, and my Georgie had an appointment there.

After walking a few blocks, I found the right building; it had an impressive stone façade and iron-work railings guarding the small balconies facing the street. After I located the correct doorbell, my cat and I were buzzed in. I carried him up a beautiful but tight spiral staircase to the third floor. At the top of the landing we were warmly greeted by two men in their thirties who welcomed me into their small but pleasant apartment. It was tastefully decorated with new, comfortable furniture and had an impressive collection of art on the wall. There were sliding glass doors at the back of the living room which opened onto a small balcony overlooking the interior courtyard of the building. It was a clean and safe place for a cat to enjoy basking in the sunlight. Jean-Bernard, who was the one I'd spoken to on the phone, shook my hand and introduced me to his partner Jean-Luc and their cat Luna. She was all black and very calm and friendly, but was a bit wary upon seeing a new animal entering her space.

Jean-Bernard spoke English fairly well and served as a translator between myself and Jean-Luc. They graciously served coffee and biscuits while the two cats eyed each other. I was impressed by how smoothly they navigated the economic divide between us. Jean-Bernard mentioned that it was customary for the giver of a cat to bring all the veterinary care up to date before the animal was transferred, but under the circumstances they offered to take care of all that. I was grateful, of course, because this was one more thing that I hadn't even thought of and obviously couldn't afford. When I took the half-bag of cat food that I still had left out of my backpack, both men stared at it, surprised. "Oh, we'll find a use for it," said Jean-Bernard without much conviction. It was bottom-shelf crap that cost one euro per three-pound bag, and I realized that they would probably not dream of feeding it to their cats. Instead, it might get tossed to the pigeons or most likely just thrown in the trash.

They immediately took a liking to Georgie and were very interested in his awful adventure with the poison. We sipped coffee in their lovely apartment and made small talk as the cats slowly became more acquainted with each other. I finally asked my hosts, "So, you two are anarchists, then?"

"Well, no. Why do you ask?"

"You said that you heard about Georgie on *Radio Libertaire*, the anarchist station, so I just assumed."

"Oh, no. We just like the music they play." Jean-Bernard said that they had been very moved by my impassioned announcement, and that they had been talking for a while about finding a companion for Luna. She was lonely and depressed when they were both at work or traveling. Hearing my announcement seemed like a sign and made them think that they could possibly help solve two problems at once.

The problem that had been weighing on me had indeed been solved. As hard as it was to say one last "good-bye" to him and rub his beautiful head one last time, I left the apartment with the knowledge that Georgie had a new, good home. A huge burden was lifted from my heart.

A couple of short days later, I was on a trans-Atlantic flight headed to Boston. As the plane lifted up from Charles de Gaulle Airport, I looked down on Paris for my final glimpse of the beautiful City of Lights. I couldn't quite pick out where, but I knew that somewhere in that maze of streets, in one of the toniest neighborhoods of Paris, if not the world, a beautiful black-and-white cat was now poised to live the good life. As for me, I was still poor, drunk, and down on my luck—but I was heading home to my next adventure and happy in the knowledge that I had some good friends who would be standing by my side.

࿇

Six months later, I was pretty much settled back into life in Boston. I'd stayed in my friend Damien's spare room for about a month and then moved to a cheap boarding house in the neighborhood. I was barely eking out a living doing construction jobs and the occasional writing gig. It was hard to make ends meet and going hungry was once again a real concern. The local Food Not Bombs collective served a meal at the anarchist community space twice a month. I showed up to volunteer to help with the cooking and serving and cleaning up afterwards but, frankly, I was also there to eat. I gleaned any free food I could from the collective's give-aways, gladly accepted any handouts or free meals from friends, and on more than one occasion resorted to dumpster-diving behind restaurants and grocery stores. Admittedly, the situation was worsened by the fact that I often chose booze over food when I had money to spend. I'd gone through a stint in a rehab program and was sober for more than a week, but then fell off the wagon once again.

Julie had been helpful, as usual, and would sometimes "loan" me small sums of money with the full knowledge that she'd probably never get repaid. I still considered her one of my closest friends, but things had definitely changed between us. She'd instituted a "zero tolerance policy" and refused to speak on the phone or be near me in person if I were drunk or hungover, which constituted a large portion of my waking hours. She and her boyfriend were also planning on getting married, so our lives were definitely moving in very different directions now.

Then one evening, I was packaging up some leftovers from the Food Not Bombs meal when Damien walked into the community center and greeted me. "Hey," he said, "I got a letter for you from France that I thought you might want to see." He handed me a rumpled envelope with a colorful canceled stamp on it. When I first landed back in Boston, I had sent postcards to people back in Paris, giving Damien's address as a way to contact me. I got a nice postcard back from Marie-Anne, but mostly didn't hear from anyone. I wasn't sure who was writing to me now, but was pleasantly surprised when I ripped open the envelope.

A color photograph of two cats cuddled up together fell from between a folded sheet of paper. One was a plump black cat and the other was a beautiful long-haired black-and-white cat with a tear-drop-shaped blaze on his chest. Georgie! He'd put on some weight since I'd said good-bye to him and his fur seemed to glisten. Tears rose to my eyes as I beheld my anarchist cat once again. Then I took a look at the letter enclosed, which read:

> Hello, our American Friend! We were listening to *Radio Libertaire* a few days since and thought of you. I found your post card and thought you might enjoy this photo to send to you. Jo-Jo as we call him now is doing very well, healthy and happy! He and Luna are in love! As you can see in the photo. Thank you for bringing him into our lives, we are loving him so much. Thanks again and take care!
>
> Your friends in Paris,
> Jean-Bernard and Jean-Luc

I turned away and wiped the tears from my face with the back of my hand. I realized that even though I was still down on my luck and struggling, I'd at least done one thing right in my life, or maybe even two. I'd helped save Georgie's life when he'd been poisoned and I had managed to save him again from the mean streets of Noisy-Le-Sec. I was overcome with emotion to think of him now, so happy and healthy, with an affectionate cat friend and living with people who loved him and took such good care of him. Georgie was living the good life in Paris, something that had eluded me. But seeing him again gave me a glimmer of hope that maybe, just maybe, life could get better for me as well.

"Caroline walked out the door and down the alley for a few blocks before emerging onto one of the streets."

(from Street Smart #3, *The Accidental Anarchist* by A.R. Melnik)

#3 The Accidental Anarchist

A.R. Melnik

Caroline was already beginning to question the wisdom of this trip. By most people's standards, it was a fairly quick one—Philadelphia is only two hours from New York City, whether you go by car, train, or bus. She'd chosen the commuter bus because it had free wifi, unlike the train, and she could work on her laptop on the way up and back. There was no driving or parking to worry about. It was not just quick, but quick and easy.

She'd chosen to do this: a spur of the moment get-away, just by herself, up to New York and back in one day. But it was already starting to bother her, wiggling like a loose tooth that just won't let you forget it. She kept turning over in her mind the various worst-case scenarios of what could possibly go wrong. She imagined James getting a phone call from a hospital in New York, where she'd been taken after a vicious subway knife attack. "No," he'd say, "you must be mistaken. My wife isn't in New York." Or the news headline, days later: "Dismembered body identified as that of missing Philadelphia woman."

She took a deep breath and tried to put these gruesome thoughts out of her mind. "I've been to New York a million times," she exaggerated, "and nothing's ever gone wrong. And if it does, I've got my cell phone. I can call someone." Who she'd call, she wasn't sure. James would still be in Philly, two hours away from helping her. She vaguely knew a few people in New York, but she didn't even have their phone numbers with her.

"What was I thinking?" she asked herself as the double-decker commuter bus pulled away from the curb and started rounding 30th Street Station. She'd left the house an hour earlier, just like she was heading to campus on any other day. She had her backpack with laptop, books, and papers slung over one shoulder, and she'd called out "See you tonight!" to James as she held the front door halfway open. "See ya!" he'd called back, just like any other day. She'd walked as usual to the trolley stop three blocks away and waited for the trolley to arrive. But instead of getting off at her usual stop, she'd stayed on for a few additional stops and gotten off at 30th Street. Hoping she wouldn't run into anyone she knew, she'd quickly headed to the side street across from the train station, where the commuter bus companies picked up passengers. She'd lingered in front of the bus with the "New York City" sign above, until the driver had called, "Hey, lady! You gettin' on or what?" The exchange of a twenty-dollar bill and a paper ticket happened quickly. It had all seemed so easy.

But now she was starting to feel anxious, maybe a six on a scale of one to ten. Maybe a seven. "Such a worrier!" she chastised herself. "Ease up and enjoy yourself a bit, will you?" She opened her laptop, logged on, and distracted herself with reading her work email. There were a couple of questions from students that she could answer quickly, a request for an assignment extension from another student that took a little longer, a reminder about a job candidate coming in that she'd forgotten about, and several other college- and department-wide messages that she could just skim. Teaching at a local university gave her the luxury of having a more flexible schedule than most jobs. This semester, she normally went to campus only on Mondays, Wednesday, and Fridays, when she was scheduled to teach. Even though it was a Tuesday, she'd decided to go in to her office anyway, to have some quiet time to grade an assignment and have lunch with her colleague Marta. James had an editorial job with a publisher downtown, but usually telecommuted from home. They were respectful of each other's space and schedules while working from home, but Caroline sometimes appreciated the "alone time" her campus office afforded her.

Caroline shot off a quick email to Marta: "Sorry, I have to cancel lunch today. Plans changed and I won't be coming in like I'd intended; hope to see you tomorrow." She then turned her attention to the stack of papers that represented the first graded essay assignment for two sections of Freshman English. She pushed a lock of greying blonde hair behind one ear and got to work. Soon she was lost in marking errors and commenting upon the students' writing; she was about a third of the way through the stack when she looked up and could see the New York skyline in the distance. They'd be there soon! She'd forgotten her sense of anxiety and was now looking forward to her spur-of-the-moment getaway to the big city.

The bus heaved to a halt in front of the Jacob Javits Center and the passengers started to gather their things and exit the bus. Caroline loaded everything into her backpack and headed down the back staircase of the upper deck then forward to the front exit. She stepped off the bus into a cool, crisp early fall day in New York: there was a nip in the air but the sun was shining brightly and the day seemed full of infinite possibilities. Caroline toyed with the idea of heading toward Central Park, but opted instead to walk south. It would be a beautiful day to just wander through the city, feeling all the hustle and bustle in the streets, and exploring anything that caught her eye. She remembered visiting a great bulk candy shop somewhere on the Lower East Side, near Orchard Street. She couldn't remember exactly where it was, but she set that in mind as a vague goal for her wanderings.

For the next hour she ambled south, peering in shop windows, eavesdropping on conversations in the streets, and feeling generally alive and free. She bought some roasted almonds from a street vendor to munch along the way. At times, she felt a bit chilled and wished she had brought a jacket with her; it was cooler here than it had been in Philadelphia when she'd left home. After a while, she turned to the west and started exploring some side streets she was unfamiliar with, finally stopping to rest on wrought iron bench outside of an apartment building. The street was surprisingly quiet, but it was a mostly residential street in the middle of the day. An alleyway opening across the street caught her attention and made her remember the "shuts of Shrewsbury" walking tour she'd been on in England a few years earlier. The tour guide had taken them down the dark and winding, almost hidden, "shuts" or alleys of the old medieval city.

"I wonder what New York alleys are like," she thought. "I don't think I've ever been in one." Deciding to embark on a new experience, she walked across the street and into the alley, finding herself in an almost maze of passages between buildings on adjacent blocks and half-blocks in between. It was fun to be "off the beaten path" of the busy city, making her way past garbage cans and the occasional locked bicycle, and looking up at the fire escapes and small balconies that dotted the higher floors of some of the buildings. She could see laundry fluttering in a few places and some potted plants that waited vainly for the sun in the dark alley. On one second-story fire escape, an orange tom cat was dozing. He opened one eye as Caroline passed, quickly assessed her as "not a threat" and went back to sleep.

Caroline skipped across side streets into the next series of alleys, and after a while she could tell that the area she was now in was more commercial than residential. There were bigger dumpsters in the alleys, wooden pallets leaning against buildings, plastic buckets full of cooking grease and rotting vegetable scraps, and stacks of empty waxed boxes. The smells were more pungent. She turned down a half-block alley that seemed to have fewer restaurants, just dotted with dumpsters and fire escapes. She was half-way down the alley when a girl came tearing around the corner from a side street, yelling "Run!"

At first Caroline wasn't sure what she was seeing. The figure was dressed in bright red and yellow plaid pants, a loose black sweater pocked with holes and runs, and black Doc Marten boots. Her head sported a wild nest of brownish white-girl dreds that seemed to be bouncing in every direction at once as she ran. It briefly flashed in Caroline's mind that "they must be filming a movie," but she knew she hadn't seen any signs of that. Caroline quickly moved out of the middle of the alley, next to a dumpster, and felt the metal door behind her jiggle as her backpack hit against it. It was one of those double metal doors meant for making deliveries, that opened to the outside and had no outer door handles; Caroline could tell that at least one side was unlocked based on its movement. Reacting solely on instinct rather than logical thought, she jumped forward and grabbed the girl as she approached.

"No!" shouted the girl, struggling against her.

"Shhhh!" hissed Caroline in response. She pulled the girl toward the door, holding her close with her right arm while she pried the unlocked side of the metal door open with her left. She shoved the girl inside, who lost balance and fell to the floor. Caroline pulled the door closed after them as quickly and quietly as possible. It was dark inside, unlit except for a yellow security light in a wire cage that was visible through a doorway on the right. It provided enough dull light that Caroline could see a sliding bolt at the top of the door. She pushed it into place.

"What the fuck?" snarled the girl on the floor.

Caroline responded only with a finger to her lips and a soft "Shhhh!" Seconds later they heard running in the alley outside, large, pounding footsteps, and men shouting.

"Where'd she go?"

"Dunno!"

"You go left, I'll go right!"

The running and pounding receded.

"Those fuckers!" exclaimed the girl.

Caroline sat down on the floor beside her, grasping the girl's arm. "We have to be quiet," she whispered. "They may be coming back."

Within a few minutes they were back, toppling over garbage cans and pounding on doors as they moved back down the alley. The two women held their breath as they heard the men getting closer. One of them pounded violently on the metal door they had just come through, and Caroline put her hand over the girl's mouth to stop her from yelling. They could hear the lid of the dumpster next to the door being opened and slammed shut again, and a man's voice calling out "Not here!" The heavy footsteps receded down the alley in the direction they'd originally come from.

"We have to be quiet and wait here," Caroline whispered again to the girl, who nodded in the semi-darkness. They appeared to be in a warehouse or some sort of a storage area, with lots of stacked boxes and wooden crates on pallets. Caroline could make out an industrial mop bucket and mop in the corner across from them, with a stack of brooms and snow shovels and other implements behind it. She couldn't even guess what kind of business this could be, but she wondered if anyone else was in the building. It was one more reason to try to keep the girl quiet.

Caroline couldn't really tell what the girl looked like as they sat on the floor against a stack of boxes to the right of the door. Even if she couldn't see her well, Caroline had no trouble smelling the girl. It wasn't the smell of sweat from the exertion of running, it was the deep-seated funk of a crusty punk, a type Caroline was familiar with from her West Philadelphia neighborhood. They openly rejected the concepts of soap and shampoo and deodorant, seemed to never shower, and took pride in not washing their clothes, which soon developed a greasy sheen. Despite the lack of hygiene, these rebellious types were secretly some of Caroline's favorites; she admired both their consistency and fortitude. She'd meet them sometimes at the local food co-op or run into them at community group meetings, but they rarely showed up in her classrooms. Higher education was apparently also something to be generally rejected, although Caroline would argue that they took this particular form of political correctness too far.

The two women sat there in the semi-darkness for what seemed like an eternity, the girl's heavy breathing finally slowing to normal and Caroline's spiked adrenaline evening out somewhat. She wracked her brain for what to do next, and wondered what she'd gotten herself into, inserting herself into this situation. But she also wondered what would have happened if she hadn't dragged the girl inside. What would those men have done to her? What would they have done to Caroline if she'd stumbled into their path as well?

She briefly considered if the girl could be a thief, chased for shoplifting or some other petty crime, but quickly dismissed the idea. What she'd heard from the men in the alley didn't seem like the words or actions of wronged shopkeepers. The vibe they gave off was dark and heavy, even dangerous. She had no idea what the story of this chase was, but her sympathies were naturally with the hunted, not the hunters.

"Why were you running from them?" Caroline asked quietly, finally breaking the silence.

The girl followed her cue and responded intently but in a low voice. "They're bastards!" she said. "They're traffickers!"

Caroline felt a shock wave go through her. "Are they trafficking you?" she asked, lightly touching the girl's arm.

"No!" the girl responded, her voice sounding irritated and starting to riseCaroline heard a noise that sounded like it was coming from the other end of the building, filtering down the hallway.

"We should leave," she whispered to the girl. "But you owe me an explanation. Do you promise not to run when we get outside?"

"OK," said the girl, dredlocs bobbing.

Caroline stood up, pulled her backpack back on, then went to the door and quietly unbolted the side that they had entered through earlier. She and the girl stepped into the alley, which even in its shadows seemed bright compared to the darkness they'd been sitting in. Caroline pushed the door shut behind them.

"Let's go this way," Caroline said, holding on to the girl's arm and moving in the direction she had originally entered the alley from, in what now seemed like a lifetime ago.

She got a better look at the girl in the daylight—she was thin and pale but seemed healthy. Her face was lightly dotted with freckles and she had clear blue eyes. She wasn't carrying a bag or backpack or anything, which struck Caroline as odd; most people, especially women, carried something for the "stuff" they brought with them.

A disturbing thought suddenly crossed Caroline's mind. This girl was, if nothing else, conspicuous. "If those men are looking for you, maybe we should try to make you harder to find?" she tentatively suggested.

"What do you mean?" asked the girl.

"Well, those pants are simply screaming 'HERE I AM!' for one thing," said Caroline.

"I like these pants," the girl replied defensively.

"I do, too," said Caroline, only partly lying. "But maybe we should try to get you looking a bit different, to be on the safe side. There's a thrift store I saw earlier, right up this block."

Caroline had noticed the thrift store before, when she was crossing the street between alleys. She turned up the block and the girl followed, trailing her into the store. A sad-looking woman in her thirties sat behind a service counter and smiled at them. The place was full of overstuffed racks of clothing, shelves of knick-knacks, and some larger pieces of furniture in the back. Yellowed florescent lighting units swung from the ceiling overheard. Christian rock music blared from a tinny sound system. The girl started rapidly pawing through a rack of clothes, almost like she was looking for something specific. Caroline decided not to hover, and found a rack on the other side of the shop that had women's coats and jackets on it. The chill outside had been bothering her, so she might as well add another layer.

Caroline tried on several things, looking at herself in a full-length mirror attached to the wall. She settled on a grey trench coat with double-breasted buttons and a belt tie. She headed back to the service desk, arriving just as the girl emerged from the dressing room next to it.

She was wearing non-descript black pants, a dark brown shirt with some sort of subtle black print that was almost indiscernible, and a cheap faux leather motorcycle jacket. "How's this?" she asked Caroline.

"You look great. You just need a hat." A hat rack was on the other side of the service desk and Caroline looked through it, pleased to find a man's XL black beret there. She plopped it onto the girl's head and stuffed the dreds sticking out the front up into the beret. The others she pulled behind the girl's ears, where they stuck out in back like a bushy ponytail. The hairstyle was undisguisable, but the hat modified the look and made the girl's face look different—less hidden, more feminine.

"Can we just wear these things out with us?" Caroline asked the woman working there.

"Sure," she replied. She came around from the counter with a pair of scissors and started snipping tags off of the various items of clothing. Then she went back behind the counter and started adding the amounts up on a grimy calculator.

The girl returned to the dressing room and came back out with her old clothes rolled in a bundle. She stuck her hand in the plaid pants' pocket and pulled out some crumpled bills and loose change, scattering them on the counter.

"Oh, no," said Caroline, quickly. "I've got this."

"OK," said the girl, sounding a bit unsure if she should be accepting the offer. But she acquiesced quickly and added on a "Thanks."

"Do you want to, um, get rid of those things?" asked Caroline, gesturing to the bundle of clothes the girl was holding.

"No way!" responded the girl with a dark look. "I *like* these clothes!"

"I can put those in a bag for you," the woman behind the counter said kindly, pulling out a used plastic bag from under the counter. To Caroline she said, "$36.65."

Caroline fished her wallet out of her backpack and pulled out a couple of $20 bills. The woman handed the plastic bag to the girl, who rolled her eyes when she saw the name on it. "Seriously? Barney's?" she complained.

"It's just a bag," said Caroline, waiting while the woman behind the counter dug through a cash box for her change. She took her change back with a "Thank you!" and a meaningful look.

Back out on the street, the two women lingered tentatively on the sidewalk in front of the store. "Let's go somewhere and talk," said Caroline. "I'm starving—what about you?"

The girl grunted noncommittally and Caroline pointed to a small diner further up the street. "Let's just duck in there for a while."

When they walked in, the older woman behind the cash register next to the door said, "Sit anywhere," and waved her hand toward the interior.

Caroline led them to a small booth beside a window looking out on the side street, pulled off her backpack and plopped down on one side of the table while the girl sat at the other, pushing her plastic Barney's bag against the window.

A waitress came by and slammed down two plastic glasses of ice water, and dropped a couple of sticky, plastic-coated menus at the end of the table. "I'll be right back, ladies," she said.

The lunch hour rush was over and the restaurant had only a few of the other tables occupied. Caroline and the girl stared at the menus in silence for a few minutes before the girl announced, "I'm a vegan."

"Of course you are," thought Caroline. She didn't reply, but immersed herself in the flapping paper clipped to the menu detailing the specials of the day. Her mind eventually turned back to the girl and the strange situation she'd stumbled into. She wondered what she needed to do next. Should she just buy them lunch and then get back on the bus to Philly? Should she go to the police? Or was there something that was more "in between" these extremes?

The waitress returned with a brusk "What can I git cha?"

"House salad," said the girl. "No egg. No bacon. Extra tomatoes. Vinaigrette on the side."

"I'll have the Rubin," said Anna. "Chips, not fries."

"Meat is murder," said the girl under her breath as the waitress walked away.

"What?" asked Caroline.

"Nothing."

Caroline sighed. The girl looked to be in her early twenties, about the age of many of her students. But she didn't really remind her of her students, most of whom seemed soft, tentative, and a little lost in comparison. This girl had harder edges to her, and exuded a confidence and willfulness that betrayed a maturity beyond her years. A couple of years ago, when she'd turned forty, Caroline suddenly realized that she was old enough to have grown children the age of the students she was now teaching. She and James never had children, opting instead to concentrate on their careers and to spend their money on their own interests. She sometimes wondered what it would be like having a nearly adult child in her life, and the girl in front of her provided an entirely new perspective on that. She realized that anyone looking at them sitting here now might easily mistake them for mother and daughter.

"I don't believe we've been properly introduced," Caroline said, breaking the silence. "I'm Caroline Wilson. I teach college English at a university in Philadelphia and I'm actually just here in the city for the day. What's your name?"

"They call me 'Mugwump,'" replied the girl.

Caroline hoped that her face didn't betray any reaction to the Burroughs reference. "OK, Mugwump. Nice to meet you. Can you tell me what the hell that was back there?"

"Those were some grade-A assholes who seriously need to be taken down, chasing me. With guns. I don't think you would have seen that."

Caroline gulped. She hadn't seen that, in fact she hadn't seen the assholes at all. And luckily, they hadn't seen her, either. But here she was, sitting in a diner with the girl they were after.

"But why were they chasing you?" she asked. "You said earlier that they were traffickers. Were they trafficking you?"

"No, I already told you that."

Caroline waited for her to say more. "They're not trying to traffick me," she continued. "They're trafficking women and girls from Thailand, and some other places in southeast Asia."

"But, why . . . how do you know?" asked Caroline, causing the girl to roll her eyes. "Maybe it would help if you just told me the whole story, starting at the beginning."

She sat there and listened while Mugwump spun her story out. She'd been a student at Hampshire College in Vermont ("hippie school," Caroline mentally registered), majoring in "Ag" because "food is important." But a trip to Thailand to study innovations in rice farming changed the direction of her interests. She'd been disgusted by the sex tourism she saw in Bangkok. "It's just a normal part of the economy," she told Caroline. "I'm definitely not opposed to sex work, when the people involved have chosen that and have agency. But most of the people I saw in Bangkok didn't really have a choice. They were young women and children, without an education, being exploited by men who took most of the money made from Western tourists."

After returning to Vermont, Mugwump found that she had a hard time focusing on her studies. A friend invited her to New York and she ended up staying, getting involved in an anarchist collective on the Lower East Side and cooking for their Food Not Bombs program. One night a young Asian woman showed up, obviously hungry and distressed. She had sat at a table by herself, eating and visibly holding back tears. She'd reminded Mugwump of some of the young women she'd seen in Bangkok, so she sat down and tried to talk with her. The girl knew little English and Mugwump had only learned a bit of Thai on her trip, but she was able to find out that the girl was Thai, that her name was Nusara, and that she'd experienced something traumatic. She was frightened and alone in a strange country.

Mugwump brought the girl home with her that night. She was ecstatic to have a shower and wash her hair, and change into some clean clothes that Mugwump gave her. She stayed in Mugwump's room, in a large run-down house shared with a number of other young anarchists, sleeping on a foam mattress on the floor. The next day, with the help of a Thai/English dictionary and some drawing paper and a pencil, Mugwump learned more of Nusara's story.

ꝏ

Nusara had lived in the country on her family's farm. They were poor, but they had enough to eat from the crops they grew. She was the oldest in a large family and she'd only gone to school for a few years, dropping out to help in the family fields. One day, a well-dressed Thai woman drove up to their farm in a big car and told her parents that she worked for a company that could provide a job for Nusara in America, being a nanny to a rich family's children. It would pay well and Nusara could send money home. She'd have a chance to learn English and the company had a scholarship program that would allow her to take classes and get an education. It had sounded almost too good to be true, but it had been too compelling to say "no" to. Nusara was sad to leave her home, her parents, and her younger siblings, but she was excited about the prospect of getting a job and being able to help her family, as well as having the opportunity to see America.

When it was time to leave, the company picked her up in a van and she traveled across the country, seeing more of her homeland than she ever had before. But she had suspected that something was wrong when she wasn't taken to the airport to fly to America as promised, but rather was brought to an industrial port. She was forced onboard a rusty, commercial-looking boat, along with the other young women that the van had picked up along the way. Her passport and suitcase were taken away from her, and she was put in a hold with about twenty other women. All of the women were crying and wailing, knowing they were in a bad situation that was only going to get worse.

There were only a few small windows in the hold, and the air was stale and fetid. There were plastic buckets to use as toilets and a few straw mats on the floor for sleeping. The food was bad and there was not enough of it. There was no water to wash with and even clean drinking water was in short supply. Despite the hardships, the women had banded together. They made sure that food was distributed equally. They comforted each other with stories of their homes and families, and their hope to return to them. They fantasized about overcoming the guard when he brought food and turning the boat around to go home, but they never had the means or opportunity to do that.

After what seemed like weeks aboard the ship, it finally came to a stop. They could hear men moving around and a lot of talking on deck. In the middle of the night, the hold was opened and the women were brought out on deck, the first time they'd been in fresh air since they'd left Thailand. They were forced to climb down a long, swaying ladder on the side of the boat, which Nusara recalled with terror. At the bottom of the ladder, she was grabbed by men who pulled her onto a motor boat where she was chained together with a group of the other women. Once all of the women were onboard, the smaller boat took them to a dark dock, where they climbed out of the boat and were herded into the back of an enclosed delivery truck.

The truck drove for an hour or more, and then they were unloaded in the alley behind some sort of commercial building and forced into a basement room. The same pattern of not enough food and not enough hygiene continued for several days. Occasionally one of the women was dragged out of the room and then would return later, crying and holding together ripped clothing. Everyone knew what was happening but no one talked about it. They tried to comfort the abused woman who returned but secretly gave thanks that it hadn't been them. One night, Nusara was awakened by a man grabbing her wrist and dragging her out of the room. Her turn had arrived, and yet it had also proven to be a salvation of sorts.

She was taken upstairs and shoved into an office. The man locked the door behind them. There was an old chair in front of a metal desk that was covered with papers, and some metal filing cabinets that the man shoved her up against, bruising her back against the metal handles. He pulled at her shirt, running his right hand over her breasts while holding her shoulder with his left. But then the phone rang. He pulled Nusara up close against him, holding his hand over her mouth while he answered the phone. She knew that the time to act was now or never. While the man was talking, she grabbed a metal stapler off the desk and smashed it against his head. He cried out and dropped the phone, as she wiggled out of his grasp. She kicked him as hard as she could between his legs, just like her friend Nin had showed her back home. The man doubled over and Nusara unlocked the office door and ran. She had no idea of where she was, but see saw a white and red sign over a door at the end of the hall and ran for it. The door opened when she pushed the metal bar and an alarm went off. She ran as fast as she could into the night.

The streets she ran through were mostly dark in the commercial area she found herself in. She saw one lit sign a few blocks away, yellow with red and black letters and a funny picture of a sandwich that had a dog's head, feet, and tail. Once she got there, she could see more lights, cars, and people in the blocks ahead, so she ran towards them. She did not even know what city she was in. She walked along the streets, not knowing where to go. Eventually she got tired, and curled up beside some steps in a back alley and slept for a while. She awakened early the next morning and spent the day walking the streets. She didn't know enough English to speak to anyone, and she did not see anyone who looked like they could speak her language. She had no money and nothing other than the clothes she was wearing. For the next few days, she scavenged food from garbage cans and dumpsters behind restaurants, and slept on the street. It was purely by chance that, on her fourth night on the street, she walked past the storefront hosting Food Not Bombs and recognized the words "Free Food." The smells coming from inside enticed her to enter.

Nusara kept insisting "Find Sheriff" after she had communicated her story to Mugwump; it was as if she had seen too many American westerns and thought that would solve the problem. "No Sheriff" was Mugwump's repeated reply. Once she understood what had happened to Nusara, Mugwump wanted to find the place where she had been held. The Thai girl was understandably not eager to return there and seemed genuinely unsure of where she had actually been. But Mugwump brought her to the Food Not Bombs storefront and started having her walk around the area with her. Nusara hid inside the hood of a sweatshirt Mugwump had given her, trying to remain unseen. Occasionally she pointed out things that she thought she recognized. On the second day of doing this, they found the yellow and red sandwich shop sign with the distinctive picture of the "hot dog" dog on it. Nusara was able to indicate the direction she'd come from when she first saw the sign, and where she'd turned to get onto that street. She was very scared to be this close to her captors, so Mugwump told her to go home and she did the rest of the reconnaissance by herself. After some scouting in the area that Nusara had indicated, she narrowed the possible location down to a few buildings on a side street a few blocks up from the sandwich shop.

She started walking by these buildings every day, as often as she could manage it, sometime lingering on the corner while pretending to look at her phone. Occasionally she'd see men coming and going from one of the buildings, and after awhile some of them started to notice her as well. Their reactions went from scowling to open abuse and threats, so she tried to keep her observations more at a distance and started coming more often at night. Late one afternoon, she noticed a large enclosed truck parked halfway up on the sidewalk behind the building. It looked like the type of truck she imagined Nusara and the other women being put in when they were transferred from the boat to here. She decided to risk coming closer to the building again and walked down the alley toward the truck. She first walked past the truck, looking in the side mirror to see no one in the cab of the truck, and glancing inside as she passed, just to make sure. Seeing no one there, she continued to the end of the block and then doubled back. Looking carefully around for signs of anyone near the buildings, she banged sharply on the side of the truck with her fist. She felt and heard the reverberation, but it seemed hollow and there was no sound in response. She left the block quickly, vowing to return after dark.

After finishing a shift at Food Not Bombs, she headed back over to the warehouse district. She was dressed all in black, including an oversized hoodie that she wore with the hood up, concealing her face like a Sith Lord. She had a set of brass knuckles in her pocket that she wasn't entirely sure she knew how to use, but they made her feel more secure. She stationed herself in the alley a couple of blocks up from the parked truck, hidden as much as possible by some garbage cans and a metal stairwell. She leaned against the wall of the building, staying as quiet and still as possible, blending into the shadows. She was standing there for hours, the cool night air helping to keep her awake and alert. Her persistence paid off a little after three a.m., when she saw two men emerge from the building and head to the truck. They unlocked the back of the truck and opened the doors, glancing up and down the street. Mugwump had held her breath, not daring to move enough to even breathe. The men returned to the building but emerged soon after with two others, hustling a group of women into the back of the truck. They slammed the doors shut and Mugwump swore she heard the click of a lock. There was some muffled conversation and two of the men got into the cab of the truck and the driver started the engine. The two men left behind returned into the building as the truck drove off. Mugwump was terrified that she might be spotted in the headlights, or that the truck would drive past her and she'd be seen, but luckily it turned at the end of the first block, before getting to her.

She waited a few more minutes, glued to her post in the alley, until she was convinced that the truck had really left and that the men inside the building weren't coming back outside. Then she sprinted away from the building as fast as she could, her hands balled into fists and her mind overcome by rage. She hadn't stopped them from taking the women; she couldn't stop them from taking the women. She was one woman in an alley with a set of brass knuckles and they were four muscular men armed with guns. On one of her earlier reconnaissance forays, a man outside the building had grinned at her as she'd walked past and pulled one side of his jacket open to reveal a holstered pistol at the side of his chest. That was when she'd made the decision to stay further away and observe from a distance. Her logical mind told her there was nothing she could do in the face of such a power imbalance, but she was still enraged by her impotence. She knew that these women and girls were on their way to the next stage of their exploitation: those considered the prettier ones would probably be sent to massage parlors somewhere and the others sold off into slavery at a sweatshop somewhere else.

ꕥ

Mugwump finished her story and finished her salad, pushing the bowl away from her. She locked eyes with Caroline across the table. "That truck I told you I saw? It's parked back on the sidewalk again, *now.* I got caught walking past it this time, and that's why I was being chased when you first saw me."

Caroline swallowed hard. "That's quite the story," she replied. "But I have to ask: if you know what's going on there, why not go to the police? Isn't there some sort of unit or department or something that works on human trafficking?"

Mugwump rolled her eyes. "Honestly, the police?" she countered. "There's no way that they don't already know what's going on, that they're not being paid off to let it happen."

"Hey, I get it," said Caroline. "I'm from Philly and I know the whole 'don't snitch' routine. I understand that dealing with the cops can be worse than dealing with the crooks, but something like this...."

"There's no good solution," broke in Mugwump. "Can't deal with the cops. Can't deal with the traffickers. But I've been working on a plan to try to force them to deal with each other. Problem is, with that truck in the alley, I have to move *now.* If the pattern holds true, it'll be gone with another group of women tonight."

"OK, well, what do you mean? What's the plan?"

Mugwump's eyes narrowed as she considered Caroline across the table. "It's complicated. All I can say is that time is of the essence...and maybe, I could use someone like you to help."

Caroline silently considered the younger woman's words for a few minutes. What kind of dangerous nonsense was she potentially getting herself drawn into? Was this another one of the anxiety scenarios she'd imagined earlier, but one that was so improbable that she couldn't have even conjured it up? Yet she felt drawn to trying to help this woman, who seemed so smart and tough and headstrong, but who also seemed to be teetering on the edge of something very dangerous.

"Alright," she finally said, deciding to test the waters. "What kind of help do you need?"

"I don't want to explain it here. Can you come meet my friend Jello at the Infoshop? It's a few blocks from here."

"Yes, I suppose so," Caroline said tentatively. She pulled out her phone and looked at the time. "2:30. I was hoping to catch the bus back to Philly by three, but I can work out a way to stay longer if I need to."

"Well, let's go then," said Mugwump, standing up and grabbing her Barney's bag.

Caroline looked at the check that the waitress had left on the table, pulled a couple of bills from her wallet and handed it all to the cashier at the front, with a "Keep the change," as she rushed to follow Mugwump out of the door.

They headed back down the sidewalk in the direction they'd come from. "I'm curious," said Caroline, "how is Nusara doing now?"

"No idea," responded Mugwump gruffly. "She totally disappeared after staying at my place for about two weeks."

"Oh, I'm sorry." Caroline was hoping she wasn't opening a wound, but couldn't contain her curiosity. "What do you think happened to her?"

"Dunno. Maybe she did finally figure out how to go to the cops. The idea of 'the sheriff' kept coming up with her, no matter how many times I shot it down."

"Ummm," Caroline murmured in response.

"Actually, it might have been the best thing. Maybe if she went to them, they'd have turned her over to ICE and best result would be having her deported back to Thailand so she could go home."

"Right, that might be best."

"Worst case would be that one of the traffickers spotted her, and that she'd be right back where she left. Or dead."

Caroline really didn't want to think about that possibility. "Could she have just gone off on her own?"

"Might have. But I think that's the most unlikely explanation. She was so grateful to me, and seemed like she'd be so lost on her own. I really can't imagine it. I don't think she would have left of her own will without telling me, or without at least saying good-bye."

They'd turned left and were heading down a street that Caroline was unfamiliar with. A few blocks later, they halted in front of an unassuming brownstone with a black painted railing in front. Almost invisible from the street, there was a hand-drawn sign in the basement window at ankle level that read: "INFOSHOP Come On Down."

Mugwump led Caroline down some steep steps to the basement area. Once they got inside, it was larger and better lit than Caroline would have expected. There was a bulletin board with an array of flyers tacked to it and a rack of pamphlets near the door where they entered. DIY wooden bookshelves filled with books lined the sides of two walls and there was a beat up four-drawer filing cabinet at the end of one of them with a sign declaring "ZINES!!!" A small table at the end of the other held a domestic coffeemaker, cans of coffee, a collection of chipped mugs, and an empty can labeled "$." A worn rag rug covered the middle of the floor and mismatched second-hand seating was scattered throughout. A thin young Black man in greasy jeans and an unbuttoned camouflage shirt over a dark blue t-shirt was slumped in a worn easy chair, one leg draped over an arm of the chair, reading a comic book. A pale young white man with curly red hair dressed in all black was sprawled in a beanbag chair under the window, reading a book. Caroline couldn't quite catch the title, but there was a photograph of an atomic bomb blast on the cover. They both glanced up without much interest when the two women entered.

"Hey, Mugwump."

"What's up, Wump?"

"Hey, guys," said Mugwump in reply. "Is Jello here?"

"Yeah, he's in the back."

"Come on," Mugwump said to Caroline, leading her through a doorway in the far wall that was covered with a piece of cloth and had a "Staff Only" sign above it. They entered a dark room a little larger than the front room, cluttered with stacks of miscellaneous boxes. Some rusty metal shelving units with old paint cans, random tools, and other objects leaned against one wall, and some large paper mâché puppet heads were stacked in one corner. A makeshift office was built out from the far corner of the room, and a line of light showed at the bottom of its closed door. They headed there and Mugwump rapped on the door. "Jello?" she called out.

"Yeah," came a voice within the office. "Come on in."

Mugwump opened the flimsy door of the office and Caroline followed her inside. The cramped space held a couple of desks stacked with papers, a couple of filing cabinets, and a messy pile of cardboard boxes in one corner. A man in who appeared to be older than Mugwump, probably in his mid-thirties, was seated at one of the desks. He had large black-framed glasses, dark hair, and a wispy beard and moustache. He read a bit "hipster" to Caroline with his green knit hat, plaid shirt, blue jeans, and brown work boots. Posters and stickers with radical messages adorned the walls of the office, including a somewhat dated poster with a picture of George W. Bush and the words "Stop Me Before I Kill Again" and an oversized yellow post-it note proclaiming "Are You Fucking Kidding Me?" A fluorescent unit overhead and a desk lamp provided strong lighting in the small room.

"Hey, Mugwump," said the man, and noticing Caroline, "Hello."

"Caroline, this is Jello Ravachol," said Mugwump. "Jello, this is Caroline from Philadelphia."

"Hello, Caroline from Philadelphia," echoed Jello.

"Hello," said Caroline, suddenly feeling a bit shy and out-of-place.

He gestured toward the other desk in the office and offered, "Have a seat." Mugwump pulled the chair around to face the other desk, and motioned to Caroline to sit. She shoved some papers aside on the desktop and perched there herself.

"Jello, they almost got me this time, man!" she blurted out. "They were coming after me with *guns and everything*!"

"They were...what?" asked Jello, confused. "Wait, slow down." Then he turned to Caroline. "*Who* are you, again?"

"I'm sorry," said Caroline. "I'm just someone from Philadelphia who happens to be in town for the day...." She was starting to feel like she really didn't belong here and once again pressed down a wave of fear that she was potentially getting into something way over her head.

"She saved me," broke in Mugwump. "She pulled me inside a building and helped me hide until they went away. I swear, Jello, they're planning a move. The truck is in the alley and it has to be today!"

Jello put up his hand. "Just...stop." He let out a heavy, frustrated sigh. "Come talk to me outside." And to Caroline, he said, "Excuse us."

"Oh, I can leave..." Caroline started to protest, but he waved her off.

"It's ok, we'll be right back." Mugwump followed him out the office door, which they closed behind them.

Left on her own, Caroline scanned more of the posters on the walls and was impressed with the variety of causes they espoused ("Support Indigenous Rights" "Workers Rights Are Human Rights" "Black Lives Matter") and the humor that many of them expressed ("Feeling Sad and Depressed? You Might Be Suffering From Capitalism" "Is It Gay In Here, Or Is It Just Me?"). She couldn't resist the temptation to peek at a few of the papers on the desk, noting some invoices from radical bookstores, an events calendar, and some scrawled incomprehensible phone messages. She could barely hear the muffled voices of the two in the other room, who were having an intense conversation if not a full-blown argument. Occasionally, she'd catch entire sentences when one of them raised their voice: "But how do you *know*?" from Jello, and "Can't you just trust me on this?" from Mugwump.

Caroline almost jumped when the door re-opened. Mugwump and Jello came in and took their earlier seats, and Jello turned his chair to face Caroline head on.

"Listen, lady, no offense, but...can you provide some sort of proof of who you actually are?"

Caroline bridled a bit at being called "lady" but said "Um, sure" and unzipped her backpack. She pulled out her wallet and produced her drivers' license. "I live in West Philadelphia," she explained. She next produced her faculty ID and said, "I teach in the English Department here." She pulled her backpack open wider and produced a sheaf of student essays. "I was grading papers on my way up, on the bus."

Jello examined the IDs that were produced and seemed especially interested in the student papers. Caroline suppressed a bit of a smile. It's easy enough to make fake IDs, she thought, but forging student papers like this would take a mastermind. Jello seemed to relax a bit after this interrogation, and Caroline felt like she'd passed a test.

"OK," said Jello, handing Caroline back her things. "What's going on, Wump? What's the plan?"

"We have to move sooner rather than later," Mugwump said intensely. "If we don't do it now, anyone they've got there now is lost and I can't fucking *stand* the thought of that! And we may not have another opportunity for weeks."

"Are you sure it wouldn't it be better to wait until night?" asked Jello.

"No. It's better to go now, in broad daylight. It's more obvious, and there will be more witnesses."

"Yeah, more witnesses. That's what I'm afraid of; more chances of getting caught."

"More witnesses to what's actually going on there, and more of a chance they'll have to actually break this thing up. It's the only way this is going to work!"

Jello's forehead creased in thought. "Hmm…you may be right."

Caroline sat silently, listening to the exchange and trying to figure out what exactly was going on. She didn't feel comfortable asking questions just yet, and decided to just hang back and observe what unfolds.

Jello shifted in his chair. "What about her? What's the deal with that?"

"She'll be the one to check the front and give the signal. We have to get the timing down, but she walks by, stops in front, and gives the signal if the light is on."

Caroline assumed that the "she" being discussed was her and decided now was the right time to enter the conversation. "Excuse me," she said. "Could you give me some information about what it is you're talking about, and how it involves me?"

They both turned to look at her. Mugwump locked eyes with her and said simply, "We're going to bomb them."

Visions of stereotypical "bomb-throwing anarchists" passed through Caroline's mind; in fact, a black-and-red graphic image of one leered down at her from one of the posters on the wall. "Bomb them?" she repeated. "Are you sure that's a good idea?"

"I've thought about it, Caroline," said Mugwump. "I've thought about it *a lot*. I really believe it's the only way we're going to be able to end this."

Caroline considered the two in front of her. Mugwump had already impressed her as an intelligent young woman with strong convictions. But she was young, and working with young adults had taught Caroline that they don't always think things through clearly or make the best choices. She knew less about Jello but he also struck her as someone who was intelligent and committed to his ideals. Still, she felt the need to be the proverbial "adult in the room."

"At the risk of betraying my own political incorrectness again," she said, "I have to ask: why not go to the police? Why not try to tip off whoever's in charge of anti-trafficking?"

"Because it won't work!" shot back Mugwump, the frustration starting to rise in her voice. "Tipping off the cops is the same thing as tipping off the traffickers. I know the local police have to be in on it. These guys could never be operating so openly like this without the cops being paid to ignore it."

"It's true," confirmed Jello. "There's a lot going on in this city that shouldn't be, because there's too many corrupt cops on the take letting it happen."

Caroline thought about what they said. She knew that there had to be corruption in the Philadelphia police department as well; occasionally she'd see a news report that indicated this or she heard some sort of rumor. But largely the whole concept was totally outside of her normal day-to-day reality. She had her middle-class home, her middle-class job, and her middle-class husband and friends. These young people were talking about an aspect of city life that she believed existed, but that was invisible to her in her own ordinary life in Philadelphia. But that didn't make it any less real.

"OK," she conceded, "but why bombing? What's that going to accomplish?"

"It's going to force it into the public's face," replied Mugwump. "It's going to mean that not just the cops are going to show up, but the firefighters and the medics are going to show up as well. Gawkers who want to see what's happening are going to be hanging around, and the press is going to show up. They'll be forced to publicly acknowledge what's going on and do something about it."

"Well, I have to admit that makes sense," said Caroline. "But you mentioned medics and if you plan on bombing this place, isn't there a real chance that someone might get hurt? How would you feel if that happened?"

"If we got some of the traffickers, believe me, I'm not going to feel bad about it," said Mugwump.

"What we have planned shouldn't be that big and the placements will be made to create the most disruption but with the lowest risk of human harm," explained Jello. "We're really not out to hurt anyone."

"'Shouldn't be that big'?" repeated Caroline. "Are you sure of that?"

"As sure as I can be of anything," said Jello. "I mean, we haven't been stupid enough to test this out anywhere, but in theory it should work."

"Hmmm, 'in theory,'" said Caroline. "What if the theory is wrong? Suppose the whole place goes up in a giant fireball and the women you're trying to help are trapped in there? What then?"

"Then I'd feel really, really bad," said Mugwump glumly. "But I trust Jello to know what he's doing and I'm willing to take that risk; I think it's actually a pretty small one."

"It's meant to be a small, targeted attack, not a massive bombing; we don't want to attract *too much* attention," explained Jello. "There's also a fire station four blocks away. We'll have someone checking to make sure that they're not already out on call before we make our move. They should be able to arrive quickly and deal with the situation before it gets out of control."

"Well, that's reassuring," said Caroline, although she was only partially reassured. "So, what exactly is the deal? What do you want from me in all of this?"

"We need someone who's able to get eyeballs on the place without seeming suspicious. It's simple, really: just stop out front and signal if the office light is on," said Mugwump. "I've seen it from before: it's always dark in the front of the building, but if someone's there, you can see the office light on, down the hallway."

"But, why me?" asked Caroline. "Can't one of your other friends help with this?"

"My friends all look like me and the cops are—how do I say this?—*aware* of us. If one of us is caught on a surveillance camera, that blows the whole thing open. You're from out of town, you've got plausible deniability, right? You don't know us, you aren't connected with us."

"Right," said Caroline. "We met entirely by accident. But, that's really all you need me to do? Just check to see if a light is on?"

"Exactly. You just walk down the street, stop in front of the building and check to see if the light's on. If it is, you give a signal to Jello, who's behind you down the block, and everything proceeds as planned. Jello signals me on the phone, and then runs past and gets the bomb to the front door. Meanwhile, at the same time, I'm delivering the other bomb to the back door. They should both detonate at around the same time."

"Wait—there are *two* bombs?"

"Yeah, of course, there has to be. We don't want the fuckers to just be able to run out the back."

Caroline sighed. She could get up and walk out now, she told herself. But her body didn't move. On some level it felt almost inevitable that she was there, and that she was going to be involved in this scheme, no matter how dangerous or harebrained it seemed. "Alright," she said finally, "show me what I need to do."

ꕥ

Caroline sat on the park bench near the wharf, two blocks up the street from the warehouse, where Mugwump had instructed her to wait; she'd just leaned over discreetly and loosened the lace on her right shoe. It had been a little less than an hour since she had left the Infoshop via the back alley. She'd slowly ambled in this general direction, continuing to sightsee and doing some minor shopping. Before she'd left, Mugwump had drilled her and Jello on the timing of what they needed to do. Caroline couldn't help but be impressed at how well Mugwump had thought this all through. She explained how to find the park bench and what time Caroline needed to be there by. Caroline knew she had to wait for a text message on the encrypted app that Mugwump had installed on her phone. It would be from their contact, indicating that fire trucks were available at the neighborhood station. If the text didn't come within fifteen minutes, she was free to just leave. If the text did come, she had to walk at a certain pace to be in front of the building at the same time that the other two would be closing in on the target destination.

"What if I get stuck crossing the street?" she'd asked.

"You pick up the pace to make up for it. Once you get up from the bench, start counting. You need to be at the end of the first block by the time you count to fifty-five. But there's some wiggle room. Jello will be coming up behind you and if he sees the signal from you, he'll signal me on the phone app to proceed. He can slow down or speed up if he needs to."

"Well, I don't know how much I'm going to be able to speed up," interjected Jello. His part of the plan was the most difficult and elaborate. He was going to change clothes in a different location, be dressed as a jogger with sunglasses, a knit cap, and a neck gaiter obscuring his identity. Once the bomb was planted, he'd run to another location to put on another set of clothes stashed there. He was at the greatest risk of being identified on surveillance cameras, so care had been taken to find locations where he could do quick changes of clothes out of sight and exit in different directions. Mugwump was most familiar with casing the rear of the building and felt confident of her ability to get in and out of the area with a minimum risk of being seen.

They'd spent time going over the plan again and again. Caroline had to repeat the plan back to Mugwump in exact detail several times in order to prove she understood it completely. They practiced counting at a certain rate and walking (and in Jello's case, running) at a certain pace in the back room of the Infoshop. Caroline had been impressed that Mugwump had worked it all out in such detail. She'd paced the whole route out ahead of time, more than once. She gauged her stride against Caroline's stride, saying "You're taller than me, so you'll cover slightly more ground with each step." She had actually measured Caroline's stride and done math to convert her own numbers into a rate that reflected Caroline's natural pace.

As far as Caroline knew, there were two other people in on the plot. One person who'd text after scoping out the fire station, and another person in their circle who wrote for the anarchist press but had also published articles in more mainstream publications. This person had already spread some rumors among local journalists about possible human trafficking in the area, but lacking any firm leads no one had really followed up on it. But he'd been tipped off to be in the area at this general time and to go to the location if a disturbance involving explosions and sirens was heard. He would start taking photographs as soon as possible, and offer copies to any other media that might show up to cover the incident.

Now Caroline sat on the assigned bench, waiting for the text message to come, or not. She tied to quell the butterflies in her stomach by concentrating on other things—the contrast of the strong sunlight and sharp wind of a beautiful fall day, and the papers in her backpack that still needed grading. Her anxiety unfortunately wasn't lessened by the guilt that kept creeping back into her mind. She'd lied to her husband earlier, and it hadn't just been on of those "little white lies" that sometimes get told in marriages to keep things running smoothly. It had, in fact, been a real whopper.

Before she left the back room of the Infoshop, she knew she needed to call her husband to let him know she'd be coming home late. James had picked up on the third ring, with a "Hello, honey."

"Hi, James," she'd replied. "I'm just calling to let you know I'm going to be running late tonight."

"Oh, really?" he'd said, sounding a bit disappointed. "What's up?"

"Oh, you know, it's just been crazy here. I got caught up in all kinds of conversations and emails, and haven't gotten to half the work I'd planned to get done."

"Sorry to hear that, hon."

"And to top it off," she'd continued. "There's a job candidate here who I'd forgotten about. Elaine was supposed to be one of the people going out to dinner with him tonight, but she called in sick. The dean asked me to take her place and, you know, I can't say 'no' to that!"

"Nah, I guess you can't. But at least you'll get a nice dinner out of it, huh?"

"I suppose. So, anyway, the upshot is just not to expect me anytime soon. Just fix something for yourself tonight, and I'll see you when I see you."

"OK, will do. Have a good time, OK?"

"I'll try! Bye, dear!"

"Bye!"

She'd hung up the phone with mixed emotions. Talking to James had felt so normal, but lying to him hadn't. She knew she'd done the right thing to check in and let him know she'd be coming home late; that was typical and expected. She honestly didn't want him wondering where she was, or worrying about her when she didn't come home by dinner time. But at the same time, she felt really bad for lying to him on this scale. She also started to turn over some of the "what if" scenarios that had been playing in her mind in the bus on the way up. Then, they had just been anxious worries; now, putting herself into this scheme made the chances of something unpleasant happening all the more likely.

After she'd finished the phone call, Mugwump had made her recite the details of the plan one more time to make sure she'd got it. The steps, the sequence, the timing all flowed flawlessly from her lips. Mugwump seemed pleased.

"Great!" Mugwump praised her with a grin. "You've got it!" She led her to the back door so that Caroline could leave unseen by the back alley. Caroline turned at the door to say good-bye and she'd seen that Mugwump's face was quite serious. "Thank you," she'd said, with a depth of sincerity.

"Um, you're welcome?" said Caroline, unsure of the etiquette of a situation like this.

"You're doing the right thing. Really."

"OK. Bye!"

Caroline walked out the door and down the alley for a few blocks before emerging onto one of the streets. She decided that the best thing to do was put the whole situation out of her mind and just behave like normal, continuing to enjoy her day in the city as an out-of-towner. She had about forty-five minutes before she had to be in place, and an alarm was set on her phone to give her a ten-minute warning. Her first stop had been a little storefront bakery that had a couple of small tables with chairs at the front. She'd gotten an éclair and a coffee from the counter and sat at one of the tables to enjoy her snack. She even pulled the student papers out of her backpack and graded a couple of them. It was a little difficult to give them her full attention, but it felt good to her to be at least a bit productive with her work.

After she left the bakery, she went up the street and stopped into a drug store, picking up a few items there. Then she continued walking and window shopping. When the alarm buzzed on her phone in her coat pocket, she knew she had plenty of time to unhurriedly move toward her staging area. She'd turned the alarm off quickly and had continued to walk, casually moving in the direction of the assigned bench.

ഌ൦ഏ

Now her phone buzzed again as she sat on the bench. She pulled it from her pocket and swiped to open the message on the special privacy app. "Dinner's ready" said the message. Caroline winched a bit at the dinner reference, but recognized it as the agreed-upon "all clear" signal from Mugwump's contact. She quickly deleted the app from her phone, got up off the bench, and started to walk in the direction of the traffickers' building.

Her mind was in high gear as she walked down the street. She was hyperaware of her surroundings: all of the colors, sounds, and smells of the street bombarded her senses. At the same time, part of her mind was in an oasis, slowly counting out her steps as she moved down the street. It was a consistent rhythm as she counted at the agreed-upon pace, almost meditative. The counting was a sea of calm as all else swirled around her.

She came to the end of the first block at exactly the count that Mugwump had predicted. There was no traffic on the side street, so she easily crossed it with no delay. She proceeded down the target block, still counting, still holding to her rhythm. But another part of her mind was succumbing to an anxiety boarding on panic. She'd already put aside any questions about "Am I doing the right thing?" but now she was wondering if Jello was coming, worrying about if the whole scenario was really unfolding as planned. The target building was coming up on her right and she moved to the side, stopping on the sidewalk near the front window. She was fumbling pulling the phone out of her coat pocket and stopped to look at it where she'd have a clear view through the window. She pretended to scroll through her phone, and as casually as possible glanced through the window. She could see a light coming from a doorway down a darkened hallway.

She leaned over and tied her loosened shoelace, giving the signal to the still unseen Jello. She stood back up and continued walking down the street. After only a few steps, she heard a dull "thump" as something hit the door of the building behind her, and a figure in running gear ran past her. Then, within a few seconds, she heard a loud double blast coming from behind her, the second one closely following on the first, which seemed further away. The concussion threw her to the sidewalk.

What happened next was a confused flurry for her. She felt people helping her up and walking her across the street. She heard sirens, saw a gathering crowd, smelled smoke. Some ambulances arrived and one of the medics cleaned a bloody scrape on her left knee and offered her oxygen. She waved it off with a shake of her head. The medic suggested taking her to the hospital for observation but she refused.

"I'm fine," she remembered saying. "I'm just a little shaken up, that's all."

"Well, rest here for a while, until you're cleared to go," replied the medic.

Firetrucks were on the scene, hoses running. The front window of the building had been broken. Caroline could hear sirens on the block behind them as well. A police cruiser pulled up and an officer got out of the passenger side. He talked to the medic and a young woman with red hair who had been one of the people to help Caroline across the street. They both gestured toward Caroline. She felt herself freezing inside as the officer walked toward her, and her mind was in a haze as he asked her some questions—her name, what she was doing there, if she'd be willing to give a statement.

The thought crossed Caroline's mind that she was being arrested as he led her to the police cruiser and opened the back door for her. "No, I'm not being arrested," she told herself, "I'm just an innocent bystander." The officer got back in the front passenger seat and pulled a clipboard with rumpled papers on it from under the dashboard. Behind the wheel was the officer's partner, a young woman not much older than Mugwump, with chin-length brown hair, looking smart in her uniform. The male officer who'd led Caroline to the car told her both of their names, but they went in one ear and out the other. He asked to see her identification and she reached in her backpack to pull out her wallet and produce her driver's license and university ID. She handed the cards to him with a twisted sense of déjà vu from having done the same thing with Jello less than two hours before. She hoped that she'd manage to pass muster here as well.

The officer examined the IDs and wrote things down on the clipboard, confirming that the information on the cards was current. He asked for her phone number and she gave him both her cell phone and office numbers. Then he asked some routine questions about what she was doing in New York and why she was in this area. She stuck to her story of having come up from Philadelphia for the day, to enjoy the fall weather and to do some shopping. Then he asked her some more specific questions about what she'd seen and experienced in the incident.

"I didn't really see much of anything," she explained. There were a few people on the sidewalk ahead of her, she recalled, and a jogger who passed by her. She didn't remember many details about who they were or what they looked like. She hadn't really seen the jogger, wasn't sure if it had been a man or a woman, but thought that the person had been wearing dark blue, or maybe black. "I'm sorry I can't be of more help," she said.

"That's alright," said the officer taking her statement. "It's a shock to be involved in something like this and that makes it hard to remember specifics. If anything comes to you later, though, give us a call." He handed her a business card over the seat back. "That's the number of the precinct, and I've written my name and the case number on the back."

"OK, thanks," said Caroline, taking the card from him and slipping it into the front zippered pouch of her backpack. "Is that everything?"

"Yeah," said the officer. "We'll call you if we need anything further."

"We're done here," said the officer behind the wheel, "and we're heading back to the precinct. Can we drop you anywhere?"

"Oh, thank you!" said Caroline, feeling a sense of exhaustion setting in. "Could you take me to the Jacob Javits Center? Right now, I just want to get on the bus and go home."

"Sure enough," said the officer as she flipped the car into gear and they moved off. Caroline felt strange riding in the back of a police car. She no longer worried that she was being arrested, but she wondered if anyone else seeing her might think that she had been.

"Um, if you don't mind me asking, do you know what it was that happened back there?" she ventured to ask.

"No, not entirely," said the officer behind the wheel. "Reports coming through on radio indicated that there were arrests made at the back of the building. There was definitely some sort of criminal activity going on there, and it might have been something like an attack from a rival gang."

"Wow," said Caroline, not knowing what more to say.

"Looks like you had the bad luck to be right in the wrong place at the wrong time," added the other officer.

"Yeah, I guess," said Caroline. "Actually, I feel kind of lucky that I got by with just a scrapped knee."

"You're right," agreed the officer. "It could have been a lot worse."

They dropped her at the end of the block near the Javits Center. "Thank you!" she called as she got out of the cruiser, turning to smile and give a little wave as the officers drove off. She stopped at a taco truck parked on the street and bought some tacos to eat on the ride home. Then she found the sandwich board propped on the sidewalk that said "Philadelphia" and stood in line to wait for the bus to take her home.

As she waited, she hugged the trench coat tighter around her. It was now dusk and the temperature had dropped. Despite having the coat, she still felt chilled in the fall evening air but was glad that she at least had it to wear. She stamped her feet on the ground and gazed across the street at the beautiful glass structure of the Javits Center. The cool clarity of the glass front of the building reminded her of an ice sculpture, so it did nothing to take off the chill. She looked at it with the familiar emotions of anger and regret that it tended to provoke in her. The events of the day, crazy as they had been, had already faded somewhat. Now she was just a woman standing on a New York City sidewalk, waiting for a bus.

The bus company representative was working her way down the line that Caroline was standing in. "Should be another ten or fifteen minutes," Caroline heard her tell a person further ahead in line. Caroline continued to hug her coat around her and stamp her feet.

"Philadelphia?" asked the representative when she got to Caroline.

"Yup," replied Caroline, as she swung her backpack down and started to dig for her wallet.

"Twenty dollars," said the representative, "should be about ten minutes."

"Thanks," said Caroline as she exchanged a twenty-dollar-bill for a paper ticket. She pulled her backpack back up onto her shoulders, just as she caught sight of an odd figure walking across the street. The person was wearing a bright orange sweatshirt with the hood up, partially obscuring their face, faded blue jeans, and red high-top sneakers. A small brown paper bag was tucked under one arm, and the figure seemed to be moving directly toward her.

"Oh, no," thought Caroline, as a feeling of panic welled up in her. "What now?"

It was clear to Caroline that this wasn't a figment of a paranoid imagination. The figure was, in fact, making a beeline toward her. She gulped and took a deep breath to try to calm herself down. She had dodged so many bullets today, she thought; could it all finally come crashing down, just as she was about to be safely on her way home?

As the figure drew nearer, Caroline's feelings of concern lessened somewhat. It was Mugwump—but what was she doing here, coming back into contact after everything that had happened today?

"Hey," Mugwump said, stopping on the sidewalk next to Caroline.

"Hey," said Caroline back, not sure what more she could risk saying to this woman.

"I just wanted to, you know, say 'thanks' again, for your help and for being so awesome today."

"There's really no need..." started Caroline, but Mugwump cut her off.

"'K, well, I wanted to give you this," she said as she thrust the brown paper bag into Caroline's hands. "It's from the Infoshop." Then she reached out to Caroline with one arm for a quick, awkward half-hug.

Caroline was surprised but tried to return the embrace as warmly as she could. She could feel what seemed to be a book in the paper bag she was holding.

"Bye!" said Mugwump, walking a few steps backward down the sidewalk before turning to run into the gathering dark.

"Bye!" Caroline called back, watching the bright orange sweatshirt recede into the night. She pushed the paper bag into the bag from the drugstore just as the bus pulled up and sighed to a stop alongside her.

Caroline had a double seat to herself again on the upper deck of the bus. She'd plopped down, dropping her backpack, the drugstore bag, and the to-go bag of tacos onto the seat beside her. She knew that she needed to grade more student papers, but didn't feel like she could concentrate well enough to consider them fairly. She had classes to teach tomorrow, and she'd just have to tell the students that she'd be a little late with this round of papers. This was the kind of thing that usually created a lot of guilt in Caroline, but right now she had to admit that it was the only reasonable course of action. Grading papers was not her priority after all she'd experienced that day.

As the bus approached the Lincoln Tunnel, she pulled out the paper bag that Mugwump had given her. Filled with curiosity, she took out the hardback book inside. The cover read: *Anarchist Women, 1870-1920* by Margaret S. Marsh. Caroline examined it closely. It had been published a number of decades ago by a university press in Philadelphia, but she had never heard of it. This copy showed signs of much use, with a worn and slightly tattered book jacket and lots of underlining and marginal notes written in the text. She read the blurb on the cover with interest:

> The anarchist-feminists and their ideology possess a significance that extends beyond anarchism and nineteenth-century popular images of it. This book examines the women who espoused anarchism and what they believed, but more importantly it seeks to understand the unique ways in which a group of women responded to the social, sexual, and economic upheavals of the late nineteenth and early twentieth centuries. The antistatist, antiauthoritarian, decentralist visions of the anarchists are an integral part of our intellectual heritage. What the women anarchists tried to do is an important part of the history of the intellectual roots of the women's movement.

Then she opened the book and started to read.

ꙮ

Caroline awoke with a start when the bus came to a halt outside of Philadelphia's 30th Street Station. The driver had turned on all the interior lights and was making an announcement that this was the final stop and to make sure you took all of your belongings with you. Caroline had fallen asleep with the book on her lap, and hurried to put it and the items from the drugstore bag into her backpack. Exiting the bus, she found a trash can and threw away the food bag and the now empty drugstore bag from her New York trip. She briefly considering ditching the trench coat as well, but it was colder in Philly now, too, and she decided to wear it home.

After a quick trolley ride and walking a few blocks back to the house, she was home. James got up from the couch when she came in the front door. "Hi, honey," he said, wrapping her in his arms after she finished locking the door. "I'm glad you're finally home!"

"Me, too!" Caroline replied, with more enthusiasm than she'd intended. "It's been quite a day!"

"Are you hungry at all? There's some leftover stir fry in the fridge if you are."

"No, thanks," said Caroline, remembering both the fact that she was supposed to have been at a fancy faculty dinner and the tacos she'd eaten on the bus while reading. "I'm stuffed!"

James held her at arm's length and considered her. "New coat?" he asked. "I don't think I've seen that before."

"New-old," said Caroline. "I left the house without a jacket this morning and it got colder than I expected, so I ducked into one of the thrift shops downtown and picked this up. Like it?"

James sniffed. "Smells a little...smoky."

"Probably from someone's fire sale," said Caroline, and James chuckled.

"Well, ready to just kick back and watch some TV with me? Glass of wine, maybe?"

The latter sounded tempting, but Caroline shook her head. "Sorry, dear, it's just been such a long, exhausting day for me. I think I'll go take a shower and get to bed early, if you don't mind."

"Suit yourself," said James, settling back down on the couch. "I hope that you get some good rest!"

"Thanks, dear," said Caroline as she headed up the steps, her familiar home suddenly having a somewhat surreal quality to it.

ꕥ

The next day Caroline was back to her usual routine, going into campus to teach her classes and putting in extra time to get caught up on her grading. The trip to New York now seemed unreal, like something she had dreamed and that had soon faded away.

But about a week after her trip, Caroline was in her office at work and decided to log onto her university library's resources and look at the electronic subscription they provided to the *New York Times*. After a little hunting around, she found the article that she was looking for, headlined "Double Bombing at SoHo Industrial Building." The article noted that small bombs had been set off at both the front and rear of the building, that three men inside had been arrested and that two of their associates not on the scene at the time had been tracked down and also arrested, and that sixteen women and girls had been rescued from the basement of the building, presumably from human trafficking. A truck had also been impounded at the scene, and authorities were investigating it to see if they could find clues to a wider trafficking network. There were no arrests made in the bombing itself, but the mayor's office had issued a formal statement that terrorism was not suspected. It was, rather, attributed to "garden variety" criminal activity by the mayor; police detectives welcomed any tips or information. The building was damaged by the bomb blasts and subsequent fires, but only minor injuries were reported, including to a visitor from Philadelphia who happened to be walking past at the time.

Well, there's my claim to fame, thought Caroline. I'm the anonymous visitor...but I guess I'm also the accidental anarchist. She picked up the worn book from her desktop, removed the bookmark, and continued to read.

#4 Stealing MacGuffin

Matthew Kastel

Chapter One

Some people are born criminals. Others, like me, are drawn into criminal enterprise by opportunity. But for now, that was in my future.

I run a forgettable one-man detective agency that usually settles for the dregs of detective work: spying on cheap hotels to catch cheating spouses or freelancing for insurance companies to expose people on disability doing things like water skiing. I may not have followed all of life's rules, but theft was something I hadn't stooped to before. I was about to hit a new low.

I was sitting alone in a blue-collar bar near the Port of Baltimore awaiting the arrival of Bert Thompson. Yesterday, Bert had sent me a cryptic email saying he was in town from Hollywood and had some business to discuss with me. Bert and I go back to my Hollywood days. That's right. You heard me. My Hollywood days.

When I finished college, I fancied myself an up-and-coming screenwriter and traveled to Tinseltown to make a name for myself. I got a little studio apartment on Sunset that I had to bolt myself into at night to keep from getting robbed by the junkies and streetwalkers who took over the neighborhood from dusk to dawn.

I lived that way for a decade. To say that work was sporadic is an understatement. I have a few things to my credit on my IMDb page but not much. To survive, I worked all the typical jobs—waiter, light carpentry, cabbie. Then one day, my father begged me to come help him with the detective agency he was trying to get off the ground. He'd just been thrown off the Baltimore PD for being a raging alcoholic. I decided to chuck show business and moved back home to Baltimore. Six months later my old man checked out of life, and I was left in charge of a detective agency, a business I knew almost nothing about.

Bert, for a brief while, was my writing partner or the closest thing I had to a writing partner. He was a good decade older than me and had more contacts with agents and producers, so I thought we would be a good match. In the end I did ninety percent of the writing and although our partnership didn't produce much more of note than one episode of a mildly successful sitcom and a made-for-TV movie that never got on air, we still got some cash for them.

That was ten years ago. But as fate would have it, within a year of my breaking up the partnership and leaving Hollywood, Bert hit the big time when he penned an indie flick about a transvestite who backpacks across Europe and finds love. It was all the buzz at Cannes. There hasn't been a day since that I haven't wondered what my career could have been like if I'd stuck with him.

After Cannes Bert got a seven-figure deal to write the screenplay for a big studio movie, which promptly flopped at the box office. Since then, Bert raced through two actress wives, so I imagine most of the money is gone, especially seeing that his IMDb page shows he hasn't worked much in the last few years. Still, he had his moment.

It was a cold fall day, and I hadn't broken out my warm clothes yet, so each time the bar door was flung open, a chill rattled me to the bones. Eventually, the wind blew in a cold blast from my past in the figure of Bert Thompson.

Bert was a big man, standing well over six feet tall and beefy, which made him look strong rather than fat. We had exchanged a few emails over the years, but it had been a long time since I had seen him in the flesh. He hadn't changed much. He must have been about fifty now, and the only hint that he had aged since the last time I saw him was some graying around the temples.

We shook hands and Bert jingled. I should explain that Bert was one of those men who wore chains and rings to the point of ridicule. It's a Hollywood thing, I guess. He also had a cheesy black mustache that made him look like a character straight out of central casting for a '70s porno.

We both ordered a beer from the bar and sat there, side by side. After we clinked glasses to toast our friendship, Bert got down to business. "I have some work for you," he said.

I sat on the edge of my barstool and salivated in anticipation. "I want you to find Mr. MacGuffin," he said, as he sucked the suds off the head of his beer.

I was surprised at how let down I felt; I thought I had left all my dreams of Hollywood behind. What had I been anticipating, that Bert had another big studio movie job and wanted me to cowrite it with him? Still, a missing person case was nothing to sneeze at. So, I pulled open my notepad and asked, "When was the last time Mr. MacGuffin was seen?"

Bert scrunched his left eye shut to think and came back with, "The last confirmed sighting of Mr. MacGuffin was 1968, give or take."

I closed the notebook, not liking where this was heading. "1968? Don't you think Mr. MacGuffin would be long dead by now?"

"Oh, I should explain. Mr. MacGuffin isn't a person but a thing."

"A thing?"

"Well, to be clear, Mr. MacGuffin is an exact replica of Rudolph Valentino's erect penis made when the great actor was still alive. It was made of plaster of Paris and then painted purple."

I was beginning to think that I was about to be stiffed and, before the night was over, not only wouldn't I have any work out of this get-together, I would also end up picking up the bar tab.

"Look. I ..." I began, before being stopped when Bert held up his hand to silence me.

"This isn't what you think. This is a very valuable piece of Hollywood memorabilia that is worth a small fortune."

"A valuable piece of Hollywood memorabilia?" I asked incredulously.

Bert nodded and asked, "You are aware of who Rudolph Valentino is, aren't you?"

"Of course," I sniffed, a little insulted that Bert would think I didn't know the first matinée movie star from the silent era, a man who could make women swoon from a glance and who died tragically young in the 1920s, breaking women's hearts all across the country.

"When it came to women, Valentino made Hugh Hefner look like an amateur. He had quality pussy hanging off of him anytime he wanted."

I should interject that Bert wasn't the type of guy who gave a hot damn about things like being politically correct or the #metoo movement. That and that alone may have been his only redeeming quality.

"Well, anyway, what's a guy to do? So many women, so little time, right? Only so much of him to go around. So, as a joke, one drunken weekend with his pals in Palm Springs, he had six of these erect penises, exact replicas of himself, made up. This way there would be more of him to go around. Get it?"

I didn't really and felt a little queasy as I took a sip from my draft, but I knew from experience not to interrupt Bert when he was on a roll.

"Now these replicas weren't a secret. As a laugh he actually named all six and would bring them to Hollywood parties. All of the show business community knew about them. They were so popular that, over time, he handed out the penises to friends as a thank you when they did a favor for him."

The bar door opened again, sending a chill our way, and we glanced toward the door before Bert continued. "Then Valentino dies and, as the years go by, all but one of these replicas disappear, presumably lost to history forever."

"And that takes us to 1968," I interjected.

"Exactly," said Bert, pointing a big meaty finger at me. "Did you ever hear of Pedro Noboa?"

"Can't say that I have."

"No surprise there," said Bert. "He was a minor character actor who did some early TV and was in some of those horrible B sci-fi movies that they used to make and show at drive-ins. He was known to have the last existing Valentino, the one named Mr. MacGuffin. He had inherited it several years earlier from an older actor he was friendly with when he died, who was one of Valentino's pals back in the day. Word was he kept this priceless piece of Hollywood kitsch on his desk and used it as a paperweight."

"A paperweight?"

Bert shrugged as if to say "to each his own."

"Anyway, Mr. Noboa was engaged to get married. In the summer of 1968, his fiancée hadn't heard from him in several days and was worried, so she convinced his landlord to open his apartment door and do a check on him. You know what he finds?"

I was about to guess, but Bert didn't have the patience to wait for my answer and said, "A dead body. And not just any dead body, mind you. Apparently, our friend, the character actor, was queer on the sly. They found him strangled to death, and he was all tied up with the usual B&D implements and had the words 'whip me' written on his ass.

"It didn't take Hollywood homicide long to bust the suspects. It turned out it was a couple of homo hustlers who were mad that Mr. Noboa didn't have the cash he promised them for his night of fun. Legend has it they took Mr. MacGuffin as a souvenir when they walked out the door after killing him. But when the police busted them, they either didn't care about Mr. MacGuffin or didn't know about it. The boys spent the rest of their lives in prison, and, according to rumor, Mr. MacGuffin then went from hand to hand, pardon the pun, disappearing for awhile only to resurface every now and again."

"Then I take it that it has resurfaced again?"

"Indeed it has, and I know who has it."

"I'm a little confused," I said. "I'm a detective, but it sounds like this isn't a mystery. What is it that I can do for you?"

"MacGuffin is right here in Baltimore," said Bert hardily. "I know I can trust you, and you have certain skills I'm sure you have acquired in your line of work that will be helpful in stealing it."

"Stealing it? Me?" I replied sharply. "No way am I getting involved in this, if it involves stealing."

Bert put his arm around my shoulder like we were old pals, saying, "Listen. What do you think is going to happen even if you're caught? The owner can't turn you in to the police, as this isn't his property. And even if he did, how much time do you think you would get for stealing a dildo that doesn't rightfully belong to anyone?"

Bert was probably right about that. With violent crime running rampant, Baltimore PD was satisfied if they could clear a homicide every now and again. Even if it did get reported, property theft wasn't exactly a high priority with Town Hall. Still, stealing was stealing. "I don't think I can help you," I said.

"You haven't heard the punch line," said Bert. "I have a guy in Hollywood who is willing to give me a half-million in cash for it. He's legit and loaded. I'll split it with you fifty-fifty if you acquire Mr. MacGuffin for me. I don't know about you, but I need a little cash to get my next project off the ground, and I'm guessing that amount of money might make a difference in your life."

I still should have said no, but by then we had switched to scotch and sodas, which must have clouded my judgment. I found myself hazily agreeing to Bert's scheme. Ah, firewater, the fuel of my introduction into criminality.

As we were walking out the door after calling it a night, I asked, "So who has MacGuffin now?"

"Have you ever heard of Cy Green?"

Indeed, I had, and the mere mention of his name scared the you-know-what out of me.

Chapter Two

The next afternoon in my office I allowed myself to think of Cy Green. I even Googled him to refresh my memory, although that wasn't really necessary. For twenty years, Cy Green had been the box office king of Hollywood, specializing as a director of horror flicks.

Just like his idol, Alfred Hitchcock, Green was obese and obscenely so, with most of his weight hanging off his belly. He had a shock of gray hair, parted on the side, that was so vibrant it screamed white instead of gray, which was in contrast to his beady brown eyes. But the most distinct feature of Green was his manner of speaking. He had a loud, commanding voice that made it seem like he was yelling even when he was speaking softly. His clipped, formal diction highlighted his perfect elocution and his flair for choosing the most apt word and pronunciation no matter the situation. When he spoke, you were reminded he was twice as smart as you, even on your best day.

In his heyday, Cy Green had ruled Hollywood with an iron fist. His ability to manufacture mass quantities of box-office bucks convinced the movie studios to look the other way and let him do as he pleased, and he used this carte blanche to be one of the worst bullies that Hollywood has ever seen. It didn't matter if you were an A-list actor, power agent, billionaire, or best boy, if you stepped on his set while he was filming you were his to abuse, and he did so at will. He screwed whoever he wanted, reduced to tears anyone who challenged him, and even reportedly knocked a studio head out cold when he dared suggest a small edit.

All this had been pretty much an open secret. But he was so terrifying that even during the present age of the #metoo movement, not one person had publicly accused him of anything improper. You didn't fuck with Cy Green.

Five years ago, two weeks after the premier of his latest movie blockbuster, *High School Graduation Fright Night IV*, Cy stunned the world by announcing his retirement. He blamed his departure on how vapid Hollywood and the movie industry had become, and, even though he wasn't yet sixty, he stated that he wanted to go out while he was still on top.

True to his word, Cy packed his bags, sold his mansions and, for whatever reason, moved back to the city he grew up in, Baltimore. He hadn't necessarily become a recluse since cashing in his chips, but he did make it a point to keep a low profile once he returned to Charm City.

Just then a shadow projected itself across my desk, causing me to break from my Google search and look up from my laptop. "Greetings," said the familiar voice coming from just outside my door.

First, to end your speculation, my office looks better than you'd imagine. It's on St. Paul Street, which is a respectable address in a not-so-respectable city. It's one of those office suites where you share a receptionist and conference room with other businesses. From the outside it looks impressive, and if you call me on the phone during business hours it sounds like I have my own secretary. In reality it's all an illusion and a cheap one at that, as the rent was affordable even to a piker like me.

"Right on time," I said.

I've known Dan since first grade when we discovered we had the same birthday and became pals. Such are the ties that bind you in childhood. After graduation we lost touch, but a few months after my dad died, I ran into him at a party given by a mutual friend.

We found ourselves chatting up the same young Latina, a temptress with seductive brown eyes and a reputation of not so much dating men as devouring them. She answered to the nickname of La Petarda, or firecracker, which fit her perfectly. In the end, she left the party with another man, leaving Dan and I alone to reconnect as we lamented where we went wrong. Since then he has been helping me out on a freelance basis at the Trowbridge Detective Agency.

Dan is black, and I'm white, a fact that we never found the need to discuss. I don't know his opinion on Freddie Grey or the Reverend Al Sharpton, and he never asks if I hope Donald Trump is going to make America great again. We also don't talk about our personal lives, families, or religion. In some ways we are nothing more than strangers passing in the street, but in certain respects we are as tight as brothers.

"What do you have for me this time?" asked Dan, tall and lean with an old school Afro. He cocked his head waiting for the answer. I had a propensity to give Dan what one would call the dirty work, work from which he never shied away. For his efforts I paid him cash, under the table, of course. I also bought a pair of Orioles tickets each opening day and then treated him as my guest. Dan backed the Birds with a passion.

I told Dan about my meeting with Bert and the proposition we had agreed on. I didn't hold anything back including that this was worth $250,000 to me. Dan, if anything, was discrete. You could hold a gun to his head and he wouldn't rat you out. He, as well as I, knew the code of the Baltimore streets by heart: stitches are for snitches. In some cities this was hyperbole. In Baltimore, if you ended up with just the stitches you were lucky.

"So, you want me to help you steal some purple penis," Dan concluded nonjudgmentally.

I nodded and added, "I definitely need your help with this. What will it take?"

I expected him to ask for half, and I was prepared to counter with $75,000.

Instead he surprised me by saying, "One dollar."

"One dollar?" I asked incredulously.

Dan shrugged, adding, "One dollar and for me to become your business partner. You keep all the money from MacGuffin, but my share will be a stake in your detective agency. I'd say about thirty-three percent of the business would be appropriate."

"Are you sure?" I responded, sweeping my arms in a grand motion to point out that my office was barren. "Some months I barely cover my nut. You might be buying into a whole lot of nothing."

"I'll take my chances," he said. "We're worth betting on."

"Sold," I said, before he could change his mind. "Tell you what, I'll make it forty percent if you do a favor for me."

"Do tell."

"There's this guy," I said. "Maybe it's my imagination, but after Bert and I parted ways last night I felt like I was being tailed by him on the way home. I didn't think much of it, but on my way to the office this morning, I saw him again. I want to find out who this guy is, and what, if anything, he's up to."

"You gotta give me more than that. You have a description?"

I thought about this for a while. Although I could see him perfectly in my head, something about his appearance rang false. "Well, he wore an expensive tan trench coat that's seen better days. He was young, maybe late twenties, early thirties, and white with unkempt brown hair and a wild look in his eyes. My impression was that he was a homeless junkie or someone trying to make you think that he was a homeless junkie."

Dan pondered this for a moment, and I knew what he was thinking. This was a city full of homeless junkies. Finding this guy could be a needle in a haystack. "OK, consider it done," he concluded. "He is as good as found."

We both sat content for a moment before Dan asked, "So when do we steal that penis?"

"As soon as possible," I replied.

Chapter Three

A few days later, well after dark, Dan and I caught an Uber to one of the few tourist areas in Baltimore, the Inner Harbor. On the ride, Dan yakked on about the Orioles' offseason moves and how next year could be their year. When it came to the Orioles, Dan was an eternal optimist. But It was never going to be the Birds' year again. Call it the curse of Jim Palmer. Palmer was the only player active for all of the Orioles' three World Championships: 1966, 1970, and 1983. Since the pretty boy ace retired, however, baseball in Baltimore, for the most part, has been downright ugly.

At one point during the ride I almost interrupted Dan to tell him I had seen my stalker again yesterday, the guy with the crazy eyes, and this time I was positive he was tailing me. In the end I kept this information to myself. Dan, like most guys, didn't like being told how to do his job, and I knew him well enough to know that if he felt like I was putting pressure on him, he would resent it.

We told the driver to let us out at the National Aquarium. Our cover, if anyone questioned us, was that we were just a couple of guys out enjoying Baltimore's nightlife. The Inner Harbor was home to plenty of restaurants and bars that were hopping late into the night, so for us to be in the neighborhood would be perfectly reasonable.

Cy Green lived in a two-story penthouse in a swanky thirty-eight-story high-rise that overlooked the harbor and was Baltimore's hottest address. His condo was a half-mile walk from the Aquarium. After we got out of the Uber, we started the walk without talking.

The plan we had come up with for stealing Mr. MacGuffin was based on good fortune. After we figured out Cy's address, Dan realized he had a good buddy who worked security overnight in the building. Two years earlier this so-called buddy had asked Dan to pick up a package from a third party and hold it for him, as he was out of town for the weekend. Unbeknownst to Dan, the *package* turned out to contain a stolen smart phone. Thanks to the GPS chip, the owner of the phone, who just happened to be a local drug dealer, tracked Dan down and beat the shit out of him before taking his property back. Dan's friend owed him big for taking the beating, and to pay back the favor he had agreed to work with us on a plan to get us in and out of the building without getting caught. Only in Baltimore would a guy like this work in *security*.

When we got within a block of the high-rise Dan got out his cell and called his friend. "Randy, my man—we're here," he said. He ended the call abruptly and jutted his chin toward the building, saying "Let's go."

Inside the high-rise, the lobby was granite and marble with high-end finishes, and sitting at the concierge station was Dan's friend Randy in a security guard's blue blazer.

After brief introductions Randy said, "On the overnight I'm the only one here. Maintenance, housekeeping, and the security supervisor are only in during the day. If we have any alarms go off, they tend not to take it too seriously. It usually takes them about forty-five minutes to get in to respond."

As planned, Randy had killed the power to the CCTV equipment in the building when Dan had called him. Without CCTV we could ransack the building with a cloak of invisibility. Cutting the power to the cameras would set off a silent alarm, but Randy assured us that if we were quick, we could be out of the building before anyone came in to restore the power to the cameras.

"Are you sure Mr. Green is out for the evening?" I asked.

"Positive. He lives alone, and I saw him last night getting into a limo. I asked him where he was going, and he told me he was going up to New York for a few days to pick up some film industry award."

I nodded, then said to Dan while looking at my watch, "Let's get moving. If we only have forty-five minutes, let's try to do it in thirty."

Cy Green was the only resident on the top two floors of the building, and he and he alone had a swipe card that allowed him up to the penthouse in the elevator. The building did have an internal stairwell that residents could use as an exit in case of a fire. The door was locked on the lobby level to prevent unwanted people from accessing it. Security held a master key for it, and Randy left his concierge post and unlocked the stairwell. "All the way to thirty-eight," he said as he held the door open for us. When the door shut behind us, we could hear him yell, "You won't need a key to get back into the stairwell to go down."

Dan and I started up the stairs at a brisk jog, which within a few flights turned into a hearty walk, and by the time we'd gotten to the last few flights, we were crawling up the stairwell clinging to the banister. It had taken over fifteen minutes to make it all the way up, but we reasoned that the trip back down would go faster. Still, there wasn't much time.

The door to Cy Green's multimillion-dollar pad was plain and simple. "OK, partner, do your thing," I said to Dan, encouraging him to break down the door.

Dan stood hunched over with his hands on his knees, and between gulping breaths said, "You gotta be kidding me. I barely have enough energy to stand."

Fortunately, I was kidding him. I had been carrying a shopping bag from Kohl's that I thought would look inconspicuous if I was seen toting it around. I had shoved the bag full of packing peanuts and some bubble wrap to keep MacGuffin safe from breakage after we stole it. Digging around to the bottom of the bag I found what I wanted, and produced the leather case containing several lock picks. I didn't know one small-time detective who was worth a damn who didn't have their own picks and know how to use them.

Green had double-locks. The first lock yielded in seconds. The second took me a good three minutes and several picks before I heard that familiar click. "We're in," I said to Dan triumphantly. I looked at my watch and guessed we had about seventeen minutes left.

It was pitch dark when we entered the apartment. I fumbled for a wall switch and found one that flooded the place with light.

"Wow," said Dan.

Wow, indeed. The penthouse had floor-to-ceiling glass windows with views of both the harbor and downtown. From this vantage point, even Baltimore looked beautiful. "Come on," I said. "We don't have time to sightsee. We have to find MacGuffin."

With two large floors to cover I was worried we wouldn't have enough time, but I scanned the room carefully. It looked like a palatial living room with trendy modern furniture that I couldn't picture the oversized Cy Green being comfortable sitting in. In the center of the room was an ornate spiral staircase that led down to the lower floor. The place was huge. MacGuffin could be anywhere.

I scrutinized the walls and saw plenty of artwork that I assumed were originals and worth a fortune. Oddly, I didn't see any photos of Green or personal items on display, nor any movie posters or anything else that would demonstrate to a visitor that not too long ago, Cy Green had been the King of Hollywood.

Then a glass case caught my eye, and I walked over to it. "Well, well," I said. "This is going to be easier than I thought."

"What do you have?" asked Dan, coming up behind me.

Inside the case, which butted up against the wall, there was a podium at eye level with a purple penis on it. The case was constructed of thick glass. At the bottom of the podium was an inscription on a silver plate that I read out loud: "Rudolph Valentino 1895–1926."

I studied the glass carefully for a few minutes, trying to see if it had an alarm and considering options for ways that we could get MacGuffin out without getting caught. While thinking this over, I sensed that Dan had walked back over to where I was. I felt a sudden whoosh of air and then heard the sound of crashing glass. While I had been contemplating, Dan had gone into the kitchen, grabbed a metal pot, and had simply smashed the glass.

The loud sound of the breaking glass was startling, but after a moment it was quiet and no audible alarm had gone off. I grabbed MacGuffin from the podium and examined it. I noticed that it must have been behind glass for a while, because it was dusty. Holding it in my hand, I gave it a few quick blows to clean it off.

Over my shoulder I could feel Dan staring at me. I quickly pulled some bubble wrap from my Kohl's bag to encase it in, then gently dropped it into the bag, making sure the packing peanuts nestled it securely. I looked at my watch. "We only have about seven minutes left. We have to get out of here."

Dan headed back toward the stairwell, but I yelled, "We don't have time to walk down. We'll have to risk it." I nodded my head to the elevator, pushing the down button. The elevator arrived quickly with a ding, and we started down as soon as I hit the button to the lobby.

Then something happened that hadn't been accounted for in our plan. When we got to the seventeenth floor the elevator stopped and a woman got on. And not just any woman at that, but a honey blonde with high cheekbones wearing a tight red dress and formal gold pumps. She was, simply put, to die for.

She seemed surprised to see us, but recovered quickly and said, "Good evening," as she entered. She had a slight English accent, and for some reason my heart always melts for women with English accents.

Being the gentlemen that we are, Dan and I backed up to allow her space to get on, which she did. When she turned to face the front of the elevator, I noted she looked as good from the back as she did from the front.

All of this should be just trivia, but when we got between the eighth and seventh floors the elevator came to a shuttering stop, and I flew forward so hard that I practically knocked this beauty over; I had to hold her up to prevent her from falling.

In the now-stuck elevator she turned to me with a smile and said, "Well, I have to give you credit. Most men aren't as creative as you when they try to grope me." Ah, a woman with a sense of humor and personality—I like that.

I should stop right now and explain something. Women, or at least certain types of women, find me attractive. I have broad shoulders, dimples, and what I have been told by one of my ex-girlfriends are dark brown hypnotic eyes. This chance encounter had serious potential.

For the next few minutes while we were stuck, we shamelessly flirted. Her name was Natalie. She was dressed up to go to a party that she said she would rather not be going to, and she had a wide beautiful smile that showed off perfect teeth when she laughed.

In the background, I could see Dan looking uncomfortable. As every second ticked by it was becoming more likely maintenance would arrive and restore power to the CCTV, and our images would be captured. If Cy Green chose to report this theft to the police we were cooked. While Dan sweated over this fact, I was having too much fun in the moment to care.

But then the elevator stuttered to life again. I tumbled into Natalie once more, and we both laughed. When we made it to the lobby, I asked for her phone number and offered to buy her dinner one night. She obliged with her number, but said, "I don't know if you have to waste money on dinner with me, since we've already achieved physical intimacy. Let's go out for some drinks and skip the pretense." Drinks it was.

Just before she walked out the front door, Natalie turned to me and said, "How will I know it's you when you call? I didn't catch your name."

"The last name is Trowbridge. First name is Phillip, but only my mother has called me that," I said. "Friends just call me Trow."

"OK, Trow," she replied. "I'll be expecting that call." Then she slipped into the night.

Randy at the concierge desk gave us a quick thumbs up, letting us know that the CCTV cameras weren't back on yet. We thanked him and he said to me, "I see you met Natalie Green."

I didn't make the connection at first, but Dan caught on quickly. "This Natalie Green. She wouldn't be related to Cy Green, would she?" he asked.

"Of course. She's his daughter."

We walked back to the Aquarium in silence, me toting my Kohl's shopping bag with Mr. MacGuffin and my picks in it. I ordered an Uber to get home, the modern getaway car for our times. As the Uber pulled up, Dan finally broke his silence saying. "You do know that girl is bad news, don't you?"

Chapter Four

Bert picked up on the third ring. "I got it," I said.

"You got it?"

"I got it!"

"Is it authentic?" he asked.

"How would I know?" I asked.

It was midnight, and I was back in my office alone after sending Dan home for the night. Pushing the packing peanuts aside, I pulled Mr. MacGuffin out of my Kohl's shopping bag and unwrapped it from the bubble wrap. I held it up, spinning it around and taking a good long look at it for the first time. "Well, I don't see any made in China stamps on it, so I take that as a good sign."

"Describe it to me."

"Describe it to you?"

"Yes, describe it to me. Take a look at it and tell me what you see."

"Well, it's purple," I said.

"How purple?"

"How purple?" I repeated quizzically. I took another look and answered my own question. "A light purple," I said. "It looks like it was darker originally and has faded over the years. If I had to describe the color now, I would use the term mauve," I said, impressed by my own vocabulary.

"Now describe the object itself."

I had to think about how best to put this. Mr. MacGuffin was remarkably detailed, with veins and the head clearly depicted. "It looks like a very thorough replication of the male unit."

"Tell me about the size," asked Bert.

"It appears to be perfectly average in length and width." I couldn't help but do a mental comparison to myself and wondered if Valentino was tempted to add an inch or two to satisfy his male ego during that drunken weekend in Palm Springs.

Bert was quiet on his end of the line, and I didn't know if I lost him, so I quipped, "Valentino looks to have been a perfectly healthy male, but certainly no Milton Berle."

"Trow, my boy, you've done it. You've done it! You have the original Mr. MacGuffin." I had known Bert for years, and I don't recall ever hearing him happier.

"So, what do we do now?" I asked. "Do you want me to put it in a box and ship it to you UPS Priority?"

"What?" he yelled. "Are you crazy?" "This is a priceless piece of Americana. If you had the *Mona Lisa*, would you slip it in a FedEx package and send it that way?"

"So, what do you want me to do with it?"

"Nothing," he replied. "I'll make arrangements to fly in from LA and pick it up in person. In the meantime, keep a low profile and guard it with your life." I didn't have the heart to tell him neither of those things was going to happen, and we hung up amicably with Bert still over the moon about Mr. MacGuffin being in my possession.

The next day I got another cryptic email from Bert that made no mention of the stolen object, only that the following morning he was catching a flight from LA to Baltimore and he wanted to see me again in the same location we had met last week.

As a precaution, I secured MacGuffin in a safe-deposit box I had, so I wouldn't have to babysit the damn thing until Bert returned. I then made a date with Natalie Green for that night.

I know what you're thinking. Dan was right: this is bad news and I should be staying as far away from Cy Green's daughter as possible. But I had to admit I was hooked and had been since the moment I fell into her on the elevator.

We agreed to meet for dinner instead of drinks because, after all, that was the gallant thing to do. She suggested a new restaurant in Fells Point, which boasted a celebrity chef who had a James Beard Award and his own cable TV show. I checked out their website and realized this date was going to hurt my wallet, but I bet on Natalie Green being worth the investment.

I got there first, and was seated at a table in the ultra-modern interior of the restaurant. I realized it was one of those places where you paid for waiters who explained every detail of the dish you ordered, and for chefs who took great pride in drizzling the bottom of the plate, as if it were artwork.

Five minutes after our scheduled date time, Natalie made a spectacular entrance. She was wearing a different red dress than the one I had seen her in last, this one less snug, but with a scoop neck showing cleavage. She caught my eye and flashed a smile, and I was taken again by how beautiful she was and rose in respect as she came to the table.

Our date got off to a bit of a rough start when she said sharply, "I think you may have an ulterior motive in trying to get on my good side."

Every straight man on a date with a beautiful woman has an ulterior motive, but I didn't think this would be a polite way to respond; instead, I innocently asked, "What do you mean?"

"I've done a little Internet research on you this afternoon and see you used to be a writer. Are you using me to get to my father, Cy Green, the famous director, in hopes he'll look at a script you're working on?"

I laughed and told a small white lie, saying "Until now I didn't realize there was a connection between you and Cy." Then I spilled the whole story of how I ended up in Hollywood, how I bottomed out in show business, my drunken dad, and how I was now quite content running a detective agency.

In all, she was sympathetic to my sad tale, which made me feel like a million bucks. Now it was her turn to talk, and for the rest of dinner she reciprocated by telling me her life story. Cy, as Natalie called him, never once referring to him as "dad" or "father," was apparently as awful in his personal life as he was on the movie set.

Natalie's mother had been a young, aspiring English actress who Cy had romanced with beautiful words and promises of movie parts, which all ended when she became pregnant with Natalie. Not only did the movie parts not come, but he shipped her back to England with a small stipend of cash and threats that she not contact him again or dare to get back into show business.

Cy even went so far as denying he was Natalie's father until she was a teenager, when her mother, finally showing some backbone, threatened to take him to court unless he publicly acknowledged her paternity Even after that connection was established, contact between Natalie and Cy was sporadic: a phone call on her birthday, lunch if he was in London on business. Cy did take financial responsibility, sending her to the best schools in England and giving her a generous allowance as an adult.

"I don't think he means to be so horrible," she said. "It's just that he is obsessive. If he wants something, he's relentless until he gets it and everything else in the world will take a back seat. That is what made him such a great film director. There were no distractions allowed, including things like wives and children. For him, it was always making his next film as perfect as possible."

I squirmed in my seat and wondered: Now that I had stolen Mr. MacGuffin from him, would his new obsession be to get it back? And to what lengths would he go? Instead of pursuing this train of thoughts, I changed the subject slightly and asked, "If he liked making movies so much, why did he walk away from the business?"

"Don't believe that nonsense that he wanted to leave while still on top of his game. Cy is never off the top of his game. The real reason is his health. Between his work schedule, his weight, and the pressure of making movies over the years, his heart is shot. His doctor told him that if he kept making movies, he would be dead sooner rather than later.

"When he moved back to Baltimore, he begged me to get involved in his life, to reconnect with him, and to keep an eye on him so he wasn't drawn back into the business. At the time I was living in Manhattan and doing well as the owner and editor of a web magazine dedicated to interior design. The last thing I wanted was to give up my life to keep an eye on Cy Green."

"So, what changed your mind?"

Natalie looked at me sheepishly and said, "Just like the *Godfather*, he made me an offer I couldn't refuse. He bought me the whole seventeenth floor in the building where we met as a down payment, and now he pays me an obscene monthly salary to be his *personal assistant,*" she said, rolling her eyes. "In the end I agreed, as long as the duties left me enough time to keep working on my magazine."

One thing about Natalie was that the more she talked, the more the rest of the world faded away. She was smart, witty, sexy, and surprisingly well-grounded. I couldn't remember the food being brought to the table, or our eating it, or any of the background noise in the restaurant. All I know is that at one point we finished dinner and the check arrived.

After the meal she offered me the opportunity to go back to her place. She had just finished building a personal movie theater that she was proud of and wanted to show it off. I agreed to go back and watch a movie with her as long as it wasn't one of Cy's horror flicks. She laughed and agreed.

In the morning, leaving her place, I felt like a new and improved man. That Trowbridge fellow with a flawed life was no more; I was reborn and nothing was going to trip me up again. That feeling lasted only until I hit the lobby, and I noticed the lobby concierge in tears. The blue-vested concierge was on the phone. I overheard him say, "I'm sorry, Mr. Green. It will never happen again. I don't know how that FedEx package I signed on your behalf became damaged. I promise to pay any restitution."

I couldn't exactly make out what Cy said back but could clearly hear him roaring his disgust on the other end of the phone, yelling at the stunned concierge. I kept my head down and got out of the lobby as quickly as possible. My day was coming with Cy, I could feel it. Whatever confidence I had built up for that encounter had just drained away.

Chapter Five

I had just wrapped up a morning meeting with a potential client and was pondering what to tackle next. The husband of the woman who wanted to hire me had died six months ago, and she swore he had squirreled away more than $200,000 in various international bank accounts to keep it secret from the IRS. The only problem was, he had done such a good job of hiding the money that now he was dead, she couldn't find the loot either.

The client had offered to give me ten percent of the money I recovered. I turned her down. First, it sounded like a job more in the wheelhouse of a detective firm that specialized in cyber detection. Second, I rarely work on commission; commission left too much of a possibility of my investing a whole lot of time for a whole lot of nothing.

My contemplation was disrupted by a ruckus in the outer office. I got to my feet to see what the was going on just as Dan forcefully dragged a guy in through the office door by the nape of his neck. The man was protesting loudly to be let go.

"Is this the guy you've been looking for?" Dan asked, pulling the guy's head up by the collar while still gripping him firmly. I took a look, and sure enough, it was the same creepy guy with the wild eyes and expensive trench coat that needed a trip to the dry cleaners.

"That's the guy," I said.

"Grab a seat," said Dan as he roughly pushed him into a chair.

I reached out and shook Dan's hand saying, "Nice job, partner. It looks like you're up to forty percent now."

I took a good look at Wild Eyes. Up close he looked younger than I thought, and he was nervous as hell. The wild eyes weren't because he was crazy or high, just scared. "OK," I said. "What's your name?"

"I don't have to tell you anything."

I didn't have time for games so I reached into the breast pocket of his jacket without asking and pulled out his wallet. "Hey," he squealed in protest.

"Let's see what we have here," I said in a mocking tone. I pulled out his driver's license. "Well, well. Your name is Evan Andrews, and you have a Virginia driver's license with an address in McLean." I looked him in the eyes and said in a drawn-out drawl, "Fancy."

Rifling through his wallet some more I found a family photo of him with his young wife, holding a baby boy. "You got a beautiful family," I said, showing the picture to Dan.

"Give that back," he said protesting, starting to get out of his seat.

"Shut up and sit back down," replied Dan as he shoved him back into the chair.

After combing through the guy's wallet some more, I said to Dan, "Well, lookie here. It seems as though Mr. Andrews is a licensed detective in DC. If his business card is accurate, he works for one of the big, high-dollar firms that has a well-known reputation for working for all the elected crooks on Capitol Hill. Now," I said, turning to Andrews, "save us all some time and tell me who hired you to tail me."

The kid looked for a second, like he might cry at the harsh way we were handling him. Then he showed a little backbone by stiffening up and saying with as much resolve as he could muster, "I'll never divulge the name of our clients. Never."

For a second I almost respected him for that, but not quite. At this point Dan chimed in, asking, "How about bumping me up to fifty percent if I get the name out of him?"

Thinking that another ten percent of my beaten down detective agency wasn't much to give up, I said, "Go for it."

With a sadistic smile Dan sang out gleefully. "Can I borrow your lock picks?"

"Sure, what are you going to do with those?"

Matter-of-factly Dan replied, "Slowly remove each of his teeth until he talks. I bet he spills the beans before I get the third one out."

Andrews looked at him coldly and said, "You don't scare me."

I pulled Andrews' head back, and Dan began to work on his teeth after forcing the picks in his mouth. Within a minute I heard a crack, and Dan shot me a surprised look that conveyed, "Whoops. I didn't mean to do that. I was just trying to scare him."

I whispered to Dan, "You're back down to a thirty-three percent share."

Andrews cried out in pain, "OK. OK. Stop! I'll talk. Just don't hurt me anymore."

"OK, Mr. Andrews. Who hired you to tail me?"

His wild eyes were back and in a trembling voice he spit out, along with a gob of blood, "That director, Cy Green."

His answer threw me for a loop, but I tried to maintain my composure and asked, "Why?"

"First, I was hired to follow a Mr. Bert Thompson while he was in town from Los Angeles, to see what he was doing in Baltimore. I followed him for a whole day and Mr. Thompson did nothing noteworthy, but he met you for drinks, so afterward I started following you, believing you might be the reason why he was in the area. Once I figured out that you're a PI,

I assumed that meant he must have hired you, so I decided to take the initiative and follow you to see if I could figure out what he hired you for."

"For your information," I said, "Bert and I are friends from way back when we were partners in another line of work. He didn't hire me. We were just two old friends catching up. Got it?"

"Got it," he said.

"Just curious. Why did Cy Green hire your firm to follow Bert Thompson?"

Andrews shrugged and said, "Don't know. I just know he wanted him followed, and he wanted a minute-by-minute update on what he did while he was in Baltimore."

I was out of questions, and Dan asked me, "So what do you want me to do with him now?"

"Like any small fish," I said, "throw him back. He's not worth the effort to scale and cook."

Dan led Andrews out of my office, where I'm sure he would hit the pavement with a tumble. I couldn't help but think of Cy Green; I figured the worst with him was going to come and come at any moment.

Before meeting Bert that night, I opened my safety-deposit box and retrieved Mr. MacGuffin, wrapping him up and shoving him into my now well-worn Kohl's shopping bag. Carrying around MacGuffin, I was starting to get paranoid, which caused me to look over my shoulder several times to make sure Mr. Wild Eyes or Cy Green weren't closing in on me from behind. I didn't have the stomach for being a thief, and I would be happy to pass on the merchandise and be done with this caper.

I arrived at the watering hole right on time and saw Bert had beaten me there. He had a corner of the bar to himself, with an empty stool next to him. He saw me and shouted, "Over here!"

Bert had a draft waiting for me, and was halfway into one of his own when I sat down next to him. For the next twenty minutes he complained about his flight and how the airline industry had gone to the dogs. When he started in on how bad the weather is in Baltimore compared to L.A., I had to put my foot down.

"Are we going to do this or what?" I asked, while reaching into my Kohl's bag.

Bert swiftly smacked my hand away from the bag whispering, "Are you crazy? We can't do this in here."

"So, where do you suggest we go?"

"Follow me," Bert said with a wave of his hand as he got off his barstool. I took a last big slug of my draft before following. It had been paid for, and I wasn't going to let it go to waste.

He led me to an alley next to the bar. It was dark and creepy and smelled of a mix of urine and garbage. If a rat the size of a fox had scurried past, I wouldn't have been surprised.

"OK, let's see it," he said.

I pulled MacGuffin out and held it up for Bert to inspect. He put on a pair of reading glasses then took out his cell phone and used the flashlight feature to inspect the artefact inch by inch. This went on for a good ten minutes as I watched in silence. Even though it was a cool evening, I could feel sweat beading on my forehead.

Finally, he put his glasses and phone away and said joyously, "I'm convinced that this is one hundred percent authentic, and we have the real MacGuffin."

Before I could respond he added, "Isn't it beautiful?"

"I'm not sure that is how I would describe it," I said, before putting MacGuffin back in my Kohl's bag.

"Trow, you did a terrific job, and you will be rewarded handsomely for your work. I'll take it now."

"Wait a second," I protested. "Where's the money? We have a deal. You get Mr. MacGuffin and I get $250,000 in cash."

"The money is in Baltimore," Bert promised earnestly. "The person who is buying it flew into town with me. He is in a hotel right now awaiting delivery. I give him MacGuffin, he gives me the cash. Then I give you your split."

"OK. Let's go meet him and give it to him right now," I replied.

"Uh, that is going to be a problem," said Bert slowly.

"And why is that?"

"Let me remind you we are in possession of stolen merchandise worth at least a half a million dollars. My client wants to deal only with me, and to keep as low of a profile as possible. I'm sure you understand that."

I did, but that didn't help my pocketbook any. I trusted Bert, but a quarter of a million dollars can even make old friends do squirrely things.

After a few more minutes of negotiating, I handed over the bag with MacGuffin in it, and Bert promised to meet me the next night at our meeting spot for the cash exchange.

I know what you're thinking at this point. I was a sucker for handing it over without getting the dough on the spot. But here's the thing. In a way I was relieved that I was handing over MacGuffin and would never see it again. Who knows, maybe not having it would keep Cy Green from tracking me down with the goon squad and working me over. Besides, I knew Bert well. He was a Hollywood guy and would never leave the area. If he split without giving me my cut, I could track him down in no time.

As he was walking away with my Kohl's bag, I gave Bert a warning. "Hey, just to give you a heads up, I learned today Cy Green is tailing you."

"Yeah? Who gives a shit? I mean what is he going to do? He can't exactly report me to the police. Besides, the guy who is buying this from me isn't exactly scared of Cy. If Cy has a problem with me, he can take it up with him."

Chapter Six

I should have been tense as I idled away the day while awaiting my rendezvous with Bert that evening, wondering if he would show with the cash. Instead, Natalie called and threw me a life preserver saying, "What do you say we get together?"

The weather had turned unexpectedly bright and warm, and we decided to celebrate this good fortune with a walk at the Inner Harbor. Baltimore was notoriously hot and muggy in the summer and cold and windy in the winter, the worst of both worlds. To let a rare perfect day go by without getting outside would have been a sin.

Natalie wore snug blue jeans and a light black sweater. It was the first time I had been with her that she wasn't dressed to kill and wearing red. Even when she downplayed it, Natalie stood out from the pack. Her honey-blond hair shimmered in the sunlight, and the dark shades she donned could easily fool passersby into thinking she was a famous actress trying to keep a low profile. People noticed us as we walked by as a couple, or at least they noticed Natalie. She looked like a million bucks.

We were both in rare moods and our conversation was easy and light. The Inner Harbor was busy with tourists and school groups taking in the sights. After getting jostled one time too many by the bustle, we naturally began holding hands so as not to get separated. We must have looked like a pair of dopey teenagers in love, and I kind of have to admit that is how I was feeling.

I treated us to some soft-serve ice cream, and we found an empty bench that had a nice view of the water. We were silent as we ate, and when Natalie spoke again her mood had turned dark.

"Cy is driving me mad."

"Oh?"

"He's impossible to deal with even on a good day, but ever since he returned from New York he has gone off the chain. If this keeps up, nice condo and hefty salary or not, I'm going to tell him to shove it and go back to life without a father." Natalie was so worked up her high cheekbones had darkened to a mix between rose and blush.

Now I had a sinking feeling in my stomach, but being a detective, I felt the need to push for specifics. "What's gotten him so worked up?"

"Who knows?" she replied dismissively. "I have my theory, but when I asked I was told it was none of my business. That would be fine by me, except that he keeps making it my business by cussing like a sailor and ranting that he is going to 'get those sons of bitches no matter what it costs' and 'no matter how many rocks he has to turn over.' I told you he is obsessive when he gets onto something. Well, this is his thing at the moment, and it is driving me mad."

It was fair for me at this juncture to wonder what Natalie really knew. After all, she had probably been in Cy's place countless times, and MacGuffin had been displayed in plain sight in his living room. What could a classy woman like Natalie have thought of such a crude phallic symbol being a prized possession of her father? Did she view it as a harmless Hollywood memento from one of the silent era's biggest stars, or did she see it as sick and perverted, something that objectified women by paying homage to male sexuality?

I also assumed that she had been in Cy's place since it had been stolen and would probably have noticed this by now. Had she put two and two together, understanding that this was what was drawing her father's ire, but being too polite to bring up such a gross subject to a new boyfriend? Troubling me further was the fact that it would probably only be a matter of time before she would ask me what Dan and I had been doing in her building that night we met.

All of these thoughts played on in me, but as she talked all I could do was to be was sympathetic and hope that she changed the subject. Eventually she did, saying, "You're very sweet to listen to me go on."

I told her it wasn't a bother, and she asked if we could get together that night. I couldn't, of course, as I had my meeting with Bert. She looked disappointed when I told her I had to work. However, I quickly got a rain check for the following day, and her face and my mood brightened.

ꕥ

I arrived ten minutes early for the meeting with Bert and ordered a rum and Coke to kill the time until he joined me. The rum settled my nerves, and it was a nice change from the draft beer that was flat and listless in this place.

After a good half-hour and another rum and Coke, it sunk in that Bert wasn't going to show. I felt stupid for being so trusting and chided myself for falling for the "I'll pay you later" gambit, the oldest bit in the book. But then I had a thought. What had Bert really said last night, something about meeting in the same spot tomorrow night? When Bert had set up the meeting for tonight, he and I were in the alley right next to the bar. It was a long shot and it didn't really make sense, but what if Bert has been waiting for me in the alley with my cash?

I flipped a ten spot at the bartender and didn't wait for change but headed straight to the alley. Looking down the alley I didn't see anything, which didn't mean a whole heck of a lot, as it was dark. "Bert?" I called out.

As soon as I said this, I heard some movement in the alley. My instincts kicked in and without knowing who was down there I started running toward where I heard the noise. Now the sound of someone running away was unmistakable, and it was clear that whoever I'd heard was heading further back into the alley. I prided myself in being fast and assumed I was making up ground with each step. Just then, however, I tripped over something large and soft and did a face plant right into the pavement.

I got up and did a quick inventory to see if I was hurt and then marshaled on. The alley came to an abrupt end a few feet away, where there was a five-foot chain-link fence. Whoever had been in the alley with me had clearly climbed over the fence and was too far gone for me to follow.

A chill came over me that had nothing to do with the night air. What was it that had I fallen over? Was my short-term memory playing tricks on me or did I really hear a jingle when I tripped? Then I thought of my old writing partner's necklaces and chains and shouted to no one, "Bert, damn it! What have you gotten us into?"

I slowly retraced my steps until I came upon a mass midway down the alley. It was too dark to see anything, so I crouched down, pulled out my phone, and flipped on the flashlight feature. "Bert?" I whispered softly, but there was no reply.

Although Bert's body was still warm, I couldn't pick up a pulse. Without touching his body any more than I had to and running the flashlight over the length of him, it didn't take a CSI to tell me that Bert had died from a single gunshot to the temple.

I was now in a major jam, and there was no way I could call this crime into the police without becoming the prime suspect myself and possibly getting arrested for a major theft at the same time. The best I could do now was stall for time and try to piece together what happened as quickly as possible. Deftly I pulled out Bert's wallet and grabbed his cell phone. Once the police IDed the cadaver as Bert Thompson, it wouldn't take them long to connect the dots to me. Taking the items that easily identified Bert would buy me some extra time. And with all the homicides stacking up in Baltimore, it might take a while before the police had the time to even figure out who they had lying in the morgue.

Before leaving the alley, I looked both ways to make sure the coast was clear and got the hell out of there.

Chapter Seven

At midnight, back at my brownstone in Pigstown, I had coffee brewing and was debriefing Dan on the events of the night, including the facts that both Mr. MacGuffin and the cash were nowhere to be found.

I had called Dan as soon as I arrived home. When he answered, he seemed to sense a problem, asking, "What's wrong?" When I said "Plenty," but couldn't talk over the phone, he said he'd be right over.

Dan had always liked my brownstone in Pigstown. I guess that's because it's near Oriole Park and when the Orioles are playing at night you can see the stadium lights from my stoop. That may sound romantic if you're a baseball fan, but on game nights people attending the games spill over into our neighborhood to park, often leaving the residents to scramble to find a spot of their own. One night of having to park your car several blocks away from your home will jade you pretty quickly.

"So, you think your buddy Bert was waiting for you in an alley with a quarter of a million and got mugged by chance?"

I pictured that scenario. Some lowlife thief rolls Bert and kills him, thinking he's getting, what, some pocket change in a satchel Bert is carrying only to find to his surprise when he opens the satchel that he has $250,000? Talk about hitting the jackpot.

"Maybe. Maybe not," I replied. "Another scenario is the guy who was supposed to exchange the money for the MacGuffin double-crossed Bert and killed him, keeping both the MacGuffin and the cash for himself, a real win-win for the mystery buyer that Bert brought with him from Hollywood."

Dan had connections with the Baltimore Police, and we had already discussed how he would try to monitor what they knew and when. Have they found the body, did they have any CCTV footage of the area, and had they IDed Bert and made the connection to me yet? Getting inside information on all of this would help me know how I could best maneuver.

Our conversation was interrupted by a clear, crisp bell tone from my door. I felt my heart jump and said, "Crap, I can't believe it. The police are on to me already."

Dan, who was peering out the corner of my blinds by my bay window, said, "That looks like no cop I've ever seen."

I walked over to Dan and snuck a peek myself. Standing on my stoop was a young white guy with wavy brown hair in serious need of a comb. He stood about five foot nothing and by the porchlight I could see that he was wearing an expensive looking Italian suit and what looked like authentic Berluti leather Oxford shoes. The outfit was impractical for a homicide detective to wear, and the shoes alone could get you killed wearing them in Baltimore.

Impatiently, the man pushed my doorbell again as he stamped his feet nervously on my stoop. Brownstone stoops have a long history in Baltimore; not that long ago the residents, despite whatever else they had going on in their lives, would wash the steps of their stoops by hand to always make sure they were bright and white. It was an unwritten competition among neighbors, each trying to outdo the other. Those days were gone, and my generation was satisfied with our stoops as long as we didn't see fresh blood on them in the morning when we went out.

"Hold your horses," I shouted. I motioned for Dan to hide in the kitchen in case this guy came in and tried to get the drop on me. If that happened Dan could repay the favor.

I opened the door saying, "I don't want any," rather curtly.

"MacGuffin. I demand Mr. MacGuffin," he shouted. I didn't need my neighbors overhearing this potentially incriminating information while Bert Thompson's body was cooling across town, so I quickly invited my late-night visitor inside my brownstone.

Inside, the visitor calmed down and took stock of his surroundings, all the while with a disapproving expression on his face. It was obvious he wasn't a fan of my interior decorating skills, which, I had to admit, were influenced more by comfort and economy rather than by a cohesive style or aesthetic.

"Just who are you, and what are you doing at my house this late at night?" I asked, trying to sound menacing.

"My name is Peter Laverany, and I made a deal with your friend, Bert Thompson. I offered to pay him a million dollars for Mr. MacGuffin. I know he is a business associate of yours, as he told me you stole MacGuffin for him. Tonight, he was scheduled to come to my hotel and make the exchange. He didn't show up, and now I need to find him. We had a deal. Mr. MacGuffin is rightfully mine. If Mr. Thompson won't fulfill our deal, I'm willing to pay you the million if you have it."

Laverany had an accent I couldn't quite place. Was it South American? Eastern European? Or was it from some other exotic locale? I figured that he was more than likely gay, as the slight lilt in his voice was setting off even my not-too-finely-tuned gaydar. You won't get noticed speaking that way in Hollywood, but in Pigstown you stand out like a sore thumb.

"Listen, pal," I said as kindly as I could. "I don't have Mr. MacGuffin, and Bert Thompson right about now is probably landing on a slab in the city morgue. If you're smart, you'll get on the first plane back to L.A. in the morning and forget all about Mr. MacGuffin."

Hearing about Bert Thompson's death didn't faze my relentless guest, who for the next hour must have gone through six cigarettes, lighting up each without asking my permission and vowing not to leave Baltimore without having what he came for. Before he finally left, he handed me a card with his cell phone number on it and told me if I had MacGuffin or could find it, *he would now pay me up to two million for it.*

When he left, I turned to Dan and said, "The nerve of that guy."

"The nerve of your so-called friend Bert Thompson," Dan fired back. "It sounds like he was going to get a million for MacGuffin, and your fifty-percent cut only amounted to $250,000. My Baltimore schooling may not be the best, but that's no fifty percent. Your old writing partner was going to rip you off."

"I wonder who else he ripped off?" I asked. "And I wonder if whoever else he ripped off didn't take it very well in the alley tonight?"

Chapter Eight

The next day Dan stopped by my office to give me an update on what he had heard from his connection in the Baltimore PD. "First, the bad news," he said matter-of-factly. "Around ten this morning someone noticed Bert Thompson in the alley and reported it to the police."

"And the good news?" I asked.

"They have no CCTV footage from the alley or nearby, and they still haven't IDed Bert yet. Best of all," said Dan with a sly smile, "Baltimore is dealing with a higher profile homicide today since one of the mayor's friends was whacked in a liquor store a few hours ago. It was a robbery that went bad, and the mayor's friend was just a poor schmuck customer who was in the wrong place at the wrong time. As you can imagine, Baltimore PD is running around frantically trying to catch the perp 'cause the mayor is breathing down the police commissioner's neck."

"Hopefully, this buys me enough time to straighten all this out first," I said.

"Straighten it all out? And just how are you going to do that?"

"I'm working on a plan right now," I said.

What I didn't tell Dan is that I had absolutely no plan, and without a plan there was not much I could do except hope for police incompetence till I could figure out how to save my bacon.

That evening I had a date with Natalie and left work early to shave and shower. The place she suggested was just a block from her waterfront condo and when I got there I was relieved to see it was a simple burger-

and-fries joint. Although she was worth it, tonight's date was more in line with my budget than the five-star eatery we had gone to previously.

I got there first and grabbed a table. A perky waitress named Molly dropped off a pair of menus after I said I was expecting a guest. Five minutes later Molly reappeared, asking, "Are you Mr. Trowbridge?"

"Yes," I said, puzzled that she knew my name.

"We just received a call from a Miss Natalie Green saying she was running about twenty minutes late. She is sending her apologies and asked that I deliver this to help pass the time." With that she handed me a draft off the tray she was carrying.

I thanked her and took a healthy slurp and pondered my next move regarding MacGuffin. Earlier that day I had Googled Peter Laverany and learned that he was a Hungarian national and loaded. He was only thirty-two years old and had made a name for himself as a financer of several successful films and, as such, the top directors and actors in Hollywood had become chummy with him, hoping he would invest in one of their projects.

According to Wikipedia, Laverany wasn't exactly a self-made man. His grandfather was tied to the commies before, during, and after the failed '56 revolution and had made a small fortune confiscating the wealth of those who disagreed with party politics. Hollywood was the perfect place for someone like Laverany.

I looked down, and my beer was finished. I assumed that at least twenty minutes had passed. I went to pull out my cell phone to see where Natalie was, and it was then that I realized I was having trouble moving my arms, which panicked me. I tried to stand, but my legs wouldn't respond. Molly passed my table with a tray of food, and I tried to call out to her, but found I couldn't speak. Although I was feeling very woozy, my mind was still coherent enough to realize I had been drugged.

"Well, well. I see the cat has got your tongue." I looked up, and saw that it was that creepy young PI, Evan Andrews. "You mind if I sit?" he said pointing to the empty seat. "I'll take that as a 'yes,'" he sneered when I couldn't reply.

"I imagine you saved this seat for Natalie. But here's a little secret, just between us guys," he said with a whisper, sitting down. "Natalie's not coming tonight. When we sent you the message that she was running late, we also sent her a message on your behalf, saying you had to cancel because something had come up."

I couldn't help but feel like a fool. If she was running late, why call the restaurant to tell me? Why not call me directly on my phone? I should have sensed the setup.

"I hope you're up for a short trip," said Andrews. "Because we're about to leave now."

The last words I remembered before it all went blank was Andrews saying, "I'm going to love what happens to you, especially after the way you and your partner treated me the other day. It cost me $2,500 and a day in a dentist's chair to save that tooth."

When I regained consciousness, I had a pounding headache and at first my eyes couldn't focus. But even in this rough state, I immediately recognized the unmistakable voice of Cy Green saying, "I believe our guest is about to join us in the land of the conscious." Each syllable he uttered felt like someone was playing very loud tom-toms in my skull.

It took me a few more minutes to shake out the cobwebs and figure out that I was in Cy Green's living room, and that my host was joined by Evan Andrews. I tried to move but couldn't. At first I thought that the drug I had been slipped was still in effect. After gaining a little more of my wits, I realized I was tied to a chair with my hands bound behind the back.

"How long have I been out?" I asked.

"Only a few hours," said Cy. Up close, even though it seemed impossible, Cy was even fatter than he appeared in pictures. He was wearing a ridiculous white suit with a red bow tie, and I wasn't sure if it was the chemicals still floating around in my brain, but he reminded me of a Macy's Thanksgiving parade-style balloon of a giant bowling pin.

"You, young man, have been very naughty. I believe you have something of mine, and I want it back." Cy leaned into within inches of my face to help make his point.

"Oh yeah, well, if I do have something of yours, I hope it's a new suit because what you're wearing looks preposterous."

Cy tilted his head back and gave a throaty laugh. "Mr. Trowbridge, you amuse me, but at the moment the only thing I care about is getting Mr. MacGuffin back. If you don't tell me where it is, I can assure you your future will be quite bleak."

"Last I knew MacGuffin was with a friend of mine, Bert Thompson. Only problem is that Bert is lying in the city morgue with a toe tag and at the moment is going by the name of John Doe. What I do know, however, is I suspect you knew my friend planned to steal MacGuffin, and you hired this clown PI," I said, nodding my head at Andrews, "to follow Bert around town and figure out what was going on. My guess is that he saw an opportunity, killed Bert while he was alone, and is going to fence MacGuffin to the highest bidder."

"Hey," said Andrews indignantly. The PI came up to me and made a fist like he was going to sock me in the face as I sat bound to the chair.

My legs were free, so before he could throw a punch, I kicked him hard in the shin. He yelped, and Cy Green let out another deep, guttural laugh.

"I thought of that possibility, Mr. Trowbridge," said Cy dismissively. "But frankly, Mr. Andrews isn't bright enough to pull something like that off. So, you're telling me Bert Thompson is dead and doesn't have what I want, and I'm telling you Mr. Andrews isn't smart enough to have it. By process of elimination that leaves only you." The smile was gone from his face, and he added sternly, "I want it back and I want it back now." His beady brown eyes bore in on me sharply.

"Why in the world do you even want the damn thing?" I asked.

Cy looked disappointed in me, and for a second I thought he was going to fly into a rage, but then he composed himself and looked serene. "For what it represents, of course. Valentino was the greatest star of his era, and he represented male sexuality at its rawest during a time when such things couldn't be discussed. And, after all, what is male sexuality, Mr. Trowbridge, but the ultimate fulfillment of greed, lust, and power?

"Imagine the history MacGuffin has been a part of. This Hollywood memento, the most unique collectible in the world I might add, was the talk of Hollywood parties during the golden age of film-making. If MacGuffin could talk, what stories he would tell!"

"You do know you're referring to a plaster of Paris penis?" I cut in sarcastically.

"No. It is more than that," rebuffed Green emphatically. "It disappeared in 1968 under the most unusual of circumstances, as I'm sure you are probably aware, which only adds to its value and mystique. After Pedro Noboa's murder, MacGuffin hadn't been seen for years, and people assumed it was lost forever. Some historians started to question whether it had ever existed at all. MacGuffin became my quest, my Holy Grail. I invested millions to track it down and followed every lead, no matter how ridiculous or improbable. I finally trailed MacGuffin down to an exotic trader in Cairo, Egypt of all places. When it came into my possession it was the happiest day of my life."

Cy Green turned away from me and held his hands behind his back as he added in that famous voice of his, "I want it back, Mr. Trowbridge, and 'no' isn't the appropriate answer."

"No," I said defiantly.

Turning around surprisingly briskly for such a heavy man, Cy looked at me thoughtfully. "You have twenty-four hours to return to me what is rightfully mine, no questions asked. If not, tomorrow will be the last sunrise you will ever see." He paused, and I thought he was done. "Oh, and one more thing, Mr. Trowbridge. If I ever see you within a mile of my daughter again, I'll personally rip your balls off."

Cy Green turned to Andrews, "Will you escort Mr. Trowbridge out of the building? I'm going to bed for the night."

"With pleasure," said the PI with a sneer. With that, Cy Green nodded politely at both of us and took his leave, waddling down the hallway.

When Cy was out of sight, and we'd heard the click of what I assumed was his bedroom door, Andrews turned to me and said, "Before I untie you, I owe you one thing—let's see how many teeth this loosens." With that he gave me his best right hook across my jaw, sending me and the chair I was tied to tumbling to the floor.

Chapter Nine

Shortly after sunrise I woke up in Natalie's bed. She lay naked on top of the covers and was in a deep sleep. I took a long look at that angelic face and heavenly body. If this was to be my last sunrise I might as well enjoy the view. Maybe Cy was right, and male sexuality was the ultimate fulfillment of greed, lust, and power, but there was something both masculine and quite right about feeling this way in the arms of a beautiful woman. This is the stuff that dreams are made of.

After getting tossed out of the high rise by Evan Andrews, I had checked my voice mail and saw that while I had been blacked out Natalie had left me a message. She was worried about the emergency that had caused me to cancel our date. I called her back and told her I was right outside her building. She promptly buzzed me in.

On the seventeenth floor she had coffee and a sympathetic ear waiting. I took a calculated risk, knowing I didn't have many cards to play, and told her the truth, the whole truth, and nothing but the truth. I started with my writing partnership with Bert Thompson ten years ago and ended with the threats from Cy minutes ago. I didn't apologize for my stupidity in getting involved in this mess, but I did say I wasn't proud of how I had been talked into it.

Pure Natalie, she was easy to talk to. When I was done she said, "If anyone is going to get their balls ripped off it will be Cy, by me." Her blue eyes had become ice cold, and it looked like she meant every word of it.

She gave me a reassuring kiss on the cheek. "Look, about Cy," she said. "One thing I learned is not to worry about his threats. He's not going to kill you or anyone else. Cy Green! Big Hollywood director of horror flicks! Sometimes he acts like life is a plot in one of his movies, but when push comes to shove, he is mostly hot air."

"So, are we OK?" I asked.

"We are fine," Natalie replied and cuddled up next to me. "In fact, I'm glad that horrible thing is gone. It was a perverted phallic symbol that represented everything wrong with Hollywood. And to think my own father kept it in a place of honor in his home, not caring how it made women, or his own daughter for that matter, feel when visiting him. It makes me sick just thinking about it. Now I can only hope that whoever took it threw it into the harbor, so I never have to see the horrible thing again."

We talked some more before we trailed off to the bedroom. It was not exactly great foreplay, but Natalie added while unbuttoning her blouse, "With a dead body involved you'll need some help. I have a friend who is a crackerjack attorney. If you don't mind, I'll give her a call on your behalf in the morning."

I didn't mind. Nor did I mind how the rest of the night went.

But now I was awake and my cell phone was rattling, so I quickly grabbed it and left the bedroom so as not to wake Natalie. Dan was on the line.

"Where are you?" he asked.

"You don't want to know."

He really didn't, and he was smart enough not ask again. Instead he said, "I have some news, and most of it is not good."

"Go ahead," I replied, bracing myself for the worse.

"The police have figured out that the stiff is Bert Thompson. They also determined he was killed by a 9mm Ruger, the kind of gun first-time gun owners buy for protection. Because of that, they aren't treating Thompson's murder as a professional hit."

"Anything else?"

"They haven't tied Bert back to you yet, but you know as well as I do that it will only be a matter of time. If you have a plan, you better put it in motion now."

"I do," I replied, "but I'll need your help."

"I'm all ears."

My plan wasn't really a plan, more of a hope. That afternoon I left a message with Cy that I had important information on Mr. MacGuffin and I needed to see him, and that he should have Evan Andrews on hand as well.

ᘓᘐ

Cy opened the door himself when I arrived and greeted me with an impatient, "Well?"

"All in good time, big man," I said, pushing my way into the apartment.

Andrews was seated in the living room and looked me over nervously. His wild eyes were back. Nodding hello to him I said, "I owe you one from last night. And you can bet I always repay a debt."

The young PI looked scared, like he knew I meant it. I could see the wheels spinning in his head as he searched for a snappy comeback. Fortunately, Cy's phone rang, saving me from a continued back-and-forth with Andrews. As planned, Randy at the lobby's concierge desk was on the other line. Cy's voice was crisp and clear, but fueled with outrage as he blurted out, "What do you mean I have guests in the front lobby who say Mr. Trowbridge told them they could come up?" Cy looked at me sourly, but then he relented and said to the concierge, "Alright, fine. They are clear to come up."

Cy gave me the stink eye and said softly but firmly enough that it seemed more like a scream, "I made a promise to you, Mr. Trowbridge. If I don't have MacGuffin back by sunrise, you'll take a permanent swim in the harbor."

"Now, don't make any promises you can't keep," I chided. "I'm the only hope you have of finding your twisted collectible that means the world to you, and as long as that is the case you won't harm a hair on my head." Cy took this in and, I swear, he physically shrank as it sunk in that I was correct. Out of the corner of my eye, I could see that Andrews was about to protest that he, too, might be able to find MacGuffin. However, before he could speak, the doorbell rang, sparing us all his bullshit.

Dan walked in first. If the shit hit the fan, I wanted someone who I could count on backing me up. Next, Peter Laverany came in. "You!" bellowed Cy when he saw Laverany.

Laverany wore a tightly tailored mod suit that showed off his youthful, slim build and made him look like an extra on an *Austin Powers* movie set. He gently stroked the lapels of his jacket and looked around Cy's living room with a jaundiced eye before declaring with his one-of-a-kind accent, "I should have known someone like you would be living in a garish penthouse like this."

Cy lunged forward, but before the men could come to blows I separated them, saying, "I take it you both know each other." This was a safe assumption on my part. Hollywood was still, at the end of the day, a small, tight-knit community.

My plan was to get all the people who had a motive for killing Bert Thompson together in the same room, and get them talking to see what shook out. Cy took the bait immediately. "I approached our so-called guest once about investing in one of my movies. He turned me down. Too bad. If he had invested, his return would have been close to four hundred percent."

"I invest in art, not crap," said Laverany, who, standing next to Cy looked like Stan Laurel to Cy's Oliver Hardy.

"You know nothing about art or filmmaking," Cy countered. "You're just an insufferable little boy playing with daddy's money."

"Boys," I scolded. "We can have this battle of the wits later. I've gotten us all together to discuss something near and dear to your hearts: the whereabouts of Mr. MacGuffin and who he rightfully belongs to."

Turning to me, Laverany said, "Where is Mr. MacGuffin? The only reason I came today is because that man," he said, pointing at Dan, "told me you had him."

"In good time," I replied. "Can we all grab a seat? I have a few questions first, and we might as well be comfortable." Staring each other down, Cy Green and Laverany finally relented and slowly found seats, joining Evan Andrews. Dan and I remained standing.

Turning to Laverany I asked, "When did you first decide to steal MacGuffin?"

"'Steal' is such an ugly term, don't you think?" he asked. He looked around for a sympathetic face, and when he couldn't find one, he continued. "I'm a legitimate businessman. About seven years ago, Mr. Green was looking for financing for his last disgraceful slasher movie and invited me over to his Hollywood Hills house for the sales pitch. After hearing him tell me about it, I had absolutely no interest in the movie, and he served me the most god-awful petit fours in the process. My night at Mr. Green's home wasn't a total loss, however; he took me on a private tour of his collectibles. When I saw Mr. MacGuffin, I knew I had to have him at all costs."

At this point Dan interrupted and asked, "Why?" This was out of character for Dan, who was usually the strong silent type. Everyone in the room somehow sensed that Dan chose his words sparingly, and a tension hung in the air until Laverany answered.

"My dear man," Laverany turned to Dan with pity, unable to fathom how sad it must be not to have the same egalitarian tastes as him. "Rudolph Valentino was the greatest male sex symbol Hollywood ever produced. He could seduce with his eyes at a glance. When the silent era ended and the actors could talk, sensuality lost something on screen that it could never get back. Did you know that when Valentino died 100,000 women rioted outside his funeral and several women committed suicide? Anything that powerful is something I want. No. Check that. Something I have to have."

Dan looked at Laverany like he was sorry he asked. To keep the ball rolling I asked, "And then what?"

"And then I made him an offer he couldn't refuse, but he did."

"And then he wouldn't take no for an answer," Cy interrupted. "For the next five years he hounded me with more offers and more money. I was sick of him. When I left Hollywood and didn't hear from him, I thought I was done with our little visitor for good."

"So…" I said, slowly putting two and two together, "when Cy refused to sell you MacGuffin and moved 3,000 miles away, you decide to steal it?"

Laverany nodded yes, totally unashamed by his admission.

"And how did Bert Thompson get mixed up in all this?" I asked.

"Because he was the right type of desperate," Laverany countered. "He was looking for funding for some ridiculous project of his. I wanted no part of it, but one could sense a pitiful desperation from Mr. Thompson. I could tell that he needed to do this project so bad he would do anything for it, and I mean anything.

"Let me explain something to you about Hollywood, Mr. Trowbridge. Desperation is its most abundant commodity. It is everywhere. People will do anything for the mere hope of success. Anything. When you have that power over someone—to make them lie, cheat, steal, murder, prostitute themselves, you name it—they will do it."

I had lived the life and knew what he was saying was true. What would I have given ten years ago just to have a buffoon like Cy Green meet with me to discuss a script I was working on?

"And how did you know someone was trying to steal MacGuffin from you?" I asked, turning to Cy Green.

"Because my disgusting little friend is right. Hollywood is a small, dirty place, where desperation is king and people would sell their first born for the hope of success. Not more than five minutes after he made a deal with you know who," barked Cy, pointing at Laverany. "Bert Thompson called me. He told me he wouldn't steal Mr. MacGuffin from me if I paid him. He said he needed money for a new project. It wasn't blackmail, he said, but an investment. As soon as his new project came to the big screen, I'd get all my money back and then some, and I wouldn't have to worry about him hiring someone to steal MacGuffin."

At this Peter Laverany let out a tsk-tsk sound, disappointed in my old friend, Bert, for not displaying honor among thieves.

"I, of course, turned him down," continued Cy.

"But now you were tipped off that a theft was possible," I said, speculating. "And you hired a PI firm to follow Bert Thompson and stop him."

"Had I insisted on a more senior member of the agency, we wouldn't be sitting here today," said Cy looking sharply at Evan Andrews.

"Hey!" said the PI in protest.

"Shut up!" countered Cy, causing Andrews to retreat like a kicked dog.

And just then it clicked. I knew who killed Bert Thompson and I knew what had happened to MacGuffin—at least I was pretty sure that I knew.

Chapter Ten

As I was going down on the elevator, I pictured Dan back in the penthouse apartment, doing his best to hold that mob at bay after I left abruptly, telling them I'd be right back.

Getting off on the seventeenth floor and taking a deep breath, I gave Natalie's door a hard knock. She answered, wearing black yoga pants and a tight red T-shirt; as usual, she looked fantastic. She didn't seem surprised to see me, but wore an expression like she had been expecting me and simply said, "Come on in."

We naturally gravitated to her breakfast nook and sat down on a pair of stools. From her nook was a floor to ceiling view of the harbor. In the distance, I could see a water taxi heading from one end to the other.

Reading my face, she asked, "Am I in trouble?"

"I think we both are," I replied, and she nodded solemnly, taking this in.

"How do you know Bert Thompson?" I asked.

"Thompson?" she shrugged. "I was hoping you would never ask."

She pouted and looked through me with those piercing blue eyes. But she went on calmly, "When Cy was in New York to receive yet another lifetime achievement award or whatever, he asked me to stop by his place once a day to make sure everything was in order. Lo and behold, the first day I checked in, I noticed broken glass on the floor and saw that god-awful penis had been taken. After inspecting the apartment, I couldn't find anything else that was missing. I was both relieved and thrilled someone had pinched MacGuffin.

"My celebration was short-lived when Cy's land line started to ring. Who has a land line anymore?" she asked incredulously. "Only old farts, like Cy," she answered herself.

"I picked up and answered, and it was your friend Bert on the line. Somehow, he had gotten Cy's home number. I told him Cy was out and wouldn't be back for several days and that I'm Cy's daughter. And you know what? Your friend was a pompous chauvinist," she added sharply.

I nodded, guessing that now wasn't the best time to go over Bert's pros and cons with her.

"You know what happened next?" she asked.

"Knowing Bert," I said, "he negotiated with you. He played both sides against the middle to see who would give him the best deal."

Natalie pointed at her nose to tell me I was right on target. "He thought that since I was a Green, I would want the damn thing back. At first, I was going to tell him to shove it. But then I calculated that if I turned him down, he would eventually get to Cy who would agree to buy it back, and that horrible dildo would be back on display. I was so close now to getting that awful object out of my life, I decided I was going to do what I could to make sure that didn't happen."

Natalie stood up now, and she must have been stressed because her English accent was thicker than normal. "I offered him a million and a quarter to buy it back. He gave me a time and place to meet for the transaction, stating that if I didn't have the money, he would pursue getting in touch with Cy. Of course, I don't have that type of money, but my plan was to talk to him and convince him to do the right thing and destroy MacGuffin, or at the very least take the original offer and be done with it."

"So why kill him?" I ask.

"How did you know?" she replied.

"The gun was a 9mm Ruger. A small gun," I added. "Just the type of weapon a woman would carry if she were heading to a shaky Baltimore neighborhood at night and was worried about her personal safety."

Natalie nodded that I was right, and her confession crushed me. Perhaps I should have figured out long ago that Natalie had done it, going all the way back to the second I felt Bert's body going cold in the alley. But until now I had held out hope that there was another explanation. And that is what love will do to you. Love will take logic and twist it like a pretzel even when the obvious truth is staring you in the face.

"As you can guess, our discussion in the alley didn't go well. I begged him to leave both me and Cy alone and do whatever he wanted with MacGuffin as long as Cy could never find it again. Bert was mad at me for wasting his time and yelled at me. I took it to a point, but when he called me 'girlie,' I guess I snapped. I pulled out the Ruger and demanded he hand the dildo over. I was going to take that preserved bit of Hollywood memorabilia and destroy it. He didn't take me seriously and laughed at me right before I pulled the trigger."

Natalie reflected on her mental image of the scene and added, "He should have taken me seriously."

"Is it safe to assume you then took Mr. MacGuffin and threw him in the harbor?"

"And how did you know that, too?" she asked again.

"Because last night you told me that you hoped whoever had it would throw it in there."

Natalie smiled warily, impressed with my detective skills. "So, what do we do now?" she asked. "You're not going to turn me in, are you?"

"We're talking about murder," I responded flatly. "Bert had his flaws, but he wasn't a monster. He was my former partner, and maybe we didn't have the type of success I had hoped for, but I owe someone who was a partner of mine a bit more than just walking away from his murder."

Silence hung in the air until Natalie filled the void. "Look. This is Baltimore, and they have more unsolved murders than police. If we hang tight, I bet they never solve this and eventually we'll be in the clear."

"Natalie," I interrupted.

Natalie snapped her finger and enthusiastically added, "I know! If the police ever ask, we can alibi each other and say we were together at the time of Bert's death. Or, I can say he tried to rape me in the alley, and it was self-defense."

"Natalie," I said more sternly.

Natalie's blue eyes were now rimmed with tears. "Trow," she said earnestly. "This is about more than just getting me off. I can't go through this again. I told you only a half of the truth about why I came down from New York to be with my father. The other part I didn't tell you was that a man I had loved for five years left me. It devastated me completely to love so deeply and then to lose it all. I thought I'd never get over it, until I met you. Please don't do this to me, to us. I know that we are just getting to know each other, but I think you feel it, too. We were made to be together. We aren't bad people, just flawed. Together—who knows—we just might be OK."

"I understand," I said, with a lump growing in my throat.

Natalie reached out and cradled my hands in hers, saying, "Please, Trow, tell me you won't turn me in."

Chapter Eleven

Dan and I were in a holding cell in central booking. A few hours before, we were outfitted with orange jumpsuits, and if we were lucky, we would get a preliminary hearing in the morning where bail would be set.

"Look at the bright side," said Dan. "They already dropped the theft charge, and if you cooperate, they'll also drop the aiding and abetting in a homicide. What does that leave them? A lousy breaking and entering rap for busting into Cy Green's place. A B&E charge in Baltimore is nothing. We'll be out before the Orioles' opening day."

Dan chowed down a baloney sandwich. We had been incarcerated for two meals so far, and we had gotten the same horrible white bread and baloney sandwiches each time. I refused to eat, so Dan took my sandwich, and also the one of a strung-out junkie we shared the cell with. So far Dan was six sandwiches in and seemed quite content.

"Even if I get a slap on the wrist," I said, "they'll take my PI's license away from me. What am I going to do when I get out?"

Dan shrugged and added optimistically, "Baltimore is for the taking. A couple of sharp guys like us? There are a million angles we can play. Something tells me we are going to be more than fine."

"Next you'll be telling me this is the beginning of a beautiful friendship."

"Nope," said Dan, who finished up the sandwich with one last big bite, "I'm telling you it's been a beautiful friendship since the first grade, and now we are just starting a new chapter."

I had to admit that there was something very Zen about Dan; nothing ever seemed to faze him. The lawyer who Natalie had called for me just yesterday was obviously out of the question now, but Dan swore he knew a friend of a friend whose brother was a lawyer and he would help us out. Best of all, this lawyer was tight with a lot of the judges in town, and his clients usually got an easier ride in court.

"Trowbridge!" a young hefty female African American prison guard yelled as she approached. "The detective wants to talk to you."

I stood up as she fished for her keys to let me out. Dan winked at her and said, "Someone is looking good today." She smiled back and my gut told me that Dan had just earned some extra baloney sandwiches the next time the meal cart wheeled around.

I was marched down a long corridor that led to one of the interrogation rooms where I was locked in and told to wait. When the guard took off the handcuffs, she asked, "Your friend, does he have a girl?"

"Not sure," I answered honestly, "but I may be available, as I'm pretty sure my girlfriend is furious with me for ratting her out." The guard laughed at that and then said something to the effect that there could be no future between us, as bringing home a white boy would be the death of her mother. The guard laughed at that as well. I was glad my trials and tribulations were bringing joy to someone.

I stewed alone in the interrogation room for a long while. It's an old police tactic. Eventually Detective Jones came into the room, throwing open the door with a loud bang. Jones was about my age, black, with a clean-shaven head. He was one of those homicide detectives who thought being a snappy dresser made him look smarter. Unfortunately for Jones, his sartorial sense was a little off and his tie clashed badly with his suit jacket, loud enough to give me a headache.

Jones was carrying a manila envelope. In it was a thirty-page handwritten document authored by me. This was the confession that I had written shortly after telling the Baltimore PD about Natalie Green, Bert Thompson, and Mr. MacGuffin.

Jones flopped the confession down in front of me and asked, "You ready to sign it?"

I nodded and replied, "Just let me read it over one last time, and add a little more about what's happened since we last spoke."

"You know it doesn't have to be a novel," he said sternly.

"I just want to be accurate. I owe that to posterity."

"Posterity?" laughed Jones as if the word on its own was one of the great punch lines ever. But I meant what I had said, and as a former writer I thought a clear paper trail penned by my own hand would best describe what I did and why. If you are reading this, then my instincts have been justified. What you are reading is my final confession.

"You know," Jones said seriously after his laughter trailed off. "Between you and me, thank you. The DA will never tell you this, but we didn't have much on the Bert Thompson murder. You may have saved me months of legwork, and even at that I'm not sure what I could have dug up would have led me to Natalie Green. The DA owes you one. When this all shakes out, I wouldn't be surprised if you and your friend got nothing more than time served."

The mere mention of Natalie's name made my heart skip. "And how is Natalie?"

"Refusing to talk without a lawyer. Hers is due to arrive any moment, and then I'll take a crack at her. But she is pretty much cooked. Between your confession and the fact that we located the Ruger with her prints on it, she is toast, lawyer or no lawyer."

I nodded and asked, "How much time do you think she'll get?"

Jones looked thoughtfully and said, "In the good old days, she would have gotten the chair. But these days, and with deep pockets and high-priced lawyers and no priors, she'll probably get twenty years. With good behavior, she could be out in ten."

I processed this and did the math, calculating how old both of us will be in ten years. "Can you do me a favor?"

"What's that?" asked Jones tentatively.

"When you see Natalie, tell her no matter what, I still love her and hope she forgives me for turning her in. And no matter how long the sentence, when her time is up, I'll be waiting for her."

Jones nodded solemnly, not sure what to make of that. He left shortly afterwards, probably to meet with Natalie and her lawyer. After he had gone, I read through my confession one last time. For the record, let me state clearly that this confession is of my own free will.

"She churned her feet faster toward the Hawaii County Ford Escape waiting in the clearing in front of the house."

(from Street Smart #4, *Pele's Domain* by Albert Tucher)

#5 Pele's Domain

Albert Tucher

Jenny's radio fussed at her. She unhooked it from her belt and kept moving through the house.

"Snap it up," said her partner. "It's getting bad out here."

"It's not so great in here, either. One more room to clear."

But the message got through. Cops didn't come any bigger or more stoic than Sammy Waga. When his voice took on that edge, they were running out of time.

She had never visited this house outside Pahoa before, but the layout of whitewashed Big Island boxes varied little. She tested the bedroom door with her palm. It felt no hotter than anything else in the superheated atmosphere. Neither did the handle. She turned it and pushed.

For a moment everything else yielded to the horror of what she saw. Jenny stared at the woman lying face up on the bed: her throat gaped open like another mouth, but this mouth was stretched in an eternal scream.

Jenny's cell phone seemed to have jumped into her hand. She started snapping pictures of everything in the room, finishing with a close-up of the woman's face with as little of the wound as she could get. This crime scene was doomed, and her phone would have to stand in for it. She couldn't help walking in the massive amount of blood, but she filed the thought away for the small hours of the morning.

"Jenny, now."

She backed out of the room and wiped her feet on the carpet before sprinting toward the front door. She couldn't afford to slip. Jenny yanked the door open and stumbled into hell.

The walls of the house had provided a little insulation against the worst of the heat. Outside, her face felt ready to melt. She looked toward Kilauea, which had been pumping lava on and off for years. But now Jenny couldn't trust the ground she stood on. Streets that children crisscrossed on their bikes had been splitting open without warning and hurling the boiling bowels of the planet into the air.

Just fifty yards away a glowing orange tide plowed through the rainforest. Some trees toppled, while others ignited where they stood. Splashes of lava leaped and sprawled like boiling surf, but no board in the world could ride this wave. The din assaulted her. Boulders banged together as the lava rolled them along. One rock exploded, and then another. Even as she ran, Jenny flinched and then wondered about the physics behind the phenomenon. If she lived through this, she might ask a geologist about it. Those were just the noises she could pick out of the crowd. They seemed to float on the roar of the earth's molten core.

She churned her feet faster toward the Hawaii County Ford Escape waiting in the clearing in front of the house. The passenger door stood open. Jenny dove into the front seat and landed with her head in Sammy's lap. Neither of them had time for embarrassment.

Sammy floored the accelerator and turned left hard. Jenny pulled her feet into the vehicle, as the passenger door's own momentum slammed it shut. She squirmed upright and looked back. The house was aflame, fully enveloped in a way that usually took minutes instead of seconds.

"Damn, girl," said Sammy. "What are you trying to do to me?"

"Do to you?"

"If the lava doesn't kill me, your mother will."

ꕥ

"Run it down for me, Officer."

Detective Coutinho held Jenny's cell phone and thumbed through the pictures she had taken. His dark Portuguese face never gave much away. He could have been looking at snaps from her vacation.

She stood by his desk, swaying a little as her feet tried to get reacquainted with an old pair of shoes from the bottom of her locker. The crime scene techs had wanted the ones she had been wearing for the victim's blood and any other evidence they could find.

"Sammy and I were clearing the neighborhood."

Residents should have evacuated the day before, but there were always holdouts, as well as people so oblivious that the eruption would come as news to them, even as the heat built and volcanic gases clung to everything.

"So, we found this one guy at home. And he starts arguing with us—how come he has to go, and his neighbor doesn't? We went to check the other house out, but we didn't raise anybody. So, we figured we'd better go in."

Coutinho tapped the phone.

"Is she the neighbor?"

"The first guy was talking about a 'him.'"

It didn't prove much. The population of the Leilani Estates subdivision ebbed and flowed with cousins and friends of cousins who needed a place to stay for a while. Some houses were for rent by the month or week.

"Recognize her?"

He held the phone toward her, and Jenny looked at the image that already had an appointment with her nightmares. She hadn't managed to exclude the wound completely from the photo, which would have to be cropped if they needed to show it to civilians. Jenny concentrated on the face, whose frozen horror must have turned to ash and disappeared under new volcanic rock by now. "Maybe. I have a feeling I might have seen her around."

But the woman's face was a quick course in Hawaiian history, combining Portuguese, Filipino, and Japanese genes. Jenny saw faces like it everywhere, including in her own mirror.

She swiped to the first photo she had taken, a framing shot of the woman on the bed.

"Look at this. Reminds me of a Viking funeral, the way she's laid out."

"Somebody put her there so she'd disappear."

"Sammy's a little pissed at me. We almost joined her."

Coutinho smiled.

"He'll come around."

ꙮ

The next morning the first thing Jenny wanted to do was vomit. She didn't think it would help, and after a moment the urge retreated. The way her social life was going, it couldn't be morning sickness, but this must be what it felt like. She turned on the radio in her Camry in time to hear that her headache and nausea came from the gases that accompanied the eruption.

The announcer didn't have to sound so damned cheerful about it.

As long as the lava flowed, calling in sick wasn't an option. Another twelve-hour emergency shift beckoned. She forced herself to get out of the car and go into Ken's House of Pancakes in Hilo for breakfast as usual. Food was the last thing she wanted, but she couldn't afford to run out of energy halfway through the morning.

Conversation was sparse in Ken's. Most people were preparing for a routine day, but they were also trying to avoid thinking about the earth turning itself inside out just a half hour away.

At roll call the sergeant passed gas masks out. The eruption had slowed overnight, but it could pick up again in a moment.

By mid-morning she and Sammy had cleared recalcitrant residents from a dozen homes and delivered more than twenty people to the Pahoa Community Center. She was about to rejoin Sammy in their vehicle, when a man accosted her. He looked familiar, but his sheepish expression wasn't one he had been wearing the last time she saw him.

"Just wanted to say thanks, Officer. I acted pretty *lolo* yesterday."

"Mr. Tanaguchi, right?"

"Did you get my neighbor out?"

"Not exactly. Did you know him?"

"Just to say howzit."

"What made you think he was there in the house?"

"Saw him go in a few days ago. Hadn't seen him since. I just figured."

"Did you see anybody else coming or going?"

"Not lately. But I ain't the type to watch my neighbors twenty-four-seven."

People who felt a need to say that were exactly the type, thought Jenny. And they were eager to talk.

"That house was kind of a problem," he said. "Owner's never there. People rent it short-term, get up to stuff. You know da kine..." The all-purpose Pidgin phrase meant anything or nothing.

"The current tenant. What does he do?"

"Don't really know. He was less trouble than some of them."

"Jenny, we gotta go," Sammy called from their vehicle.

Jenny thanked the man for his time and then joined her partner.

"Where to?" she asked Sammy.

"Back to Leilani. Might not be as tense today."

They reached the grid of streets and turned toward the lava flow, which hunkered like a sullen crocodile the size of an Airbus. And that was just the small part they could see. A crust of brand-new rock had already formed on the beast, but dozens of glowing orange eyes gave glimpses into its pitiless soul.

For now, it was moving only inches per hour. She and Sammy started with the house closest to the flow. This time Jenny stayed with the vehicle. One of them had to. The lava could decide to speed up again without bothering to notify them.

She watched Sammy as he banged on the door and got no response. He went to the right side of the house and shaded his eyes with his cupped hands as he peered inside a window. He must have seen nothing out of line, because he went around back.

Seconds later he came back into view looking ready to heave, as if he had encountered a concentration of sulphur dioxide in the back yard.

"Another one," Sammy yelled to her. "Call it in."

"Another what?"

Sammy just shook his head, and a punch of adrenaline hit Jenny in the gut. She got on the radio.

ജ്ജ

Coutinho stood looking down at the new victim.

"The lava was on our side this time. Wish I knew who to write the thank-you note to."

Jenny didn't remind him that the islands were the goddess Pele's domain, including their lethal innards. It might sound flippant.

This victim was giving her a worse feeling than even the very bad circumstances warranted. The woman also lay face up on the bed as if laid out for a funeral pyre, exactly like the first victim. Her throat was in the same condition. And both women were island ethnic mixes like Jenny herself.

This time the crime scene technicians were giving everything the complete work up, while Coutinho, Jenny, and Sammy searched the house. Jenny kept glancing out the window at the lava.

"Killed here," said Coutinho when they finished. "Like the first victim."

"Moke must have a vehicle," said Sammy. "Wouldn't want to get trapped here."

"Moke or tita," said Coutinho.

Bad guy or bad girl. Jenny had thought it herself but had decided not to bring it up yet.

"Can't canvas the neighborhood," said Coutinho. "Not after we made everybody leave. Question is, did the moke figure on that, or was he just lucky?"

"Or she," said Sammy.

Jenny decided she liked it when they did her job for her.

ꙮ

But the next morning she was the one who found the first victim on a Facebook page set up for local residents to connect with each other and with loved ones. Jenny usually treated breakfast as personal time, but her habits had to yield to the emergency. And social media could hold crucial information.

"Has anyone seen my sister?" read the post.

Several photos of Rainie Fruehauf in happier times accompanied the query. Her sister Randi had posted from Las Vegas. Nothing surprised Jenny about that. At some point in history an economic refugee from Hawaii had landed a casino job in Vegas and then recommended his cousins and their friends, until the traffic back and forth had worn a trail in the ocean.

At headquarters Jenny found Coutinho alone in the tiny office he shared with Detective Kim, who had been detached to Kona Division for a while. Coutinho had been policing the eruption like every other cop, but his exhaustion wasn't showing yet.

"That's interesting," he said. "I tracked down the owner of the house and got the name of his most recent tenant. Gentleman named Malachi Pereira. He took off for Vegas right about the time when you were trying to save him from the lava."

Some detectives hoarded information, but Coutinho regarded a case as a teaching moment. With her, anyway.

"Sounds like he decided to leave in a big hurry."

"He left the place empty. And we know what they say about nature and a vacuum."

"Squatters," said Jenny. "I guess there's going to be even more of that for a while."

She thought about it.

"So did Malachi leave because of the murder, or did he just make an opportunity for somebody else?"

"We'll have to ask him when we find him," said Coutinho. He paused, as if preparing himself. "Right now, I'm going to reach out to the sister."

He typed into Messenger. "I doubt it will take long."

Jenny looked at her watch. She had five minutes before roll call. Maybe she could listen and learn. But four minutes passed before the phone on Coutinho's desk rang. He put it on speaker for her, which was also like him.

A male voice sounded from the phone. "Who's this?"

"Detective Coutinho, Hawaii County Police. Is Ms. Fruehauf there, please?"

"For why you want her?"

That single sentence identified the man as another transplant from Hawaii. Jenny thought back to what she had seen on Facebook and recalled an island face on a man hovering over Randi Fruehauf. He looked as if he did a lot of hovering.

"I really need to talk to her. What's your name, by the way?"

Suspicion traveled almost audibly across the ocean.

"Levi."

"Levi what?"

"Hold on."

"Hello?" asked a female voice.

"Ms. Fruehauf? I'm afraid I have bad news for you."

Jenny's watch told her she couldn't stay for more. Her disappointment was mixed with guilty relief. These notifications were part of the job, but she avoided them if she could. Coutinho would do the hard stuff and then fill her in about what he learned.

ഋഗ

The next morning at headquarters Jenny concentrated on putting her right foot forward and then her left. It amazed her how much this methodical approach accomplished against her exhaustion. Commitment and tenacity carried her into the station and halfway to the women's locker room, but Coutinho intercepted her.

"Need to pick your brain," he said. He studied her and added, "Over coffee."

She liked the sound of that. Drinking coffee would involve sitting.

He led her to the detectives' bullpen and pointed at an empty chair. For a giddy moment she felt like a little girl in Daddy's armchair, but that was a feeling she didn't intend to share.

Coutinho skipped the creamers and the sugar, and she did too, even if she would have preferred them. If drinking her coffee black was the price of admission to the big leagues, she would drink it black. She waited for him to start.

"Rainie Fruehauf was from Kona, originally. I remember you were detached to Kona Division for a while."

"Three months last summer," she said. "And you know what? That jogs my memory about our second victim. I saw her once coming out of a corporate crash pad in Keauhou."

Vacation condos packed the smaller town just south of Kona.

"J.D.L.R," she added. Just Doesn't Look Right. No cop needed it spelled out.

"No contact card?" asked Coutinho.

"I remember I was cuffing some moke. He didn't want to see things my way. I had to let her slide."

A contact card recorded an encounter that didn't lead to an arrest. If she hadn't been busy, Jenny would have stopped the woman as a way of telling her the cops knew a hooker when they saw one.

"She doesn't seem to have taken a bust. Her prints aren't in AFIS."

"How about Rainie Fruehauf? If I ever saw her, I don't remember."

"Her sister told me a lot. Rainie went through a bad patch. Lost a job, boyfriend ran out on her."

"Let me guess," said Jenny. "Taking the money and leaving the debts."

It was the story behind a lot of prostitutes at the escort level. In Hawaii they might earn three or four hundred dollars an hour, but little of it stuck to their fingers.

"What was the job she lost?"

"Housekeeper at a vacation condo complex in Keauhou. According to Randi, Rainie had an issue with a guest. A male guest who put the moves on her."

"It happens," said Jenny.

"But this incident happened at night, and she worked days. I didn't rub Randi's face in it, but it sounds like a hooker dispute with a john. The management of the place must have come to the same conclusion, because they didn't back her."

"Drugs?"

"The sister doesn't think so, but she didn't know about the other stuff either. According to her, Rainie was starting to get her act together. She mentioned a job offer on this side, which she liked because it wasn't in Kona."

"So, two hookers from Kona. Maybe ex-hookers. Both dead in Puna."

Jenny thought about the possibilities. The worst case was a serial killer, the kind who liked prostitutes because they made cooperative victims. Going off with strange men was part of the job description.

"What was she going to be doing?"

"Real estate."

"Heard that one, too." Hookers looking to transition chose a field that took anyone who was hungry.

"And," said Coutinho, "it can be as dangerous as hooking." More than one woman realtor had found herself alone in a property with the wrong man.

"I'm going to look at applications for realtor's licenses. See if Rainie was following through."

"And maybe there's another recent application. Somebody like our other victim."

Coutinho grinned. "Thought of that."

Jenny felt herself turning red. "I figured."

And of course, Sammy had to show up at that moment, when she was looking as if she had just asked Coutinho out on a date and been turned down.

"Can I borrow my partner, Detective?"

"She's all yours."

༺༻

For a second day the lava cooperated, and so did the local residents. The state had decided to let anyone who hadn't already evacuated stay for now, and in the shelters aloha prevailed. The cops held their breath about that, because nerves would start to fray sooner or later.

It didn't mean Jenny got a rest. It meant she went back on routine patrol. Women still went into labor, residents still called about ominous odors, and the mokes still looked for cars and homes to break into. So, she drove alone in her personal Camry with a blue cone on the roof and a backlog of mileage reimbursement forms under the seat. She found she missed Sammy's grumpiness and the way his three hundred pounds made the vehicle tilt toward him.

Dispatch sent her to a Toyota dealership with a complaint about a missing salesman and a RAV4 that might have gone with him. Jenny had bought her car at the same dealership three years earlier.

The sales manager remembered her. He should. He had been bugging her ever since to trade her car in, dangling some preposterous offer for a vehicle that already had more than fifty thousand hard miles on it.

"Officer, howzit?"

"Mr. Peres."

"You here about my missing vehicle?"

She had expected a little more tact from him about his priorities, but never mind.

"You also have a missing salesman?"

"Not a salesman. A *wahine*."

Jenny began to get that detective feeling.

"A woman."

"Yeah. I told them that on the phone."

"Things get garbled. What's her name?"

"Jackie Gutierres."

"What's she look like?"

"I can show you."

Peres led her to his office, where the usual group photos of the sales team decorated the walls. Jenny's eyes went straight to her second victim, third from the left. She couldn't help looking for a premonition of the victim's miserable fate, but it didn't show. It never did.

"When did you see her last?"

"Day the eruption started. Last time we had any customers to speak of. She took a prospect out for a test drive in my RAV. I hope she still has it."

"You're just reporting this now?"

"Been trying all week. Couldn't get through to anybody."

Unfortunately, that was plausible. "Who was the customer?"

"Kona guy. Little weird that he came all the way over here, but I'm not going to complain."

"You have the copy of his license?"

Peres opened a desk drawer and riffled files.

"Oswald Peltier. Keauhou address."

Jenny looked around and spotted two security cameras, one covering the entrance and the other the sales area. She would check outside for more surveillance.

"Those work?"

"Sure."

She got on the phone to Coutinho.

ഗ്ദ

Jenny stood behind the detective and watched the screen over his shoulder. Jackie Gutierres and the middle-aged man displayed an indefinable ease with each other.

"They've met," she said.

Coutinho paused the video.

"You're sure you never saw him before?" he asked Peres.

"Definitely. Remembering people is part of my job."

"What did he drive here? You must have tried to hold his car keys."

Peres grinned without shame, and Jenny remembered him trying that old car salesman's trick on her.

"He said a friend had dropped him off. What the hell, that could be good if he's marooned and desperate."

Coutinho grunted and restarted the video.

Jenny watched Jackie get up and leave the frame for a moment. The man waited at her desk. He was about fifty and impressively fit. Jenny had seen it before. The military had a major presence in Hawaii, and this man had put in his time, maybe in an elite unit. He looked around the showroom and for a moment gave the camera the perfect angle on his face.

"How smart is that?" said Coutinho. "He leaves his name and address and a mug shot."

"Well, he was thinking we'd never catch on. Both victims were supposed to burn up without a trace."

"True, but he's still way overconfident. Lucky for us."

Peres was looking more and more troubled.

"What's happened to her?" he asked.

"Mr. Peres," said Coutinho, "she won't be coming back."

He had the manager call up the exterior cameras. Jenny saw nothing but Jackie minutes closer to death, as she and the man drove away. He was a prudent driver, pausing to look both ways before pulling onto the highway.

Then the door opened, and a Japanese couple in their sixties came in. Peres got up and put on a salesman's smile that Jenny found grotesque in context. But his departure gave the cops some privacy.

"This raises some questions," said Coutinho. "Are there other victims we don't know about?"

"Let's make a list of jobs that are risky for women," said Jenny. "That could give us a rough idea."

She hadn't known she was going to blurt that out until the words emerged. But it was true. Sometimes a woman trying to make a living had to take a chance on a male stranger. Prostitution wasn't the only such occupation. It just made the principle especially stark. And then there were the dangers posed by men who weren't strangers.

Coutinho raised an eyebrow and waited for more, but she had made her point.

"Well," he said, "we're letting people back into their neighborhoods to see what they can salvage. We'll just have to see what they find."

Pele must have heard that and found it funny, because she started the lava moving again that afternoon. Visits by residents were canceled, and the cops put their gas masks back on.

When Jenny climbed into the departmental Escape, Sammy gave her a dour look.

"Didn't we just do this?"

Underneath the words was grim anticipation of another body laid out on a bed. Every time Jenny pounded on a door or peered through a window, she held her breath. But she found nothing.

As they drove to the next street, Jenny's radio crackled, and Coutinho's voice said, "See if you can find Mr. Tanaguchi. Bring him in."

Jenny didn't ask what was up. She knew he wouldn't tell her over the radio.

"That's interesting," said Sammy.

Tanaguchi was still passing the days at the Pahoa Community Center. He seemed eager for a change of scenery, even at the police station. The desk sergeant directed them to Interview Two, where Coutinho met them.

"Can I get back out there?" Sammy asked.

That was Sammy. Detective stuff didn't interest him. Street policing did.

"Sure, Officer."

Coutinho had a civilian clerk set up Tanaguchi in Interview Two with coffee and a couple of malasadas from the best Portuguese donut truck in Hilo. He led Jenny to the hall outside the room.

"Randi Fruehauf is in the hospital. Somebody beat the hell out of her."

"She going to be okay?"

"It looked bad for a while, but they think so."

"How do we know about it?"

"When this first came up, I asked a Vegas detective if Randi had come to their attention. She hadn't at that point. But he remembered and called me back."

"Do they know who did it?"

"She says she didn't know him. Description could be anybody."

He called up a DMV photo on his laptop. "Here's Malachi Pereira."

"Did the Vegas cops find him?"

"We're behind the curve on this. He's back. United has him flying into Kona yesterday."

"Interesting," said Jenny. "Never seen him before."

"Let's see what Mr. Tanaguchi can remember."

The witness had just crumbs left from his donuts. "I never talked to Malachi that much," he said.

"He ever complain about business? Brag about it?"

"I don't think he was hurting for cash, but that's all I know about that." Tanaguchi paused for thought. "I know the guy owns the house. He complains about his tenants a lot, but Malachi didn't sound any worse than the rest of them."

"You see any visitors?"

"Yeah. Sketchy-looking mokes a couple times. Puna rats." Low-level local bad guys. "Matter of fact, one of them broke into my house a while back. Found him asleep on my couch. Whole place smelled like pakalolo."

"Did you get his name?"

"Nah. But I called you guys. It was funny as hell watching that big cop wake him up."

"Officer Waga?"

"Yeah. That's the one."

Jenny radioed Sammy, who remembered the incident.

"Harvey Koana. Wasn't even the first time I found him like that. When he ain't couch surfing, he's usually hanging at Isaac Hale. Should I bring him in?"

Coutinho nodded, and Jenny relayed the message.

When Sammy arrived with the young man, she recognized him. She spent a fair amount of time at the beach where small-time marijuana dealers spent a lot of theirs. In the interview room Koana struck a tough guy pose, which made Jenny feel even more tired. Coutinho seemed to feel the same.

"Harvey, spare us the attitude. Today we don't care about your business. We just need to pick your brain about Malachi Pereira."

The young man sat in sullen silence.

"Of course, we could decide to make a project of you. And if you make us go to the trouble, we're really going to come down on you. Clear?"

"Yeah," came after a moment.

"What's Malachi into?"

"What's anybody around here into? Pakalolo."

"Pimping?"

"How'd you know?"

"Harvey, we're the cops."

"He was bragging about that, but I didn't believe him."

"Why not?"

"Where's he gonna get these girls?"

"Seen him lately?"

"He just got back from Vegas."

"Why'd he go there?"

"No lava. What you think?"

"You stuck around."

"No cousins in Vegas."

"So, he's back."

"His cousin was getting on his nerves."

"Okay, Harvey, where's Malachi now?"

"I ain't his mother."

"Harvey. Remember what I said?"

"His house burned up."

"We know that."

"So, I don't know where he is right this minute. But I told him he could stay with me for a while."

"He take you up on it?"

"I'll know tonight."

"Harvey," said Coutinho, "when you see him, tell him we need to talk to him. And the longer it takes, the less he's going to like it when we find him."

ꕤ

Police headquarters didn't look like home anymore.

The governor had finally activated the National Guard, partly to give the police a break. Many of the cops were starting to look like extras from *The Walking Dead*. But now military fatigues were showing up all over the station, as the Guard coordinated with the cops.

Coutinho had given Jenny coffee again.

"What's our next step, Officer?"

"I think we need to send a picture of Oswald Peltier to Kona. See if he's the man Rainie Fruehauf had the dispute with."

Coutinho smiled and nodded. "It'll be better if we go."

"We?"

"Yeah. Now that we have some help, we can act like detectives a little." He made a sweeping gesture that took in the military personnel and all the extra comings and goings.

Jenny had been looking forward to a day off, but an ambitious junior officer couldn't pass up an opportunity like this.

They left at five the next morning on little sleep, for Jenny, at least. The detective assignment had kept her mind working most of the night. Her body was clamoring for coffee, and when they reached the small town of Na'alehu near the southern tip of the island, she made herself look straight ahead. If she cast a longing look at the Punalu'u Bake Shop, Coutinho might think she wasn't ready for the big leagues. But he turned into the parking lot. "Malasadas are mandatory," he said.

The donuts didn't disappoint, and neither did the southern route to Kona, with the best ocean views on the island. In Kona they fought the local traffic to Division headquarters.

Coutinho led her through the gauntlet of male appraisal. These men hadn't seen her in the months since her detachment there had ended, and it seemed to make her new meat all over again. Jenny allowed herself a moment of relief at the prospect of going home soon.

Just ten minutes later a uniformed officer delivered the warrant they needed. The young man was even newer than Jenny's time in Kona Division.

"Thanks, Officer…" Coutinho looked at the young man's name tag. "…Bowman."

"Scott," said the officer to Jenny. He waited.

"Jenny," she said, wondering why it felt as if she had lost a point.

Coutinho drove, as they backtracked the few miles to Keauhou. Parking was always difficult there, with the condos occupying almost every square inch of ground. Coutinho somehow turned half a space into a whole one. Jenny climbed out of his Camry, and right away the sun began cooking her hair. By three in the afternoon she would feel ready for spontaneous combustion. These days she was getting enough of that feeling from the lava. Coutinho glanced at her and seemed to read her mind.

"At least the ground here cooperates."

Of course, volcanoes had created this side of the island too. They had been dormant for thousands of years, but Pele could decide to wake them up.

The manager of the complex was a Filipino bantamweight boxer type. Jenny played him some of the video from the Toyota dealership on her phone.

"That's Mr. Peltier," he said.

The manager took a key ring from a hook on the wall and led them across the interior courtyard to a staircase. On the second floor he opened a door for them. "All yours."

It wasn't going to take long. The place looked barely inhabited. Peltier didn't seem to have used the kitchen, even for pouring milk on cold cereal. The trash can was pristine.

"No TV," said Jenny. The bedroom held a single cot. "What was he, a monk?"

"Just military," said Coutinho.

That was a type they knew well.

Peltier did have a laptop computer, which rested on a card table in the middle of the living room. A folding chair and a desk lamp were the only other furnishings in the room.

Coutinho opened the computer, which started right up. Peltier hadn't password protected the screensaver or his files, and he had only one file in My Documents. Coutinho clicked on it and began to read.

"Interesting stuff," he said after a while.

He got up and let Jenny take the chair. The single file was hundreds of pages, and she decided to skim it first. But passage after passage grabbed her attention. She started reading some of them aloud.

"The people of Hawaii have lost their way, with their pollution and the destruction of their patrimony. Extinctions of the native species are a sign Pele will punish them."

"One of those," Coutinho said. He didn't have to explain. Many outsiders found island culture fascinating, but some became deranged on the topic.

When Peltier wasn't ranting, he reminisced about his transactions with local prostitutes. Jenny glanced at the cot in the bedroom and grimaced. It reminded her of college dorm sex on beds that could accommodate two bodies only if they were stacked.

Peltier's love of island purity and his attachment to commercial sex struck a dissonant chord, but he didn't seem to hear it. Three women came up repeatedly under obvious professional aliases. From his comments on their appearance, Jenny thought two were probably Rainie and Jackie, and the third a woman who resembled them. Jenny had known more than a few men who had a type when it came to women. If Peltier's type was one seen everywhere in these islands, that was convenient for him.

All three women had told him about their plans to relocate and get out of hooking. When Jenny had started meeting women in the business, usually while arresting them, she had been surprised by how much they talked to anyone who would listen, even johns. Maybe they did it to keep the silence of a strange man from filling the room.

Peltier seemed to approve of their plans. Jenny had seen that too. A john justified his hooker habit to himself by telling himself he was trying to help the women.

Then Pele dominated the ravings again.

"That would be the start of the eruption," said Jenny.

"The file was last updated a day into it," Coutinho replied.

"Harvey Koana said Malachi was pimping. Maybe he met Rainie and Jackie in Hilo."

"He could have been trying to draw them back into the business. Some of them relapse when they can't match the money they used to make."

Jenny thought about it. "

And when they did, Peltier got pissed enough to kill them?"

"This isn't hanging together yet. What we need to do is find the third woman, and hope she's in shape to tell us."

The National Guard personnel were putting additional boots on the ground in the eruption zone, but they were also complicating things. Their culture differed from law enforcement. To get along with them, cops now had to become diplomats as well as doctors, nurses, lawyers, social workers, and maybe anthropologists and sociologists. And when it came to diplomacy, Jenny noticed a willingness on the part of male cops to defer to her.

Of course, it didn't stop them from doubting her abilities in other areas.

"The residents can leave if they want," she told a Guard captain at the Pahoa Community Center.

The captain was a woman from Honolulu, and she was making a point of acting like a hardcase. Jenny thought she might have something to prove to the men under her command, but that wasn't a police problem. Keeping the emergency shelters calm was, and running them like prison camps wasn't the way to do it.

"Then they head right back to the neighborhood," said the captain, "and we have to go rescue them again."

"Most of them won't. A few will, but, hey. If civilians didn't do dumb stuff, we'd be out of a job."

Jenny tried a man-to-man smile. It fell flat, but she thought she had defused the situation for now.

That was until she heard a female voice screaming outside the Center. Jenny hustled outside to see two young Guardsmen frog-marching a young woman toward the entrance. The woman was objecting in vulgar terms. Jenny planted herself in their path. The young men looked uncertain of their next step, and she thought she could get the initiative away from them.

"What's up?"

"Caught her in a house we already cleared."

"Doing what?"

The young man reddened, and his partner looked at his shoes. "She wouldn't say."

And they couldn't figure out how to make her.

"We thought you might know her," said his partner.

The Guardsmen looked disheveled, and Jenny saw scratches on their faces and forearms. The two young men had just learned the hard way that a small package could contain a lot of fight, and police work was harder than it looked.

"Okay, I'll take her."

She had never seen such relief on a young male face, not even when her father had been affable to her prom date.

Now Jenny evaluated her prize. She saw a basic island beauty with mixed ancestry, just like the two murdered women. And this young woman had been doing something in a no-go zone that she refused to talk about. Jenny could think of several explanations, but one had been on her mind a lot lately.

"What's your name?"

"Miriam."

"Miriam what?" Sometimes the game got exhausting, but a cop still had to play.

"Soares."

"How long have you been doing this?"

She made a point of using the vague phrase favored by women in the business. "How long have you been hooking?" would have sounded like a challenge and produced sullen silence.

The young woman still gave her a suspicious look.

"I don't care about your business," said Jenny. "Right now, I've got bigger things to worry about."

"Couple of years, off and on."

"Off and on?"

"I thought I was out of it. But waitressing wasn't paying the bills."

"Are you from Kona?"

"Yeah, how'd you know?"

"Do you know Rainie and Jackie?"

"Sure. Haven't seen them in a while."

Jenny reminded herself that a lot of people had been in no position to follow the news.

"You won't be seeing them," she said.

"Oh," said Miriam in a small voice, then something occurred to her. "I haven't seen Malachi, either. Is he okay?"

"Good question. Tell me about your client today."

"He found me on the message boards. Not through Malachi. Said he wanted something special."

"What was that?"

"Do it in the lava zone, with all the noise and stuff. He said it would get him off."

"And you said yes?"

"He said there was a thousand in it for me."

Miriam frowned.

"This is the second time we didn't connect. He's gonna find somebody else."

"When was the first?"

"Couple of days ago."

"You would never have seen the money. You're lucky those soldier boys found you first."

Miriam's mouth moved, but nothing came out.

"Know him?"

Miriam looked at the picture of Peltier.

"Yeah, that's Oswald, from Kona. A little weird, maybe, but nice enough. As they go."

"You seen him over on this side?"

"If you know everything, for why you ask me? Yeah, he found me at work. Said he was proud of me for making it. But then he wanted a date for old time's sake."

Miriam gave Jenny a look with sisterhood in it. "What is it with them?"

"Men?"

"I mean, it didn't surprise me, but why do they always try to have it both ways?"

"You figure that out, give me a call."

ꕥ

"It's still not making sense," said Jenny. "She already knew Peltier. Why would he approach her online like a new john?"

"Digital trails are hard to get rid of. Maybe he knows that, and he wanted to look like somebody else—in case we ever caught onto it."

Coutinho didn't look as if he had convinced himself. Peltier had been careless with his name and face in the Toyota dealership. Now all of a sudden, he was a shrewd planner?

"Let's find him and ask," said Jenny.

"The problem is," said Coutinho, "it's a big island." Hawaii County cops said that a lot when a moke was eluding them.

"He didn't get his thrill this time," said Jenny. "Maybe we can get him to come to us."

Coutinho looked at her for a long moment. "You mean a decoy operation?"

"I'm his type. Like the other three."

"We need to think about this. I don't want your mother coming after me," he said, giving her a sharp look. "What?"

Jenny's smile widened. "Sammy's afraid of my mother too."

Coutinho didn't think about it for long. They had no alternative. "Let's set it up."

The internet had remade prostitution along with everything else. It took the tech people just an hour to give Jenny—or Leila, as she decided to call herself after the Leilani Estates—an online presence in *The Erotic Review*, *Best GFE,* and a website of her own. There were even templates available online for making escort sites.

GFE, she learned, stood for "Girlfriend Experience," a concept she would grapple with another time. The websites taught her another term: a "hobbyist" was a man who spent a lot of time and money on prostitutes at the escort level.

She and Coutinho settled in at a table in a coffee shop in the Prince Kuhio mall. They didn't know how tech savvy their suspect was, and they couldn't risk being traced to police headquarters. The detective was following the action on a clone of Jenny's laptop.

Leila already had messages. They expected a brief window of time before the hobbyist community realized she was virtual. By then they hoped to have made contact with the one john they wanted. The men were reckless with their personal information, which surprised Jenny but also helped in the screening process. A man who wanted her to come to his home or office or hotel room wasn't their target.

And then it arrived in an online chat room. "If you're feeling adventurous, you can make three times your rate. I'm talking about going to the lava zone. Up for it?"

Coutinho nodded to her. She decided not to remind him they weren't on the phone, and the moke couldn't hear them.

"Sure," she typed. "Where and when?"

He gave her an address in Leilani Estates.

"How about now?"

She and Coutinho had talked about this. She would need to stall the man to let her backup get into position without tipping him off.

"I have classes until two. Three o'clock?"

That was Jenny's idea. She had heard a lot of young women in this business posed as college students to give the johns some extra titillation.

"Okay, but no island time." He wanted three to mean three, and not whenever Jenny happened to get there.

"I didn't see any cops, but park a couple of houses away, just in case they come by."

"Three times my hourly rate is a thousand."

"It's a thousand, fifty," he typed back. "Don't sell yourself short."

"Smooth," Jenny said to Coutinho.

"It's not like he plans to pay you."

ꕥ

Where had all these cops come from?

Jenny's friend Patsy Inaba used Coutinho's office to wire her up in privacy. When Jenny emerged dressed in her hooker outfit, every male officer in Hilo Division seemed to have nothing to do but loiter nearby.

She didn't get it. The modest top, shorts and sandals were nothing she wouldn't have worn off duty, which was the point. The street prostitutes of Waikiki were blatant about what they did, but women at the escort level dressed to blend in.

So, the men had come to peek at her looking like a whore who didn't look like a whore. And they didn't even seem disappointed.

Maybe sex is all in the mind.

"We don't really have anything on him yet," Coutinho said for the third time.

The repetition was a little annoying, but he was right. The Guardsmen had interrupted the suspect's plans for Miriam.

"Get him talking until he lets something slip."

"Got it."

"And if you even see a knife, that's it. You know what to say."

"Knife." She could probably remember that.

Her backup, officers borrowed from Kona Division, had already driven off in their undercover vehicles. No one was supposed to be out and about in the Leilani subdivision, but the local element that ignored the government on principle drove battered RAVs and Wranglers.

Sammy was too well known in Puna go undercover. He muttered some more about Jenny's mother and critiqued her appearance.

"Damn, girl, they should send me in. I look more like a hooker than you."

His flagrant concern touched her.

She was driving a Nissan Versa that Coutinho had found somewhere. Maybe Leila really was a college student. There was the house she wanted. Guard personnel had already scrawled "Clear" on it. She drove two houses past it and parked in the front yard.

Nobody in this normally nosy neighborhood came out to investigate. It was eerie.

As Jenny got out of the Versa and started toward the house, she read off the makes, models and license plates of six vehicles that didn't belong to her backup. Coutinho would run the plates. Residents had left some of them behind, but maybe one belonged to the man they wanted.

At the front door she paused for a moment to breathe and calm her butterflies.

"Going in," she said.

She pushed the door open, and right away the house spoke to her in a silent language that cops learned on the job. This wasn't going according to the plan. Jenny considered backing out, but she had only a feeling. If her instinct turned out wrong, and she aborted the operation for nothing, Coutinho's understanding would hit her harder than a reprimand.

She started going through the house room by room. Her hands felt strangely light and empty. She had spent the first twenty-four years of her life without a gun, but two years as a cop had wiped those years clean.

It had become habit to leave the bedroom and its nasty surprises for last. For that reason alone, she decided to shake things up and go there first. And of course, this time she found nothing.

That left the kitchen.

"Hi," said Jenny. "I'm Leila."

She knew the man at the table from photographs. Maybe that was why her voice stayed level, and her pulse didn't surge. In the flesh he still looked fit for his age, roughly fifty, and he perched on the chair like a man who didn't sit often, or for long. He would be hard to handle.

"I'm Oswald.

She hadn't expected him to use his real name. Maybe he wasn't concealing anything from her because he didn't intend to leave her alive. But somehow he didn't feel like a threat.

"We mentioned some money," she said.

He shook his head impatiently.

"I'm not him. I'm here to save your life. Not that my track record on that has been very good."

"Why do I need saving?"

Now was the time for his obsessive rant about saving her soul from the fate worse than death. But he shook his head.

"And I'm not one of those, either," he said. "I'm talking about your life, not your soul. He's already killed two friends of mine."

"Who?"

"Rainie and Jackie."

"No, who killed them?"

"That's the problem. I don't know."

His face let his frustration show.

"I just missed him the other day. He must have seen something that spooked him."

"Come with me," said Jenny. "We need to talk someplace else."

"You go. I'm going to wait a while longer. In case he still comes."

Jenny saw three choices. She could spend more time on persuading him, she could identify herself as a police officer, without knowing how he would react, or she could say, "Knife."

But Coutinho gave her a fourth choice, which was to do nothing. He appeared in the doorway of the kitchen with two uniforms behind him. One of them was Scott Bowman, the young man she had met in Kona. The other was probably a loaner from Kona as well.

Coutinho gave Peltier his stony cop look and then aimed it at Jenny. "You're both under arrest. Conspiracy to commit prostitution."

For now, he wanted to keep Peltier believing she was a hooker. She tried to look stoic and resigned, as if the occasional bust was part of her business model.

Bowman cuffed her. He did it right. Jenny hadn't felt steel on her wrists since her academy days, but the experience hadn't improved. The young men led her out of the kitchen and then out of the house.

The cuffs had to stay on until they were out of sight. Jenny found nothing to like about walking on tricky ground without her hands free to catch herself if she fell. But the young men kept a firm grip on her biceps. They walked her all the way to her Versa. Jenny rattled the cuffs on her wrists.

"Somebody want to get these off me?"

Nothing happened, unless young men staring and mentally undressing her counted as something.

"Um, today?"

Jenny kept her tone level and light. Showing concern would be a mistake.

But no one made a move toward her with the handcuff keys. A third young male officer appeared.

"The operation is over. So is the joke."

They kept running their eyes over her and in those eyes, she saw the reflected glow of the lava and something else as old as the planet: the glint of predators spotting their prey.

Would they really do something here? They were the cops, the people who were supposed to stand in the way of the pack mentality of young men. But these cops were also young men, and their adult supervision had already driven off.

She needed to suspend her disbelief. If this was a breakdown of civilization, she was a cop, and it was her job to handle it. She started planning her counterattack. It didn't look promising. She'd be lucky to get one groin kick in, and her flimsy sandals wouldn't accomplish much.

Which one would move first? Would guessing right do any good?

"Need some help, girlfriend?"

Patsy Inaba came bustling up to her with a key ready in her hand. In a moment Jenny's hands were free.

"You guys couldn't make yourselves useful?"

Jenny knew the tone of a woman making light of a situation that wasn't light at all. She had used it herself, hating herself as she did.

"Come on. Coutinho wants you."

Patsy hustled Jenny into her car. Neither spoke, until the young men began to shuffle away. Jenny started to breathe.

"Coutinho went back to headquarters," said Patsy finally. "He does want you."

"Okay." Jenny told herself to stop resenting Coutinho for leaving her. Not even he could foresee everything.

Patsy went to her vehicle. Jenny drove off and felt her heart rate slow. By the time she got back to headquarters, she had decided not to tell Coutinho anything about her close call, if that was what it was. He would believe her, but the young cops would support each other and simply say that she couldn't take a joke.

Patsy had done enough already; Jenny couldn't make her go public. But that left Jenny with one more thing to watch for over her shoulder.

She went to the bullpen. She didn't see Coutinho until she focused on the monitor for Interview Two. He was sitting across from Oswald Peltier.

"I read your diary," said the detective. "Interesting stuff."

"That's private."

"Not in a murder investigation."

"How many times I got to tell you? I didn't kill them."

"Several problems with that. You knew both victims. And now we find you right where we were waiting for the killer. How did you know where to be?"

"Educated guess. He's been using that neighborhood. I staked it out until I saw the young lady." Peltier looked proud of himself. "I know a prostitute when I see one."

Jenny's eyelids drooped with weariness. No one was around to hear Peltier's words, but he had immortalized them on video. Soon they would spread all over the station.

"Okay," said Coutinho, "if you didn't kill them, who did?"

"I'll tell you again. I don't know."

"Was it Malachi?"

"I never met him, but I guess it's possible. Maybe he found out they were working off the books. His books, anyway."

Peltier had a point. Pimps could turn murderous with a woman who cost them money.

Coutinho studied Peltier until the man started to squirm. "Let me show you something."

He opened a laptop on the table and turned it to face Peltier. Coutinho pressed play and sat back.

"That's you and Jackie Gutierres. Later that day she was dead. You want to explain what's going on here?"

"I was just looking in on her. She was at her new job, so I told them I was in the market for a car."

"Wasting her time like that?"

"I do need a new vehicle. I would have bought it from her."

"Who was the friend who dropped you at the dealer?"

Peltier didn't blink at Coutinho's detailed knowledge.

"I walked there, but car people think you're weird if you walk. Like maybe I don't know anything about cars, and they can overcharge me."

"So, you found Jackie and went off for a test drive."

"And we talked. She said she was doing well, but she offered me a date."

"Like old times."

"Right."

"So, where did that happen?"

"It didn't. She got a call on her cell. Then she said she had to do something. She'd make it up to me that night."

"What was it?"

"She didn't say."

"What do you think?"

"I think it was the killer offering her a lot of money."

"So, what happened?"

"She dropped me at my hotel and drove off."

"Anybody see this happen?"

"The desk clerk was looking right at us when I got out. She might remember."

Coutinho backed up and picked at Peltier's story, but he couldn't pry anything loose. He got up and said, "Sit tight, Oswald."

He came out and found Jenny in the bullpen. "What do you think, Officer?"

"I think I believe him."

"I do, too."

He could have looked happier about it.

"He was in the no-go zone. We can stretch the point and hold him for a while on that, but the...well, we don't want to think about it."

She knew what he meant. A cop shouldn't hope for another murder, but nothing else would move the case forward.

ꝏ

Jenny had finished her shift and changed out of her uniform. She was driving home when her radio crackled and the dispatcher spoke. No one answered. Police manpower had stretched and finally snapped.

"I'll take it," said Jenny.

A cop was never off duty.

An anonymous caller had reported a man breaking into a house in the neighborhood. The caller shouldn't have been there to see it, but he had, and now someone needed to check it out. If it had been just a property crime, the cops could have practiced triage. But they were holding their breath about another murder.

Jenny stopped her Camry and looked toward the lava. It had taken another overnight breather, but it was now back to munching its way through forest, houses, cars and anything else it could find. Once again, she would have to move fast. She got out and approached the house.

The ground lurched sideways. Jenny flexed her knees and threw her arms out in a surfer's pose. But she was riding supposedly solid ground, not a wave. So this was what an earthquake felt like. The TV news reported minor temblors all the time, but this was the real thing.

She went through the steps—the knock on the door and then the circuit around the house, peering in through windows. Jenny then tried the front door handle, which turned. Someone had left in too much of a hurry to lock up—or maybe someone wanted company.

She radioed for backup, but she heard what she expected. "ASAP, Officer." The dispatcher didn't sound hopeful.

This was Jenny's show. She had to go in, but that didn't mean with her eyes closed. First, she cleared the other rooms, off-duty weapon in hand. She found nothing, but someone had just been here. She could feel it, even if she couldn't see it.

The ground shook again. This time she cringed at the noise of a jet liner revving its engines as it rolled up to the front door of the house. Okay, it couldn't be that, but it was the only comparison she could think of.

She went back to the front door and stopped just short of death itself.

A new fissure had opened up, and the blazing bowels of the earth were doing their best to climb out. Jenny grabbed the door frame to stop her forward momentum, as her eyes closed instinctively against the merciless heat. She forced them open to look for her car and a path to it.

Her Camry was gone. Pele had swallowed it whole.

"Bitch," said Jenny.

The goddess must have heard her. The lava leaped up from the fissure and reached for her with fiery claws.

As Jenny backed into the house, she looked to her left and saw the flowing lava closer than ever. For a demented moment she thought the flood from Kilauea intended to duel the fissure for supremacy. The winner's trophy would be Jenny, if she didn't get moving. She holstered her off-duty weapon for speed and ran through rooms as familiar as if she lived there herself.

The last thing she needed was an obstacle, especially one with the mass of this man. He was easily Sammy's size. Before she could stop, she ran right into him. He caught her bicep in a painful grip. Jenny leaned away and looked up at him.

There was a lot of him to take in, but she knew him. She had seen him on Facebook, hovering over Randi Fruehauf.

"Levi," she almost said, but she stopped herself. A better time to spring her knowledge on him might come later.

He stared down at her until she wondered whether he ever blinked. "Lava's getting close," she said.

"We have a few minutes."

"For what?"

"The cops saved you yesterday. I saw you getting busted. You and Peltier."

"He knows your name too. He must have told the cops. Don't make this worse."

"Save your breath. He doesn't know me."

"If you have the money, we can still do it."

"What money?"

He kept staring. Now Jenny understood the instinct that had made her keep up the hooker act. He would expect a cop to have a gun, but he might get careless with a prostitute.

His grip showed no mercy, but he was letting her angle her right side away from him so he couldn't feel her weapon against his body. Now she had to pick the right moment to use it.

Levi maneuvered her out of the doorway and started to drag her toward the bedroom. He looked away from her and toward their destination. The distraction gave her the opening she needed. Jenny drew the gun and fired into his side, under his right arm.

He roared with pain and shoved her away from him. Jenny fired again. Maybe she missed, or maybe the bullet gave up somewhere in his three hundred pounds of muscle and fat. He charged her, and she fired a third shot.

Then he was crushing her against the wall. Construction in some of these houses was so shoddy that for a moment she hoped he would propel her right through the sheet rock. But the wall held. He mashed her flat, until her breath left her.

Jenny's revolver had three rounds left, but they would do her no good if she couldn't free her arm to shoot. She tried to turn her body one way and then the other to win some room to maneuver. It wasn't working. Her arm stayed pinned down at her side.

But she found she could bend her right leg and slide it up the wall, which got her foot out of the way. She put a bullet into his left leg.

He bellowed again, but he kept pressing her into the wall.

"Police! Don't move!"

The voice was young and male. Levi pulled her away from the wall, wrapped his arm around her, and tried to swing her in front of him. Jenny didn't plan to serve as anybody's human shield. She put another shot into his side, and when his grip loosened for an instant, she dropped and rolled.

And as she went, she got a look at her backup.

It was Scott Bowman. Scott, the would-be rapist.

He was aiming his S&W 9mm at Levi, who breathed hard and glared back at him.

"Down," said Scott.

The moment seemed to last hours, but then Levi got down on his knees. He walked forward on his hands until he was prone. He did it well for a man with five bullets in him. Jenny thought about the single round left in her revolver. It wouldn't have accomplished much without perfect placement and a lot of luck. Was she now going to need it for someone else?

Bowman took his handcuffs from his belt and tossed them to Jenny. She knee-walked to Levi and straddled his bulk as she cuffed him. Bowman kept his aim steady. Jenny nodded at him, and he took his radio from his belt. He called for more backup and an ambulance.

"Meet us outside Leilani."

The urgency in his tone got Jenny moving. She regained her feet and bent down to hook her hand under Levi's arm.

"Up. We have to go."

But he weighed three times her hundred and twenty pounds. She looked toward Bowman.

"Come on. Grab an arm."

He took Levi's other arm. They pulled in unison once, twice, three times, but the man was too heavy for both of them.

"Leave him," said Bowman. "We gotta get out of here."

"You're a cop," said Jenny.

Her tone lashed him into shamefaced fury. If Jenny lived through this, she had made an enemy for life. She looked down at Levi.

"Help with your legs," Jenny ordered him.

"I'm shot."

"Whose fault is that?"

It took agonizing moments they couldn't afford, but Levi got his uninjured leg under him and supplied enough additional lift to get him upright.

"Out the back," said Bowman.

"No kidding," said Jenny. She didn't plan to challenge the fissure out front again.

"What kind of vehicle?" she asked.

"We've got an Escape."

Jenny exhaled in relief. The three of them would fit, assuming the limping six-legged beast they were making could get out of this house in time. She thanked Pele for the layout of a standard island box. She knew exactly where the back door was.

Halfway across the small back yard she heard a whoosh that penetrated the general din. She turned her head and saw the house fully aflame.

Bowman's departmental Ford Escape waited on the road behind the house. It took more sweating and cursing to heave Levi into the rear seat in his handcuffs, but she refused to trust him with his hands free.

Then she was in the passenger seat beside Bowman at the wheel, and the vehicle was moving. And within minutes she began to get that bad-date feeling. It stood to reason, with a man who had already proven he was someone to be avoided.

"I guess you're still on loan to Hilo," she said. Why was it always up to her to deescalate?

"Yeah."

Anger flared at his monosyllabic manly man bullshit. She put up with it every day, but maybe today was the day she had enough. Whatever it was, it was about to make her blurt. She wondered what would come out, but she didn't feel like stopping it.

"We're cops," she said. "This is how cops act. We back each other up. You know it, and now I know you know it."

"You almost got us killed."

"Protect and serve. Even the bad guys."

He turned his head and glared, but she gave him her own cop look right back. What the hell. The best she could hope for was a stalemate, but maybe that was good enough.

ꝏ

Coutinho found her in the waiting room at Hilo Medical Center.

"He's stabilized."

"Is he talking?"

"Not so far, but I don't think we need him to." He paused. "Randi Fruehauf admitted it: Levi was the one who beat her up. Wasn't the first time, but she had always stayed out of the hospital before. I checked the flight manifests, and he was here on our turf for both of the murders. She claims she didn't know."

"When he wasn't there to pound on her, she probably couldn't afford to wonder why."

"It would be nice if he felt the need to explain himself at some point. I mean, what was this about?"

"Maybe he came here so he wouldn't kill her. He wanted to keep her around for more punishment."

And here, with the deadly bowels of the earth to tell him murder didn't matter, Levi had felt at home.

"Nice guy," said Coutinho.

"I wish he was the only one."

"...I am sweating and coughing all over the place from the dust and dirt blown up by the leaf-blower. The theaters get worse as I go along..."

(from Street Smart #6, *"Make the Bear Be Nice"* by Stephen St. Francis Decky)

#6 "Make the Bear Be Nice"

Stephen St. Francis Decky

My job is cleaning the theaters at the Deptford Super-6 Multi-Plex Cinema in Deptford, New Jersey. I do it seven nights a week because I'm trying to save enough money to get my own apartment. Right now, I am not living anywhere.

Cleaning theaters can be gross but it's kinda neat being alone in such a huge place all night. Plus, I actually like cleaning. When I was still living at home, I spent at least an hour every night cleaning something — the bathroom or the living room or the kitchen, which was always a mess because my dad is such a slob. I didn't get paid anything for cleaning at home, but at the movie theater, I get nine dollars an hour. Because there's nobody to supervise me at night, I get paid for eight hours no matter what, even though I usually finish everything up in less than four. I spend the rest of the time sleeping on one of the couches in the lobby. They're very soft and way more comfortable than the backseat of my car.

In the daytime I drink coffee and drive around. Sometimes I buy CDs to play in the car but I'm trying not to spend too much money so if I can, I just steal them. I also steal food.

ꕥ

It was three months ago that I got kicked out of my house. The last night I was there, my dad grabbed my neck and slammed me against the wall in my room. He was only wearing his underwear when he did this. He was so mad and the room was kinda dark but the reflection of the light from the hallway made his eyes glow orange.

"I'LL FUCKIN' KILL YOU" is the very last thing he said to me.

I spent the next couple of days wandering aimlessly and feeling terrible but then I got the job at the movie theater and right away I started feeling better—mostly because it meant I was making money but also secretly because I finally had something to clean again.

ꕥ

Sometimes in the daytime I see Jimmy Kirkos. He's a waiter at the Freeway Diner and I knew him in high school but we were never friends back then. We're sorta friends now, I think.

"How's the movie business?" he asks me today.

"Kinda messy," I tell him.

He's on his break and sitting in the booth across from me. We've both got coffees and grilled cheese sandwiches.

"Must be cool workin' with no boss around," he says, raising his eyebrows. "Betcha could have a pretty decent party."

"Oh, but I couldn't. I'd get in trouble." I take a bite of my sandwich and wait until I'm done chewing it to say: "Besides, it's been way too busy lately."

The reason it's busy is because it's summer and there's a lotta kids' movies out. All the theaters showing kids' movies are extra messy, and it takes me a little longer every night to get done. I tell Jimmy this, then add, "It's gonna be even worse when *Make the Bear Be Nice* comes out."

"Christ, that friggin' bear," Jimmy grumbles.

There's been a lotta hype about *Make the Bear Be Nice*—it's supposed to be the biggest summer kids' movie ever, and there are posters and signs and ads for it everywhere. People have been talking about it for months and everybody knows the plot: It's about a girl who finds a cuddly bear in the woods and brings it to her house. He is very nice but can't help accidentally knocking shit over and breaking things so her dad gives her an ultimatum: *"Make the bear be nice, or he's out."* The bear in the ads is *really* cute.

"I wonder if it's gonna be good," I say to Jimmy.

"You're fuckin' kiddin', right?" Jimmy replies. "It's gonna be total shit. It don't matter though, it's gonna make a fuckin' kabillion dollars no matter what. Ya know why?" He stops to light a cigarette, then says: "I'll tell ya why. It's because people are fuckin' *dumb*."

"Maybe it won't be all that bad," I say.

"Yeah, right."

When his break is over, I finish my coffee and pay the bill. I'm just getting into my car when I hear somebody call my name. I look up, and Jimmy is standing on the steps outside the diner.

"Hey, gimme a call some night, will ya? We'll go get hammered."

"Alright," I say, even though I don't have his number.

ഇ൬

The next few days are kinda busy at the theater. In spite of this, I break my all-time FASTEST-CLEANING RECORD on Tuesday night by finishing in just under two hours and fifty-eight minutes. That's including the extra mess from the two kids' movies playing—*The Look-Ups* and *Prince Kebby's Castle*—as well as spraying the windows and changing all the urinal cakes in the men's room. I sleep soundly in the lobby all through the week, but on Friday I wake up all of a sudden when I hear a car pull into the parking lot and stop right outside the window.

Instinctively, I grab a broom and start sweeping out a spot at the corner of the lobby, just under one of several giant *Make the Bear Be Nice* posters. There's a jangle of keys in the front door and the manager, Miss Ellie, walks in.

"You're still here?" she asks.

I have no idea what time it is and my head's foggy from sleeping so I can only nod.

"You're gonna have to pick up the pace startin' tonight," she says, shaking her head, which makes her many earrings jingle. "*Make the Bear Be Nice* is gonna show in Theaters 1 through 4, and we're adding on late shows to play in all 6 theaters over the weekend. They won't be letting out 'til 1:15 so you're gonna get a late start."

"I can do it."

"I hope you can," she says. "You've been doin' good work and I'm counting on you to make sure the place looks nice, no matter how nasty it gets. And believe me, it ain't gonna be pretty." She pokes my chest with her index finger then adds: "Make sure you get lotsa rest."

"I will."

She nods. "I'm gonna write you in for an extra two hours every night this week—as long as you keep up the good work." She waves one of her many ring-covered fingers at me then starts walking across the lobby. "Now finish up and get the hell outta here."

"Yes, Miss Ellie."

I wait until I hear her go through the door to the office at the end of the hallway before throwing my broom in the closet. I usually take a couple minutes to wash myself up and brush my teeth in the men's room, but there's no way I can do it today. I leave the theater feeling tired and gross.

When I pass the clock on the bank at the end of Multiplex Road, I see that it's only 10:09 a.m., and because I have absolutely nowhere to go and nothing to do, I stop at the store and buy a paper to see what movies are playing in the city.

ꕥ

It's a long day and I spend most of it walking around and wishing I had an apartment. I would not need a big one or a lot of furniture: Only a chair and a desk and a real bed to sleep in. After living there for a while, I could probably have a bookshelf and maybe a kitchen table.

When my legs start to hurt, I buy a ticket to see the new Dracula movie that's playing everywhere but I fall asleep during the previews. When I wake up, Dracula is telepathically making some poor guy pull off another guy's head so I close my eyes and conk back out to the sound of the people behind me saying "*Oh my gahd*" and "*What the fahhhck*" over and over.

All the lights are on when I wake up again. There's an usher walking up the aisle and gathering trash so I make to get up so I can move out of his way.

"Relax," he says, waving his hand. "Stick around if ya want, next one's startin' in ten minutes."

"Oh, OK, thanks."

I stay awake to watch the movie this time but it's not all that good so I leave in the middle of it and walk to a bar on the corner. I'm not really old enough to buy drinks but the bartender doesn't ask me for ID so after ordering a grilled cheese sandwich I also ask for a beer. He brings it to me and I drink it. It's pretty good.

By the time I finally get to my car and start heading back over the bridge it's almost midnight. Because of the late shows I won't be able to start work yet so I stop at the Freeway Diner and am surprised to see Jimmy is working because he usually only works in the daytime. The place is packed.

"Gonna have to sit at the counter," he says to me, frowning. "We been packed all day—*'cuz a that fuckin' bear*. I'm on double-overtime."

There are a pair of old-lady waitresses working and one of them brings me a coffee, which is all I want. It would be nice to talk to Jimmy, but because he's so busy it's just not gonna happen. It's not until I've finished my third cup and the clock on the wall across from me says it's 1:15 on the dot that I stand up.

Jimmy follows me to the door. He rips a page out of his checkbook and hands it to me. There's a phone number written on it.

"Whenever you wanna get fucked up," he says.

"OK, sure," I tell him.

He winks and I leave.

ഌന്ദ

There are still cars in the parking lot when I get to the theater but I wait until the last of the employees leaves before getting out and using my key to get in. The first thing I see is a giant *Make the Bear Be Nice* standee by the window, which wasn't there when I left this morning. The bear's arm is moving back and forth and every once in a while, his eyes light up and turn sorta yellow. The trashcan beside him has been overturned; popcorn boxes and soda cups are spread out all around it. The carpet is totally covered with trash and stains for as far as I can see. I walk through it really slow because I've never seen such a mess in my whole life.

The theaters are much, much worse. I go through every one of them with my mouth open and my head shaking back and forth, with posters and signs for *Make the Bear Be Nice* flashing all around me.

"*It's impossible*" is alls I can think.

There's no time to waste at all so I literally run to the broom closet and get out the leaf-blower, which is what you use to blow all the trash in the theaters to the front. It's the first time I've ever had to use it on the lobby and that's not a good sign. By the time I've gotten to the theaters it's already closing in on 4 a.m.

"*There's no way you can stop,*" I tell myself. "*You have to work harder than you've ever worked before, AND YOU CANNOT STOP 'TIL IT'S ALL DONE.*"

For the next five hours, I am sweating and coughing all over the place from the dust and dirt blown up by the leaf-blower. The theaters get worse as I go along: there's candy stuck to half the seats and pools of spilled soda everywhere. Theater 4 smells like vomit and it's not until I go to wipe off a seat with a rag and hit a big chunky wet spot that I find out why. I have to run to the men's room when this happens and I waste two precious minutes washing my hands and trying to think of nice things to keep myself from barfing.

But in the end, I get the job done. The dumpster outside is filled to capacity so I'm hoping the trashmen come today to empty it. I am just climbing into my car when I see Miss Ellie's car pull in off of Multiplex Road and speed toward her parking spot, which has a special sign in front of it that reads *RESERVED FOR MANAGER.*

ꕤ

This day is even longer than yesterday because I'm totally exhausted and there's nowhere to sleep. I try parking in the lot of my old high school, but even though I'm buried under dirty clothes in the backseat some kids spot me and start pushing the car back and forth until it feels like it might tip over. They are giving me the finger when I drive away and although I want to tell them they might die alone and in agony someday, I just drive away instead.

I'm too tired to go to the city so I get a coffee to go from Burger Dan's on Route 41 before heading to the local Shopper's Paradise Supermarket to steal some food.

I'm shoving a bag of cookies into my pants when my dad walks into the aisle.

It's too late to pull the bag out and I'm too confused to run, so I just stand there 'til he looks up and notices me.

"Yo," he says, nodding his head and trying to look tough with a shopping basket fulla toilet paper in his hand. "The hella you doin' here?"

"Shoppin'," I say.

"No shit? Where you livin' these days?"

"At my friend's house," I say.

"Oh yeah?" His eyes look funny under the bright fluorescent lights and even though I want to I can't turn away from them. "What friend? You ain't got any friends—I know that."

"I'm stayin' at Jimmy Kirkos' house."

"Jiminy Who? Jiminy Cricket?" He shakes his head. "Hate to tell you this, kid, but Jiminy Cricket's not real—he's a grasshopper in a cartoon."

There is always this feeling around my dad that I'm about to get physically injured. It could be a punch or a shove or both. When I was living at his house this feeling was always there, and no matter how nice I was being or how good I did in school it wouldn't leave.

"I gotta go," I say.

"Where you gotta go?"

He grabs my arm and I stop and close my eyes.

"You ain't goin' nowhere," he tells me. "I seen your car at the movie theater every morning the past coupla months. You think I'm stupid? I pass it every day comin' back from work." I don't want to look at his face, but I do. My eyes start to water. "I want'cha to come home," he continues. "Ya can't hide from me, I'm your dad. I know what you're up to."

"I'm not up to anything. Let go," I say.

"*Let go*," he says, making it sound like I'm a scaredy-cat. I have to push him with my free hand but the motion makes the bag of cookies go *POP!* in my pants and just like that a wave of crumbs is rolling into my underwear and down my legs.

"The fuck was that?" Dad says.

I push him again, with both hands now, and his head bonks against one of the shelves. He shouts some kinda threat, but I can't hear it because I'm crying and running for the front doors with little pieces of cookies and cupcakes and all the other shit I stole spilling outta my pockets and shirt and pants.

ᴥ

The only other thing to do today is to get as far away as I can so I drive all the way out to where my Aunt Bette lives in Cumberland County and park in the woods across from her house. My legs and belly are itching from all the crumbs down there and even though I know Aunt Bette would be happy to let me use her bathroom to get cleaned up, I'm too embarrassed to knock on her door. I lay down in the backseat and fall asleep scratching myself and every once in a while making a pathetic kind of whimpering lonely animal sound.

When I wake up it's so dark that I can't even see my own hand so I climb up into the front seat and start the car. The clock on the dashboard says 1:20 a.m. and I stare at it for a minute trying to think why this is bad and then I remember I'm thirty minutes away from the theater and already late. I back up out of the woods and drive as fast as I can back to Deptford.

There is no way the theater can be worse than it was yesterday but—amazingly—it is. The trash is piled so high in the lobby that I trip twice before I even reach the hallway. The amount of energy I'm gonna need to do all this is almost impossible to think of so I just stop thinking about it and get to work. *"You cannot mess this up"* is what I keep telling myself, but by the time the sun comes up I'm not even halfway done. My arms are aching so bad I can hardly even hold up the leaf-blower when I reach Theater Six, but it's almost 9 a.m. so I just keep working even though my head is hurting and my legs feel like they're gonna snap off and every once in a while I get such a heavy feeling of sadness that I just wanna stop and melt into the gum and melted gummy-bear-stained carpet.

But there's still no way I'm gonna stop. I just work and right as I'm hauling the last few bags of trash out to the dumpster, I hear the sound of Miss Ellie and the morning crew walking into the lobby to start the next day's work.

ᴥ

I'm too tired to drive all the way to Aunt Bette's again so I go to the Freeway Diner and park out back by the dumpster. I'm sleeping in the backseat totally covered up with dirty clothes when the front door opens and somebody climbs in behind the wheel.

My hair's all over the place and my eyes are hardly able to focus, but I know right away it's Jimmy.

"The fucka ya doin'?" he asks. "The manager saw your car out here and wanted to call the cops."

"Sorry," is alls I can say.

"You alright?" He leans back a little to give my face a good look, then says: "You don't look alright. It's that fuckin' movie, ain't it? *Make the Bear Be* DEAD. Fuck." He lights a cigarette, shaking his head back and forth. "Look, man, I wish I could let'cha stay here but my boss is a jackass. This is the first break I had all day and I been on since eight in the mornin'."

"What time is it?"

"Little after two." He leans back and reaches into his pocket then pulls out a set of keys. It takes him a minute but eventually he yanks one of them off of the keyring and holds it toward me. "Here, take this. You know where Almonesson is?"

"Uh-huh."

"Right. I live at the end of Cooper Street, across from the Krazy Kat. There's no driveway or anything, there's just a hole in the sidewalk and a buncha dirt and trees but there's a mailbox at the end with KIRKOS written on it." He pushes the key into my hand. "Just use the key if nobody answers. My sister's there but knowin' her she's prob'ly sleepin' in fronta the TV. I'll try callin' 'er first."

I am clutching the key tight in my hand when Jimmy opens the door and climbs out.

"You'll prob'ly be gone before I get there, so try and stop by tomorrow. Maybe me and you can go out and have a couple drinks, figger out a way to kill that fuckin' bear forever."

He gives me a thumbs-up and closes the door. It takes some effort but eventually I manage to crawl up to the front seat and start the engine. In the rear-view mirror, I can see Jimmy lighting a cigarette while pissing against the dumpster. He throws another thumbs-up as I pass.

❧

I drive past the house three times before I spot the mailbox with KIRKOS written on it. The hole in the sidewalk is so deep that the front end of my car goes *KA-THUNK* and my head bangs against the ceiling when I hit it. The house is small and almost totally hidden by trees. I park right in front of it and get out.

Jimmy's sister is standing in the doorway with the door open. She is short with blonde hair and rolled-up sleeves. She's smoking a cigarette.

"Hey, Buddy," she says. "Jimmy called 'n said ya need a place to rest?"

"Is it OK?" I ask.

"For sure. I'm Robin." She reaches out to shake my hand and for just a second I take it.

Inside the house it's pretty gross. There's beer and soda bottles all over the place and also a smell that's sort of like chicken soup but not really. A TV is on with the volume way up but Robin turns it down with a clunky remote.

"Siddown. You wanna beer?"

"Oh, no thanks."

She is pointing to a couch with all sorts of clothes and bags on it so I push some stuff aside and take a seat. On the TV the Phillies are playing a game against the Mets. There is a break in the game and a commercial for *Make the Bear Be Nice* comes on.

"Jesus, this mothafuckin' bear," Robin says.

There are other chairs in the room but Robin sits down on the couch right next to me. She doesn't smell bad but being close to her makes me realize how bad I stink: It's the same stink you get in a gross movie theater, a syrupy kind of old food smell mixed with sweat and buttery popcorn.

"Do you think I could maybe take a shower?" I ask. I've been making sure to clean myself up every day in the men's room at the theater and I even have a bar of soap and a washcloth hidden under one of the sinks there. In all honesty, though, it's been three months since I've taken a real shower.

"Oh yeah, for sure," Robin says, grabbing a can of beer from the floor and shaking it before taking a sip. "Bathroom's right down the hall. You got clean clothes?"

I have to think a minute before I say, "I don't know. I'll have to look in my car."

"Well, bring all your dirty stuff in," she says. "You can wash it while you're gettin' cleaned up."

"Really?"

"Yeah, we got a washer/dryer in the kitchen. Go 'head, grab your stuff." She shakes her beer and takes another sip.

Outside, I gather up all the clothes in the backseat and carry them back to the house, feeling like this is all too good to be true.

Robin is waiting at the door.

"Jimmy didn't tell me you were so cute," she says, not really looking at me. "It...could be a problem."

I almost laugh but I hold it in. Robin stretches the door open a little further so I can squeeze through it. Our eyes meet briefly as I pass but I don't know what that means.

ꕥ

The bathroom smells awful and feels like a TV crime scene. There is pee in the toilet and a black ring around the bathtub. The shower curtain has black stuff all around the bottom of it. When you look up close, the black stuff is wet and fuzzy.

I turn on the water and take off my clothes.

I'm afraid to touch anything while I'm under the water, so I just sorta stand there for a while and let it wash over my hair and skin. There's some pieces of soap at the bottom of the tub and a couple of shampoo bottles, but mostly alls you see is cigarette butts—they're in the soap dish and in the little shower rack and also clogged up in the drain.

I get out of the tub after a couple minutes. All the towels have black stains on them so I use my dirty t-shirt to dry myself. I'm standing in the middle of the bathroom, still dripping all over the place, when the door opens and Robin walks in.

"I'm not gonna look," she says. She's holding a hand up to her face but I can see a little space between her fingers and the watery glitter of her eye behind it. There's a clean towel in her free hand and she's holding it out toward me. I take it and wrap it around my middle.

"Your stuff's in the dryer," she says. "You hungry?"

"A little."

"I'm makin' baked mac 'n cheese. It's in the oven right now but it'll be done in, like, fifteen/twenty minutes." She exhales smoke, but turns her head left so's not to blow it in my face. "Maybe you could take a nap 'til it's done?"

I don't know what to say because I'm more nervous than tired right now, but I can't stand in the filthy bathroom anymore so I follow Robin to a doorway in the middle of the hallway and walk in behind her. There's a kids-size bed pushed up against a wall but no light so it's hard to see anything else except piles of stuff all over the floor.

"I'm not that tired," I say.

"Yeah, right," she tells me, staring right into my eyes with a funny smile. I turn away and look toward the bed, then lean down on it. It's been three months since I slept on a real bed. This one's tiny, but right now it feels voluptuous.

I lay down on it all the way and within seconds I'm out like a light.

ꕥ

When I wake up, I'm struggling to breathe and for a second I feel like it's because I'm having a panic attack but then I realize there's a terrible smell coming from somewhere and when I look out into the hallway alls I see is smoke.

"I think something's burning," I say.

From the living room, I can hear a beer can hit the ground followed by Robin yelling "Ah, shit!"

She stumbles into the kitchen and turns off the oven, which has thick black smoke pumping out of it. My eyes are all watered-up so it's hard to see, but I find the back door and open it before making my way all around the tiny house, tripping over plates and bottles while opening up the windows. I'm still only wearing a towel so when I'm done, I pull my clothes out of the dryer and walk back to the bathroom. The clothes are not completely dry, but it doesn't matter. I get dressed quickly then carry what I'm not wearing out to the car.

It's dark out. I'm teary-eyed and having trouble breathing because of all the smoke. There's the sound of somebody coughing behind me and then Robin comes out through the front door and sits down on the top step.

"Sorry, I conked out on the couch," she says, then coughs again. "I bet if we scrape the burnt parts off, the mac 'n cheese'll still be good. Whaddya think?"

"I gotta go to work."

"Right now?"

I'm standing on the dirt lawn and looking up at her and I'm completely confused. There is one part of me that wants to run away but another part that wants to sit down next to her and tell her stuff, and listen to her tell me stuff. Instead, I just stand there for another minute.

"I know the house is gross," she says. "I'm gonna clean it, eventually. Someday. We've had a lot goin' on here lately, though. I don't know if Jimmy told'ja."

What Jimmy told me was that their mom died a few months ago. It was the thing that made us be friends, I think. My mom died when I was in high school, so I was sort of able to tell how he was feeling.

"We got insurance money from it but Mom's lawyer tried to rip us off, so we had to get another one," she says. "The money's still coming but prolly not 'til September. I'm figuring I'll start cleanin' up toward the end of August."

Alls I can do is nod.

"C'mon, come back inside and have dinner with me," Robin says. "Twenty bucks says you're hungrier than I am." She coughs, then adds: "You're definitely lonelier."

ꕥ

The black stuff peels off the top of the mac 'n cheese pretty easily, and although the rest of it's a little dry, it's not bad if you dip it in ketchup. I'm starving anyway so I eat two bowls of it on the back porch while Robin smokes cigarettes and drinks beer in the chair across from me.

"Jimmy talks about you a lot," she says. "I sorta remember you from school but I graduated the year before you and him were seniors. Your hair was always fucked-up and you looked like you were stoned all the time, that's alls I remember."

"I wasn't ever stoned."

"It's what you looked like."

I don't like to think about high school because it wasn't much fun. My mom was sick for a long time and for a long time after she died, I pretty much just wanted to die too. It wasn't until Dad kicked me out of the house and I got the job at the theater that I really felt like I even wanted to be part of the regular world again.

When I'm done eating, I volunteer to do the dishes but doing the dishes only makes me want to clean the kitchen, so I do that, and with Robin's permission, I gather up all the trash from the bedroom and the living room and haul it out to the curb in clunky white trash bags. The entire house still needs to be rubbed down with some kind of de-greaser and vacuumed, but it's getting late and I have to go to work soon.

"I'd love to stay and clean the bathroom," I say, meaning it.

"Come back tomorrow and do it," she says. We are standing in the living room and she is looking at me in a way that's both pleading and confused. "Seriously—come back, OK?"

"For sure," I say.

❧

The mess at the theater is impossible to explain; I feel weak and insignificant before it, like I'm having some kinda existential crisis. There's no time for that kinda crap, though. I was running too late to stop by the diner for coffee before work, but I'm so hyped to have taken a shower and eaten a home-cooked meal that I'm able to clean like I've never cleaned before.

It felt kind of energizing to have met Robin too, but I should mention that I don't really like girls. I mean I like them and respect them and like being friends with them, but I don't like them beyond that. I'm not sure I like guys either, but I get the feeling sometimes that later on I might. More importantly, it's been a long time since I had a truly best friend and I would be really interested in having one right now.

The sun is just coming up through the windows in the lobby when I carry out the final trash bag. I go back inside to lock everything up but instead of going out to my car and driving away, I lay down in the lobby and fall asleep with the whirr and grind of the *Make the Bear Be Nice* standee echoing behind me.

ཌྷ

What wakes me up is the sound of something banging against the window. I stand and grab the broom beside the couch and make like I'm sweeping for a second, but then I stop and look around. The front door is still closed and there's no sign of Miss Ellie.

There's another BANG against the window.

Slowly, I move toward the curtains and pull them apart. What I see is the big round face of my dad staring in at me. He waves for me to come outside.

ཌྷ

"I want'cha to come home," is what he tells me. We're sitting on the curb outside the movie theater and I have no idea what time it is. Alls I know is it's early.

"I'm gettin' an apartment next week," I tell him. It might not be a lie. If my check is as big as I'm hoping it will be, I should probably have enough for a down payment on my own place. When I think about it, I can almost smell it: it will smell clean and nice and also it will be very quiet.

"Oh, so now alla sudden you're all grown up, right?" Dad says. "Gonna get your own apartment and all that. Who the hell's gonna rent a place to you?" He pauses to light a cigarette before adding, "You're just a little friggin' punk."

His car is parked next to mine in the parking lot. Every once in a while, a car passes on Multiplex Road but none of them belong to Miss Ellie.

"I'm not a punk," is what I tell him. "Mom always said I was smart."

It's quiet for a long time and I'm able to think about the house and Dad and how different things have been since Mom died. When she was there, I never thought about leaving; I only thought about going to college and studying to be a teacher, which I think would be a great job for me. But after she was gone, Dad got quiet for a few months and then he turned mean. It wasn't long before the only thing on my mind was running away.

"Alright, you're not a punk," Dad says. "If your mother heard me say that, she'd punch me in the mouth." He shakes his head a little, then huffs out a big smoky breath and adds, "I don't mean to be such a jerkoff. You lost your mom, but I lost my wife. I known her since I was your age and..." He pauses to rub his face. "You just don't know what it's like."

"I need to get my own place," I tell him.

It takes a while for him to respond. "No, you don't," he says. "You got a place; I ain't even stepped foot in your room since you left. I got money in the bank, but I got nothin' to spend it on. I don't even drink anymore; I just work and go to sleep." He puts his hand on my shoulder for a second and I'm scared he's gonna hug me, but instead he just stands up and says, "It's been three years—three years since she died. If she knew how things turned out, she'd...she'd kick me in the friggin' nuts." He crushes out his cigarette before adding: "I'm only tryna say I'm sorry."

I can tell he wants to look me in the eyes, so I just keep staring at my hands which are sticky and red in spots from touching melted candy.

"Whenever you're ready," he says, "you come home. I ain't goin' anywhere else, so you know where to find me."

When I look up his eyes are all bloodshot and watery. We stare at each other for a second and then his hand comes out toward me. I have just reached out to shake it when Miss Ellie's car pulls into the lot.

ꕥ

I drive out to the woods across from Aunt Bette's house and sleep until it's dark. There's still plenty of time before I have to get back to the theater, so I drive to Jimmy's house to see if Robin might want to get dinner. The front door is open and I can see her drinking beer on the couch.

"Come in," she says. "I was thinking of you earlier so I went out and bought all kindsa cleanin' stuff."

This is without a doubt the most thoughtful thing anyone's done for me in a long time.

"There's some bread and cheese and stuff if you wanna make a sandwich," she adds.

"Oh yeah? I'm pretty hungry—I could prob'ly eat three of 'em."

Together, we finish half a loaf of bread and all the cheese in the fridge. When we're done, we go through everything she got at the grocery store, which feels like genuine treasure: there's a big bottle of Colonel Pine's Pine-Scented All-Purpose Cleanser, a 12-pack of Generally Nice Brand paper towels, a Bonus-Pack of Jonny-Sponge rainbow-colored sponges, and a couple more bags full of bathroom, kitchen, and multi-use cleaning supplies and implements. Together, we start scrubbing down the kitchen, though after a few minutes Robin sort of sits down on the kitchen table, smoking a steady stream of cigarettes while I continue cleaning. It's a long time before either of us says anything, but in between our eyes meet a couple times and I smile a little and so does she.

ꕥ

I head off to work a little later, and as I'm pulling into the diner for some coffee, I realize I haven't seen Jimmy since he gave me the key to his house. He nods to me when I step inside and joins me at a booth a few minutes later.

"So what's it like fuckin' my sister?" is the first thing he says to me.

Jimmy's eyes are red and there is sweat all over his arms and hands. He has been working for fourteen hours straight but he doesn't look tired at all: he looks insane.

"That definitely didn't happen," I say.

"Liar."

He winks and slurps from the coffee cup in front of him.

"I'm serious," I say. "She's pretty cool, though."

"I know," Jimmy says. "I'm just ridin' ya. I know you're a decent kid, you ain't like that. The problem is girls are animals. Guys like me an' you don't have a chance against 'em. If you got money, they'll take it. If you ain't got that, they'll just take somethin' else—your balls or your brains or both. It's a scientific fact: *Girls make you dumb.* Look it up."

I'm not sure where Jimmy got this information from and I definitely don't agree with it but I nod anyway, mostly because he looks even more bonkers than usual.

"Look, Robin's a goofball but she's my sister and I love 'er." He looks me square in the eye then adds: "Don't get 'er upset, OK? We been through a lot this year."

"I definitely won't."

He is taking another slurp of his coffee when a man with a gigantic moustache leans out of the kitchen and says, "Hey Jimmy, break over." He disappears before he can see Jimmy holding up his middle finger.

"I'm gonna wrap a fuckin' plate around somebody's face tonight, just wait," he says. "We'll talk later."

He gets up and puts his apron on but I stay in the booth to finish my coffee, which tastes really refreshing and nice.

When I get done work in the morning I drive to the mall and steal some CDs then listen to them while driving to Glendora. As I'm turning onto my old street, I realize that this is the first time I've been this close to the house since Dad kicked me out. I was only meaning to drive past it—just to see if it still looks the same—but when I see his car is not in the driveway I pull up in front of the curb and just sit there for a minute with the engine still running. The lawn has not been mowed all summer and the grass looks like a jungle, with burnt patches spread out all over it. The little flower garden beside the steps is totally overrun with weeds and there is a giant wasp nest hanging down next to the gutter near the driveway.

I turn off the engine and get out of the car, heading straight for the garden.

Half an hour later, I'm still kneeling in the dirt with my hands all dried-out and black and I'm sweating from the heat of the sun on my head. It takes almost two hours to finish pulling all the weeds. When I'm done, I grab the hose from the side of the house and give the whole garden a good watering because I know there are still flowers in there somewhere.

After taking a long drink from the hose, I walk to the backyard and pull the lawnmower from the shed. The gas tank is more than half-full and the engine starts on the first pull. It takes a while to get through the backyard because there are a lot of rocks beneath the grass and they keep getting caught and shutting down the engine. Also, one of them flies out and hits me right in the balls, and for a second it feels like I got stabbed with a knife there. I step behind the shed for a quick exam and everything looks alright, but it still aches a little.

I check the clock on my dashboard when I'm done with the front lawn and am surprised by how much time has passed: It's almost three o'clock, and my entire body is coated with a film of dirt and sweat. I take another drink from the hose then give the grass a good watering before climbing back into my car. For a while, I just stare at the house, because it would be nice to go inside and take a shower but even though I still have a key—it's jingling right there on my keyring right now—there's no way I'm ever gonna step into that house again.

ꕤ

There is no answer at Robin's house and I'm about to walk back to my car when the door suddenly opens and she is there. Only one of her eyes is open and there is a sheet covered with pictures of giraffes wrapped around her.

"Were you, like, rollin' around in a dumpster?" she asks.

"I mowed my dad's lawn," I tell her.

She yawns and says, "I was up 'til like nine this mornin'. Jimmy freaked out and kicked a hole in the wall last night and then we just sat around drinkin' 'til he had to go to work."

"You want me to come back later?"

"No, stay here. Take a shower and then come talk with me on the back porch."

I say "Alright" and then follow her into the house.

There is no way I can take a shower until the bathtub is cleaned so I fill the tub with hot water and bleach and throw the shower curtain into it. While it's soaking, I scrub out the toilet and clean the walls and mirrors, then sweep out all the trash that's gathered on the floor. When I'm finished mopping, I drain the tub and scrub it. All the nasty stains are gone from the shower curtain, and by the time I step into the shower and turn on the water, the whole bathroom looks and smells like new.

ᘓᘐ

It's almost eight o'clock when my stomach starts growling from hunger. We are sitting on the back porch and Robin is smoking a cigarette.

"Dude, you gotta start eatin' more regular," she says, tapping my belly. "That thing's tryna tell you somethin'."

"Maybe we could go out somewhere?" I say.

"That's cool, except I gotta bring Jimmy's car to the diner. I drove him in this morning, he was too fuckin' drunk to drive."

I shake my head.

Robin says, "You prob'ly think I'm a lazy bum but the thing is I don't need a job right now—what I need is time to think. I want the next part of my life to be better than the last part, and I got this time right now to think about how I'm gonna make that happen." She taps out her cigarette, then adds: "Anyway, things are gonna change once that money comes."

"I totally never thought you were a bum."

"I know it, and I know I don't need to tell *you* this, but I got nothin' to hide and I don't need any judgment."

I nod because losing somebody affects everybody different and even after all this time, I still don't know how to put it into words.

It's almost a full minute later when I ask: "If youse got money comin' why is Jimmy working so much?"

"It's 'cuz he's *fucking nuts.* I don't mind that part, though—there's no way I'd be able to live here if he wasn't gone half the day." She fakes a shiver, then adds: "Soon as we get that money though, I'm gettin' my own place. Nothin' fancy, ya know? Just a place in like Woodbury or Haddon Heights, somewhere I feel good and safe and can think about what I'm gonna do next."

"That's almost exactly how I feel about living right now," I tell her, and it's the truth.

"Maybe we could find a place together?" she says.

It takes me a minute but after thinking about it I tell her: "No, I don't think that's a good idea. Not now."

"But we could live somewhere close," she says.

"Yeah," I say. "I can picture that."

ꕥ

We could go almost anywhere to eat but because the diner is so close and Robin has to bring the car there, it's where we go. We get fries and grilled cheese sandwiches and we're almost finished when Jimmy sits down next to Robin and pours the entire contents of a small bottle of Yukon Jack into a glass. He winks and taps the glass against my coffee cup then takes a drink.

"Look, I got a plan," he says. "I been thinkin' about it all day. I was gonna do it myself but since youse are here, maybe we could all do it together."

"Do what?" Robin asks.

I look at Robin who looks at Jimmy who nods at both of us and smiles.

"I wanna go to the movies," he says. "There's a 9:30 show—if we leave in like fifteen minutes, we could definitely make it."

"What movie?" I ask.

"Dude," Jimmy says. "You know what movie."

Robin starts shaking her head right away. "No, no, no, no fuckin' way," she says. "There's no way I'm payin' to see that stupid bear."

There is saliva hanging out of both sides of Jimmy's mouth and his hair is totally slick with sweat. His eyes are bulging and staring into my face. He leans forward a little.

"I think I can get us in for free," is alls I can say.

ꕥ

The line for tickets is very long, so I lead Jimmy and Robin around to the back of the theater and use my key to get in through the entrance behind the dumpster. This opens up into the front of Theater Six, so we sneak out into the hallway and down to Theater 4. There are no ushers around and because the place is so packed, nobody really notices us.

The movie is not very good. The story is so flat you can pretty much tell what every actor's gonna say before they even say it. Still, the crowd seems enchanted, and when the bear tells the girl he's sorry for blowing up the washing machine and that he loves her, you can even hear some kids start to cry.

Jimmy is sitting to my left and groaning out loud through most of the movie. Every once in a while, somebody turns around and says "Shhh!" but Jimmy just gives them the finger or tells them to buzz off. Robin is on my right and every time Jimmy says something I can feel her tense up.

We are a little over an hour into the movie when, pretty much outta nowhere, Jimmy says, loudly: "Fuck you, Bear."

On the screen, the girl's dad is pointing at the bear and yelling. The bear's eyes are all moist and the little girl is holding his hand. Inside the theater, several people have turned around to look at us.

"THE FUCKA YOU LOOKIN' AT?" Jimmy yells at them. "I AIN'T TALKIN' TO YOU—I'M TALKIN' TO THE BEAR."

A man right in front of us stands suddenly, blocking out the screen. There are kids on both sides of him and they are both crying and shouting "DADDY, NOOOO!"

"Listen," the man says, waving his finger in Jimmy's face. "I've had just about enough of you—"

Jimmy grabs the finger and twists it up.

There is a snapping sound and right after that, the man lets out a howl that makes the whole theater erupt in nervous chaos; some people begin running for the doors while others yell for everyone to shut up and calm down.

Jimmy stands and pushes the man in front of us to the floor, which knocks the giant tub of popcorn on his armrest into the air, spraying popcorn everywhere. I try to grab Jimmy's arm but he pushes me aside and lifts a giant-sized cup of soda from the seat next to him then hurls it at the screen. The bear is just hopping onto a bicycle and riding away from the house when the soda hits: It makes a thunderous *SPLASH!* but on top of that you can hear everybody in the crowd shouting "NO!" and "STOP IT!"

There is soda spilling all down the bear's face when he crashes into a tree and starts to cry.

"YOU FUCKIN' PEOPLE ARE IDIOTS," Jimmy hollers above everything, and with real sincerity in his voice. "THIS IS THE STUPIDEST FUCKIN' MOVIE EVER MADE, AND YOU *KNOW* IT!"

He's in the aisle now, and the light from the screen gives a clear view of his silhouette reaching in toward the seats and knocking buckets of popcorn all over the floor. A few people try to grab him but he only shoves them away.

"FUCK THE BEAR!" he screams above all the other screams. "MAKE THE BEAR GET FUCKED! YOU GUYS ARE SUCH FUCKIN' IDIOTS!"

He is all the way up in the front of the theater now, jumping up at the screen and banging his fists against it. I'm kind of in shock and also scared that I might get in trouble because I helped Jimmy get in for free, but at the same time it's pretty dark in here and everyone is pretty much in shadow. Plus, there's just so many people and it's hard to move until all of a sudden I feel Robin pulling at my arm and the next thing I know we are both running down the aisle toward the screen. By this time the entire audience is on their feet and several people are trying to pull Jimmy to the ground. He throws some punches then grabs somebody's arm and bites it.

There is blood all over his face and his fists when Robin grabs him from behind and starts pulling him toward the front EXIT. I'm right behind her, holding onto her shirt, and I have to use my elbows and also kick some people to keep them from stopping us.

As soon as we're outside, I start running around the building toward the parking lot. Jimmy is screaming "DIE MOTHERFUCKER" over and over, but it's Robin's hand I feel on my arm as we turn the corner and make a beeline to my car.

Jimmy is still screaming when I start the engine and screech out toward Multiplex Road.

ꙮ

It feels like a lot of time has passed but it's really only just after eleven when I pull into the dirt outside of Jimmy's house. He's not screaming anymore but he's mumbling and crying and when me and Robin try dragging him into the house, he bites my leg and kicks Robin in the chest so we just leave him in the dirt and go inside.

"You see that?" she says. She's nodding out toward the driveway as she shakes a can of beer sitting on top of the TV. "That happens three, four times a week. I mean it's not always at the movies or in public? But there's always something he's goin' over the top about. When Mom was still here, she used to punch him—I mean she'd just like haul off and punch him in the face. Sometimes it knocked him out cold." She takes a drink from the can and tells me: "Maybe that's what it is—maybe he got brain damage from all them punchouts."

I'm almost scared to leave her alone when it's time to go to work, but Robin says it's alright. She locks the door as soon as I'm out.

When I get to the car, Jimmy is still lying beside it.

"Jimmy," I say.

One of his eyes opens but he doesn't say anything. It's a little chilly out and I can't just leave him here in the dirt, so I half-lift, half-drag him onto the porch then cover him with a blanket from my back seat.

There are a pair of police cars in the parking lot at the theater when I arrive, so I park near the back of the lot and walk toward the front door. Miss Ellie is standing outside with her hands on her hips and a big frown on her face. She asks me if I know anything about what happened at the 9:30 showing of *Make the Bear be Nice* but I tell her "No."

"The screen in Theater 4 is wrecked," she tells me. There's a cop standing right behind her and although I should be scared, I'm not. "Just clean it up like you usually do, but leave the screen alone. We'll have to see about getting a new one this week." She looks pale and sick and when she puts her hand on my shoulder, I jump a little. "This whole fuckin' bear thing has been a nightmare," she tells me.

Alls I can do is nod. The cop behind her starts asking her questions, so I walk down the hallway and pull the leaf-blower out of the closet. As far as I'm concerned, it's time to get to work.

ꕥ

The cops linger for another hour or so, but by the time I've got the first three theaters cleaned up, the place is empty. In the morning, I drive to a convenience store on Route 41 and carry a pair of coffees back out to the car. I also buy a newspaper, and am not surprised to find the incident at the movie theater reported on the front of the Local News section.

Jimmy is still on the porch, curled up in the blanket when I pull into the driveway.

"What time's it?" he asks.

"Almost eight."

"I'm late for work."

"I can drive you there if you want," I say, "but it might be better if you just call in sick."

I tell him about the story in the newspaper: What it says is that there will be an official investigation and that if anybody knows anything about what happened, they should call the Deptford Police.

"Fuckit," he says, taking a sip of the coffee while rubbing his head. "Fuck the fuckin' diner, I quit. I shoulda quit a long time ago."

"Maybe you oughta take a vacation," I tell him. "Just a couple days, ya know? You could go to the beach."

"Maybe, yeah," he replies. "You're right, I should take a break. I think I'm tryna kill myself."

"You don't deserve that."

"You're right. I don't."

I help him stand up. He's weaving a little, so I help him with his housekey and hold him tight as I push the door open. The sound of Robin snoring from the little bedroom echoes through the house.

Jimmy stomps toward the couch and flops down onto it.

"I got another plan," he says, pointing his finger toward the ceiling. "If that movie's still out when I get back? I'm gonna rent a bear-suit and stand outside the theater. When the kids come up to shake my hand, I'm gonna just…push 'em down."

"You might feel different later," I say.

"Ummph."

I wait until his breathing levels out before walking down the short hallway to the little bedroom. Robin is curled up under the giraffe sheet and when I lay down next to her, she squeaks then wraps her arm around my neck and presses her face up to the side of my head. This is how I fall asleep.

In the afternoon when we wake up, Jimmy is gone.

༄༅

My big check comes on Thursday, and by then I've already got my apartment picked out. It's right off of Haddon Avenue in Haddonfield, and even though most places there are kind of expensive, this one's totally in my range, with the heat and hot water included. It's not very big: there is one big room with a kitchen in it and then a little back room with a window that is totally blocked out by a big tree outside. As soon as I step into the place, I know it's meant for me. I have my checkbook with me and the landlord is only too happy to take a down payment. When I get back to my car I have to laugh out loud because this is totally like a dream come true. It's so great.

༄༅

Four days later, Jimmy calls home from somewhere down the Jersey shore.

"He says he got a job makin' pizzas but he'll come back to deal with the insurance stuff when it's time," Robin tells me, hanging up the phone. "I can't tell if he sounded happy or drunk."

"It was totally both."

"Oh, right."

We are sitting on the edge of the couch a little later, watching a Phillies game, when she says, "You still gonna come see me after you move into your new place?"

"Oh, yeah, absolutely," I say, meaning it.

"I don't know how to feel about you, but I know it feels good to be together."

I feel exactly the same way, and when her hand touches mine it starts off like a handshake but it's a long time before either one of us lets go. It's a pretty good feeling.

༄༅

I get the key to the apartment on Monday. It takes me twenty minutes to move all the stuff from my car to the apartment, and I spend the next couple of hours roaming the junk shops in Collingswood, looking for furniture. I only find one small table but later on, before work, I stop and grab a futon mattress from a second-hand store in Runnemede. It takes a minute to fold it up into the trunk but once it's in and I'm back in the car, heading to the movie theater, I know I'm set.

I spend the whole night daydreaming of sleeping in my own place: *In this dream, I wake up and drink a cup of coffee while listening to the radio and thinking about the day ahead. It's just a regular day, but even though it seems normal, there's still a chance that something great might happen.*

Eventually there is a knock on the door and when I answer it, Robin is there. She's carrying a couple of books and wants to go down to the café on the corner to have breakfast. This sounds like a great idea, so I lock the door and follow her out onto the sidewalk. I'll have to go to work later but there's a lotta time before that, so almost anything could happen ...

I wake up just as I'm carrying the last bag of trash out to the dumpster. The key feels weightless in my pocket, and I seriously just cannot wait to get home.

"He moves the bottle away from her reach, laughing and shaking his head..."

(from Street Smart #7, The Day is Gone by Shelonda Montgomery

#7 The Day is Gone

Shelonda Montgomery

The Ditch

"He dead?"

"Don't know."

"Looks dead to me."

"Lips all purple like he dead. Eyes open," Walter says, eating a red freeze-pop which is now just juice.

He and Earl look at Charlie Jackson, a man from their neighborhood. Walter's little brother Lawrence sits on the gate and tries to stretch his neck so he can see. Walter lets the freeze-pop go. It hangs from his lips. Charlie's body lies in the ditch, his mouth and eyes open. A bloody sheet covers half of his naked body. His chest and head are out and flies swarm around his open eyes and mouth, buzzing loud.

Charlie owned a grocery store that sells a bunch of the usual things: bread, butter, cold cuts, hog head cheese, milk, corn bread, and hot corn chips. Walter and Lawrence's mother Norah regularly buys milk and two pounds of ground beef from Charlie's store. Several people in their neighborhood have died in recent weeks, which Norah hates. Today it's Charlie. Last week it was Ann Turner, a local laundromat owner.

"They killed Ann," Norah had told her husband Thomas, who shook his head in disbelief. Norah, Thomas, Walter, Lawrence, and Fay, the baby, live in apartment 603 in one of high-rise projects. The hallway smells like urine because people frequently urinate there.

It had been different when Thomas and Norah first moved into the building. The halls were pristine. The floors were urine-free. Someone urinating on them would have made a person call someone's grandmother, and their grandmother would have made them clean it up. Back then, the mere sight of a chewed-up clump of gum on the hallway floor would have warranted a stern finger wagging. The neighborhood itself was not the best, but it was better than many. The people were not always the friendliest, but they looked out for one another. There was a common respect. A common decency. There were no discarded dead men in ditches. Back then, Norah and Thomas were young and happy and full of life. They married soon after meeting and then they had Walter. In time, Lawrence was born. Then Fay. They were happy. They laughed and loved in their small apartment.

Today Norah had let Walter and Lawrence walk home from school because Walter often asked to be allowed. In the past, Norah had always said "No."

"Norah, let the boys go," Thomas had said this morning.

Norah looked at the boys long and hard. "Yes, but go to school and come straight home," she told them.

When they got out of school, Walter said they were going to take a short cut home with his friend and classmate Earl, who also lives in their building.

"Why his lips always dry and peeling, like his Mama don't ever give him no grease?" Lawrence whispered to Walter about Earl as they walked from the school. Walter flicked Lawrence's head in response.

Earl gets off of his bike, puts it down, and climbs over it, still holding the handlebars. He walks over toward the ditch to get a closer look, picks up a rock, and throws it at Charlie. The rock bounces off Charlie's shoulder and lands on the grass. They all watch to see if he moves. He does not. The ditch is shallow, and if someone stands near the edge, they will fall in. Lawrence starts climbing down off the gate.

"I said stay right there! If you get up, I'm 'gone pop you upside your head," Walter yells.

Lawrence sits down.

"I wanna' see," Lawrence says. The other boys ignore him.

"I think he dead, too," Earl says, his half-smooched lint ball-filled hair is thick all over his head as if his mother does not comb it.

"Looks dead," Walter says, tilting his head to look at Charlie. His shoelaces are untied.

"Touch him," Earl says, scratching his face.

"I ain't touching him! You touch him!" Walter says.

"I *know* I ain't touchin' that man!" Lawrence says.

Walter quickly turns around and stares him down. "I ain't touching him!" Walter says again, this time as if he is mad.

Walter walks over, gets a stick, and starts poking Charlie; the freeze pop is swinging back and forth, hanging from his mouth between his teeth. He pokes Charlie's chest.

Earl watches closely. Walter takes the freeze pop out of his mouth, "Did he move?"

"Don't think so," Earl says, kneeling with his hands on his knees, his feet wide apart, to get a better look, balancing himself on the sides of his blue sneakers.

Walter hands Earl the stick, rubs his hand together, with all fingers spread out, and wipes them on his worn-out blue jeans, knees faded white and starting to tear.

Earl, his eyes bugged out, takes the stick and slowly pokes Charlie in his side. They stand still, waiting for him to move.

"Can I do it?" Lawrence asks Walter.

"Nope," Walter says, his eyes focused on Charlie.

"He dead; bet the police did it. My daddy say the police always killing black folks. Bet the police did this," Walter explains, walking up real close and looking into Charlie's stale wide-open eyes. Dark, dried and fresh, bright red blood are in the corners of his mouth. "Yeah, he dead."

"How you know?" Earl asks.

"Look at his eyes," Walter says pointing. "He dead and that's how stuff be looking when it be dead. He dead. Saw a dead bird and a dead cat. Once even saw a dead bullfrog in the middle of a road. His back half was crushed by a car. His mouth was open and eyes was looking *just* like that. All dead and gone. Glassy and full of tears that's about to fall but don't."

Earl puts his hands on the knees of his brown corduroy pants and looks real close, but is careful not to tilt over and fall on Charlie.

"He stink!" Walter says, frowning and fanning his nose. Earl frowns and nods, agreeing. Although he does not smell anything, Lawrence fans his nose too.

Earl gets on his bike and starts riding real slow, so slow that the pedals shake.

"Come on," Walter says. Lawrence grabs his book bag and runs to him. They walk beside Earl. Walter leans his head back and drinks the rest of his freeze pop, his shoelaces dragging behind him as he walks.

ꕤ

Of all the police officers in Chicago, the department only sends two to the crime scene. Charlie's wife, Lana, was told that he was dead and ran out crying on Fourteenth Place without shoes, her hair undone and standing out like tired weeds all over her head.

"Lord, please help him!" she says, running through the crowd.

Lawrence watches from the kitchen window, sitting on Norah's lap, playing with her hand, holding his blue and white spin top.

Norah bought the blue and white spin top for Lawrence when they were at the grocery store together earlier in the day. There was candy inside of the package as well.

"You're eating that candy *too fast,*" Norah said, as she watched Lawrence tear into the package, grab the candy, and stuff it into his mouth until his jaws protruded like a squirrel harboring nuts. Walter ate some of his candy very slowly and put the rest into his pocket. He has been eating it throughout the day.

"No," he said to Lawrence, when he asked if he could have some. Fay chewed on the corner of her unopened bag of candy. She put the plastic corner in her mouth and chewed very slow. Norah took it from her and put it on the top cabinet shelf beside a white box that's partially covered with brown, dried-up water stains. The box is filled with old plastic spoons and forks.

"Can I have some of Fay's candy, Momma?" Lawrence asked Norah

"No, sit on down and eat your own, boy," she said. Lawrence stood and looked at Fay's candy with his head held back, and thought about the best ways he could climb the cabinet and get the candy.

Fay, wearing a pink shirt with a bird on it, now sits with her nose pressed against the kitchen window. Her hair is full of braids with pink barrettes on the tips that match her shirt. She has a dried-up jelly stain on her cheek.

"What are you looking at?" Norah says to Fay.

She puts Lawrence down and he drops his blue and white spin top. It rolls on its side across the floor. Norah walks over and looks at the crowd of people gathered beneath their window.

"What's going on out there?" she asks, looking down at the crowd. Lawrence sits on the floor under the table and tries to reach his spin top. He sees it under the radiator behind his mother's leg. Norah looks at Fay's face, gets a napkin, wets it, and wipes off the jelly stain. She looks out of the window again.

"I wonder what is going on," she says with her pinky finger in some dust that's in the corner of the brown, paint-chipped windowsill.

"Must have found Mr. Jackson," Walter says, looking down at a sheet of paper, doing his homework. He puts his pencil down. "Nineteen, twenty, twenty-one, twenty-two, twenty-three," he says counting on his fingers. He erases an answer and writes in a new one.

"Mama," Lawrence says, trying to reach past Norah's leg to get his top.

"What do you mean…they must have found Mr. Jackson?" Norah asks, her eyes wide open, and her head to the side.

"Someone killed him," Walter says, looking at his paper and writing. "Been in the ditch all day. Me, Lawrence, and Earl saw him hours ago," he says, writing with his head down. "We *been* found him, Mama. The police be too late for stuff," he adds, curving his lips and scrunching his nose.

"What? Walter! Look at me!"

Walter looks at Norah, his fingers wrapped around his orange pencil tight. His eyes are big. His other hand is flat on the paper as if the wind is going to come through the window and blow it off the table.

"What...do...you...mean...you, Lawrence, and Earl found him?" Norah says with her eyes blinking mad. She's holding a blue and white worn-out checkered dishcloth, from which strings hang and water drips as she moves her hand.

"Someone killed him and threw him in the ditch. We found him. The police probably did it," Walter says as he starts slowly writing a crooked "49" on his paper, trying to make it straight.

"Mama," Lawrence says, looking up at Norah from under the table, wanting her to move so that he can retrieve his spin top. She does not move; rather she unknowingly stands in his way as he tries to reach the toy. Norah stares at Walter, her eyes wide and still.

"Mama!" Lawrence yells, looking up at her on his hands and knees.

Thomas walks in from work. Fay runs over to him, wobbling as if she is about to fall. He grabs her and picks her up.

"Why are you just telling me this now?" Norah says to Walter. "And my baby was out there, too. Did he see it?"

"I guess...Mr. Jackson was dead, Mama. His lips was all purple. I bet the police did it," Walter says again, shaking his head and looking at his homework. He puts the pencil's eraser on his lips and reads the next math problem.

"What happened?" Thomas asks.

"Charlie Jackson was killed. Walter, Lawrence, and Earl found him long before the police did, and Walter is just now telling me."

"What? Is that what all that mess is out there? Street full of people," Thomas says looking out of the window from across the room as he slowly puts Fay down, letting her feet drop to the floor. She reaches up for him to pick her up again, but he stretches his neck like an ostrich and looks toward the window.

"Yes. And Walter and Lawrence found him. And did not tell me anything. I see all those people out there," Norah says, pointing to the window, "and Walter says they were out there because of Charlie Jackson. Walter, you don't keep that stuff to yourself! You understand me? You tell me when you see stuff like that!"

"Where was he, Walter?" Thomas asks.-

"In the ditch. Dead. Somebody killed him," Walter says.

"What did you and Lawrence do?"

"I made Lawrence sit on the gate. Then Earl and me poked Charlie with a stick. Then we all went to the store. Earl bought a juice 'cause his Mama gave him a quarter this morning. I brought Lawrence and me some bags of chips. Hot ones. Didn't have enough for juice and chips because I was seven cents short."

"You could have gotten yourself and your brother hurt out there,

Walter!" Norah says. "Did you touch him?"

"Noooooooooo," he says shaking his head. "I wasn't touchin' him. He was dead, Mama. And he was stinkin'," he adds, frowning and writing.

Thomas walks to the window and looks out. He is wearing his work uniform and worn-out steel-toe boots. The steel part is partially showing through the ripped and worn leather.

Charlie Jackson's body is still in the ditch with the white sheet covering it. There is yellow tape around the crime scene. The two cops walk around the body as if they are busy working, but they are not. They look at their watches and write on their note pads. Hundreds of people stand around and attempt to look at Charlie and gossip about who they think did it. They stand, try to look past the police, frown hard, and whisper in each other's ears. Then they stand with their noses turned up and their arms crossed, as if they had solved the murder.

Thomas shakes his head, his hands deep in his pockets fidgeting with his keys, which jangle and bang against coins.

Outside, Lana tries to run through the police tape, but a man grabs her. She falls to her knees, screaming. The man holds her around her waist in order to restrain her.

Norah shifts a little. Lawrence reaches for his spin top. Norah quickly picks him up so that he does not burn his hand on the radiator.

A Needed Change

"We have to get out of here, Thomas. This is too much," Norah says, tying her scarf on her head and looking in the bathroom mirror, preparing for bed. It is 10:34 pm. She turns around and looks at Thomas, who sits on the bathtub without a shirt, wearing brown slacks which are unbutton, his bare feet pressed against the white and black linoleum floor. "The kids didn't need to see that…and Walter did not tell us…did not say one thing…like it was nothing," she continues.

"They've seen stuff like that before," Thomas says.

Sheturnstohimandlookshiminhiseyes."Theyain'tneverseenadeadbody! They don't need to see that! We have to get these kids out of here!" He looks at her tired face, her frown lines growing deeper and dark circles forming around her bulging eyes. He stands up, hugs her tight, and rubs the back of her head. Then he closes his eyes and rests his head on hers.

"That's what you want?" he says rubbing her shoulder. She nods. They both stand silent. "Then we'll get out of here. I'm going to do everything in my power to get us out of here," he says, his eyes still closed as he slowly sways with her.

Norah smiles and wraps her arms around his bare waist, his body slim and muscular; his skin, a deep hickory, is warm, sweaty, and soft.

"We'll get out of here, OK?" He looks down at her round face and small eyes, her short and heavy frame. "OK, Baby?" he asks. She nods with her head deep in his chest. He kisses her scarfed head.

Peanut Butter and Jelly

"Boy, get down from there!" Thomas yells.

Walter is standing on the kitchen table, holding an open loaf of white bread. The bread bag swings in one hand. The red twist tie is in his other. Thomas stares him down.

"What are you doing up there?"

Walter looks at his father and does not say a word, his eyes wide and sweat forming on his forehead. "Get down!" Thomas says again, blinking and struggling to adjust his eyes to the light. He stands there in his tan pajamas. He was on his way to the bathroom but stopped when he saw Walter.

"What are you doing up there?"

"Making a peanut butter and jelly sandwich," Walter says, his voice low and soft, nervously trawling the twist tie between his fingers. "Peanut butter up there," he says, pointing to the wooden cabinet above the kitchen table.

"You gone hurt yourself. It's 2:38am in the morning," Thomas says, looking at the clock hanging near the sink. "Come here." Walter walks across the table barefoot and stands there, his toes trembling as they peer over the table's edge. Thomas lifts him down.

"What if you would have hurt yourself?" Thomas asks. Walter stands silently, looking at the wooden cabinet, then the floor.

Thomas stares at him. Walter stands there in his dark-blue airplane pajamas and a light blue robe, which is oversized and hangs off of him.

"Didn't your Mama cook y'all dinner?"

Walter nods.

"But you still hungry?"

Walter looks down.

Thomas walks to the cabinet, takes out the peanut butter,-and places it on the table.

"Get two plates," he says, his voice strained and hoarse.

"OK," Walter says and gets two plates. Thomas places two slices of bread on each of them, then takes the jelly out of the refrigerator and places it on the table.

"Which one do you want to spread? Peanut butter or jelly?"

"Jelly."

"OK." He opens the jar of jelly and sets it in front of Walter. "I'll do the peanut butter." Thomas opens the jar of peanut butter, his huge knuckles around the cap. Walter slowly spreads jelly on two slices of bread and Thomas slowly spreads peanut butter on two slices of bread.

Walter picks up a wooden chair, but can barely carry it to the table. Thomas helps him. They pass each other a slice of bread and press it down on the other.

"You scared your mother today," Thomas says.

"I did," Walter says and tilts his head to the side as he slowly sits in the chair.

"Yep. I need you to tell us when you see stuff like that, OK?"

"OK."

Walter reaches over and presses down on Thomas's sandwich, his dark brown fingers spread out as he presses gently to ensure that the peanut butter and jelly are well mixed. Thomas watches, silent.

"We are going to move out of here," Thomas says

"Where we moving to?"

"Not sure yet, but a place safer than this."

They both sit silent. Both look at the sandwiches on their tan glass plates. Thomas's plate is chipped on the left side.

"Bet the police did it," Walter says.

"Bet the police did it, too," Thomas says with a smirk on his face. Walter smiles and nods.

They pick up their sandwiches and take bites as they sit side-by-side in the dim kitchen, chewing and giggling.

Sky Diving

Norah sits on a concrete bench in the small neighborhood playground, holding Fay on her lap. Thomas sits beside them, wearing his brown work uniform and work boots. Nearby, Walter pushes Lawrence on a swing. Both are dressed in huge fall jackets. Walter's is blue and Lawrence's is red and black.

"So, what do we do now?" Norah asks, her hands around Fay's waist.

Thomas shakes his head. His eyes are low, yellowish, and filled with red veins. He takes off his hat and clenches it so tight that his brown fingers turn red.

"Faster!" Lawrence yells. Walter pushes harder.

Thomas looks at the ground, focusing on the brown and yellow leaves, trembling with the breeze.

"We'll get through this, Thomas," Norah says and rubs his hand; his brown work gloves laying on his thigh shake as he slightly moves. He looks at her hand and takes it into his.

"You'll get another job. You always do," she says. "We've been through hard times before. This is just another thing that we'll get through. OK? We'll live on beans and rice if we have to."

"We have to postpone moving until I find something else," he says, biting his top lip, digging his teeth into the flesh.

"I know," she whispers. She touches his face; his chin is hard and broken with lines, his scruffy beard is graying.

He slouches on the bench and looks around. Some distance away, a young man is selling drugs to an older man, drug addicts and alcoholics sit and stand and walk in a daze, and a group of teens stand on the street corner. Thomas wipes his forehead and stares at the line of liquor stores, abandoned boarded-up buildings, and deserted store fronts that used to be shops and restaurants.

"I'll get us out of here in time," he says, tears forming in the corners of his eyes. Norah closes hers and nods.

"Faster!" Lawrence yells again. Walter pushes harder.

Walter gives Lawrence a big push. When the swing is high in the air, Lawrence jumps out, afraid. He soars into the air and lands on his hands and knees, his fingertips deep in the gravel and leaves.

"Lawrence!" Norah yells. Norah and Thomas quickly jump up and run to Lawrence. Norah carries Fay, whose arms and legs swing in a pink jacket and pink corduroy pants. Lawrence cries and the tears runs down his face. "Lawrence!" Norah says, breathing heavy, her eyes big.

"*Boy,* get up!" Thomas yells as he pulls Lawrence up by his arm. "Why did you let him do that, Walter? A man looks after his family. You need to look after him."

Walter stands in disbelief and looks into his father's eyes. Then he looks at Lawrence, whose tears run from his eyes, down his cheeks, and onto the gravel and colorful, dirty leaves.

"Lawrence, why did you do that?" Norah asks, shaking, as Thomas brushes him off. "Don't do that again!" Lawrence stands in the middle of the gravel and the leaves, bleeding from a cut on his hand. The blood runs down his fingers and thumb.

Walter, his black cap crooked on his head, stands as if in a trance with his eyes wide and his mouth slightly open, staring at Lawrence's hand. Norah shakes her head in disbelief, takes a tissue out of her purse, and wipes at the cut. Fay stands wobbling beside her, holding her pants leg and trying not to fall. Thomas picks her up and places her under his arm as if she's a football.

"Hold his hand, Walter," Thomas says, shaking his head and breathing heavy. Lawrence cries softly, his cut hand snuggled in Walter's pocket, clutched tight.

ജ്ഞ

"Don't do that anymore," Walter says, holding Lawrence's hand. They are at home in their small bathroom. Lawrence, silent, looks at Walter, frowning. "Mama say put some of this on it," Walter says, holding a bottle of rubbing alcohol.

Lawrence snatches his hand away. "That's gone burn," he says, looking at the bottle of alcohol and holding his wounded hand behind his back in a balled fist.

"You have to be a big boy and let me put this on you. Come on," Walter says and reaches for Lawrence's hand.

"No! It's gone burn!" Lawrence pulls his hand away again, still looking at the bottle of alcohol. Tears roll down his face and mucus slides from his nose. His chubby stomach is poking out from underneath his long-sleeved green shirt and hanging over the rim of his hand-me-down blue jeans, the pant legs rolled up to his ankles. Walter reaches into his pocket and takes out a plastic toy bubble. In it is a little green car. He brought it from a laundromat vending machine when he and Norah did the laundry.

"I will give you this if you be a big boy and let me put this on you," he says and shows Lawrence the bubble toy with the car inside. Lawrence stares at the toy with his mouth open and eyes sparkling. "You want it? OK, Mama say I have to put alcohol on your cut to kill the germs," he says, holding the bubble in his hand like it is a valuable treasured prize. Lawrence nods, tears still in his eyes. "OK, you can't cry. You just have to let me put it on you, ok?" Lawrence nods again. "OK, give me your hand…I have to wash it first, OK?"

They watch as the water runs over Lawrence's hand, washing the blood from the open wound and running down the drain.

Walter takes a huge yellow towel from the towel rack and dries Lawrence's hand thoroughly. Lawrence watches, silent, his eyes focused on the towel. Walter carefully pours some rubbing alcohol on a cotton ball and takes Lawrence's hand. Lawrence's eyes, big and watering up, stare at the cotton ball.

"Don't look at it!" Walter orders. "Look that way," he says, pointing to a spot in the corner of the bathroom, between the door and wall. Lawrence turns his head and looks into the corner.

"Like that and keep looking that way," Walter says.

"OK." Lawrence braces himself so hard that the veins protrude from his neck. He stands with his fingers spread out and hand shaking.

Walter quickly rubs the alcohol-soaked cotton ball on Lawrence's cut. Lawrence grimaces with his eyes closed and begins to cry.

"Here, here, here," Walter says and gives him the toy bubble. Lawrence takes it and looks at the green car inside, closely and carefully, as Walter places a bandage on the small cut. "Don't do that anymore, OK?" He looks into Lawrence 's eyes as he rubs the bandage to ensure that it doesn't fall off. "You could have killed yourself," he continues, tearing up. "I have to look after you better. Don't do that anymore, OK?" Walter stands, slightly taller than his brother. Lawrence nods.

"Open this," Lawrence says, giving Walter the bubble toy and wiping the tears from his face and the snot from his nose with the back of his hand. Walter opens the toy and hands Lawrence back the bubble and the green car.

"Mama and Daddy said we not moving yet, so we have to be more careful. You can't be doing crazy stuff like that, OK?" Walter says.

Lawrence nods and runs out of the bathroom, excited. He holds the green car in one hand and the snot-covered bubble in the other.

Having a Party

Thomas is singing with his eyes closed. Sam Cooke's "Having a Party" blasts from the record player on the dresser.

Now Thomas is slowly dancing in the middle of the living room floor, holding a half-finished bottle of whiskey. The whiskey bottle's black top is on the end table, next to a dark green, leaf-shaped ashtray with a small, dingy-white chip on the side. There's a burned-out cigarette there. Thomas's white dress-shirt has the top buttons open; it's wrinkled and part of it is hanging out of his pants. Under his white wrinkled shirt, there's white T-shirt stained with bright yellow sweat. Thomas has been looking for a job for weeks, but has not yet found one.

"They keep telling me 'no,' so I need a drink when I come home," he said to Norah one night. Now every day when he comes home, he grabs a bottle and sits around with his head down, sucking his teeth and drinking. Thomas continues singing, but stops to take a sip from the whiskey bottle. The setting sunlight shines through the yellow curtain into the living room. Thomas sings, wearing an old brown beat-up wide-brimmed hat, his black, wrinkled tie loose around his neck. "Come on, Lawrence," he says, reaching out to his son.

Lawrence looks at his father and smiles. "Come on y'all, help Daddy," Thomas says. The children get up and start dancing with their father, trying not to fall. Thomas dances, staggering beside them. He had gotten up at 5:00am and was out all day. When he came home, he was holding a brown paper bag that was dirty from the cigarette stains on his hands, twisted tight, and shaped like a bottle. "Everybody dance now," Thomas says, taking a sip from his bottle and moving side to side.

"We dancing," Walter says, his eyes closed and face contorted as if he feels the music like his father does. Their Grandma says that Walter is tall, dark, and lean like Thomas. Lawrence is short, brown, and round like Norah. She describes Fay as light yellow. She had bent down and looked at Fay. "She came here not looking like nobody."

"Come on, kids!" Thomas says. Lawrence shakes and kicks his legs.

Thomas picks up Fay, who reaches for the whiskey bottle.

"You want some of this?" he says, holding the whiskey bottle out to her. "You can't have none of this." He moves the bottle away from her reach, laughing and shaking his head, his face full of sweat, rolling down his forehead, nose, and arm, and into the rolled-up sleeves of his wrinkled shirt. Whiskey is heavy on his hot breath. "Having a good time dancing to the music," he sings, rocking with Fay.

Norah walks into the living room and looks around. There is paper everywhere and the furniture is out of place. The music is so loud that the walls shake. Thomas is holding Fay and staggering with the whiskey bottle in his hand. The whiskey is now nearly finished. Walter and Lawrence are dancing beside him. Norah looks at him, her eyes like slits, her jaw puffed out. She walks over, turns the record player off, and takes the whiskey bottle out of Thomas's hand. She takes Fay from him and puts her on the floor. Then she takes Thomas's hand into hers and starts leading him toward their bedroom, holding him up so that he does not fall.

"No baby, we are having a party," Thomas says slowly, his eyes low and drooping. He wobbles back and forth and bumps into the corner of the couch.

Although the music is off, Walter continues dancing with Thomas. Fay and Lawrence are dancing as well. Fay mainly jumps and laughs in an attempt to do what the older children are doing. Lawrence holds her hands and moves with her from side to side. "Dancing to the music." Thomas closes his eyes and puts his hands in the air, his hat nearly falling off his head. Norah stands silent and looks at them all. She walks to the record player, turns it back on, then walks back to Thomas and wraps her arms around him.

She sings like she's Sam Cooke and rocks slowly with Thomas. He opens his red eyes and looks at her, smiles and kisses her, moving his hips from side to side.

ꙮ

"Take off his other shoe, Walter," Norah says as she removes Thomas's right shoe. Walter slowly unties the left one and takes it off. Thomas sits asleep on the couch, snoring loud with his arms folded and hands in his armpits. "Get your sister, Lawrence," Norah whispers as Fay starts to climb on top of Thomas, stepping on his stomach. He does not awaken. Norah takes off his tie and shirt, placing them on the arm of the couch to take into the bedroom with her later. "When he finds a job, he will feel better. Then we are moving." Norah had told the children before Thomas came home.

"Ready?" she now asks. Walter and Lawrence nod that they are ready. They pick up Thomas's legs, and push his lower body up as she pushes his upper body down onto the couch. Fay pushes, too, but Thomas does not move. Norah puts a blanket over him and turns off the light, holding his folded shirt and tie in her arms up to her chest. "Come on," she whispers. The children follow, leaving Thomas in the dark, snoring into his armpit and hand.

Another Day

"Norah!" Thomas yells from the living room. He has been searching for a job all night and has just returned.

Lawrence had stood by the window, waiting for him. Finally, his son spotted him, rained-soaked with his hands in his pocket. He quickly turned the corner and rushed toward their building's entrance. "Daddy!" Lawrence yelled from the window, but Thomas did not hear him.

"Lawrence, get out of that window," Norah had said.

"Norah!" Thomas now yells again from the living room. Norah walks in. Thomas sits on the couch, taking off his boots, hunched over.

"How'd it go?" Norah asks. "Did you find something?"

Thomas shrugs his shoulders, takes a wet, smashed pack of cigarettes out of his pocket and puts them on the end table along with a wrinkled newspaper with job listings circled in red pen and crossed out with a black one. He leans back, places his foot on his thigh, and scoots down. His face sags as if it is melting, his blood-clotted eyes are low.

"Are you hungry?" Norah asks, "I made stew and potatoes." He does not answer. He rubs his eyes and stares at his fingers. "We'll get through this, Thomas," Norah says. She puts his boots in the closet and closes the door.

Postponed

2:38a.m. Norah lies in bed alone. Thomas walks into their small dark bedroom. He takes off his hat and places it on their dresser. Then his watch. He places it beside his hat and a dim lit lamp. He takes off his slacks. Then he slowly unbuttons his shirt and takes it off. He folds his slacks and shirt and places them on a wooden chair beside their bed. He sits on their bed with his back to Norah. "I found a job," he says, his voice low. He pauses. "It's pretty far from here. Outside of Chicago." He looks at Norah, who looks him in his eyes. He looks away and faces the wall. Both are silent. "I will send you some money every two weeks for the kids." The dim light on the dresser illuminates their figures, their faces—the sweat on Thomas's forehead as it rolls to the tip of his nose and falls. "I'm going to move out there first...then I'll come back for y'all...then we gonna move outta here, Norah."

"Thomas, what are you saying to me?" Norah says, turning on her side.

"We moving, Norah. I found a job and we moving," he says.

"When?"

"A few weeks. A few months...when I get things worked out. I'm going down there first. Then I'm coming back for y'all...I'm going down there today."

"Today? Norah sits up. "Why you going today? Why can't we all go there together? Today? What you mean, *you going down there today*?"

"A buddy got something set up for me. I start Monday."

"What buddy?"

"A buddy."

"Who is this buddy? And why can't we all go down there, Thomas?"

"Norah, I just said I'm going down there first…then I'm coming back for y'all."

"Is this buddy a woman?"

"That ain't important."

"Ain't it?"

"I told you my plan."

"Why can't we go too? I can get these kids up and we can all get out of here."

Thomas shakes his head, "I gotta go first. You know…see how things are down there... then come back for y'all."

"How long is that gonna take?"

"Not, sure…." he says, looking around the room. "But you might have to start looking for a better job...you know...for the kids."

"I thought you said you was gonna send us some money?"

"I am, but I don't know for how long."

"Thomas, you make it sound like you ain't coming back"

"Naw....I'll be back…soon as I get on my feet. Don't know how long that's gonna take. Just give me some time."

"Thomas, don't do this to us," Norah says, her voice cracking and shaking and banging against her throat.

Thomas takes her hand in his. She pulls it away. He drops his head and places his hands on his knees. He sits without a shirt in blue boxers, his back to Norah.

"Thomas, what's going on? Can you just please tell me?"

"There ain't nothing here for me!"

"We here! What are you talking about?

He looks at her. "I know you are. You've always been. You a good woman. And we got some good kids."

"Thomas…"

"I just…I need to do this…for me."

"Do what?"

"Go down there."

"For how long?"

"I don't know."

Norah closes her eyes and clutches the pink and orange blanket to her chest, her hands shaking and warm from her racing blood.

She climbs out of the bed. The scarf on her head is tied with bow in the front. She is wearing a white, lace-trimmed nightgown and puts on a pink flowered robe that is missing a button. She bought the robe from the Goodwill store one Sunday after church, and realized that a button was missing when she got home. Now, her hands shake as she struggles with the remaining buttons and ties her robe. She walks into the kitchen. Thomas sits on the side of their bed in his blue boxer shorts, his hands firmly positioned on his knees, his bare feet firmly pressed against the floor.

ℵ

Norah stands beside the kitchen sink, holding it tight for fear that she might fall. She stares, in a daze, at the wooden cabinet. The only source of light is that of the street light peering in through the small kitchen window. The rest of the house is dark. The faucet, which has rust around the edges and knobs, slowly drips. Norah walks into the dark living room and sits on the sofa. The sound of the dripping faucet is accompanied by that of drawers opening and closing and metal hangers screeching against metal poles. Footsteps. Norah closes her eyes and focuses on the sound of the dripping water. The bedroom is again silent. Now, she feels Thomas's presence in the doorway. Although the living room is dark, she knows he is fully dressed and wearing his wool coat, insulated boots, hat, and gloves, and is holding a suitcase. Both are silent.

"I can't raise them by myself—I need you to help me raise them. I need you to help me. Please, Thomas," she says, her voice soft and trembling. Tears run down her lips, chin, and onto her white, lace-trimmed nightgown and pink flowered robe that has a missing button.

"Thomas," she says.

His suitcase brushes the closing door.

A Bag of Chips

"Momma! Can you take me to the store?" Lawrence asks, sitting on the kitchen floor, flicking a spoon around as if it's a toy. The spoon fell when Norah began washing the dishes. Norah stands in front of the sink, scrubbing a black pot with a steel pad. She looks down at him.

"Why do you want to go to the store?" asks Norah, submerging the pot in the greasy, soapy dish water and scrubbing it again. As she scrubs, sweat runs down her neck and water splashes on her white blouse.

"To buy some chips," Lawrence explains. "So, can we go?"

"No, because I just bought you some chips yesterday," she says.

"Can Daddy take me?"

Norah puts the pot, with a burnt spot still at the bottom, into the dish water and wipes her hands on her blue jeans, something she always tells the children not to do.

"Lawrence, get up."

Lawrence gets up and looks at her, still holding the spoon. She takes the spoon out of his hand and puts it in the greasy dish water. "I want you all to sit on the couch with Mama…Walter, bring Fay." Walter takes Fay's hand and guides her to the couch. He picks her up, puts her down on the couch, and sits beside her. Lawrence walks over and sits down, his hands behind his back. Lawrence and Walter both look at Norah. "Daddy doesn't live with us anymore," Norah says.

Walter nods as if he is aware that his father has left.

"OK?" Norah says, looking at the children.

"Where Daddy at?" Lawrence asks. The whites of his eyes are showing almost fully.

"He just doesn't live with us anymore," Norah says.

Lawrence looks at Norah and places his hand between the couch's cushions, because he does not know what to do with it. One by one, he pulls items from underneath the cushion: a penny, a receipt, a bright pink barrette, a blue crayon, a ketchup packet. He places the items on the side table. Norah looks at him.

"Y'all put on your shoes and coats so we can go to the store," she says. Lawrence smiles, pulls his hand from underneath the couch cushion, and runs to his bedroom to put on his shoes.

Earline

"Ain't Miz Earline crazy?" Lawrence asks when they first spot Earline turning the corner as they walk down the street.

Norah grabs the children's hands, her grocery cart, and starts walking fast. "Come on y'all… Earline's coming." She pulls them up the street in the opposite direction with each swift step.

But Earline quickens her step and rushes up the street, trying to catch up to them. Norah looks back. She and the children begin running.

" Norah!" Earline calls.

At first, Norah acts as if she did not hear her.

"Norah! is that you?" Earline calls, hot on their tail. Still they run. "Norah!" Earline calls out, louder and louder. Running is no use, so Norah and the children stop.

"So, Norah, how are you?" Earline asks, standing before them now.

"Fine, Earline, how are you?" Norah answers.

"Fine," Earline says, then looks at Norah and the children. "It's just that I have not seen you in a while." She is holding tightly onto a white purse and wearing a black church hat and flowered dress. She's waiting for Norah to tell her business, because she feels that it is her right to know everything about everyone. "How is Thomas?" she asks and touches Norah's arm with the tips of her fingers, aware that Thomas has left. Everyone knows they were trying to move when Thomas left.

Norah smiles. She stands holding the handle of their metal grocery cart full of groceries. The bottom of the cart is bent because it once doubled as a stroller for Lawrence. Earline, her eyes wide, stares at Norah.

"How is he?" she asks again. She leans in a little with her arms folded, turns her head to the side, and squints. "See, Dolorous told me that you and Thomas broke up. I told her…that was not the truth!" Earline presses her lips tight.

"It was nice seeing you, Earline," Norah says. "Come on y'all," she says, taking Fay's hand. Lawrence puts his hand on the handle of the grocery cart. A spotted banana is on top, sticking up from one of the bags. They start walking. Walter walks beside them, holding a brown paper bag full of groceries in his arms. A carton of orange juice and a box of cereal sticks up from the top of the bag, which he holds so tight that it bends and starts to tear on the side. They all walk across the street, leaving Earline standing with her arms folded, still waiting for Norah's answer.

ꕥ

When they get home, Norah walks into her bedroom and sits on her bed. She grabs the sides of her red blouse, pulls it over her head, and stares at a white coffee cup that is on the bedroom dresser. Beside the cup is the lamp and her black Bible, which has a missing cover; some of its pages are wrinkled and loose, tucked inside of it. Beside the Bible are a spool of red thread, a needle, a yellow opened envelope, and three safety pins. Norah sits in a daze, wearing a black, faded, stretched-out bra, her shoulders hunched over, her red blouse hanging from her wrist and touching the floor.

ꕥ

When they get home, Walter takes Fay's big pink and white coat off of her and puts it on the couch. He tries to help Lawrence take off his coat as well, but Lawrence tells him, "It's broke."

"Hold still," says Walter, holding the zipper in his hands, trying to work a small piece of the coat's fabric out of it. "Now, hold your head back'"

He's on his knees in front of Lawrence, who holds his head back so his chin does not get snagged in the zipper. Once Norah zipped it up and snagged his chin. He fell to the floor screaming and hollering. "I'm gone die," he had yelled, rolling around and kicking his legs.

"You got it?" he now asks his brother, looking at the ceiling, sweating, his lips dry.

"Yep," Walter says and zips Lawrence's coat up and down again. Fay sits in front of the dark television and watches it as if it is on. She sits, looking at it closely. Walter stands on a chair, puts their coats on hangers, and hangs them in the living room closet. Lawrence turns the television on and sits down next to Fay. She looks at him, then at the television, her eyes shining.

Now Walter folds the metal grocery cart and puts it into the pantry. Then he takes the groceries out of the bags and starts putting them away.

"Lawrence, turn the TV down a little, Mama's taking a nap," he whispers, putting a carton of eggs and a pound of ground beef into the refrigerator. Cereal, greens, spotted bananas, cornmeal, apples, tomatoes, bread, butter, fish, and a carton of orange juice sit on the table beside the bunch of wrinkled grocery store plastic bags and some big brown paper bags.

"OK," Lawrence whispers and turns the television down slowly, careful that he does not wake his mother.

Come Morning

Norah lies in bed perfectly still and looks at the ceiling. Tears rest in her eyes, roll down the side of her face and onto her pillow. She rises up and, with her head hung down, sits on the edge of her bed and places her feet in her plush white slippers.

Fay is laying on her back on the floor, playing with her toy doll at the entrance to Norah's bedroom. Norah, eyes red, looks at her.

"Fay," she whispers. Fay gets up and walks to her, her doll underneath her arm.

"Who's that?" Noah says as she points to the doll, her voice hoarse, "Can Mama see her?"

Fay looks at her doll. Norah, gently takes it into her hands and looks at it closely. The doll is cotton with long, black yarn hair. Her complexion is caramel. Her lips are red and smiling. She has big, black eyes. Red shoes. And white socks.

There ain't nothing here for me: Thomas's words echo in Norah's mind. As she plays with her daughter, her tears fall on the doll. Fay watches. Norah looks at her and rubs the dolls hair. "Where are your brothers?" Norah asks. Fay returns her mother's glance and touches the doll's hair. "Boys, come here! Walter! Lawrence!" Norah tries to say this forcefully, but her voice is strained and low as if it slipped from her and fell to the floor at her feet.

Walter walks into the bedroom, almost completely dressed. He holds a blue sweater in his hand.

"Yes, Mama?" he says, sitting next to her on the bed. He's wearing blue pants and a blue shirt and black shoes. He has so much grease in his hair that it shines—he's dressed both himself and Lawrence. With his head down, he slides his feet from side to side against the floor.

Lawrence wipes his eyes with the back of his hand as he walks into the bedroom, stands in front of Norah and places his hand on her knee. Norah looks at her children: Fay, trying to take the attached shoe off of her doll; Walter, sliding his feet from side to side; and Lawrence, fully dressed, now yawning, one hand on her knee and the other picking at the corner of his eye.

"What do you all want for breakfast?" she asks, her heart pulling in her chest. Hot. Her un-scarfed, tangled hair droops like shriveled weeds bruised and beaten by the sun and heavy rain. She has tears in her baggy eyes, with wrinkles underneath and dried-up tear blotches on her cheeks.

"I'll fix breakfast, Mama," Walter says.

She looks at him and touches his face. "No, I'll make breakfast. Can you set the table for Mama?" she asks Lawrence.

Lawrence runs out of the room. Fay picks up her doll and follows, trying to keep up. Walter looks up at Norah with tears in his own eyes and wipes her eyes with his hand. He hugs her, his eyes closed, his shiny afro brushing against her chin.

"Come on, help your Mama up," Norah says. Walter puts his sweater down beside him and gently holds Norah's forearm and elbow as she lifts herself from her bed. They slowly walk into the kitchen. Walter's arm is around Norah's waist tight, trying to hold her up. She walks a little, pauses, rest herself on the door frame, and tries again, Walter is at her side, gently guiding her steps.

ꙮ

The smell of eggs, bacon, and oatmeal spill through the kitchen. As Norah cooks breakfast, she watches Walter comb Fay's hair, her head tilting with each stroke from a blue comb.-

"Hold still," Walter says, "Let me see." He steps back and looks at her hair from a distance, trying to see if both sides are even. "You have to hold still," he says as he walks back, and then carefully parts her hair. He holds a lock of hair between his fingers and braids it, holding the comb in his mouth. An open jar of grease is on the couch inches away from them, its black top to the side of it. Rubber bands, barrettes, and bobby pins are in a faded, white plastic butter bowl beside the open jar of grease and its black top.

Lawrence lies on the floor on his stomach, one leg kicked up on a stool, drinking a strawberry juice box and watching morning cartoons.

Norah looks at them all, takes a deep breath, and stirs the oatmeal. The bacon and eggs sizzle in the frying pan.

Ain't Got Here Yet

"Mama's looking for a job," Lawrence says, sitting at his grandparent's kitchen table, staring at his food.

Walter looks up at him and shakes his head. "I know that already."

Their grandfather had picked them up from school.

"She supposed to come get us, but she ain't got here yet," Lawrence adds.

"Stop talking to me," Walter says.

Norah has been looking for another job for some time, but still has not found one. Now the children's grandfather sits in his chair, asleep with his mouth open. Lawrence stands over him, looking into his mouth, waiting for his mother.

"She ain't got here yet. Called and said she was coming, but she ain't got here yet," Lawrence says again. Walter ignores him and eats his dinner as if Lawrence had not said a word.

Fay is asleep in their grandparents' room. Now, their grandmother comes out of the bedroom with big pink rollers on one side of her hair. The other side is freshly curled and shiny. The soft smell of oil sheen floats about her like a cloud.

"Lawrence, are you done with your food?" She walks to the kitchen table and looks at Lawrence's plate. His steak and potatoes are gone, but his baby carrots are still there.

"Lawrence, eat these carrots!" she says. He walks to the table, sits down, and looks at his hands, his jaws puffed.

"Your Mama will be here soon, so when you are both done eating, get your things together. She'll be here any minute," their grandmother says.

"OK, Grandma," Walter says, eating, holding his fork tight, his mouth open and chewing wide, his head so low to his plate that his chin almost touches his food.

Their grandmother walks back into the bedroom, taking a roller out of her hair.

Lawrence walks over to his grandfather and looks into his gaping mouth again. His grandfather sits there with his head leaning back against the chair, snoring hard. Lawrence drops a carrot in his mouth. His grandfather makes a sound as if he choking, jumps up, and spits the carrot out into his hand. He looks at it closely to determine what it is. Then, he looks at Lawrence, his eyes wide and full of fire. He takes off his belt.

Just then, someone knocks on the door. Lawrence runs to it, hoping it's his mother. He opens it and Norah is standing there, looking at him. She walks in and Lawrence runs behind her, grabbing her coat.

"Get over here!" yells her father at Lawrence. He's nearly stumbling and falling as he holds the belt and tries to catch Lawrence.

"Daddy, what he'd do?" Norah asks looking around, almost out of breath.

"What's going on?" their grandmother says, rushing out of the bedroom. She's taken out another roller and the pink spongy part of it falls off and rolls beside a couch leg. Her bare feet slap against the floor, loud.

Their grandfather sits back down in the chair, still holding his belt in his hand.

"What did you do?" Norah asks, looking down at Lawrence.

"I gave Granddad one of my carrots because I can't eat them all by myself," he says, swinging the front of her coat and looking up at her.

Their grandfather leans back, shakes his head, and closes his eyes, his legs crossed and hands folded on his stomach.

In a Moment

"I'm coming, Walter," Norah says. Walter holds the elevator door open for her. She quickly rushes through the door, holding a bag of groceries and unzipping her purse for her keys. The elevator goes up; the door opens.

"Thomas!" Norah says. Thomas stands outside of their door at the end of the hallway, looking at them.

"Daddy!" Lawrence screams and runs to his father. Norah stands, holding Fay's hand. Walter stands beside them.

"I was hoping ya'll still lived here," Thomas says and walks toward them. Norah looks at him. Into his eyes. He looks down. Then up again. He stares at Walter, who holds his stare then takes his mother's hand. He then looks at Fay. Norah opens the door. She, Walter, Lawrence, and Fay walk into the apartment, then away from the opened door. Thomas walks in, closes the door, and looks around. Most of the furniture is the same and in its original place. Norah puts the bag of groceries on the kitchen table. She takes off her coat and hangs it up. Walter takes off his coat and helps Lawrence and Fay out of theirs. He hangs them all up. Norah takes a carton of milk out of the brown paper bag and puts it into the refrigerator. Thomas, silent, stands by the door. He takes a napkin out of his pocket and wipes his mouth, staring at Norah, who sits in a brown chair that is beside the kitchen window. She looks at Thomas, who now watches Walter as he takes the remaining items out of the grocery bag: a bag of apples, a carton of orange juice, butter, and a bag of corn meal. Walter takes Lawrence and Fay by their hands and guides them into a bedroom.

"Thomas, what are you doing here? Norah says with her hands pressed into her thighs, her knuckles resting on her newly formed rolls.

"I wanted to see you and the kids," Thomas says, his hands in his pocket and his coat under his arm.

"For what?"

"Y'all been on my mind." He touches the arm of a chair and looks at it, then back at Norah. "I'm sorry, Norah."

"Thomas, don't come in here after disappearing for months and tell me you're sorry."

He looks down.

"But I am, Norah. I should have ended things better," he says, his voice soft and low.

"*Why* are you *here*?"

"I feel it's time to be here. Time to explain to you why I left. I was going through some things and didn't know how to handle it.... Losing my job and you wanting to move. I was under so much pressure."

"I was, too."

"I know…I know. I made a mistake. I should not have left."

"Did she put you out? Is that it?"

He looks at her, licks his lips, and stares at his shoes.

"Is it?" Norah says.

"It ain't about her," Thomas says.

"The hell it ain't!"

"I'm trying to talk to you. What's done is done, but I'm here now."

"Thomas, these are your kids and you can see them any time you want. You don't need me to tell you that."

"Norah, you can't raise these kids by yourself. You, need me here to help you."

"You don't have to be here to help me."

"But I want to be. I'm home, Norah."

"You can see the kids any time you want."

"Can I see you?"

Norah gets up, puts water in the burnt pot, places it on the stove, and lights the burner. She takes a piece of catfish out of the refrigerator, washes it, and places it on a platter. Her back is to him. He watches her, wringing his brown skullcap in his hands. He has sweat on his brow, which rests and runs down the bridge of his nose. He rubs his eyes, puts on his hat, and leaves as Norah pours corn meal on the fish, covering it completely.

The Hall

"Just sit right here. Walter, please watch them," Norah says. The children sit in black plastic chairs in a long hallway that has blue-carpeted floors and white walls inside of a posh downtown building. Norah's hair is pined into a ponytail and she is wearing a dress shirt, a black skirt, a blazer, and black dress shoes for a job interview. She brought the children with her because she could not find a babysitter. Earlier she took out their winter clothing and wrapped them up. "Got to get this good and tight, so the Hawk won't get you," she said, as she tied Lawrence's scarf.

"The Hawk?" Lawrence turned around quickly, asking, "What's that?"

"Yeah, what's the Hawk, Momma?" Walter said.

"The blood-chilling wind out there is called the Hawk. It's cold, quick, and hunts in Chicago. We've got to wrap up so it won't get us."

"Oooh, Momma! The Hawk be hitting people in the face real hard. One time, I could not even feel my face it was so cold. 'The Hawk' got me. He whacked me in the face and almost knocked me down. You had to hold me Momma because I was going to go flying across the street."

"I remember that," Norah said, and smiled. "See, that's why we have to warp up. OK?" Lawrence and Walter nodded.

Now they sit in the hallway as Norah puts Lawrence's blue and gray gloves together and rolls them into a ball. They came here on a bus in the snow. "The big mean green," Norah said, describing the CTA bus to the children. "Always late and even later when it's cold. Especially when there's snow on the ground. It's extremely late then. Too late," she said.

"Wait right here," Norah said to the children as they stood at the bus stop. "Hold their hands, Walter." Walter grabbed one each of Lawrence's and Fay's hands and held them tight. Norah stepped into the street and searched the distance for an approaching bus. She stood looking down the street and rubbing her hands together, shaking with the cold. The children were shaking too, even Fay.

"It's the Hawk," Lawrence said, his voice horse.

Walter nodded. The ground, streets, houses, cars, tree branches, everything around them was covered in snow.

"Nope," Norah had said, walking back to the sidewalk. As she spoke, some of her body heat, like a tiny white cloudy ball, bounced off her lips and escaped into the air.

They waited for some time before the bus came. When it came, they were so cold that their noses were running and their eyes were full of frozen tear drops. They boarded quickly. Walter and Lawrence ran to two seats that were next to the window. Lawrence was on his knees looking out of the window. He pulled his scarf down from his face, so that he could see, and wiped the window with his glove. Norah stood at the front, paying the bus driver their fares. The bus driver looked at his watch, punched the time on her transfer, and gave it back to her.

"Lawrence, sit down right," Norah said to him, as she sat beside him. He stretched his legs out in front of himself and sat correctly in his seat. Norah held Fay on her lap.

Now, Norah stands beside the black plastic chairs in the hallway, making sure they did not drop any of their things on the floor. She takes off Fay's gloves and puts them into a bag. She then takes some tissue out of her purse and wipes Fay's face. Lawrence holds on to the pole of a floor lamp that is to the side of him and slides down his chair to the floor.

"Lawrence, get up!" Norah says. "Get … up!" She picks him up by his arm and sits him back down in the chair. "Listen to your brother," she says, wagging her finger at him. All of their coats are on a chair beside them in a huge pile. About five plastic grocery bags are on the floor, with extra clothing and food inside of them. Some bags are doubled because there are holes in them. Three of the bags are tan, two are white, and all have the names of stores on them. Walter pulls the bags over by him and puts them between his big black and blue boots. Lawrence's boots are blue and gray. Fay's are pink and white. "I will be out soon," Norah says.

"OK, Momma," Walter says, looking up at her, still trying to ensure with his foot that all of the bags are between his boots.

Norah walks over to Lawrence and kneels down. "Stand up for Momma." He stands up in front of her. She starts fixing his sweater, then wipes his hair and pats it down, careful not to mess up his part. "Lawrence, I want you to listen to your brother, OK?"

He nods as he rolls his tongue against his jaw, reaches back and touches his chair, which has a bumpy seat. Norah takes his chin in her cold hand. "Lawrence, do what he says, OK?" He nods, sits down, and rubs his hands on his chair, smacking his seat. Norah picks up her purse and walks down the long hallway into an open office. Lawrence slides down his chair, holding the lamp pole.

ꟷ

"You want this one?" Walter asks, pulling an apple cereal bar from one of the plastic bags.

"No," Lawrence says and looks into the bag. Walter takes out a strawberry bar and an apple bar and holds them up to Fay. She takes the strawberry one out of his hand, but she does not know the difference. She just takes it because it is closest to her. Walter opens it for her and gives it back. Lawrence takes another strawberry one out of the box that's inside of one of the plastic bags and gives it to Walter to open for him. Walter opens it and gives it back to Lawrence. Norah had told them that they could eat the cereal bars if they were hungry.

Walter starts re-packing the remaining bars and placing them into a bag. Lawrence sees an open door down the hall. He walks over to it and stands in the doorway, eating his cereal bar. A white man sitting at a desk, writing, looks up at him. Walter walks over, grabs Lawrence's hand, takes him back to his chair, and sits him down. Lawrence hits Walter on his arm. Fay gets up from her chair. Walter picks her up and puts her on his lap. She almost falls, but he holds her tight around her waist.

"You want another one?" he asks, holding another cereal bar up to her, which he dug out of the plastic bag, which has crumbs at the bottom. She nods, although her first one is still unfinished.

"Where the juice?" Lawrence asks.

"In one of the white plastic bags," Walter says.

Lawrence bends down, gets a juice out of one of the white plastic bag, and opens it. The white man that was sitting at the desk in the office now stands in the doorway and looks at them. He is chubby. A patch of thick brown curly side hair partially circles a bold spot. A few strings fight to make their way to the other side of his hairline, but get stuck in the middle. He is wearing a white shirt with the sleeves rolled up to his elbows, and a loose black tie. He has a wide face that curves and twists like a bull dog. He stands and stares at them with his eyes low, his bushy eyebrows twitching, and his mouth moving as if he is mumbling or chewing on his tongue.

Walter opens a juice box and gives it to Fay.

"What are y'all doing out here?" the man asks with his hands in his pockets, his brown pants legs flooding, revealing his black socks.

"Waiting on our Momma," Walter says. "She down there." He points down the hall to the other office. The white man looks down the hall and back at the children. Walter stares at him hard, locking eyes with him. Lawrence gets up.

"Sit down, Lawrence!" Walter says, his eyes still locked on the white man. Lawrence sits down. The white man nods at Walter, walks back into his office, and closes the door.

Norah hurriedly walks down the hallway, smiling. "OK, come on." She takes Fay's coat from the chair and starts putting it on her. Walter and Lawrence start putting on theirs. It's the third time they've done this routine this week. Walter and Lawrence put on their hats and gloves and Norah ties their scarves tight around their faces.

Walter pulls his scarf away from his mouth. "What happened?" he asks, his black skullcap covering his eyebrows.

"I start next Wednesday," Norah says, smiling.

Walter's eyes widen. "So, we gonna move soon?"

"Yep," Norah says, still smiling. Walter smiles back and puts his scarf over his mouth. They all go outside and battle the Hawk, walking fast with their scarves tied tight over their mouths, pushing through the snow.

A New Day

"It is not the best, but it is better," Norah says to Walter, Lawrence, and Fay. They stand staring at a two-story brownstone apartment building, where they will now live. The building is on a quiet street in a peaceful neighborhood where crime, although present, is not as high as where they came from. The streets are lined with nice houses and brownstone apartment buildings with freshly mowed lawns, elaborate flower beds, shrubs, and hedges. There are trimmed trees that line the walkways. Movers are carrying boxes from the van into the brownstone apartment building.

"This our new house Mama," Lawrence says, looking up at the building.

"It's our new apartment," Norah says, with tears in her eyes.

"Why it's not as big as the other one we use to live in? The other one went way, way high," he says, demonstrating with his hands, elevating them.

"Because this is not a project," Walter says, looking at Lawrence. "The other building was a project. Right, Mama?"

"It was, but it severed us while it did," she says.

"Momma, did we move because the police was going to kill us like they killed Charlie?" Lawrence asks, squinting, his finger up to lips, his jaw puffed.

"No, the police did not kill Charlie," Norah says.

"I bet they did, Momma. They be killing black people," Walter says, nodding.

"Some do, but Charlie was not killed by the police. Charlie died because some people wanted his store and he did not want to sell it. There was a lot money being made on that little corner. The police found the people who did it and arrested them. Lina was behind it. They arrested her, too. They also killed Ann. Everybody knew that laundromat was making money."

"Did they die because they were Black, Mama?" Walter asks.

"No, greed killed them. Greed doesn't care about race. It just kills. We moved because there was too much crime and I want you all to have better. Like I said, this isn't the best, but it's better. And when I go back to school and finish, we're gonna have even better."

Blinking rapidly, Lawrence and Walter up look at her. "OK?" she asks and takes a deep breath. They nod. She looks around and watches as the movers carry in the last few boxes. Fay pulls on Norah's coat. Norah picks her up. "What do you want?" Norah asks, smiling and looking into Fay's eyes. Fay smiles and puts her head on her mother's chest. Norah looks at the brownstone. "Let's go inside," she says.

"Me first!" Lawrence says.

"Walter, hold the door!" Norah says. Walter runs toward the building.

"I'LL get it," Lawrence yells, running after Walter who makes it to the door first and opens it.

Fay struggles to get down. Norah assists her, allowing her feet to touch the pavement.

"I'll get it!" Fay repeats, wobbling and running toward Walter and Lawrence.

Norah looks around. "Thank you, Lord," she says.

"Come on, Mama!" Walter says, holding the door. Lawrence and Fay stand in the hallway. Norah walks in. The door slowly closes behind them as they hold hands and walk down the hall together.

I felt a sudden whoosh of air and then heard the sound of crashing glass. While I had been contemplating, Dan had gone into the kitchen, grabbed a metal pot, and had simply smashed the glass.

(from Street Smart #4, *Stealing MacGuffin* by Matthew Kastel)

About the Contributors

R.A. Bolo is a pseudonym of two people who live in West Philadelphia, one of whom identifies as an anarchist, and both of whom love their cats.

Stephen St. Francis Decky is a multimedia artist and writer whose work has appeared in festivals, collections, and museums internationally. As a technical collaborator, he has worked on video installations in Boston, New York, and Montana, and has taught animation and digital media courses at several schools, including Tufts University and Lycoming College. He currently lives and works in upstate New York.

Carolyn Gates currently lives in Belgium and works as a freelance translator, mostly for educational materials and board games. Dr. **Jean-Philippe Gury** is a teacher for French National Education, currently teaching in Luxembourg. He is also a teachers' union representative and a board game designer. Together, Carolyn and Jean-Philippe are the parents of three Franco-American teens.

Daniel Hales is the author of *¿Cómo Hacer Preguntas? or How To Make Questions: 69 Instructional Poems in English* (Frayed Edge Press) and the hybrid novel *Run Story* (Shape&Nature Press), as well as three poetry chapbooks. His poetry, flash fiction, and hybrid writing have appeared in a variety of journals. He rocks out with *The Frost Heaves and Hales*, *The Ambiguities*, and *Umbral*, and is also a visual artist. He lives in western Massachusetts.

Robert P. Helms is an independent historian based in Philadelphia. He has previously edited and annotated the memoirs of Philadelphia anarchist Chaim Weinberg (*Forty Years in the Struggle*; Litwin Books, 2009) and edits the Guinea Pig Zero and Dead Anarchists websites. Most recently, he was co-executive producer of the *Murder at Ryan's Run* podcast (2021).

Matthew Kastel lives in an undisclosed location in suburban Maryland with his beloved black lab, Hershey...and the rest of his family.

Alison M. Lewis is tthe Frayed Edge Press publisher, and editor of the *Street Smart Series.* She lives in Philadelphia and enjoys reading, cats, and long walks to nowhere.

A.R. Melnik is a long-time West Philadelphia resident. All of her trips to New York have been planned in advance.

Shelonda Montgomery is a Chicago-based writer. Her works have appeared in the journals *Sinister Wisdom, Akikiro, Prevention at the Intersections, The African-American Review,* and the poetry anthology *Urban Voices.*

Bruce Orr received an MFA from the University of the Arts in 1994, and a master's degree from Hahnemann University in 1996. He's run a comics press and has been involved in several arts collectives, mural programs, and puppet design and performance groups, including Puppet Uprising, Spiral Q, Mudeye Puppet Company, and Raw Art Works. He currently works in Beverly, MA with a public arts program and as a senior art therapist.

Jean-Bernard Pouy is a popular French author, best known for the *Le Poulpe* ("the octopus," also a play on words evoking pulp fiction) series of detective stories, featuring the distinctively anarchistic sleuth, Gabriel Lecouvreur. His short writings made available in train stations were the original inspiration for the *Street Smart Series.*

Albert Tucher is the author of the Errol Coutinho/Big Island of Hawaii series of novels, which includes *Blood Like Rain, The Place of Refuge, The Hollow Vessel,* and *The Honorary Jersey Girl.* He also writes about prostitute Diana Andrews, who has appeared in almost 100 hardboiled stories and the novella *The Same Mistake Twice.* He spends every possible moment in Hawaii.

www.ingramcontent.com/pod-product-compliance
Lightning Source LLC
Chambersburg PA
CBHW071526120726
47907CB00013B/1087

* 9 7 8 1 6 4 2 5 1 0 4 3 0 *